Toasting Cora

Cassandra Miller

Chelsea K Publications
Edmonds, WA
Copyright © Cassandra Miller, 2006
All rights reserved.
ISBN 0–9755721–0–5
ISBN 978-0-9755721-0-8

Printed in Canada

Cover designed by Lisa Torrence

Acknowledgements

This book was written with the absolutely essential assistance of the following people:

The Tall Women— Jodi Henderson, Donna Modine, and especially Elaine Blackmore, my editor and voice of reason.

Adam Long, my son and the most insatiable reader I know, for honest yet kindly guidance.

The many women who served as inspirations for Cora… may we all age so gracefully and gratefully.

Laura Robinson and Josh Miller, my stepchildren, who continue to enrich my life beyond all expectations.

And always and forever, my husband Rob, who supported, nurtured and made possible this impossible dream.

Many thanks to Ralph Bruksos, fellow author and kindred spirit.

To Rob

Oh, the comfort, the inexpressible comfort of feeling safe with a person; having neither to weigh thoughts nor measure words, but to pour them all out, just as they are, chaff and grain together, knowing that a faithful hand will take and sift them, keep what is worth keeping, and then, with a breath of kindness, blow the rest away.

– George Eliot

CHAPTER ONE

One by one they filed out the door, slid into their cars and headed toward their "real lives." Another workweek was over at last and they all felt a little lighter as they smiled and waved to each other. "See you Monday," and "Have a great weekend," they recited, the ambitious, the dutiful, the numb, all at their happiest on Friday afternoon.

And each of them, as they left, bade farewell to the mystery girl, predictably still sitting at the desk in her tiny glass office. The pretty girl that no one really knew.

She was pleasant enough, certainly, her co-workers all agreed. When approached, she wasn't standoffish exactly, and she consistently observed copier and fax machine etiquette. If she took the last of the coffee, she always made a fresh pot. She was always willing to assist others when asked. Still, not one person had been able to unearth any juicy details about Hallie McLaren, either from the office grapevine or from the lady herself.

No one knew her secret.

Hallie was at once a part of and separate from the daily routine, though she noticed it more than anyone else. By 8 A.M. each day the office clamor— voices, telephones and various gadgets— rose and fell in an indistinguishable buzz. Somewhere around four-twenty, the machines became identifiable once more and, at the magic hour of 4:30, their electric hum was silenced altogether. Voices, too, once again took on distinct character as their numbers dwindled.

With a smile frozen on her face, Hallie nodded at each good-bye as the familiar strangers went off to their other lives. She wondered sometimes what those lives were like. What did these quasi-acquaintances do outside this accounting firm? Something exciting, she hoped, something that might make up for their drab and dreary jobs.

Hallie had never wanted to be an accountant. But she had effortlessly excelled at all things mathematical throughout her school career and so her mother had pushed her in that direction. "It's a solid business career, Hallie. You will always be able to make a living as a CPA— especially since you probably won't have the good sense to marry well." Hallie knew she didn't want to work with numbers for the rest of her life, but she hadn't had a viable alternative in mind when it was time to register for college; there was no dream left that her parents hadn't scoffed into silence.

So, nearly ten years later here she was, sitting at the desk in her cubicle-sized office, speaking to a client on the phone and watching her co-workers leave. On her desk was a single framed picture: her cat Cleopatra, Cleo for short.

The phone call took up the better part of an hour; when it ended Hallie strolled through the office to make sure she was the only one there. Occasionally, one of the more ambitious managers or managers-to-be would work late. But today was Friday; everyone was eager for the weekend to begin.

Hallie, however, looked forward only to this: being alone in the big, empty office. Hallie was thought of as a hard worker— that was why she had been recently been awarded an office with an actual door. She did work hard, it was true, but no one knew the real reason she stayed late so often.

Satisfied she was alone at last, Hallie locked the doors and closed the blinds, then kicked off her shoes and climbed on to the receptionist's desk. That desk was the largest and sturdiest, so it was the obvious choice for Hallie's purpose. Standing tall, high over the many workstations, photocopiers, printers, fax machines and water coolers, Hallie imagined a concert hall packed with people, electric with anticipation. Hallie cleared her throat once, and sang.

She sang from her heart, from her belly, as she had been taught in the clandestine voice lessons she had taken two months earlier, her private New Year's resolution. She sang in sorrowful joy, in sweet and perfect pitch, loving the way her voice filled this empty room. At home in her apartment she only hummed softly, afraid her neighbors might hear through the thin walls. But here, in the stillness of the after-hours office, Hallie sang with abandon. She sang old songs and new, Big Band, torch and New Age rock, whatever occurred to her that particular day.

She timed her daily concert to last until seven o'clock, no later. That gave her time to come down from her makeshift stage and her performer's high; carefully, she replaced anything she had moved on the receptionist's desk, gathered her belongings, locked the door and walked to her car, just before the cleaning crew arrived.

For two years now, this had been Hallie's routine on most weekdays. She had been with the firm for over a year when, working late one night she had begun humming and noticed the acoustics in the office. When she was sure she was alone, she'd taken a deep breath and begun a slow, silky ballad. From that night on, the empty workstations had transformed each day into hushed phantom fans, waiting for another performance.

Hallie had always loved to sing, but it hadn't been a habit for a very long time. She'd sing in the car sometimes, following along to the songs she liked on the radio, but that felt reflexive, like driving itself. Her voice was rusty that first night in the office, creaking and more rigid than she'd remembered. She'd promised herself right then to sing more often, loud and proud. But alone, of course: only to an inanimate audience.

While Hallie occasionally harbored silent dreams of stardom, she did not really believe her voice would carry her that far. No, her voice simply was not that special. If it had been, surely her parents would have recognized and nurtured such a talent. They wouldn't have discouraged her.

Her mother's voice: that was a different matter. Hallie's earliest memories were given context and focus by the soundtrack of her mother's songs. "Wedding Bell Blues," hummed while washing dishes at the kitchen sink, six-year-old

Hallie on a chair beside her, drying a plate. "Don't Rain on My Parade" filled the house as Hallie's mother dressed for a party, and Hallie, age ten, watched and listened in silent awe. "Your mother could have been a star," Hallie's father was fond of saying. "She could have been another Barbra Streisand. But she had you, instead." Hallie's father always grinned and winked when he said that.

As a freshman in high school, Hallie would sing along with her favorite records. Her ability to sound like famous singers surprised her; she hit all the notes and held them as long as she wanted. She felt in command of her voice, pushing it harder, challenging it with more and more difficult songs.

She was so excited by the way she sounded that one day she called her parents into her room. "Listen to me sing! I think I'm really good! I think I could really be a singer! Okay— here comes the song." She sang along to a particularly challenging tune written by Smoky Robinson and recorded by Linda Ronstadt, "Ooh Baby Baby." A friend from school had played it for her one day, a discovery from her parents' record collection, and Hallie had fallen in love with its sad, sweet melody. She had practiced and even worked out some harmony with the recording. Proud and excited to share her gift with her parents at last, she couldn't wait to hear their responses, see their eyes shining with pride. But before the song was even over, they began to laugh. Hallie stopped singing, turned away from them and lifted the needle from the record.

Seeing Hallie so deflated, her mother had tried to make her understand. "Honey, singing careers are for people with really *exceptional* voices— Like Julie Andrews or Lena Horne. I'm sorry, honey, but your voice just doesn't have that spark. God has a plan for you, Hallie. That's why He made you so good with numbers."

That evening, Hallie had overheard her parents talking. Her mother sighed deeply. "If only Hallie had been born with a voice like mine." Standing silent in the dark hallway, Hallie held her breath. One hand instinctively went to her throat, and she stepped backward, retreating to her room. She sat on her bed and nodded, finally understanding that she would never be in her mother's league; it had been silly pride, thinking that she too could be so talented. *Poor Mom,* she thought. *I must be such a disappointment to her.* Hallie was an only child, so there would be no superstar sibling to fulfill her mother's dream. Hallie had been her last chance.

So Hallie, clearly unable to trust her own mind, stopped wondering what she would be when she grew up, and obediently took the path laid out by her parents— and God, of course. Except for her move to Seattle and her failed marriage, Hallie had exhibited few rebellious tendencies. Now, fully aware that her parents would not approve of voice lessons and furtive office performances, she simply didn't tell them, or anyone else, her secrets.

Hallie's commute typically took forty minutes, and nearly an hour on Fridays when weekend travelers added to the gridlock. Friday nights were lonely these days. She had two close friends in the area, but they both had steady boyfriends. Occasionally, they called to arrange a lunch or dinner during the week, but weekends were boyfriend-only time. Hallie understood and accepted this, but wished Lonnie and Kim had not both found a man at the same time. Hallie herself wasn't even looking for one.

She stopped at her mailbox, then jogged up the stairs to her apartment door. Slipping her key into the lock, she could hear Cleo's manic greeting. Hallie locked the door behind her and walked into the kitchen, Cleo trotting close behind. While Hallie looked through the mail, then in the refrigerator for dinner ideas, Cleo was annoyingly underfoot. Finally, Hallie looked down at her. "Hi, kiddo." She sat down and allowed the sleek black cat to settle on her lap. Cleo lifted her head to meet Hallie's hand, closed her eyes and began to purr. Hallie sighed. "Well, what are we going to do this weekend?"

Hallie's apartment was in a small town north of Seattle; if she stood on her toes, Hallie could actually see a glimpse of

Puget Sound from her balcony. She could walk to the beach in just a few minutes. On cool, cloudy weekends she would walk on the shore for hours; in nice weather, the crowds took over and quickly drove her away.

Hallie was continually amazed at the enormity of the beach, the water, and the tidal pools teeming with life, visible only if you knew where to look. Under a rock she might see a baby Dungeness or rock crab, krill, clams, even tiny eels or sea stars. She would study the boulders on the sand, covered with living barnacles. Up close, she could hear them snapping, catch their serrated smiles moving in their hard round shells. Once, she spotted a seal not far from shore, watching her curiously.

Today, a brisk March wind kept all but the most determined beach walkers away; Hallie had the beach almost completely to herself. On days like this she sometimes sang on the beach too, warily and more restrained than in her safe and empty office.

Scattered along the sand with miles between them were the other devotees: vague figures shrinking into the distance. Hallie walked slowly, breathing in the salty air, watching the waves roll lazily to the shore.

Faintly, she heard someone's chimes tinkling in the breeze. The soft tones brought a song to Hallie's mind and she hummed a few notes. She looked around once more to ensure that no one was close enough to hear and began to sing. Her voice, accompanied by the waves, seemed to blow away as each note escaped her mouth. She sang louder, stronger. At last she lost herself completely to the song, forgetting everything but its beauty. On the last triumphant note, held long and high, Hallie, performer and audience, giggled and applauded, then threw her hands up in the air, twirling in the sand. And then— she stopped cold in her tracks, nearly tripping over her own feet.

She was no longer alone.

2

"Bravo! I'd clap for you, too, my dear, if I didn't think I'd fall over in the process," the old woman said, lifting her walking stick. "That was marvelous! I didn't get to hear the whole song, but the finale was gorgeous. Do you sing for a living? I'm afraid I've lost track of the newer artists. You're probably quite famous, and I've completely embarrassed myself."

Hallie was irritated, mostly with herself. How could she not have noticed this slow-moving old woman? She was not exactly inconspicuous: wide-brimmed hat with a huge fake sunflower tied in place by a yellow ribbon, matching purple and yellow tunic and Capri pants. Her lipstick was bleeding red toward her nose, an odd reverse-motion visual effect. But her smile was wide, her eyes round, pale blue and kind. Hallie's frustration, mostly due to her own embarrassment, eased a bit. She tried to smile.

"No, I'm not a singer, famous or otherwise. I live a few blocks away."

"Then we're practically neighbors! My house is just up the beach a ways. I try to get out every day, keep the blood flowing through these old limbs. The beach seems to be getting longer every year." She sighed, nodding at the long stretch ahead, then looked back at Hallie. "So you really don't sing professionally?"

"No! No, I just— well, I just sing for myself, really. But I've taken a few lessons, so I sang for my instructor too. People used to tell me I wasn't very good. But I love to sing, so I do it when no one's around. I don't want to bother anyone, it just makes me happy. I'm sorry— I'm babbling, aren't I?"

"Not at all. But I can't imagine who those people were. Hearing you sing made me happy too. Very happy. You have a gift. I hope your singing teacher told you that. If not, I'm glad I did. Someone has to! And you have to believe it. Really believe it, in your heart, your soul." She shifted her walking stick to her left hand and offered her right one to Hallie. "I'm Cora. Cora Rouget."

"Nice to met you, Cora. I'm Hallie McLaren. Sorry, I didn't catch your last name?"

"It's pronounced Rozhay but looks like Rouge with a t on the end. It's French. Anyway, when I heard you I was about to turn back, to go drink a cup of tea. I'd love it if you'd join me. What do you say?"

Hallie's impulse was to stick to her routine and politely decline the kind offer, but she found herself unable to form the necessary words. Instead, she said, "I would love a cup of tea. Thank you."

They walked up the beach at Cora's surprisingly brisk pace. "Hallie," she said. "What an unusual name. I hadn't heard it before that lovely actress became famous— Halle Berry, isn't it?"

"Yes, but I spell it with an 'i-e'."

"Even better. I think it's a little more feminine that way." Cora walked on, remarking on the coolness of the wind, the beauty of the water and islands in the distance, the Olympic Mountains across the Sound. Hallie listened to Cora's animated chatter, watched the long spiral of her white ponytail swing below her hat. Cora was clearly in love with the Seattle area, and in particular Edmonds, where she had lived for more than fifty years.

Hallie learned that Cora's husband had been a doctor. Cora had urged him to retire after his first heart attack. "We had the money, we could have traveled more, gone on grand adventures together. But he just couldn't bring himself to give up his work. And, he worked long hours, didn't eat well at times, didn't exercise enough. He died at 55. I'm still angry with him. I miss the stubborn fool. Ah, here we are!" She motioned toward an enormous Victorian home, one Hallie had often admired.

Hallie opened and held the gate for Cora. Daffodils, hyacinths and crocuses danced with the wind, dipping toward the walkway. Cora paused, breathing in the green fragrance of the newly mown lawn. "We'll go to the side door, Hallie, over here." Cora tried the door, found it locked, and knocked twice.

The door opened almost immediately. "Oh! There you are! Ready for lunch?"

"No, I think just some tea for now, thanks. Hallie, this is my housekeeper Marion. Maid Marion, isn't that funny?"

Marion rolled her eyes at the old joke and smiled at Hallie. "Nice to meet you. What kind of tea would you like?"

"Oh, anything would be fine, thank you." Hallie felt strange being served by a maid, but Cora and Marion seemed very comfortable in their respective roles. Marion brought the tea in a beautiful ceramic pot, cups perched on their matching saucers, cream and sugar in crystal pitcher and bowl, dainty cookies and biscotti "just in case," all on a shiny silver tray. They drank their tea in a sunny bay window on a cushioned built-in seat. "Your home is so beautiful, Cora," Hallie said. "This is exactly the kind of house I'd like someday."

Cora smiled. "Thank you, Hallie! I'll take you on a tour after we have our tea. There are some lovely rooms on the upper floors you might like to see. You know, I've thought about selling this big old thing and moving into a condo. It would be the practical thing to do. But I can't quite seem to take that step. For one thing, I'd have to let Marion and Tom go— Tom takes care of my lawn and flowers. I'd hate to do that. And, I love the view." Hallie followed her gaze, taking in the gray-blue Puget Sound, the islands and mountains Cora had named on their walk to the house. "This has been my home for so long; it would be difficult to say good-bye."

She watched Hallie for a moment, waited until their eyes met again. "So. Tell me about these horrible people who told you you're not a good singer."

"Oh, they're not horrible, they just wanted me to be safe and comfortable. They didn't think I should pursue singing as a career, that's all."

"Ah. Your parents, I presume? Well, that wasn't their choice to make, now was it? I swear, parents do more harm than good most of the time. It's a wonder more children don't hate us once they're grown and gone."

"Do you have children, Cora?"

"Yes, I have two: a daughter in California and a son in New York, off pursuing their own dreams. I also lost a baby in my fifth month. Would have been my eldest. I still miss her. They didn't tell me, but I'm sure it was a girl, just had a feeling about it. I've imagined what she would look like today. She'd be 53 years old, can you believe it?"

Hallie's smile had vanished; she had suddenly become completely absorbed by something inside her teacup. "Hallie?"

Hallie raised her head, glanced at Cora and quickly looked out the window. "I'm sorry, I don't know what's wrong with me," she said quietly.

"Yes you do. Why are you crying, my dear?"

Hallie breathed in deeply. No one in her present life knew the secret she was about to tell this stranger, but she was going to tell it just the same.

"I lost a baby, too, Cora. Six years ago. I got married, moved out here from Michigan, and got pregnant right away. It wasn't planned, but we were so happy about it. Anyway, when I was almost three months along I woke up cramping and bleeding. Joe, my husband, called for an ambulance, but the baby was gone by the time I got to the hospital. They checked, and there just wasn't a baby anymore.

"We hadn't told anyone that I was pregnant yet, we were waiting until after the first trimester. After I lost the baby, I couldn't bring myself to tell my parents. I told my supervisor at the time— I hadn't been working long enough to have sick leave and I had to explain why I needed time off. Otherwise, no one knew. It was as if there had never been a baby.

"That's how Joe dealt with it, too, like nothing had happened. He said, 'It just wasn't meant to be, Hal.' He even said, 'There was probably something wrong with it, Hallie. It's better this way.' He didn't seem to feel anything, Cora." Hallie met Cora's eyes at last. "And he wouldn't let me grieve. But the more he tried to make things seem normal, the worse I felt. I needed him and he wasn't there. I tried to make him understand how much I loved and missed our baby. How much I needed him to grieve with me. He told me to stop wallowing so we could get on with our lives. Finally, he said we should just try again. I resisted at first, but I thought if we could make another baby together maybe things would be all right. But I couldn't get pregnant! We tried for over a year and I cried every month when my period came. My periods seemed to get worse and worse, too, but Joe said that was my imagination.

"Then one day I came home early and caught him with his assistant. His secretary! That tired old cliché! They were half naked and kissing on the couch. I just walked into the bedroom, packed a suitcase and walked out. I stayed with my friend Lonnie for a month, until I found a place of my own.

"A few days later after I left, Joe called me at work and I agreed to meet him for lunch. I thought he would beg me to give him a second chance, but he didn't want me back at all. He just said he was sorry I found out the way I did and that he would work with me to divide things up equitably. He said he hoped I could get it together and have a happy life. I told him I hoped he would grow a conscience." She paused, looking at her knees. "I'm sorry, Cora. I'm babbling again."

"Don't you apologize, sweetie pie. I am so sorry for all you've been through. All this and you're only, what, 25, 26?"

"I am about to turn 29. Monday is my birthday. I was 23 when I lost the baby. The thing is, no one knows about this. I've never told my parents. Even Lonnie never knew about the baby. It feels really good to be able to talk about it. Thank you."

Cora's eyes narrowed. She picked up a box of tissues from the coffee table and offered Hallie one. "Hallie, we meet people for a reason. Maybe you needed a new friend. You've got one." She reached for Hallie's hand, held it tight. "I don't warm up this fast to everyone I meet. There's something special about you. I'm so glad we met today." She touched Hallie's cheek, then straightened her back again. "You know, Joe probably felt tremendous grief for your lost baby. He just told himself not to show it, even acknowledge it. To admit that he grieved would mean that the loss was real, and he couldn't face that. So he couldn't abide your grief either. He was probably afraid of his sorrow, afraid it would be too painful to bear. So, first he tried to fill that emptiness with another child, and when that didn't happen he pushed you away. He convinced himself that you were the problem. I'd bet my bottom dollar that young Joe has gone through a string of relationships since then and just can't understand why he can't find the right girl.

"I came very close to leaving my husband after the miscarriage. He behaved almost as badly as Joe at first. But in the end he realized that we needed to grieve our loss together before we could move on. Much later, he said that the experience, as painful as it was for us, had a powerful influence on the way he responded to his patients. We had Christina a year after it happened, and Barry four years after that. I am so fortunate that we— Jack and I— were able to work through it all and stay together. He was quite a guy. You just haven't found your Jack yet, Hallie, but you will." Cora nodded and smiled, sipped her tea.

"So— you stayed out west after the divorce," she continued. "That couldn't have been easy."

Hallie smiled. "No, my parents were pretty angry about that! But I felt I would be taking a step backward if I moved back to Michigan. I have friends back there that I miss, but being that close to Mom and Dad again— I couldn't do it. They mean well, I suppose, but they are so controlling. I knew my life would never really be my own if I moved back there."

"So you have your job, your own place, a few friends and a few secrets, one of which is that you love to sing and you do it well. What kind of work do you do?"

"I'm an accountant, a CPA. I work at a little firm in Kenmore. That's where I really sing. I make sure I'm the last one in the office and I just belt out one song after another until the janitors get there. Pretty crazy, right?"

"The only crazy thing I've heard is that you don't share this talent with the world. Why are you afraid to sing in front of people?"

Hallie had never been asked this question; it took a while for the honest answer to form in her mind. "I'm afraid people will laugh at me or tell me I'm terrible."

"And what would it mean if someone said that you can't sing?"

"It would mean that the one thing that brings me joy is just a lie. My dream would die."

"What dream, Hallie?"

"I don't know; singing in front of people, I guess. Having people tell me I'm good. I guess I just want to have an opportunity to sing in front of a big audience and have them clap and cheer for me."

"And what would it mean if they clapped and cheered for you?" Cora asked.

"It would mean… it would mean that I'm good."

"Ah. Validation. Proof that your parents were wrong."

Hallie looked at Cora's pale, unblinking eyes. Could they see her thoughts? Was Cora staring straight into Hallie's soul? "I guess that's part of it. I think I'd prefer to be thought of as a talented singer than a really good accountant."

"Why is one talent better than the other?"

"Well, hundreds of people wouldn't pay to watch an accountant crunch numbers. People admire creative talents: musicians, actors, dancers. I'd like to be admired like that."

"Adored by the masses? Your name in lights?"

Hallie laughed. "Adored by someone would be nice, Cora. It's been a long time."

Cora slid closer to Hallie on the window seat. She put a soft arm around Hallie's shoulder. "And it would be easier to adore you as a singer than as a number-cruncher?" Cora sighed and squeezed her closer. "Patience, dear. Mark my words, you'll be adored. Don't know about the auditorium full of fans, although I'm sure you could make that happen, but trust me— someone will break through that wall you've got around you. Someone will care enough to chip away at it until one day you'll find those last few bricks have toppled down. You just have to take a few steps toward people now and then, let them get a closer look at you.

"One more thing before I step down from this creaky old soap box of mine. If someone said you couldn't sing, it would be a person with no taste, a mile-wide jealous streak, or just very poor judgment. You are a talented singer, Hallie, and no one can take that away from you."

"Thank you, Cora." Hallie took a deep breath, sat up and reached for another tissue. What kind of work did you do, anyway? Were you a psychologist or something?"

"Good guess, dear, psychiatrist actually. I was much more existential in my approach than was the fashion back then. Now, the powder room is down that hallway, second door on your left. You freshen up a bit and I'll have Marion fix us a little lunch."

They spent the afternoon sharing more details of their respective histories. Hallie marveled at how completely at ease she felt in this stranger's home. Hours drifted by comfortably and Hallie was surprised when the room seemed suddenly dim. Cora turned on a nearby lamp. "Please say you'll stay for dinner," she said. "No, no, it's no trouble. I insist. After dinner, I'll take you on that tour of the house I promised and then I'll have Tom drive you home."

"Thank you, Cora. For everything."

"You're welcome, dear. I'll just let Marion know there will be one more for dinner."

Hallie walked back down the hall toward the bathroom. Several black and white pictures hung in a row on the wall. She'd barely noticed them before, but this time she looked at each one carefully as she passed. In one, a little girl and boy played in a plastic wading pool; in another, they were dressed as ghosts for Halloween: Christina and Barry, no doubt. Next came older versions of each child, dressed in graduation gowns, mortarboards and tassels, Christina carrying roses, Barry with his arms around two other graduates. Then, a stunning couple, probably in their late thirties: she with raven curls and dark lips (deep red, Hallie was sure), he much taller and wearing a fedora. Even in the faded, colorless photo it was clear they were glowing, thrilled to be in each other's company. *You just haven't found your Jack,* Cora had said. Hallie shook her head. *Can't hope for something like that,* she thought.

Suddenly, pain: a piercing stab in her lower abdomen. Then, a vague sense of falling, and finally, blackness.

In the kitchen, Cora and Marion heard Hallie fall to the ground.

3

Moments later, Hallie woke to see Marion kneeling beside her. "What happened? Are you all right?" Marion asked.

Cora appeared next. "She fainted, but came to right away," Marion told her.

Cora took in a deep breath and looked at Hallie. "Did you hit your head on anything? Does it hurt?"

"No, nothing hurts. I'm fine," Hallie said and started to get up.

"Here, let me help you," Marion said, holding out her hand. Hallie took it and allowed Marion's strength— which was considerable— to pull her up.

"Were you dizzy? What do you remember?" Cora asked.

"It's nothing. I just need to go to the bathroom."

"Oh, I see. Hallie has another secret?" Cora scowled at her. "This has happened before?"

Hallie felt the telltale warmth between her legs. "Really, I just need my purse and a bathroom." Another searing cramp doubled her over.

"Marion, please go retrieve Hallie's purse from the living room." Cora turned back to Hallie. "I will then walk you to the bathroom myself and stand outside until you emerge in one piece. Deal?"

Hallie smiled. It had been a long time since someone had wanted to take care of her. "Deal. Thank you."

From the bathroom door, Cora and Hallie walked back to the living room together. At Cora's insistence, Hallie settled in to a huge overstuffed chair. "Curl up in that, dear. You'll be more comfortable. Put your feet up on the ottoman. Do you have anything for the pain?"

"Just some non-prescription anti-inflammatories. That was my doctor's latest suggestion. Anyway, I felt this coming on and took a couple of ibuprofen in the bathroom earlier. I'm sure they'll kick in soon."

"You know, of course, that this is not normal menstrual pain."

"My doctor seems to think it is."

"Nonsense. Is this the only doctor you've seen?"

Hallie rolled her eyes. "Not even close. I've seen five in the last three years. Some of them thought it might be that endo something…"

"Endometriosis."

"Right. But I had an ultrasound a couple of years ago and it didn't show anything. So I keep getting this 'Just rest, use a heating pad and ibuprofen.' One of the doctors I saw actually said, 'Some women just have cramps, honey.' Can you believe that?"

"Amazing. You've described your symptoms?"

"Yes, *ad nauseum*. My latest doctor asked what color my menstrual blood is. I really hadn't paid that much attention, and I told him I thought it looked normal. What's normal? He said, 'Well, that doesn't sound like endometriosis to me.' So he's not going to do anything either. But I'm ready to try someone new again, because this is really starting to interfere with my life." *My life? Yeah, some days I can't even climb onto a desk to sing to a bunch of office furniture.*

"I'm no expert, of course, but I believe I read somewhere that ultrasound images are not the best way to diagnose endometriosis. Listen, I know a wonderful ob/gyn I'd like you to see, if you don't think I'm meddling too much. I'll give you her card before you leave."

"Thank you, Cora. I appreciate it. You know, it seems incredible that we just met today. It's like I've known you for years."

Cora smiled, reached out and patted Hallie's leg. "Sweetheart, we've probably crossed paths in many lives. This kind of connection doesn't happen every day. Now that we've found each other in this life, I believe we'll always be friends. Hey— I promised you a tour of the house, but I doubt that you're feeling up to climbing a lot of stairs right now. Let's save that for your next visit, shall we?"

When they sat down to dinner, Cora had Marion put a pillow behind Hallie's back so that she would be more comfortable. To Hallie's surprise, Marion and Tom joined them. Sitting around the table, no one seemed like servants; this felt like a gathering of family. Cora steered the lively conversation through dinner and dessert. Hallie was so grateful; she had planned on a frozen entrée and a video.

But Cora's energy waned at last; Hallie noticed her drooping eyes and insisted it was time to go. Tom offered to drive her without even knowing that Cora had already volunteered his services. Once he learned that Hallie lived just a few blocks up the hill from Cora's, he was adamant, in fact: "I'm going right up there on my way home anyway. It won't be any problem." Hallie thanked them all for their hospitality.

At the door, Cora pressed the doctor's business card into Hallie's hand. "Please call her. If they tell you she's not taking new patients, mention my name. Once in a while that's good for something." Cora took Hallie's hands in both of hers. "Please don't hesitate to stop by anytime. I mean that. I would love to see you just as often as you can manage. You take good care of yourself, Hallie."

In Tom's old truck, riding the short but immeasurable distance from Cora's home to her apartment, Hallie found herself choking back tears. She felt Tom watching her, swallowed and said, "She's amazing, isn't she?"

"Cora? She's great. I've been working for her ever since her husband passed. Guess it's been about twenty-three years now. When was it you met her?"

"Today, on the beach. She was walking and I, well I was singing. She heard me, and we started talking."

"Ah, yeah, she's easy to talk to. She seems pretty taken with you, Miss. Hope you don't take that for granted. She's a nice lady, but she's lonely. No doubt about that."

"Well, she's got you and Marion. You all seem close. Oh, turn right here. My apartment is the third building on the right."

"Yeah, guess you could say we're close." Tom pulled over to the curb in front of Hallie's building. He looked Hallie in the eye. "In fact, we'd protect her from anyone who might hurt her or take advantage of her. You can bank on that." He nodded toward Hallie. "Well, you have yourself a good night, Miss."

Hallie closed the door on the truck and walked toward the apartment building, thinking about Tom's implicit accusation. At the top of the stairs, she turned around once. He was still there, watching her. Inside her apartment, she locked the door. She was relieved when she heard his truck rumble away.

4

Pain interrupted Hallie's sleep several times that night. Her flow was always heavy, but this seemed extreme. Waking up for the fifth time, she decided to give up on sleep completely. Her digital alarm clock read 5:23. She pulled on socks and put her bathrobe on over her pajamas, cleaned up and brushed her teeth in the bathroom. She turned on the TV, made herself some chamomile tea (someone had told her it was helpful for cramps) and planted herself on the sofa. Cleo joined her, and Hallie pulled her close, enjoying the warmth and vibration of her contented purring.

Hallie and Cleo stayed there most of the day, rising only for food and bathroom breaks. At noon, when Hallie's stomach began rumbling, she sat up, getting ready to head to the kitchen. The phone rang, startling her. *Oh God, it's probably Mom.* She stood, debating. *Do I answer it or not?* She decided not to postpone the inevitable, went to the kitchen and lifted the receiver. "Hello?"

"Is this Hallie?"

"Yes." She felt a little disoriented. It wasn't her mother. She knew this voice, though; hearing it felt like… home. But whom did it belong to?

And suddenly Hallie knew, just as the voice spoke again. "It's Cora, sweetie. I hope this isn't too presumptuous, dear. I just wanted to see if you are all right today. I've been so concerned about you."

"Cora! Oh, it's so nice to hear your voice!" She started to say she was fine, but decided once again to be honest with Cora. "I'm actually in a lot of pain today. Didn't get a lot of sleep. I'm just lying around with my cat. This will be my worst day. I'm sure I'll be better tomorrow. But thank you so much for calling!"

"You're welcome, dear. Do you need anything from the store? Can I bring you a hot-water bottle? Some food for dinner?"

"No, really. I have everything I need. I just went grocery shopping a couple of days ago, so I'm well stocked. Thank you for the offer, Cora."

"If you insist you can manage all right, that's fine, but it would be no trouble to run some things over for you. So don't be polite, be honest."

Hallie swallowed hard, close to tears. There was actually a human being on the planet who had spent time thinking about her today and who wanted to help her. Hallie thought this was possibly the sweetest gift she had ever received. She took a deep breath. "No, Cora, really. I don't need anything. But I am so grateful that you asked. Thanks again. And I am going to call that doctor tomorrow, first thing."

"Good girl. All right, then, at least let me give you my number so you can call if you change your mind."

Hallie took down Cora's phone number as directed, thanked her again, and hung up. She stood at the kitchen counter a moment, staring at the phone number. Underneath the number, she wrote 'Cora,' tore the sheet from the notepad and tucked it under a refrigerator magnet, comforted. Cora was only a quick phone call away.

Hallie's dreams were vivid that night, as they often were when she was in pain. She passed from one dream to the next, like moving through different rooms in the same hazy, haunted house. In one, a beautiful little girl ran down the beach, looking back at Hallie and laughing. Hallie was overcome with love and pride, and realized this was *her* little girl. But she kept running, running away from Hallie. Fog grew thick and Hallie couldn't see her anymore. She tried to follow the sweet sound of her baby's laughter, but it grew dim, distant. Hallie ran, crying, pleading with her little girl to stop, to come back, but it was too late. She was gone forever.

The dream shifted, and Hallie was in Cora's front yard, surrounded by countless men, all with Tom's suspicious face. One approached her, too close, and screamed in her face, "I know what you're up to. I'll never let you hurt her. Never!" His fist pounded into her stomach while the other Toms closed in on her.

She tried to object: "I'd never do anything to hurt Cora. She's my friend!"

Suddenly, another shift. Now, the men with Tom's face were surrounding Cora. One began to hit her; another kicked her in the back, knocking her to the ground. Hallie watched in horror and amazement when, as each blow struck Cora, Hallie herself felt the pain.

Crying out, Hallie woke, safe again in her bed. But the pain continued, worse than it had ever been. She glanced at the clock: 4:19. Two more hours to sleep, if she could. She waited for the cramping to ease a bit, then threw back the comforter and went to the bathroom for more pain relievers. The light hurt her eyes. Closing the medicine cabinet, she looked in the mirror. Her reflection stared back, hollow-eyed and pale. "Happy birthday," she said. Exhaling deeply, she filled a glass with water. She put the pills on her tongue, toasted her reflection and drank.

Shuffling back to bed Hallie thought, *Maybe I won't go to work today.* She tried to remember the last time she had taken sick leave. She hadn't, not at this job. It was her first job in Washington, when… *when I lost my baby. Almost six years ago.* She shook her head, banishing those stubborn memories once again.

Sitting on the edge of the bed, Hallie resolved to call in sick. It wasn't a lie, after all. She would call Cora's doctor friend and make an appointment. Then she wouldn't have to deal with the obligatory birthday show at work. Someone may have already ordered a cake, but that's what it was about for most of them anyway: an excuse to leave their desks for cake, coffee and idle chats about the weather and what movies they'd like to see. *They won't even miss me,* Hallie told herself. She reset her alarm clock for 8 A.M., when her supervisor would be arriving at the office, and crawled back into bed. Within minutes, Cleo jumped onto the bed and nestled into the warmth of Hallie's body, but Hallie was already asleep.

She did not stir until the alarm clock burst into radio babble. After calling her supervisor, Hallie made a cup of tea to drink with her cereal, and curled up with a blanket— and Cleo— on the couch. She spent the entire morning engrossed in daytime television: the talk shows— *My Stepsister Slept with My Best Friend's Husband*— and the soaps. She was feeling a bit better; the cramps were still intense, but not as frequent. Curled up with Cleo's purring warmth against her, she was comfortable. If the phone rang, even once, she resolved not to answer it; it would probably be a solicitor anyway. But she had no contingency plan for a knock on the door.

The knock was loud, insistent. Hallie groaned, hesitated, then moved Cleo, went to the door and peeked out the peephole. Flowers. Someone was standing at her door with a huge bouquet of flowers obscuring his—or her— face. *Probably has the wrong apartment.* "Who is it?"

"Delivery for Hallie McLaren?"

Lonnie sent flowers for my birthday! Or maybe Kim? She opened the door, greeted the uniformed deliveryman whose name, Stan, was embroidered on a patch over his left shirt pocket. She signed the receipt as he directed, and took the flowers from him, an enormous basket of spring blossoms in bright reds, yellows, purples and blues, and started to close the door. "Ma'am? There's more in the truck. I'll get it for you."

Hallie put the flowers down on her kitchen table and came back to the door. This time Stan was carrying two large baskets, one in each hand. "They're kind of heavy, Ma'am. Can I bring them in for you?"

"Please!" Hallie directed him to the kitchen counter and fished through her purse for a tip. She might have been a bit generous; Stan smiled for the first time as he backed out the door. She shrugged and locked the door behind him, then turned to examine her mysterious treasures.

Two baskets: one filled with fruit, cheeses, crackers, smoked salmon, champagne, crystal glasses and various condiments, the second with chocolate truffles of every imaginable variety, coffee beans and tins of cocoa. There was no card on the food baskets, so she checked the flowers. There it was, tucked in among the perfect blooms. 'To Hallie: Have a wonderful birthday! Love, your new friend and admirer, Cora.'

Stunned, Hallie sank into a chair at her kitchen table. How did Cora arrange all this on such short notice? And why? Why would she go to such trouble— and expense— for someone she had just met? It was no wonder that Tom had been so protective of her. Someone could easily take advantage of such generosity.

Hallie grinned. It was her birthday! Something to celebrate. She sorted through her treats, put the champagne in the fridge and made a snack of some of the fancy crackers, cheese and fruit, savoring the tastes and smells of her little birthday spread. Putting away the food, she considered possible ways to thank Cora. Nothing seemed adequate. Cora had given her so much: an entire birthday celebration, delivered to her door.

At last Hallie thought about the chilling champagne. Picking up the phone, she dialed Cora's number. Marion answered: "Rouget residence."

"Hi, Marion. This is Hallie McLaren. Do you remember me? I was there on Saturday, I met Cora on the beach?"

"Yes, of course. How are you feeling, Hallie? Cora's been quite concerned about you." Her tone was brisk, but cordial.

"I'm much better, thanks. Is Cora available?"

"Please wait, I'll check."

"Thank you," Hallie said, but too late: Marion had already put the receiver down. Moments later, Hallie heard Cora's voice.

"I'll take it in the living room, dear! Hallie? I'm so glad you called! How are you, sugar pie?"

"I'm feeling much better now, Cora. The pain seems to be subsiding. I'm calling to thank you for the wonderful gifts you sent! I've been nibbling on the goodies, and the flowers are so beautiful! You really shouldn't have gone to so much trouble, but I appreciate it. You made it feel like my birthday."

"I'm so glad you're enjoying your treats. I just couldn't bear the idea of your spending your birthday alone and in pain. I had to do something! I hoped you'd stayed home today— I took a chance on an early delivery."

"But how could you arrange all this so fast?"

"I have a wonderful friend who is a florist in the area. She specializes in gift baskets. She was happy to whip something together for me."

"Well, it was all perfect. Thanks again for everything. Listen, do you drink champagne? Because I really don't want to drink the whole bottle myself, and I would love to share it with you. I can bring it down there. What do you think?"

"I'd be delighted! But I don't want you to come down here; I want you to stay in your comfortable clothes and in your own surroundings. I will have Tom drive me to your apartment. Don't you dare lift a finger to tidy up. I'll bring dinner and we'll toast your big day. How about 7 o'clock?"

"That sounds wonderful, Cora. But don't bring dessert. We can munch on some of those truffles you sent me."

"All right, dear. Oh, I meant to ask: were you able to get an appointment with Dr. Shaw?"

Dr. Shaw! The business card Cora had given her! Hallie had meant to call that morning. "I haven't called yet, Cora, but I'm going to. I've been really lazy today, and it just slipped my mind. I'm glad you reminded me."

"Poor thing! You've gotten so used to this pain that you don't think about looking for help anymore. Well, I promise you it will get better. You make that call, and I'll see you at 7. Bye, sugar pie!"

Hallie called Dr. Shaw's office immediately. The doctor was taking new patients after all, so it wasn't necessary to drop Cora's name. Hallie made an appointment for March 31, exactly three weeks from today. She wrote the appointment down in her planner. *Life without this pain?* she thought. *That would be something to toast!*

Hallie sighed. Looking around, she decided she would disobey Cora's directive after all, and began to straighten up her apartment, just a little.

5

Cora knocked on her door at precisely 7 P.M., accompanied by Tom. They had stopped at a local Italian restaurant and ordered food to go. Cora brought salad, bread and a pasta entrée for each of them, along with a bottle of Sangiovese from her own collection. "We must have a glass of red wine with dinner. We'll drink the champagne with dessert!"

Tom helped Cora serve dinner, then grumbled a terse good-bye. "Oh, never mind him," Cora said, closing the door behind him. "He's a bit grouchy today. Let's eat!"

Over dinner, they chatted about wine, movies, political issues and music. Hallie was amazed at the vast knowledge Cora had accumulated on a wide variety of subjects. Yet she seemed more interested in Hallie's interests and opinions than in sharing her own.

Even as she delighted in her new friend's company, Hallie found herself wishing that Cora was a little closer to her own age. Young as she seemed, Cora had to be close to 80. How long could Hallie reasonably expect Cora to be in her life?

"You've stopped eating, dear. Are you in pain, or just full?" Cora asked.

"I was just thinking."

"Thinking is good. Anything you want to share?"

Hallie looked at Cora's eyes. "Life really is short, isn't it Cora?"

Cora smiled. "Honey, it passes in the blink of an eye. That's why we have to make the most of it. It sounds trite, I know, but we hear it a lot because it's true; each day must be lived as if it is our last, because it truly might be. Death is not to be feared; it's just the matching bookend of birth. We're all born and we all die, that's one of life's few certainties. So we simply can't afford to spend our days afraid or sad. We must embrace life, embrace each other, be the best people we can possibly be; do the best with what we have; step up to the plate at every opportunity and hit that ball right out of the park. Listen to that: a sports metaphor, speaking of trite. But you get the idea. Besides, I love baseball, don't you? I think the Mariners really have a shot at the World Series this year. Maybe we can go to a game sometime, wouldn't that be fun?"

Hallie laughed and ate another bite of her fettuccine. Cora had traveled from the meaning of life to America's pastime in one philosophical stream. Hallie felt honored that this wonderful woman had chosen to spend precious time with her. *Stop wishing for things you can't have. We were born in different generations, and Cora probably has less time left than I do. Can't change that. Enjoy what you have.*

"Well, if I eat anymore I won't be able to have even one of those lovely truffles, and that simply wouldn't do. Let me clear the table for you, and then we'll break open that champagne," Cora said.

Hallie tried to argue, but Cora insisted she sit down and relax. "Just put the dishes in the sink then, and I'll wash them tomorrow. Thanks, Cora."

Cora insisted on leaving the Sangiovese with Hallie ("You enjoy it, sweetie. Red wine is good for the heart."). Hallie had carried the basket of truffles into the living room, and now Cora took the champagne out of the fridge. "Shall we uncork this on the balcony?"

"Sure. I'll get the glasses."

Hallie opened the sliding glass door to her tiny balcony; Cora stepped through it first, followed by Hallie.

"Here, let's trade," Cora said, giving Hallie the bottle of champagne and taking the flutes from her. "Would you do the honors, sugar pie? I would, but my hands would ache for hours."

"I've never done this before, but I'll try." Hallie removed the foil cover, then untwisted the metal guard over the cork. "Okay, now what?" Hallie asked.

"The secret," said Cora, "is to turn the bottle, not the cork."

Hallie followed her instructions, and the bottle opened with a quick pop, a little vapor, and no bubbling over at all. "I did it!" Giggling, she poured the cold bubbles into the glasses Cora held.

Hallie took one of the flutes and Cora lifted hers to the sky. "To Hallie McLaren, a beautiful, wondrously talented 29-year-old on her birthday. To your brand new year!" They clinked glasses, and sipped. "I'm so glad you were born, Hallie. Now, let's go inside and have some chocolates. It's a bit chilly out here."

They sat on the sofa in Hallie's tiny living room, chocolates laid out on the coffee table in front of them. "I love your apartment, Hallie. It's warm and tasteful." Cora looked around. On the wall behind them was Hallie's only work of art: Van Gogh's *Irises.* Cora smiled. "I've always loved that painting, too. I've intended to buy the damn thing for years; but when I see it in art shops, stop and really look at it, I end up feeling so sad I just can't do it. The poor man must have felt so dreadfully alone. How long have you had it, Hallie?"

"I bought it when I moved in here. After Joe and I split up. He hates Impressionism. It was a declaration of my independence, I guess. I love it, but you know it makes me sad too. It always makes me think of Joe and…. well, a lot of things I'd rather not think about. I've thought of getting rid of it, but it was really expensive. I paid to have it framed and everything. I've been telling myself to stop being silly, it's just flowers for heaven's sake!"

"Oh, no, it's much, much more than that, my dear." Cora popped a truffle into her mouth, savored the rich chocolate taste. She took a sip of champagne, held the flute between her hands. "I've always believed, even when I was very poor, that we should surround ourselves not just with objects of beauty, but with those that bring us joy. Something that triggers a happy memory, even if it's just a lovely rock from a stroll by the ocean. Or something that somehow feeds the soul, lifts the spirit. I have a silly glass paperweight with a fluffy white dandelion gone to seed, preserved inside. You know, the little round things that float through the air? Children make wishes on them and blow them away. My daughter gave me that one year for my birthday, one of the first years she actually bought a gift with her own money. When I opened it, she said, 'It's magic, Mommy! The wish never blows away!' That silly paperweight means more to me as any string of pearls or diamond ring. I try to look at it every day. It fills me with joy— calms me, brings me peace.

"You know, I sent you all this food because I didn't know what else to give you for your birthday. Now I do. When you have a chance, next weekend maybe, I'll take you to my favorite art shop and we'll pick out a new print for your wall. My treat. Don't argue, I insist. It'll be fun!"

"Cora, you are too generous. You've really made my birthday special already."

"Tell me: what good is having money if I can't spend it the way I want?"

"All right! I give up!"

"Good girl."

When the champagne was nearly gone, Cora called a taxi. "I'd walk if it wasn't so dark," she said. "I hope I haven't kept you up too late, dear."

"No, of course not. Thank you so much for coming!"

They chatted and nibbled on truffles until the cab driver knocked on the door. Hallie watched Cora walk down the stairs to the taxi. "I'll call you about next weekend!"

Cora turned, looked up and wiggled her fingers. "I'm counting on it!"

Hallie closed and locked the door, smiling. Cleaning up after their little party, she looked at her watch. Ten-thirty already. She shook her head, amazed. She'd had fun tonight. She was never uncomfortable with Cora, not for a moment. *Cora may just be the best friend I've ever had.* For some reason, Hallie blinked back tears at this thought.

It didn't even occur to her until the next morning that no one else, none of her other friends, her parents, no one seemed to have acknowledged her birthday at all. Only Cora. *Could that really be?* But then she remembered that she hadn't checked her mailbox today or Saturday. Grabbing the key from its hook beside the door, she ran down the stairs to the row of metal boxes and opened the door on the one assigned to her.

There they were, all present and accounted for. Return addresses from her parents, her two best local friends, and a couple of friends from Michigan on pastel envelopes: she had not been forgotten.

Back in her apartment, she laid them out on her kitchen table and opened them. Cards reading "Happy Birthday to a Special Person," "Happy Birthday to a Dear Daughter," "Happy Birthday to a Wonderful Friend." A check floated down from her parents' card, and Lonnie had included a gift certificate for Nordstrom. Kim's gift card for Gene Juarez was enough to cover a pedicure— one of Hallie's favorite indulgences. She grinned. Things were looking up; her pain was gone, for now anyway, and suddenly she felt loved, her connection to the rest of the world seemed a little less tenuous. On the way to work, she sang along to every song on the radio— with feeling.

6

There were a dozen messages waiting for Hallie at work, among them birthday greetings from her mother, Kim and Lonnie. Each one had called only once. Funny, it hadn't even occurred to them to call her at home. Hallie thought about

Cora's words— "someone will break down that wall you've got around you.... You just have to take a few steps toward people now and then, let them get a closer look at you." *She's right. I've been so closed off, so distant. Even my friends don't know me very well. But that's going to change, starting today!*

Work kept her busy all morning. When her clock read 12:30, she looked at her phone. *Time to take that first step.* She called Lonnie at the gym where she worked; Lonnie herself answered. "Jodi's Gym, this is Lonnie!"

"Hey! It's Hallie. Thanks for the birthday present and card. Sorry I didn't get back to you yesterday."

"You're welcome! Yeah, where were you? Did you play hooky for your birthday?"

"Actually, I was in a lot of pain yesterday. But you'll be happy to know I've gotten the name of a new doctor, and I've made an appointment."

"Well, hallelujah! It's about time! So, not much of a birthday, huh?"

"It turned out okay. But listen, I was wondering if you'd like to get together tomorrow night. I have an idea for something to do that's kind of wild and different."

"Hmmm, I'm intrigued. Do tell!"

Hallie paused, took a deep breath. "How about karaoke?"

A sign above the door of the Mexican restaurant down the street from Hallie's apartment boasted KARAOKE EVERY WEDNESDAY NIGHT, 8:30-12:30. Hallie had noticed it many times, had promised herself that she would get on that stage someday. How better to let her friends get a "closer look" than to invite them to her debut?

Lonnie had been excited about the idea, said she had gone a couple of times before and it had been fun to listen to people sing: some sang well, some were horrible but still having fun. She suggested they call Kim also, and the three of them would go together. They had agreed to meet in the bar at

7:30, have some dinner and be ready for the festivities to begin an hour later.

Now, Hallie was trying hard to enjoy her dinner and hide her shaking hands. Kim and Lonnie seemed unaware of her nervousness and chattered on about their boyfriends. "I don't know about Jeff. I'm thinking of calling it quits," Kim said, stirring her margarita with a straw. "He's starting to take me for granted! And, it's okay for him to spend time with his friends, but he's jealous of every minute I choose to be away from him. That is not a good sign."

"He sounds controlling, Kim. Who is he, your father? Your boss? What is it with guys anyway? Everything's cool for the first couple of months, and suddenly he's telling you where you can go and who you can go with. Steve, too! I'm like, 'whoa, wait a minute. I've been on my own a long time, buster. This is MY life. You want to be part of it, fine, but I am not going to arrange my life around what you want.' I mean, we've been going out, what, three months? And he's telling me he loves me and wants a future with me. That's scary. And of course, there's the old double standard like you said, Kim. 'I'm my own man, but you're my woman.' The old caveman thing. I am not putting up with that! That's why it's so important for women to have a decent career: so men can't control our fate."

Hallie smiled politely and inserted the occasional sympathetic murmurs of "mmm" and "right, right" as they spoke, discreetly checking her watch periodically. Now, the dinner dishes had been cleared, their drinks refreshed; her watch read 8:28.

Suddenly, there he was: the host. He tapped the microphone in his hand, then said, "Testing, testing." Satisfied, he turned to the audience. "Good evening, everyone! I'm Karaoke Kyle, your host for the evening. I'd like to invite you all to pick out your songs from the booklets that are now being passed out— one per table, please. Along with the booklet you'll find a supply of song request slips. When you find a song you'd like to sing, just write down the title, the number listed beside the song, and your name. Then turn them in to me, and get ready to sing!"

Lonnie rolled her eyes. "Is he cheesy or what?" she whispered. Kim nodded and motioned toward Hallie, who was already looking intently through the list of songs.

"Hey, are you going to sing, Hallie?" Kim asked.

Briefly, Hallie looked up. "Oh, uh, yeah, I thought I might."

Kim and Lonnie, stunned into silence, watched Hallie continue her search, then scribble the requested information on the slip. Without meeting her friends' eyes, Hallie took a deep breath, slid out of the booth and delivered it to Karaoke Kyle, who was launching into a heartfelt rendition of "After the Loving," but smiled and took the slip from her.

Kyle's song seemed agonizingly long to Hallie's friends, but was over much too soon for Hallie's comfort. Her heart was beating hard; she was sure everyone in the room could hear it. *Calm down!* she told herself. *You're going to be fine.*

Lonnie took her hand. "Hey. You don't have to do this, you know."

"Yes, I really do."

Karaoke Kyle wrapped up his Humperdinck impression and the music faded away. "Okay! The first brave soul has already come forward. Everybody give a great big hand to Hallie!"

This was it. Hallie was going to sing in front of her friends. In public— a full house, no less. *Why is it so crowded?* Lonnie and Kim touched her arm as she stood from the table. She stepped up, onto the stage, took the microphone from smiling Kyle, who nodded toward the monitor, where the first verse of the song she'd chosen had appeared. The music started; her cue was coming. *Okay, here I am on the desk in the office. No one is here, it's just the fax machine and me. I can do this.*

Hallie owned the song; it was hers from the first note, and she knew it. Suddenly she no longer had to imagine the empty office, and she stopped staring at the monitor. She looked at the audience, met people's eyes. She felt invincible.

As the music faded, there was a split second of silence. Then— a burst of applause. Cheering. Someone yelled, "More! More!" Hallie smiled at them and gave the microphone back to Kyle. He grinned.

"All right! Great job, Hallie! Hope we'll hear more from you!"

The clapping and cheering followed her back to her friends. Someone gave her a high five as she passed. She slid back in the booth across from Lonnie and Kim, who just stared at her. "Well? How was I?"

Then they were both talking at once. "How were you? Great! Fantastic! Why didn't I know you could sing?"

"You've been holding out on us! If I could sing like that I'd let everyone know! What are you going to sing next?"

The night flew by. Hallie sang seven times. Kim and Lonnie became her loudest fans. Kim joined her for a duet once, but Lonnie refused: "I know what my talents are, and singing is not one of them. You would be so sorry if I went up there."

Near the end of the night, Karaoke Kyle himself asked Hallie to sing with him. "Ooh, Kyle's sweet on you," Kim whispered.

After the duet, Kyle thanked Hallie for making the evening so enjoyable and invited her back the following week. As he was taking the equipment down, he called her over. "Hey, you're really good. Would you be interested in hosting?"

"No, I don't think so. But thanks!"

"Wait! Will you come back sometime?"

"Yeah, I think so. Thanks."

Lonnie and Kim were waiting at the door. "He's really got it bad for you, doesn't he?" Kim nudged Hallie, laughing.

"He might not be bad looking if he wore something decent and didn't slick back his hair like that."

"Seriously, though, don't forget us little people when you're rich and famous, okay Miss Diva?" Lonnie laughed.

"Just think, Lonnie, we'll be interviewed on TV someday. 'Yes, I knew Hallie McLaren when she was an accountant. That's right, an accountant.' I'll tell Mary Hart how you were discovered by Karaoke Kyle in his green polyester suit."

"Okay, okay you guys. Thanks for being my personal cheer squad tonight. It was fun." They said good-bye in the parking lot. Hallie watched Lonnie and Kim drive away in their respective cars, then turned to walk home. She couldn't stop smiling. *Cora! I can't wait to tell Cora!*

As she had promised, Hallie called Cora to arrange a trip to a local art store that weekend. Hallie was in awe; the walls of the shop were covered with beautiful works of art by famous masters and by aspiring artists from the local area. Pottery and glass items were displayed on multi-level stands. Everywhere she looked, Hallie drank in beauty.

She took her time, allowing her eyes to explore the displayed prints, paying careful attention to the emotions evoked by each one. Cora watched, smiling, occasionally offering information about an artist or technique. Choosing one print was difficult, but Hallie eventually settled on a northwest artist's watercolor: an Impressionist-style field of wildflowers, framed in brick red.

Cora, not wanting to influence Hallie's decision, had reserved her own opinions; now, paying for the print, she was clearly delighted. "I met this artist once. She's brilliant! I have two of her paintings myself. I just knew we'd have similar taste!"

Over lunch, Hallie described her public singing debut. "When I sang the first time, I looked at my friends' faces. They were so shocked! They really thought I was good! And everyone cheered and yelled for more when I sang. It was so much fun, Cora. I thought of you the whole night. If I hadn't met you, there's no way I would have had the courage to get up there. Thank you."

Cora grinned back, her lipstick bleeding slightly, just as it had the day she found Hallie on the beach. Impulsively, Hallie reached over with her napkin and wiped off the straying color. "Oh, thanks, dear. I keep forgetting that damn lip liner. Anyway, what I was going to say of course is that you did it yourself. All I did was point out the obvious: that you are a gifted singer and that you should share that wonderful voice of yours. I'm just so proud of you! That was a big step you took, singing in front of strangers. Even more important, you sang for your friends. I'll bet they felt much closer to you by the end of the night. You gave them a glimpse of how special you are. Good for you!" Cora squeezed her hand. "Now, eat your tomato bisque before it gets cold. It's absolutely delicious."

7

The last day of March dawned gray and wet. Hallie had hit the snooze button on her alarm clock three times, but now, forcing herself out of bed, she shivered. Her appointment with Dr. Shaw was this morning. She would have to hurry to get there by nine o'clock.

Time usually spent reading outdated magazines in doctors' waiting rooms was taken up with three pages of forms to be completed by all new patients. Hallie was impressed by the thorough history this doctors' office requested. She turned in the completed forms to the receptionist and was about to sit back down when her name was called; a medical assistant ushered her to the examination room, asked questions, took her blood pressure and advised her that the doctor would see her in a few minutes.

Hallie hoped the surprise she felt didn't register on her face when Sarah Shaw entered the exam room. She was petite, maybe five feet even, very pretty— and very young. Possibly younger than Hallie. "Hello, Hallie is it?" She looked up from the chart in her hand, held out her other one. Hallie shook it, nodding. "Nice to meet you. So you've had some pretty extreme menstrual pain for quite a while now? How long exactly?"

"About six years. And it keeps getting worse."

"Keeping you awake at night?"

"Sometimes. Sometimes I fall asleep okay, but then I wake up because of the pain. I've blacked out a few times. My last period was three weeks ago and it was really bad. I actually stayed home from work. I've never done that before."

"Uh huh. It says you've been taking anti-inflammatories— ibuprofen, acetaminophen, naproxem sodium, that sort of thing?

"Mostly ibuprofen."

"Does it help?"

"Sometimes it takes the edge off, but no, it doesn't really help a lot."

"Okay. I'm pretty sure you have endometriosis. You have a few options. You could take birth control pills— they sometimes ease the symptoms. There is also a birth control injection you get once a month that people have had some success with. Or, we could go in and take a look surgically. It's a laparoscopic surgery. We go in through a small incision in your belly button, and one or two other incisions a little lower. We fill up your abdomen with a carbon dioxide gas so that it's easier to see in there. A tube with a little light on the end of it is inserted so we can look around for endometriosis and cauterize—actually burn— any we find. So you'd be diagnosed and treated at the same time. Recovery is usually pretty fast; you'd have a few days of soreness and in a week you're close to fully recovered. After the surgery, any endometriosis you have should be gone, unless it's too extensive to get it all the first time, or it's attached to places I can't get to, like internal organs. Endometriosis does recur pretty frequently, but in some cases it never comes back. What do you think?"

Hallie was stunned. Six years of suffering, seeing sage old doctor after doctor, and here before her was an impossibly beautiful young woman not only validating her pain, but giving more useful information in thirty seconds than she had heard since her symptoms first appeared. Tears escaped her eyes before she could blink them away and suddenly she was sobbing. "I'm sorry! I don't know what's wrong with me, I just... Thank you for the information. It's been a long time in coming."

Dr. Shaw sat on a round, wheeled stool and scooted closer to Hallie's chair; she reached for a box of tissues on the counter and offered Hallie one. "Don't apologize." Her voice was gentle, her eyes soft. "You've been dealing with this for a long time. I understand your frustration. I wish I had more options for you. Listen, you don't have to decide today, but if you've been in extreme pain for several years now it might be a good idea to get in there and take a look."

Wiping her nose, Hallie nodded. "Let's do the surgery. It sounds like my best bet."

Dr. Shaw left for a moment, then brought in her schedule, offered Hallie three dates in June. "I'm sorry I'm booked up so far out. June is the best I can do."

"That's okay. The earliest is the 12th? That's a Thursday?"

"All the dates are Thursdays, that's my surgery day. That gives you Friday and the weekend to recover. With a desk job, you should be able to work Monday or Tuesday. So the 12th is it then? That will be at 11 A.M." She wrote it down in her scheduling book. "One more detail. I have to call the hospital and book an operating room. If there's a problem I'll let you know. If you don't hear anything different before then, you need to get there about two hours ahead of time. You can't eat or drink anything from midnight on. I'll give you a sheet with all the pre-op instructions and possible complications from the surgery. Any surgery carries some risk, of course, there's always a possibility of a negative reaction to the anesthetic. I want you to read the information really carefully and get back to me with any concerns. Do you have any questions right now?"

"Yes. What exactly is endometriosis? I don't really have a clear picture of what's going on in there."

"Well, the lining of the uterus is called the endometrium. Normally, that tissue builds up each month and then sloughs off during your menstrual period. In endometriosis, endometrium-like tissue is found outside the uterus, usually on the ovaries, fallopian tubes, pelvic area or around the uterus itself. Those cells become lesions, nodules or implants. During your monthly cycle, the endometriosis cells tend to react to the same hormonal changes as the lining of your uterus; they build up, then break down. But they don't have any way to leave the body each month, so there can be bleeding and inflammation in those areas. Adhesions can form, as well as scar tissue. So with all those cells sort of stuck, becoming inflamed, bleeding and causing other problems in there, the pain can be really severe."

"What causes it?"

"We don't know. It's still a mystery. Any questions about what I've told you, or about the surgery or anything?"

"How do you burn the endometriosis?"

"With a little laser. It's very precise. Anything else?"

"Nothing that I can think of."

"Well, call me later if you think of something else. Are you okay?"

"Yeah, I'm fine. Sorry about all the blubbering."

"Don't give it another thought. I'll be in touch, and the hospital will call before the surgery date to go over everything with you. Oh, by the way, I was going to ask if someone referred you to me?"

"Yes, actually it was a friend of mine. Cora Rouget."

Dr. Shaw smiled. "Cora's a friend of yours? Isn't she a wonderful woman? She was a real pioneer in the field of psychiatry; one of her articles was required reading in one of my college classes. She's been kind of an adopted grandmother to me for quite a while, even helped me through medical school. I haven't called her for a few months; I really have to do that. I'll thank her for the referral. It was nice to meet you, Hallie. I'll see you soon."

Back home, Hallie picked up the phone and dialed her parents' number. She should have called when she got her birthday card and check, she knew, but now she would have two reasons to call, and maybe she could postpone the next one for a few weeks. "Mom?"

"Hallie! So you didn't forget our number. Did you get your birthday card?"

"Yes, thank you so much, Mom. I also wanted to thank you for the money. It was a nice surprise."

"You're welcome. I didn't know what else to do for you, since I don't know what you need. What did you buy with it? Clothes?"

"Nothing yet, I haven't had a chance to go shopping. And I'm waiting for a sale," she added before her mother could suggest it.

"Oh. That's a good idea, I suppose. Well, your father isn't home, but I'll tell him you said hello."

"Great, thanks. Mom? I also wanted to let you know that I'm going to be having surgery in June. It's just a minor procedure, nothing to worry about, but I thought you'd want to know."

"An operation? What for?"

"Well, remember I told you that I've been in a lot of pain during my period? It's been getting worse. I found a new doctor who thinks I have a condition called endometriosis. She's going to perform the surgery— she'll be able to diagnose the problem and fix it at the same time, if that's what it is."

"A lady doctor? Are you sure about her? I've never even heard of that disease. What if she's the kind that just does surgery to make money, even if it's not necessary? That happens, you know. I saw it on *60 Minutes*. You're gullible,

Hallie, I've always said so. Don't you know you should always get a second opinion? It sounds fishy to me. I've always had terrible cramps and no one ever told me I had a disease."

"Mom, I've been to a lot of doctors about this and she's the first one to offer any real explanation."

"That's what I mean! What makes her so much smarter than all the other doctors? Maybe she made up this disease! These young doctors are greedy. Don't come running to us when the bill comes."

"She didn't make it up, Mom. I've heard the term from other doctors before, but they just didn't think I had it. This doctor thinks I may have had it for a long time. I think it's worth having surgery to find out. My medical insurance will cover it, Mom."

"Oh."

Hallie held her breath, hoping the insurance trump card would end the argument.

"So when is this happening?" her mother asked at last.

Hallie exhaled. "June 12th. It's a Thursday, and then I'll have all day Friday and the weekend to recuperate."

"I suppose you want me to come out there."

Hallie swallowed hard; her mother didn't even try to hide her lack of enthusiasm at the prospect. "No, Mom. I'll be fine. I've got friends who can take me there and pick me up. It's a minor procedure. I'll be back on my feet in a few days. I just wanted you to know."

"Okay. Of course if you still lived here *I* could take care of you. Oh, it's just as well I suppose. I'm pretty busy these days. By the way, did I tell you that Ted Clark died? Cancer."

"Who was Ted Clark?"

"You know Ted. Barbara's husband? Barbara, from my bridge club. Honestly, Hallie, you must remember Barbara— red hair, talks non-stop?"

"Yes, Mom, I remember. I just don't think I ever knew her last name."

"There's so much cancer now. I read an article in the paper about how the population is aging. That's why there are so many diseases now. Cancer, sugar diabetes, Lou Gehrig's, you name it." She sighed. "Well, life is short. You live from one problem to another, and then some horrible disease comes along and makes you wish you had those little things to worry about again.

"Well, thanks for calling, Hallie. Good luck on your operation. My soap is coming on, so I have to go now. I'll tell your father you called."

"Bye, Mom." Click. Her mother never said good-bye anymore. When had she stopped? Had she ever said it? Hallie couldn't remember.

The obligatory call was over and it had actually been relatively painless, but Hallie was once again very grateful to be living so far from Michigan.

8

The next two months flew by. Work seemed easier, somehow, and Hallie herself seemed… lighter. Her co-workers asked repeatedly if she had changed her hair or lost weight. Three different men began to ask her out, rather persistently. One of them, Ben Lawson, began to bring her coffee and little gifts. He seemed nice. Hallie was actually considering acquiescing; what could one date hurt?

Lonnie and Kim insisted on a karaoke night every couple of weeks. Hallie felt a little more comfortable each time. As she sang more often, her range expanded. Her voice was stronger than ever.

She and Cora spoke every few days and met for lunch or dinner often. During one of their phone conversations, Hallie was sharing the details of her most recent karaoke triumph when she was suddenly struck by a glaringly obvious oversight. "Cora, you have to come next time! I'm so sorry I haven't thought to invite you before! I have no idea what I was thinking. Please say you'll come! I'd love to have you there. I wouldn't be doing this if not for you."

Cora laughed. "I thought you'd never ask. I was actually close to inviting myself. I thought you were afraid I might not be comfortable around so many young people, or in a bar. I don't much care for smoky bars, it's true, but to hear you sing? Wild smoking horses couldn't keep me away! Have you set a date?"

Plans were made to have Tom drop Cora off at Hallie's the following Wednesday so that the two of them could walk to the Mexican restaurant for dinner and Karaoke Kyle's show. They were to meet Kim and Lonnie there. That morning, Ben knocked on her office door. "Hi, Hallie. I couldn't help but notice that you like this color." He held out one perfect lavender rose. He smiled as she took the flower from him and held it to her nose. "Listen, there's this really great Italian restaurant in the University district. I haven't been there, but my friends say the food is great. Why don't we just check it out together tonight? I'm not trying to be pushy, but I'd love to spend some time with you. Couldn't we just have dinner and talk?"

Hallie smiled, staring at the floor until he was finished. "Thank you. For the flower and the offer. And I'd like to, I just— well, I have plans tonight."

"Oh, hey, I'm sorry. I didn't know you were seeing someone. Pretend I never asked." Ben turned quickly, clearly wanting to escape.

"No! Ben, it's not a date! I'm meeting some friends for dinner, and then— well, then I'm singing in a karaoke bar."

"Really? You sing?"

"Yeah, we've been going every other week lately. It's fun! Tonight is special because a really close friend of mine is coming for the first time. She inspired me to start doing this, so it's going to be great to have her there. Uh—" *Invite him! Don't think, just do it!* "Uh, you could come too, if you're interested. It's the *Dos Amigos* in Edmonds. We're meeting for dinner at 7:30, and the show starts at 8:30."

Ben smiled even wider. "I know where that is. Sounds great! I'll be in front of the restaurant at 7:30, okay?" He reached out, touched her arm. "I can't wait to hear you sing!"

"A man? Well my goodness, what's his name?" Cora and Hallie stood outside the restaurant, waiting for the others.

"Ben Lawson. I work with him— well, not directly, he's in another department. Remember I told you that all of a sudden I was getting all this attention at work? Three men asked me out in a matter of days. Ben was one of them, but when the others gave up, he kept asking. Today he gave me a beautiful rose. It's purple! Lavender, my favorite. I've never seen a rose that color. He said he'd noticed I liked the color— I wear it pretty often— and I had this impulse to invite him tonight. I just didn't talk myself out of it before the words spilled out. "

"I think it was a good impulse, dear. I noticed the rose at your apartment. It's lovely. I'm looking forward to meeting this young man."

"But now we're going to have a crowd. I told Lonnie and Kim about it and they're having their boyfriends come down after dinner. I hope you don't mind."

"Not at all, sweetie pie. I hope *they* don't mind having an old lady around. I'll try not to spoil their fun too much."

"No chance of that, Cora. I haven't met these guys yet. Let's hope they won't spoil *our* fun!" Hallie put her arm around Cora's shoulder and squeezed.

"Hallie?" She looked up and saw Ben. "It is you. Hi! I'm sorry I'm so late; I guess I don't know Edmonds as well as I'd thought."

Hallie looked at her watch: 7:36. "It's okay, Ben, it's just a few minutes. Ben, this is my friend Cora Rouget, the one I told you about. Cora, Ben Lawson."

He hesitated, cleared his throat, nodded. "Nice to meet you, ma'am."

"Oh, for heaven's sake, call me Cora, Ben. Very nice to meet you too." Cora reached out and shook Ben's hand. Firmly. "Hallie, what do you say we wait inside for your other friends? I'll spring for the first round of margaritas."

Shortly after they were seated, Kim and Lonnie arrived. They too stammered when introduced to Cora, but she quickly put them at ease.

On previous karaoke nights, Hallie had met Lonnie and Kim in the bar. This time, Hallie had made reservations in the restaurant area for dinner before the show started, to minimize Cora's exposure to cigarette smoke. Looking around, she noticed some familiar faces— other karaoke singers who'd apparently had the same idea.

The dinner conversation was lively and interesting. Hallie watched Cora, fascinated by her ability to make each person feel special. Cora asked Ben, Lonnie and Kim all about themselves and seemed to hang on every answer. Occasionally she would pat Hallie's hand as she spoke of their friendship and Hallie's talent. Cora's audience was enchanted. Hallie learned a great deal about her friends that night, Cora included.

Time passed quickly and suddenly Cora nudged her. "It's almost show time, Hallie! Let's get into the bar and find a table."

Karaoke Kyle wasn't hosting; it was a woman Hallie had not seen before, Deedee. When she called Hallie's name the first time, Cora squeezed her hand. "Break a leg, sugar pie!" Ben, Lonnie, Kim and Cora cheered and whistled as Hallie took the microphone.

She had chosen a slow, bluesy ballad and as the introductory notes played Hallie said, "This is for Cora, a true friend." Hallie sang with power and emotion, style and strength. The crowd was silent, watching her. She met Cora's eyes; they were shining in the dim light. Ben sat beside her, grinning in open-mouthed amazement. *This is magic,* Hallie thought. *I'll remember this moment forever.*

Applause exploded as the last note faded and Hallie returned to the table. Cora stood and hugged her, saying nothing. Kim, Lonnie, and Lonnie's boyfriend Steve, who had arrived shortly after the song began, stood clapping and cheering. Lonnie introduced him to the rest of the group and they returned to their seats.

Ben alone remained standing, staring at Hallie as she sipped her margarita. "What?" she asked.

"You are incredible! Do you have any idea how good you are? Why are you an accountant? It's an outrage! You should have a recording contract. You should be a star!"

"Would you sit down, please? Thanks, but sit!"

"Seriously, though, haven't you ever thought of pursuing a singing career?"

Hallie glanced at Cora. "Not really. Hey, this is a big step for me. I never used to sing in front of people. Other than a singing teacher, Cora was the first to hear me in a very long time."

Cora nodded. "Yes, and I had to be very sneaky to make that happen."

Ben saw the two women smile, sharing a secret. "Well, I feel pretty lucky to be one of the chosen few. Thanks for inviting me, Hallie."

When Kim's boyfriend Jeff arrived, the two couples decided to move on, leaving Hallie with Cora and Ben. Hallie sang several times, taking song suggestions from her friends.

At midnight, Cora called for a taxi, and Ben and Hallie waited with her outside the restaurant. "Midnight feels so much later than it used to. Damn shame. It was lovely, my dear. You're a sensation! Please call soon; we'll have lunch. Ben? Wonderful to meet you. I hope our paths cross again soon." When the cab arrived, Hallie walked with her and opened the door to the backseat. Before she climbed in Cora asked, "Sweetie pie, isn't your surgery coming up soon?"

Surgery. Hallie hadn't thought about it for weeks. Since March, when she'd fainted in Cora's house, Hallie's monthly pain had continued to be intense; but it had been slightly more manageable, and she hadn't taken any more time off from work. Now the surgery was less than two weeks away. "That's right, June 12th. Guess I need to prepare myself for that, don't I?"

"Call me this weekend and we'll talk about it. It'll be fine, honey, I promise. Sarah's a wonderful surgeon." Grasping Hallie's hand, Cora gave her a quick kiss on the cheek. "Ta ta, sugar."

Ben caught up with Hallie and they returned Cora's wave as the taxi pulled away. "Sorry for eavesdropping, but did I hear something about surgery?" Ben asked.

"It's nothing, just a minor procedure. I'll be home the same day."

"Are you sick, Hallie?"

"No, I'm fine. Really! It's female problems. Isn't that what they used to call it?"

"Okay. Let me know if I can help. I mean, you'll need someone to help take care of you after the surgery, right? Please let me help if I can.

"So— do you want to go back in and wow the crowd one more time, or are you ready to call it a night?"

"I think I'm ready to head home. I live a couple of blocks away, I walked here."

"I'll walk with you."

"Thanks, it's not necessary."

"What kind of date would I be if I didn't see you safely to your door?"

Hallie faced him. "Okay, you can walk me to my door. Period."

Ben took her hand. "I wouldn't ask for anything else tonight, scouts' honor."

Smiling, Hallie allowed her fingers to curl between his, and they walked slowly toward her apartment building.

At the door, Ben touched Hallie's face. "You are an amazing woman. I know I've already said this, but thank you for inviting me tonight. I had an incredible time and I really want to see you again. Please say you'll see me again."

Laughing, Hallie said, "Okay, I'll see you again! I had a really great time too. "

"Really?"

"Honest. But as for the 'amazing woman' thing, you don't really know me yet. I'm not all that amazing."

"Well, maybe you don't see yourself clearly. I know we don't know each other very well yet, Hallie, but I want that to change. I hope you'll let me learn all about you."

Ben leaned toward her, kissed her softly. *Oh, God,* she thought. *It's been so long, but I remember feeling this way. I remember...* The kiss ended. She opened her eyes. Ben exhaled slowly. "Can I see you this weekend? Friday?"

"Yeah, Friday would be fine," she whispered.

"We can go to dinner right after work if you like. I'll take you to that Italian place I told you about. Okay?"

"Sounds great. I'll see you at work tomorrow. Good night, Ben."

He kissed her once more, briefly, and touched her hair. "'Night."

She watched him walk down the steps to the sidewalk and back toward the restaurant, where his car was parked. Inside her apartment, she scooped Cleo up and twirled her around. "Hey, kiddo! What a night I've had!" She giggled. *Giddy,* she thought. *I am downright giddy!* Pouring a glass of milk, she wondered if she would be able to sleep at all.

9

Hallie did sleep that night; in fact she slept very well. Vague memories of sexually charged dreams followed her into morning consciousness, but as she tried to retrieve the details they slipped further and further from her grasp. She could guess who the star of the show had been, however.

Suddenly uneasy, she sat on the edge of the bed. *How could I be so careless? How can I just rush in to a relationship with a guy I barely know? What's wrong with me? Okay, it's not too late to back out of the date on Friday. So it's been a long time since I've had sex— what is it, two years? No, more like three. So what! Start thinking with your head, Hallie. Don't lose it over a pair of pretty brown eyes.* She nodded, satisfied by her new resolve, and rose to get ready for work.

But then he was there, in her office waiting for her when she arrived, grinning. "Here you are! Ready to assume the identity of your alter ego, the quiet accountant, but I know it's just a cover for the dynamic diva you really are. You look beautiful, Hallie." He stood, reached out and touched her hair, exactly the way he had the night before.

Hallie tried to steel herself against all that charm, tried not to return his smile, but seeing his face, his glow at catching his first glimpse of her, she couldn't quite remember the reasons she should be rejecting him. "Hi, Ben. You're here early."

"I couldn't wait to see you. Here." He handed her a small box that had been on her desk. "I saw this at the coffee shop on my way in and it just seemed to call your name."

"Ben, you have to stop giving me things all the time! But thanks." She opened the box, pulled out a white coffee mug. Written on the side were the words *Superstar in Disguise.* She laughed. "Pretty good disguise, I'd say. Thanks. I love it."

"You're welcome. Hey, I was thinking: is there any reason to wait until tomorrow to go to dinner? Why not tonight?"

"I'd like that."

"Great! I'll come get you at 4:30 and we'll head out. It shouldn't be too busy, but I'll make a reservation anyway. In the meantime, what are you doing for lunch?"

"I brought my lunch today— it's in the fridge. Thought I'd get a little ahead on work, since I'm going to be taking a couple of days off for my surgery."

"Okay, but you need to get out of here for a few minutes, right? How about we just go for a walk? I'll come get you about 12:15."

"Okay. See you then." Ben squeezed her hand and closed the door behind him. Hallie sat behind her desk and looked up to see him waving at her through the glass wall.

Having her door closed brought a strange quiet to Hallie's office. She usually kept it open, half-listening to the familiar buzz of background noise, almost enjoying its ebb and flow; but now she needed to be productive, and the sudden absence of office din felt like an unbidden answer.

It was a busy morning, and when Hallie finally came up for air she was shocked to see it was already noon. She went to the staff kitchen to get her lunch from the fridge and ate at her desk while checking her e-mail.

True to his word, Ben knocked on her door a few minutes later. They walked on a path in a nearby park, asking about each other's past, flirting and holding hands. It was truly warm today, a hint of summer's approach on the breeze. When they arrived back at the office, flushed and laughing, their co-workers smiled knowingly and quickly turned away, trying to seem nonchalant.

Rumors intensified when Ben once more appeared at Hallie's office door at 4:30. No one could remember Hallie leaving on time, let alone escorted by a man. Until recently, the general consensus around the office had been that Hallie was pleasant but a definite workaholic. Some had theorized that she was secretly gay; after all, she had never volunteered any information about her private life. The upper management group was notoriously conservative. Perhaps she was afraid of the consequences of "coming out" at work, they'd speculated. She was obviously ambitious, working late as often as she did.

But Hallie's behavior had changed these last two months. She had begun to wear more colorful clothing. She was smiling more, engaging in conversation, asking people about themselves and even answering their questions about her with only slight hesitation. When two of the more eligible bachelors in the firm actually asked her out, Hallie turned them down as expected but seemed to keep the door slightly open for another try.

Now, Bachelor Number Three, the most eligible of all, Ben Lawson had stepped in and slammed that door shut, at least for now. Several women in the office had enjoyed flirting with Ben and a couple of them had dated him a few times, but they had not seemed to connect and the relationships had quickly fizzled. Now, some felt a few envious pangs, witnessing his obvious infatuation with Hallie blossom; but, as beautiful as she was, Hallie was simply too kind, too helpful to be hated, even if she was a bit distant. So, while the office was abuzz with gossip about Hallie and Ben, the tone was not malicious; rather, the air hummed with electric surprise and delicious anticipation.

Hallie was not exactly oblivious to the office vibes, but they were a minor consideration. She felt compelled to slow down this thing with Ben and resolved to do so each time he disappeared from view; but in his presence her determination seemed simply to evaporate. Here he was now, at exactly 4:30, tapping on her door.

She sighed. "Come on in." He opened the door, removing the barrier between them. "I have just a couple of things to finish up." Hallie tried not to look up as she felt him approaching. She stared hard at her desk, stacking papers into neater piles and his hands appeared, moving closer. Ben's hands took the stack from Hallie's own, tapped it on her desk and placed them neatly next to the other piles. Hallie saw one of his hands rise to her chin, lifting it gently until her eyes were once again lost in his.

"Hey, listen. It's obvious that you've been hurt. I realize you've been out of the dating scene for a while and that you're a little scared. Hallie, I am not in a hurry here. I don't want to scare you off, but I am seriously smitten. I think we could really have something special, you and me. I promise you, we are going to take things slow. We'll take one step and when you're ready we'll take the next one. So, come with me now. Leave your work until tomorrow. We're going to have a delicious meal, a bottle of red wine and a long conversation. Then I'll bring you back to the office where your car will be waiting and I'll say goodnight. Okay?"

Hallie nodded, amazed. Was she always so easy to read? Or was he just particularly intuitive? At any rate, his plan sounded absolutely, irresistibly, rational.

On their way out the door, it occurred to Hallie that it had been nearly a week since her last after hours 'concert.' The last few times, she'd told herself she needed the practice for karaoke. But it had started to seem downright… silly. Standing on the receptionist's desk, she had looked over the rows of cubicles, and as always tried to imagine a sold out concert hall. But all she saw was an empty office, devoid of people. She had forced out one song, but could not dredge up any phantom applause. She missed the real thing.

"I'm glad we're getting here early," Ben said as he pulled into the parking lot of *Mirabella's*. "I've heard it's really popular, and a little noisy when it's crowded."

The restaurant had just opened and some of the bus-people were finishing up last minute preparations. The hostess seated them immediately. Opening the wine list, Ben asked, "What kind of wine do you like? Light and fruity or deeper, richer flavors?"

"I don't really know much about wine. So far, I haven't met a red wine I didn't like."

"A girl after my own heart. Okay if I pick one then?"

"Absolutely."

Ben ordered an Amarone. During the tasting ritual, he explained to Hallie that it was from Tuscany, that it was an intense wine with cherry overtones and a hint of spice. "Be careful, though, the alcohol content is a little higher than in most wines." He nodded his approval to the waiter, who then poured for Hallie.

She sipped, savored the complexity of flavors on her tongue. "Ben, this is the best wine I've ever tasted!"

"Yeah, it's one of my favorites. It'll be even better once it has a chance to breathe." He swirled the wine in his glass. "You were kind of quiet on the way here. What were you thinking about?"

"I don't think I want to tell you. It's embarrassing."

"Come on. I'll tell you something embarrassing next."

"It's silly. You'll think I'm nuts."

"Never."

Hallie sighed. "Okay. At the office, when everyone else is gone at the end of the day, I sing sometimes."

"What do you mean? You sing in your office while you work? I do that, sing along to the radio sometimes, even though people beg me not to. How can that be embarrassing?"

"No, not like that. I close all the blinds, lock the doors, stand up on Stella's desk and really belt one out."

"You stand on Stella's desk? Now that's gutsy. Do you make sure you put everything back the way it was? You must, or we'd all hear about it. So why do you sing to an empty office?"

"Well, I used to do it all the time. Remember I told you that I never used to sing in front of people? Until Cora heard me one day. The office was one place where I could really sing with abandon and without fear that anyone would hear me."

"A voice like yours and you were afraid someone would hear you?" Ben shook his head.

"Terrified. I took singing lessons a while back, but I didn't really throw myself into it completely. I did all the exercises and learned to sing more from my diaphragm, learned techniques for developing my vibrato, and that was all helpful. But I was holding back. I'm sure my instructor thought I was pretty average.

"Anyway, one day I was on the beach. I thought I was alone; it was windy and cold. So I sang. And Cora snuck up behind me to listen. At first I was really annoyed when I saw her, but we started talking and suddenly I found myself having tea in her house. We became friends instantly. Cora can— and I know this is going to sound strange— she can see inside my soul. She just seemed to know me from the moment we met. Because of her, I'm singing in front of my friends, strangers too. I'm opening up more. I'm even dating!" Hallie grinned. "But what this was all leading up to is that I don't like to sing in the office anymore. It seems stupid now, and… unnecessary. I sing alone in my car, and that feels good. I sing alone in the office and it's like I'm trying to hide something. I don't want to hide anymore. Cora convinced me I don't have to."

Ben touched her fingers. "I'm glad you met her."

"Oh, so am I. Cora says that we meet people for a reason, that she and I were meant to be friends. She always makes me feel so wonderful. You know, I was sick at home on my birthday, and she sent me all this food, champagne, chocolates, fruit, and flowers— the biggest bouquet of flowers I've ever seen. Ben, I had just met her two days earlier! She is such a wonderful, caring person. I feel so lucky to have her in my life."

"I'm sorry you were sick on your birthday. You caused quite a stir at the office, you know. There was a lot of speculation going on."

"What was your theory?"

Ben shrugged. "Considering how rarely you call in sick, I thought you probably really were. I'm glad Cora was there for you."

"Hey it's your turn! Something embarrassing!"

"That's not fair. You have an incredible voice and your secret was that you sing. You shouldn't be embarrassed about that, ever. But, okay, I'll keep my promise. Here goes: I have been watching you for over a year. I tried probably a dozen times to talk to you and I couldn't bring myself to get past, 'Hi, how are you?' I even called my sister and asked her how to approach you."

"Really? What did she say?"

"Um, actually she said, 'Ben, I can't talk— the twins need to be fed. Just ask her out! What's the big deal?' But back then I thought that if I asked at the wrong time or in the wrong way, I'd chase you away forever. Was I right?"

"Well, yeah, you probably were. I convinced myself a long time ago that I didn't need or want a man in my life. Men bring trouble and complications. I told myself that I had my work, my cat, my friends and my secret singing sessions and that I didn't need anything else. Then Cora came along and everything changed. I changed, I can feel it. I feel alive for the first time in six years. It feels good."

"I saw you change. One day, you just glowed. You were always beautiful, Hallie, but now it's as if someone lifted a curtain that you were hiding behind. It was as if I couldn't tell the curtain was there until it was taken away— and the light around you was just blinding. I know that sounds pretty corny, but that's the best way I can describe it. The first thing I thought was 'Oh no, she's already seeing someone!' But I had to try.

"So now there's a question hovering over this table. You said you feel alive for the first time in six years. Obviously, something really awful happened to you six years ago. If you want to tell me about it, I'd love to listen. But no pressure, remember? We move at your pace. It's completely up to you."

Hallie sipped her wine. "Six years was a pretty specific time frame to mention. It just slipped out." A lump formed in her throat and she felt a knot starting to take shape in her stomach. She shook her head, swallowed hard. "No, I'm not ready for that. Talking about it is just too hard."

"It's okay, Hallie. Really. Just know that I'll be here when you are ready." He nodded at a point over Hallie's shoulder. "The waiter's been watching us. I think he's hoping we'll open our menus soon."

Hallie laughed. "Maybe we should oblige." Her throat had opened again, her stomach untwisted. With the menu open in front of her, she considered her options.

10

Aside from her initial nervousness, Hallie's first dinner alone with Ben was wonderful. They slid easily into comfortable conversation. Hallie found that she truly enjoyed Ben's company.

His curiosity about her seemed endless; his questions covered her musical taste, favorite foods, colors, artists, animals and activities. It was exciting and flattering to be the focus of such intense interest. "But hold on!" she said suddenly. "I know almost nothing about you! It's your turn now."

He laughed. "You know I'm an accountant and that I like Italian food and red wine. Okay, there's a little more to the story. Ask away."

"You said you have a sister who has twins. Do you have any other siblings?"

"I am the oldest of three. My sister with the twins— they're two-year-old boys, by the way, Nate and Jonah— is 30. Her name is Rachel. She's a social worker, married to Sam, a lawyer, and believe it or not, a great guy. My youngest sister, Natalie, is 27. She did some modeling a few years ago, some catalogue work, a couple of commercials too. She was dangerously close to anorexic for a couple of years. The family stepped in for an intervention at one point and she was able to work through it, thank God. She went back to school and became a nurse. They both live in Seattle.

"My parents are retired. My dad was a doctor and my mom was a nurse before they got married. They do the snowbird thing— they come up here in the summer and have a place in Arizona for the winter. My dad seems like a pretty tough guy on the outside, but he really has a heart of gold. He's stubborn, argumentative and a little out of touch; we all love him a lot though. Mom's a worrier but very kind. She thinks the only way we'll be happy is if we all do what Rachel's done: get married and have a family. I've never introduced her to any of the women I've dated because I knew she'd be planning the wedding the next day. And I haven't been that serious about anyone yet." He smiled, almost shyly.

Hallie returned his smile, then looked at the table. "Your younger sister is 30, so how old are you?"

"I'm 34, as of April 28. I know you're younger, but how much younger?"

"I turned 29 in March."

"That's not a huge age difference, right?"

"No, it's not bad. Okay, another question. You asked me about my favorite animals, but you didn't offer your own opinion. This is very important: do you like cats?"

"I haven't really been around cats very much; we had dogs growing up. But I'm not anti-cat or cat-phobic or anything. You said you have one, right?"

"Yes I do. Cleo. She's great. She always greets me when I come home and she loves to cuddle. She has this really loud purr and actually drools when I pay a lot of attention to her. You'll like her, I'm sure of it. So, what is your favorite animal?"

"Probably golden retrievers. We had one when I was a kid: really a cool dog. But I like whales a lot. Bears too. I love watching the grizzlies at Woodland Park Zoo. Have you been there?"

"No. I keep meaning to go, but I just haven't gotten there yet."

"All right then, we'll go together. Okay?"

"I'd love to. I've heard great things about it."

"How about Saturday?"

"Okay. That sounds great."

"Any more questions?"

"Yes! What do you love to do outside work? Any hobbies?"

"I ski— downhill, not cross country— and I like to hike. I like to get out of the city, up into the mountains. I have a couple of buddies I golf with once in a while. What do you like to do? Other than singing, of course."

"I've skied a couple of times with my friend Lonnie. I loved it. I used to hike a little when I was in college. Nothing too extreme. I go walking on the beach almost every weekend and I work out pretty regularly. But I'd like to challenge myself physically a little more. Hmm, why is it that the conversation always comes back to me?"

"Because you're fascinating. Because I want to know everything about you. Because I could listen to you talk forever." He lifted Hallie's fingers to his lips and kissed them softly.

Hallie smiled. This time, she didn't retreat from his intensity; she drank it in.

True to his word, Ben drove Hallie back to the office parking lot after dinner, pulling up beside her car. "Here you are, m'lady."

"Thanks for dinner. I had a wonderful time. I'm glad I came."

She felt his kiss in her entire body. Their tongues touched, sending sparks flying to her fingertips, her toes. She responded hungrily, wanting more. Wanting him as she hadn't wanted anyone since Joe. Desire filled her mind, pushing out all other thoughts. *Follow me home, Ben. Stay with me. Love me tonight.* She opened her mouth to let the words out, but he spoke first.

"Hallie. I want you, you know that." She nodded. *Don't say anymore, let's not be cautious, let's just let it happen.* But she knew he was going to continue, and he did. "I just want this to be perfect. I want you to be ready. I don't want to jump into this too soon and ruin it. We have time. A long time, I hope. I think we should wait. Think about it. You think so too, don't you?"

There it was: the Voice of Reason. Hallie knew he was right. They had plenty of time. She leaned back against the seat. "You're right. God, I'm so embarrassed."

"No, no, please don't be." Ben reached for her, pulled her close. "You don't know how tough it was for me to say all that. I was just as carried away. But it will be even better when we're ready. Right?"

"Yes. Absolutely."

"So dinner again tomorrow?"

Hallie laughed. "Are you sure you don't want a break from me?"

He kissed her softly. "See you in the morning."

Hallie started her car and let it warm up a little. She noticed that Ben waited in his own car until she pulled out. Smiling, she turned up the radio and started toward home.

11

The office gossip machine was fueled up and humming when Ben and Hallie left together for the second day in a row, but now they were simply having too much fun to notice. Hungry for details about each other, hours disappeared until they were the only patrons left in the restaurant. They sat, grinning, glowing. Making plans for their zoo date the next day, they were already eager for more time together.

Saturday morning, Hallie woke too early, unable to close her eyes again. She fed Cleo, cleaned the litter box, cleared away the dishes that had been in her sink how long? Three days maybe? Looking around, she noticed dust that she swore hadn't been there the day before.

Hallie went into a cleaning frenzy. Cleo glanced up from her food dish, still crunching, curious about all this activity. When the apartment was at last grime-free, Hallie stepped into the shower to do the same for herself. Picking out her clothes took longer than expected. She stood, looking into the mirror, applying her mascara. Seeing her face, she stopped. *This is what happy looks like.* "Hey," she said aloud. "I remember you."

This time, Ben was exactly on time. He stood in front of her door with his hands behind his back, grinning. "Hi! God, you look beautiful. Here, these are for you." He held out a long, gold box.

"Thank you! What is this? Come in!" Hallie put the box down on the kitchen table and opened it. Inside were twelve long-stemmed lavender roses. "Ben!" She touched one of the petals. "They're incredible. Thank you so much." She opened a cupboard door and reached for her only vase. It was a little short, but big enough around to hold the roses.

Hallie ran water into the vase and added the flowers, then joined Ben in the living room. He was looking at the new framed print on the wall. "I like your place. It looks like you."

Cleo had appeared, seemingly from nowhere, and begun weaving in and out of Ben's legs. "Uh, Ben, meet Cleo. She's so funny, she just has to check out new people."

Kneeling down, Ben ran his hand over Cleo's back. "Hello, Cleo. Wow— her eyes are amazing. They're huge!" He stood up, still watching the little black cat.

Hallie walked to him, took his hand and kissed his cheek. "Ready to go? I can't wait to see the zoo!"

It was a perfect day for the zoo: warm and dry, not too hot. They arrived early enough to avoid a huge crowd. Walking along the paths, fingers entwined, Ben showed Hallie some of his favorite exhibits. They saw kangaroos, wallabies and emus, and in the African Savanna area giraffes roamed with zebras and worried-looking Patas monkeys. One exhibit was housed inside, where dim lights encouraged nocturnal animals to engage in their normal nighttime activities. Here they saw reptiles, bats and three-toed sloths feeding and climbing.

Ben saved his favorite area for last. Up close, the grizzly bears' size was startling, their grace surprising. Next-door was an observation area with windows into both the bear and the otter enclosures. When the otters were in the water, they were nose to nose with the viewers. Hallie was fascinated, watching them crack open shellfish on rocks resting on their bellies. When lunch was over, they frolicked in the water and chased each other on the land, seemingly for the sole purpose of having fun. Hallie laughed, watching a pair wrestle and splash into the water, rolling and wiggling like children at a neighborhood pool. Ben smiled, enjoying her delight.

A young mother, carrying an infant in a sling and pushing a toddler in a stroller, stopped next to Hallie. She pointed at the otters and said: "Look! Do you see them swimming? Those are otters."

"Awdas," said her little girl.

"That's right!" her mother answered.

Ben looked back at Hallie and saw a different expression now. The childlike, unselfconscious joy he had witnessed a moment ago was completely gone. Hallie smiled at the children, but it was a sad, troubled smile. He put his arm around her and she looked at him. "You okay?" he asked.

"Mm-hmm. I'm fine." Gradually, she seemed to shake off whatever shadow had descended and was completely herself again by the time they left.

"Well, what do you think of the zoo?" Ben asked as they walked through the gates.

"I love it! It's really impressive. It's huge! I really enjoyed it. Thanks for bringing me." She squeezed his hand.

"Thanks for coming. I knew you'd like it. Sometime we'll have to go to the Point Defiance Zoo in Tacoma. They have beluga whales and polar bears down there. They're pretty fun to watch. So— are you hungry?"

"Famished."

They bought sandwiches at a sub shop and sat down on a bench overlooking Green Lake, a popular spot with a paved perimeter for walking, running and in-line skating. The sun felt much warmer now and Hallie closed her eyes, lifting her face to it. "Mmm….feels like summer's on its way."

"Is summer your favorite season?"

"I suppose. I like warm weather. I really enjoy all the seasons though. Fall is so beautiful with all its color. I love snow, though we don't get too much here."

"Ah, but the mountains are so close you can have snow whenever you want. We can go skiing this winter if you'd like."

"I'd love that. So what about you? Is winter your favorite time of year?"

"Probably. I do get pretty excited when the temperature drops in the fall. But I enjoy warm weather, too. Especially if I can spend time near water."

They were quiet for a few minutes, eating and watching the procession of exercise enthusiasts circling Green Lake. Hallie felt completely content, until the next question from Ben. It was a simple one, but it chilled her instantly.

"So Hallie, have you ever been married?"

Why was this so difficult? She had been seeing a lot of Ben in the last few days; it was a reasonable question. "Uh…"

"Hallie? You're white as a sheet. Are you okay? I'm sorry, was I overstepping?"

"No! I'm okay. Remember when you asked what happened six years ago?"

"Yeah, and you said you couldn't talk about it yet. I'm sorry, I didn't know."

"It's all right. Really. Just because it's hard doesn't mean I shouldn't tell you." Hallie put the rest of her sandwich in the wrapper and laid it on the bench. She began to speak, slowly at first, searching for words, then gradually let go of caution and told him everything. Just as it had with Cora, sharing her story felt like surrender to Hallie. Another piece of the wall crumbled; she could almost hear it fall.

"I still grieve for my baby. Sometimes my arms ache with emptiness. I dream about her once in awhile. Cora said that Joe probably wasn't as heartless as he seemed, that he was just afraid of his pain so he pushed me away. Hearing that helped somehow. I don't hate him anymore. I actually pity him a bit." She wiped away a tear and looked up at Ben's face.

"I'm sorry, Hallie. I knew you'd been hurt. I wish I could take it away. But I can tell you that I would have responded differently. Not all guys are self-absorbed jerks. Maybe Joe was afraid of feeling pain. I'm not. It's part of life; the highs and the lows are both part of the bargain. If you and I had made a baby, I would've been so thrilled! I love kids and I want more than anything to have a couple with someone I love. To lose one— it would be tough. I'm so sorry you went through all that alone. Listen, you don't have to keep anything from me. If you're feeling sad and missing your baby, you can talk to me about it. Okay? I'll be here."

Ben lifted her chin until she saw his dark eyes and... she believed him. For a moment, she truly believed what he said, believed in *him*. She nodded. And she knew without a doubt, she could love this man. Maybe she'd finally overcome the fundamental distrust of men planted by Joe so long ago. She had adopted a belief that men were amoral beasts, had accepted the assumption so completely that she hadn't even been fully aware of its existence. Until now, when this glaring contradiction forced it into her consciousness.

But she had believed in Joe, too. She had trusted him completely, placed her life in his hands. How could she have been so wrong about him? What made her think she was right about Ben now? Maybe it was her judgment that couldn't be trusted.

"Hallie? What's going on? What are you thinking about?"

Suddenly, all Hallie wanted was to escape. She wanted to be home with Cleo, curled up on the couch and watching her favorite weepy movie about impossible love. She wanted to leave this man, who'd probably just end up hurting her, and never look into his eyes again. "I'm thinking about everything I have to get done today. I really should go home. I can just get a taxi so you don't have to drive me." She stood up and threw the rest of her lunch into a nearby trashcan. "Thanks for the zoo and everything. It was fun. I'll just call a cab on my cell phone and have them pick me up at the tennis courts. Thanks again." She turned away and started walking. Fast.

She winced when she heard Ben running after her. He appeared in front of her. "Wait a minute. What happened? I'm not going to let you run away from me so easily. Hallie, we've got something good happening here. What's got you so scared?"

"Scared? I'm not scared. I just don't think it's a good idea for us to see each other anymore."

"I don't believe you. I saw it back there, you were feeling what I felt. You started to let me in and then you slammed the door in my face. Did I push too hard?"

"You don't understand. I can't do this again. I thought I could, but I can't."

"Do what? Care about someone? Fall in love? Do you really want to pass this by? Hallie, please, look at me. We've only been together a short time and I have never felt this way about anyone. I want to see where it goes. It would be wrong to piss it away, don't you see that? Hallie, I would never hurt you. You can trust me."

Hallie turned her back to him, her arms folded tight across her chest. She shivered, suddenly cold. Ben reached out, touching her back, and she stepped forward, shook him off. "I don't think I can take that chance," she whispered.

"Yes, you can. We both know you can. But if you convince yourself that you'd rather be alone than risk being hurt again, we'll both lose. Maybe you'll tell yourself that it's all for the best, that you were smart to push me away, but I'll know the truth. I'll know that we could have been great together. I'll compare every woman in my life to you and none of them will quite measure up. We'll be two damaged people that will always wonder what could have been. See, it's already too late for me, Hallie. If you decide we can't see each other anymore, you will be hurting me, and I can't believe you won't be hurt too." He touched her shoulder. This time, she turned around to face him. "Hallie, I'm scared too. I'm afraid of loving you and having it go wrong somehow. But I'm terrified of not trying. I want us to give it everything we've got and hold on tight. Isn't that what you want too?"

Hallie knew he was right; it was already too late. Breaking it off now would hurt them both. If he was secretly a selfish, unfeeling oaf, he was certainly good at hiding it. Could she risk everything and truly trust him? *What kind of person do I want to be? Closed off, emotionally dead? What would Cora do?* Cora, she knew, would throw all caution to the wind in the name of love. *What if Ben is right for me—what if he's my Jack— and I drive him away? Cora would never forgive me.*

Hallie summoned all her courage and looked into Ben's face once more. Never, not even in the early days with Joe, had she seen such intensity in a man's eyes. *Surrender.* It was her only thought as she leaned forward just enough for Ben to open his arms and pull her close. "Hallie," he whispered, holding her tighter. "I promise you won't be sorry. Just please don't ever do that to me again."

Hallie closed her eyes and rested her head on his chest. "I won't. Just don't let go, okay?"

"Never."

They stood, clinging, swaying a little. Finally, they began walking on the path around the lake, arms wrapped around each other. They talked about everything and nothing in particular, stopping here and there to watch ducks or geese bobbing on the water. The sun was hanging low, just above the horizon, when Hallie realized she had forgotten all about being afraid.

12

After several consecutive warm, sunny days, the morning of Hallie's surgery dawned chilly and gray. Lonnie had made arrangements to drive her to the outpatient clinic, and Ben would take the afternoon off to be there when she woke up after the surgery. He had wanted to be with her the entire day, but Lonnie had set aside the morning when the surgery was first scheduled, and Hallie felt she couldn't renege now.

She had to be there by 9 A.M. and the surgery was scheduled for 11. She glanced at the clock: 8:10. Sleep had been difficult all night; she'd been awake since 6:30. No food or water was allowed all morning, she had been instructed. She wished Lonnie would arrive so that she could stop thinking about food.

Moments later, Lonnie knocked on the door. They had about ten minutes before they had to leave. "Nervous?" Lonnie asked.

"A little, but..." Hallie's answer was cut off by the phone.

"Bet I know who that is!" Lonnie smiled, picking up a magazine and pretending not to listen.

"Hello? Hi, Ben. Yes, I'm fine. I was just telling Lonnie that I'm more excited than nervous. The idea of not being in pain so often is pretty enticing. No, really. I'm feeling good. Just hungry and thirsty! Okay, I'll see you when I wake up. Yes, they said it should take an hour, so noon is perfect. No, there's no need for you to get there earlier. Thanks for doing this. Okay, see you then. Bye!"

"Wow. He's got it bad, doesn't he?" Lonnie asked, looking up from her magazine.

"He seems to. And he's not the only one!"

"Oh my God! Never thought I'd see the day. Good for you! Although, I do worry sometimes. Doesn't he just seem too damn good to be true?"

"Yeah, he does. But he's convinced me that he's for real. Things are heating up pretty quickly and it's a little scary, but I can't let that get in the way of what might be the best thing that ever happened to me."

"Hallie, believe me. He's not perfect. He'll show his warts sooner or later. They all do. Until then, enjoy the wave of new guy euphoria. It's always a fun ride. Speaking of which, we should fly."

At the day surgery center, Hallie checked in at the reception desk and sat down to wait for her name to be called. Lonnie seemed more nervous than Hallie, swinging her legs, drumming her fingers on her knee, leafing through magazines so fast she could barely even see the pictures. When a nurse opened the door and called, "Hallie McLaren?" Lonnie jumped to her feet first.

Hallie stood. "That's me. Lonnie, you don't have to stay. Go do something fun before you have to go back to work. Ben will be here soon, and I'll be fine until the surgery."

"Well, if you're really sure."

"Yes. Go! Thanks for bringing me."

"Call me tonight and let me know how it went. I'll be thinking about you." She squeezed Hallie's hand, then held up her crossed fingers. "Luck, luck, luck. Love ya!"

Hallie followed the nurse into the pre-op area. They went around a corner, into a dressing room with a curtain door. "Here's a gown, robe and slippers. Take everything off, your watch and jewelry too, if you're wearing any, and put it all in this bag. Put the robe on so that it opens in the front. Leave the bag here, we'll take care of it. When you're ready, open the curtain and I'll come take you to your bed."

As Hallie slipped out of her clothes, she noticed that her hands were shaking. Why was she nervous now? *Come on, you've been fine all morning. This is no big deal, it's a routine surgery. Shake it off.* She put the gown on as instructed. It was warm, a pleasant surprise. The robe, too had been heated a bit. The "slippers" were actually thick socks with rubber stripes on the bottom to prevent any falls on the slick hospital floors. She remembered a similar pair of crocheted slippers she had as a very young child, perhaps three years old. She would pretend they were skates, sliding on the hardwood floor, spinning, careful to avoid the imaginary roses thrown by the invisible, admiring audience. Hallie closed and tied the robe, took a deep breath and opened the curtain.

The nurse, Carol, led her to a bed with the head lifted so that Hallie was in a sitting position when she climbed up. Carol took her blood pressure, explaining that they were expecting a low reading because of the lack of water in her system. She then excused herself, saying she would return shortly. Another nurse appeared then, and connected her to an IV— for nourishment and fluids, she said. She also slid a clip onto Hallie's middle finger, to measure the oxygen in her blood. She brought magazines for Hallie to read.

Halfway through the first one, a man appeared beside her bed. "Hallie McLaren? Hi." He shook her hand— the one not hooked up to the IV. "I'm Dr. Masson. I'm going to be your anesthesiologist. Now, have you ever had an allergic reaction to any medications?"

"No."

"Have you ever been under general anesthetic before?"

"No, I haven't."

"Have they weighed you yet?"

A nurse appeared. "I was just going to do that, Doctor."

"Okay. How tall are you, Hallie?"

"I'm about 5'7"."

The nurse had wheeled an electronic scale over. "Step on this, please."

Hallie stood on the scale. *131 pounds.*

Dr. Masson wrote down the information. "Okay, Hallie. What's going to happen is this: when Dr. Shaw gets here, she'll come in and go over the procedure with you, and answer any questions you might have. When we're all ready, we'll take you to the operating room. I'll add the anesthetic to your IV, and you'll go to sleep very quickly. Next thing you know, you'll be waking up in recovery. I'll send a sheet of instructions home with you. With general anesthetic you can feel groggy for a while, and some people feel a little nauseous. So eat bland, boring food the first day or two. Is someone here who can take you home afterward?"

"My boyfriend is planning on being here about noon, when the surgery is over."

"Will he be taking care of you the rest of the day?"

"Yes."

"So is it all right if we share information with him? Because you probably won't remember much from when you first wake up."

"Yeah, that's fine."

"Okay, any questions for me?"

"None that I can think of."

"I'll see you in the operating room, so if you think of something you can ask me before I knock you out. Okay?"

"Yeah. Thanks."

Hallie leafed through magazines, trying to ignore the soreness around the IV needle. Forty-five minutes later, she looked up to see Dr. Shaw approaching. Wearing a gray raincoat over a black sweater and pants, she didn't look much like a doctor right now. Hallie marveled again at how young and pretty she was.

"Hi, Hallie! How're you feeling?"

"I'm fine. Maybe a little nervous."

"Hopefully we'll have some answers for you today. I'll talk to you after the surgery and let you know what we find in there. Then I'll want you to call the office for a follow-up visit in about a week. I understand you've arranged for someone to take you home and stay with you for the rest of today?"

"Yes, my boyfriend, Ben. He'll be here at noon."

"No, I think he's here now. In fact, he's asking to see you. Nice looking guy, dark hair?"

"That's him, but he said he'd be here when the surgery is over."

"Well, he's here now. So I did tell you that the surgery would take about an hour? That's on average. It could take longer, just depends on what we find. I just don't want you to be startled if you wake up later. Also, remember I told you about the gas we use to inflate your abdomen so we can look around in there a little easier? Sometimes some of the gas remains inside and causes shoulder pain after the surgery. I'm a real stickler for getting that stuff out, but sometimes people report a little shoulder pain. Just wanted to let you know that could happen. Any questions?"

"None that I can think of."

"Okay. I am going to go get ready. Someone will come get you in a few minutes. Do you want the nurse to bring in your boyfriend?"

"Sure. Thanks, Dr. Shaw."

Ben walked through the door moments later carrying balloons and flowers in a vase. "Hey, beautiful!"

"You're amazing. What are you doing here so early?"

"Well, I knew I wouldn't be able to concentrate at work anyway. I wanted to make sure you're okay. Are you?"

"Yes, I'm fine. They've been really great about explaining everything and telling me what to expect. My doctor just went to get ready, so it won't be long now." She glanced at the clock on the wall. "Is it really a quarter to eleven? That was a quick two hours." She squeezed Ben's hand. "I'm glad you're here."

Around the corner came her escorts, two nurses and Dr. Masson. "Are you ready Hallie?" he asked.

"Yes, I think so." They unhooked everything except the IV and one nurse helped Hallie move the tower around the obstacles beside her bed. Hallie turned to Ben. "See you when I wake up!"

"I'll be there," he answered, and kissed her forehead.

Hallie and the IV tower followed the procession down a corridor to the operating room.

Walking through the swinging doors, Hallie suddenly expected a crowd to yell "Surprise!", welcoming the guest of honor to a strange costume party. No one did, but Dr. Shaw and two assistants turned to greet her. Paper masks covered their mouths, but she could see their eyes crinkle in reassuring smiles.

One of the nurses helped Hallie onto the table. Surrounding her were lights, machines and monitors. "Hallie, we're going to open your gown and scoot it up a bit under you," another nurse said.

Hallie nodded. They tucked her gown under her and covered her with a blanket.

"How you doin'?" Dr. Shaw asked.

"I'm fine." *How many times have I said that today?*

Dr. Masson leaned over and looked at Hallie's face. "Hey! Did you think of any questions?" She shook her head. "No? All right. Are you ready? I'm going to start the anesthetic now. You're going to be feeling sleepy pretty quickly, so we'll say good-bye now. Okay?"

Hallie nodded. She watched him put the anesthetic into her IV. *Magic sleeping potion,* she thought. She expected them to have her count backwards from ten or something, like she had seen so many times on TV. A nurse smiled at her again, and she had just enough time to think *Strange, I don't feel sleepy at all.*

"Hallie! Are you with us?"

"Is she awake?"

"I think she's coming around, Doctor."

"Hallie? Time to wake up!"

Opening her eyes, the first thing Hallie saw was a round, institutional black and white clock on the wall. It read ten minutes after two. It blurred, then disappeared as Hallie's heavy eyes closed. With great effort, she opened them again. Still ten minutes after two. She looked up at the nurse and Dr. Shaw standing over her. "Your clock is wrong," she said.

Dr. Shaw smiled and shook her head. "No, that's the correct time. Your surgery took longer than we expected. It took about three hours. We found a lot of endometriosis, Hallie. I'll go into more detail when you come see me in my office, but for now at least we have a clear reason for all the pain you've been in."

"So I'm not crazy?"

"No, not at all. How are you feeling?"

"Sleepy. My mouth is really dry, too."

"I'll get you some water," said the nurse, and she moved quickly out of Hallie's view.

"Remember, you're going to feel groggy and maybe a little sick to your stomach for the rest of the day and possibly into tomorrow. That's just the anesthetic; it's perfectly normal. I'll give some instructions on your care to your boyfriend, okay? I'll go get him now."

Hallie closed her eyes again. They felt so much better closed. The nurse's voice said, "Here's your water. I'll help you sit up."

This did not sound like a marvelous prospect to Hallie, but opening her eyes was slightly easier this time. She scooted forward on the bed, slowly, and the nurse arranged the pillows behind her. "Okay," she said, "lean back. Is that comfortable?"

Hallie nodded. The nurse wheeled a table over, on which she had placed a paper cup full of water. Hallie took a sip. It tasted wonderful. Realizing exactly how thirsty she was, Hallie drank half the water before the nurse said, "Just drink a little at a time for now and see how it settles on your tummy."

Ben walked in. Dr. Shaw was beside him, talking, and Ben was looking at a piece of paper in his hand. Looking up, he grinned at Hallie.

"Hey, how's my sweetheart?"

"I'm fine, just really tired."

Dr. Shaw patted her hand. "The surgery went really well. We were able to cauterize all of the endometriosis we found. Right now, you are disease-free. Chances are it will come back, but it has been known not to recur. We'll hope you're one of the lucky ones. I've told Ben what to expect for the rest of today; he has some written information about the surgery and about the anesthetic. I've also given him a prescription for some pain meds. Don't be brave. Take them before the pain gets too bad. I want to see you in a week. Then we'll go over everything in detail. For now, just relax and let the anesthetic wear off a bit. The nurses will watch you and let you know when you can go home. Okay?"

"Thanks, Dr. Shaw."

"You're welcome. See you in a week!"

Ben sat with Hallie as she gradually became more alert, ate crackers and drank more water. From crackers she graduated to chicken noodle soup; its warmth felt comforting. Then one of the nurses took her blood pressure and announced it was at last time to go home. She fetched Hallie's bag of belongings and helped her dress while Ben had her prescription filled at the clinic's pharmacy. He brought the car around to the closest entrance. Hallie stood slowly, turned and sat in the requisite wheelchair for the ride to the car. Nurse Carol was assigned to wheel her outside; she held the chair and watched as Ben helped Hallie stand up and walk to his car.

Now that the anesthetic was beginning to wear off, Hallie was feeling a little pain. She wasn't able to stand up completely, and had to laugh at her Quasimodo-like gait. Laughing hurt too though, and not just in her abdomen. She was feeling just a twinge of that shoulder pain Dr. Shaw had warned her about. She slid into Ben's car and pulled the seat belt across, clicking it in place.

Smiling at Carol, she waved good-bye as Ben closed the car door and walked around to the driver's side. Hallie thought about Carol and the other nurses, going on with their workday, treating and comforting the people coming and going, coming and going. It was a gift, she reflected, the ability to touch someone so intimately, yet so briefly.

Hallie and Ben pulled away from the curb, and Carol was already back inside, pushing the wheelchair toward its next occupant, while Hallie's thoughts shifted to the couch and cat waiting for her at home. She looked at Ben. Ben, who was now driving her there, balloons and flowers in the backseat.

She smiled and touched his arm. "Thanks for doing this."

He glanced over, smiling back at her. "I'm happy to be here. I was getting a little worried about you when the surgery took so long. Dr. Shaw said it might take a little longer for you to recover because of all the work they did in there. You just relax and let me take care of you, okay?"

"Sounds good." Hallie closed her eyes, still smiling.

13

It was nearly 4:30 when Ben helped Hallie up the stairs to her apartment. He fetched a comforter and pillows from her bed, ran past Hallie and arranged them on the couch. When she was settled in, he returned to the car for the last load. With the balloons in the corner behind the couch and the flowers on the kitchen table, he sat down at Hallie's feet.

Cleo, displaced from the bed, had been following Ben ever since. Now, seeing Hallie on the couch, she jumped up and lay next to Hallie's legs on the comforter.

"Are you in a lot of pain?" Ben asked.

"Actually, yeah I am. It's worse than I thought it would be. I think I'm ready for a pain pill."

"Coming right up." From the kitchen he called, "Hallie, it says take one or two tablets every six hours as needed. Do you want to start with one and see how you feel?"

"That's a good idea." Ben brought her the pill, a plate of crackers and a glass of water. "You're supposed to take them with food."

"Thanks."

"Are you comfortable?"

"Yes, thank you."

"Okay, don't move. Anything you want, just say so. What sounds good for dinner?"

"I'm supposed to eat bland food tonight. I have some frozen entrees. There's a chicken fettuccine that would be fine."

"No, I want you to have real food. I'll figure something out; is it okay if I just scout around your kitchen?"

"Of course. I think I have some hamburger and a couple of chicken breasts in the freezer."

"Want the TV on?"

"Sure."

Half an hour later, good smells were coming from the kitchen. Hallie was watching a sitcom she normally didn't like but which now seemed hilarious. "I think one pill is just fine, Ben! I'm feeling much better!"

He peeked around the corner. "Hallie McLaren, are you stoned?"

"Maybe a little. The pain isn't quite so intense now."

"That's good. Remember, it will be time for another one at 10:30, then hopefully you'll be able to sleep. Uh, Hallie? I really think I should sleep on the couch tonight. I don't like the idea of you being alone all night. What do you think?"

"That's fine. It will be nice to have you here when I wake up. But what about work tomorrow?"

"Well— I have a confession to make. I took tomorrow off too."

"But Ben, Cora said she'd come by tomorrow to see if I needed anything. You don't have to waste your vacation time on this!"

"It's not a waste, and besides I haven't really been taking all my vacation days. I have to take at least two more days off before the end of the year or I'll be over the maximum bankable hours and I'll lose them. So you've given me a very good reason to avoid that! Cora can still come over. I'll run out for groceries while she's here."

"Why haven't you taken any time off for so long?"

"I've taken a day or two now and then, but the idea of going on a two week vacation by myself just doesn't appeal to me all that much. I was thinking about getting some friends together for a ski trip this winter, but haven't planned anything yet. So really, I need to take some days off and I can't think of a better way to spend them."

"Okay, if you're really sure about that. I don't have a lot of extra blankets, but there's a sleeping bag in the front closet. Hey— what smells so good?"

"You'll see!"

Hallie watched TV cuddled up with Cleo, who was now curled next to her sound asleep, and finally dozed a bit herself until Ben tapped her shoulder. "Hey you, dinner's ready. Do you have a TV tray?"

"No, but there's a little table in my bedroom that might work."

The table was perfect— just tall enough for Hallie to reach comfortably from the couch. Ben put her plate on it along with a fork and paper napkin. "It's nothing fancy; I hope you like it."

Hallie had to smile. "How could you possibly know that meatloaf and mashed potatoes are my all time favorite comfort foods? Thank you."

"Anytime. What would you like to drink? I'm boiling water, would you like some tea?"

"Perfect. Lemon, please. It's in the…"

"Cupboard above the stove. I found it. I'll be right back."

Hallie looked at her food. He had even put butter, salt and pepper on her potatoes, and the meatloaf had tomato sauce on the top, just the way she made it. She nudged Cleo off the couch, then took a bite. "Bland can be quite wonderful, don't you think?"

Ben brought her the tea, then sat down at the table with his own plate. "Are you comfortable?" he asked one more time.

"I'm fine."

Throughout the evening, Ben doted on Hallie. She was in no position to object. When she moved or laughed, the pain reminded her of the reason for all this attention. Inevitably, the time came for Hallie to venture to the bathroom. She postponed the trip as long as possible but finally broke the news. "Guess what? I really have to go to the bathroom."

Ben stood and fairly leapt over to her. "Here, take my hand."

She reached for his hand with both of hers. He held her arm with his other hand. Slowly, she moved her legs until her feet touched the floor and gradually, gently, Ben helped her to her feet.

"You okay?" he asked.

"I think so. Let me see if I can do this on my own." She took a few steps toward the bathroom door. "I'm okay. It hurts, but I can do it."

"Okay, but you yell if you need me."

No wonder they told me to wear sweat pants, she thought as she eased them down over her belly, which was now much rounder than she had ever seen it. A bandage covered her navel and two smaller strips hid spots on her lower abdomen. If she drew a line between the three bandages, there would be a triangle on her stomach. She wondered what the incisions looked like, but she wasn't supposed to take the bandages off for twenty-four hours; she couldn't actually imagine trying now anyway, the area was so tender.

Hallie had never thought much about the mechanics of urinating. Now, to her amazement, it was clear that some effort involving the abdominal muscles was required in the process. The pain brought tears to her eyes. As she stood and pulled her underwear and pants back up over her swollen belly, she would have traded this pain for even her worst cramps.

She flushed, washed her hands and glanced at the mirror above the sink. *Ugh! Who is that?* Her face was white, her eyes rimmed in pink. She considered brushing her hair, but remembered that her brush was in the cupboard under the sink. Bending down was not an attractive prospect. The hair could wait.

"Are you okay?" Ben called.

"Peachy. I'm coming out."

Emerging from the bathroom she said, "Please tell me it will be worth it."

He put his arm around her and she leaned against him, grateful for his help back to the couch. "I'm sure it will be. Dr. Shaw said you've been dealing with a lot of pain for a long time. It's bound to be better now. Once you heal from the surgery, you're going to be in great shape."

Lifting her sweatshirt over her belly, she showed Ben how far it protruded. "Look! It's like I'm five or sixth months pregnant!"

He leaned over and kissed her forehead, her nose. "You'll be beautiful pregnant."

"You think so?" Hallie grinned at him.

He nodded, not moving, staring straight into her eyes. "I love you, Hallie. You know that, don't you? I don't want to scare you or anything; I just wanted to say it."

Taking his hand, she pulled him closer. He sat beside her, on the edge of the couch. "I love you, too, Ben. I love you so much."

Tucking one arm behind her shoulders, he held her gently, gratefully, kissed her hair, then unwound himself from her and adjusted the pillows behind her. "Comfortable? Can I get you anything?"

She shook her head. "I have everything I need."

14

Ben had given Hallie another pain pill at 10:30 just as he'd promised, then helped her into bed, tucked her in, turned off the light and left the door open just a little. He uncurled Hallie's sleeping bag on the couch and watched TV until he felt his eyes droop. Cleo happily switched from one bed to the other throughout the night.

After a restless night spent half listening for Hallie, Ben woke up one last time. Dim light and birdsong told him that morning had finally arrived. No noise yet from Hallie's room, though. He hoped she'd been able to sleep.

He rolled up the sleeping bag and walked to the bedroom door. Peeking in, he saw her face, eyes closed and peaceful, her chestnut hair wild around her. *She loves me.* He smiled. Watching her from the doorway, he saw her eyes open. "Good morning! How are you feeling?"

"Um..." She shifted, lifted her head from the pillows. "Oh! It hurts. A lot."

"Wait right there. I'll bring you some food and a pain pill."

He brought toast, juice and water, and her pill. When Hallie began to feel its effects, he helped her to the couch. "How's that?"

"Better, thanks. But..."

"What do you need?"

"I hate to say this, but I feel really grungy. I think I'd like to take a shower. I just need to tape some plastic over my incisions."

"Gotcha." Ben rummaged through the kitchen drawers. He found a plastic bag, scissors and tape. The bag was large enough to cut two squares: a double layer to fit over Hallie's belly. She lifted her pajama top and lowered the elastic waist of the bottoms to uncover all three incisions. There was some redness around each bandage, and her stomach was still a bit distended. Hallie positioned the plastic and Ben taped it on, then gently covered the area with her pajamas. "Ready?" he asked.

She nodded, took his arm and stood up. "I'm okay from here."

"Okay, but I'll be listening. Yell if you get into trouble. Do you want me to get some clothes from your room?"

"Yeah. Bottom right drawer of my dresser. My gray sweatpants. I think the top's in there, too. My underwear is in the top left drawer, socks in the top right."

Hallie walked into the bathroom and took a clean towel from the shelf. *Bottom shelf. Why did I put these on the bottom shelf?* It hurt to bend, but she managed. Ben appeared at the door as she was slowly straightening back up. "You sure you're up to this?"

"Yeah. I know I'll feel better when I'm clean."

He handed her the pile of fresh clothes, bra and panties on top of the pile. The intimacy of the situation struck her suddenly. Here he was choosing underwear for her when he had never even seen her in anything more daring than a pair of shorts and a t-shirt. She wondered if the same thoughts had occurred to him. Was he blushing, just a bit?

As if in answer, Ben grinned. "You have nice underwear. I thought pink cotton would be more comfortable today than your black lace."

"How considerate," she laughed. "You're right. I'm not exactly feeling seductive right now."

"Flannel pj's are sexy on you, though." He turned on the shower, adjusted the temperature and closed the curtain. "You're all set. I'll be listening outside." He kissed her nose and stepped out.

When Hallie emerged from the bathroom in a cloud of steam, toweling her hair dry, she felt warm and refreshed, but ready to recline. Ben had just tucked her in again on the couch when the phone rang. "The cordless is in the bedroom," she told Ben. "Go ahead and answer it if you want."

He picked it up on the third ring. "Hello? Hey, Cora." Ben's voice got louder as he walked the phone in to Hallie. "Yeah, she's awake. Even took a shower this morning. I think she's in a lot of pain, but she's a trouper. Yeah, I think she's expecting you, but you can talk to her. Here she is."

"Hi, Cora!"

"Hello, sweetie. Feeling a little delicate?"

"It does hurt, more than I expected really. But Ben is taking good care of me. Are you still coming over?"

"Absolutely. Just wondering if you need anything."

"No, nothing. Ben is going to go get some groceries while you're here. He thinks I shouldn't be alone yet."

"Good boy. All right, dear. I'll be there in about an hour."

Moments later, the phone rang again. This time, Hallie answered. "Hello?"

"Hey! It's Lonnie! You were supposed to call me last night! How'd it go?"

"Sorry. I completely forgot to call. It went well, I guess. It took longer than they thought it would. It's definitely endometriosis. They found a lot of it in there, but they managed to get rid of it."

"Get rid of it? Will it come back?"

"Yeah, it probably will, but things should be better for a while."

"Well at least you know, right?"

"Yeah! It's good to know I'm not a hypochondriac, or a wimp."

"When do you see the doc again?"

"I have to call today to make an appointment. I was still pretty groggy when I woke up, so Dr. Shaw said she'd go into more detail when I see her."

"Makes sense. So how are you feeling now?"

"I'm sore, but the pain pills help. Ben is here, and Cora's coming by, so I'm being well taken care of. Hey, thanks for taking me and checking up on me."

"*De nada.* I'm sorry about running out on you so fast. I'm just not very comfortable with the whole hospital thing. But if you need anything, give me a jingle. Okay?"

"I will. Thanks again."

Hallie hung up and once again, the phone rang almost immediately. "This has to be my mom." She took a deep breath before answering. Ben saw her shoulders droop.

"Hello? Hi, Mom. Yeah, I'm fine. The surgery went well. I do have endometriosis. Yes, it really is a disease. What? Well, maybe you do have it, Mom. Really? I had no idea your periods were so painful. But aren't you going through menopause now? Still having periods regularly? Well, talk to your doctor. Mom? It's time for a pain pill, so I'm going to hang up, okay? I'm sorry about your friend, but I really don't think I'm going to get addicted to pain pills. Well, I'll try to be strong this one time, Mom. I'll talk to you next week after I see the doctor, okay? Bye!"

Hallie tossed the phone onto the far end of the couch. "Aaaaaaah! It's always about her. I know she's my mother, but I really don't like the woman very much. Is that terrible?"

"No, just honest. I'm glad you decided to move away from her. Being a mother doesn't automatically make someone a good person. But your obligatory conversation is over for today. You've met your quota."

"Thank God!"

Cora tapped her signature code on the door. Hallie always knew when it was Cora; she knocked in a particular rhythm: tap, taptap, tap, tap. Ben opened the door and there she was, bright red windbreaker and lipstick to match. Ben took the huge paper shopping bag from her and invited her in.

"How's our girl? Ah, there you are. Well, you look awfully pale. Are you in a lot of pain, sugar pie?"

"A fair amount. The surgery took three hours instead of one. Dr. Shaw told Ben my recovery would probably take a little longer than she originally thought."

"I would imagine. Just being under anesthetic that long takes its toll, let alone all that work they did in there. So what happens on Monday when Ben goes back to work?"

"I'm sure I'll be able to take care of myself by then."

"Maybe so, but you shouldn't have to. I'll tell you what. Tom and I will pick you up on Sunday night and you will come stay with me for a day or two."

"Cora, I appreciate it, but really…"

"No objections. We'll fix up a spare room upstairs. There's a bathroom right across the hall. You'll have all the privacy you need, and you won't be alone. Please, Hallie. Do it for me. I just can't bear the thought of you all alone and in pain."

Hallie smiled. "Thanks, Cora. I'd love to stay with you."

"Wonderful. It's settled. Now, look at the goodies I brought!" From the bag Ben had put on the table Cora brought out a teapot, several varieties of tea, a large plate of cookies, plus some lavender bubble bath, flower-shaped floating candles and French-milled soap. "We're going to have a little tea party while Ben runs his errands. The rest is for a nice long soak in the tub when you're up to it. It's just the thing for a sore body. I'll put the kettle on!" She headed for the kitchen.

Hallie shrugged. "She thinks of everything!"

"Well, I know you'll be in good hands when I'm gone. Not that I want to leave."

"It's only Friday. We still have all weekend." Ben knelt beside the couch and kissed her, then nuzzled her neck. "I'm going to go get those groceries. I'll be back soon. I love you." He kissed her forehead, then got his jacket from the closet. "Cora, I'm taking off. I'll be back in an hour or so. Take good care of her."

"I certainly will. See you soon, Ben."

The kettle whistled and Cora brought the teapot full of hot water into the living room. "I brought all my favorite teas, so I'll like anything you choose."

Hallie opted for peppermint. While it steeped, Cora seemed deep in thought. "Cora? Everything all right?"

"Hmm? Of course. I was just reminiscing a bit. It's so wonderful to see a young couple in love. He's a good one, Hallie. I can tell. Clearly, he's crazy about you. How do you feel about him?"

"I'm completely loopy about him, Cora. When I'm not with him, I think about him constantly. He is so loving and attentive. He's taking such good care of me through all this. He showed up early when I had surgery and took today off without telling me ahead of time. He seems perfect. My friend Lonnie, you remember her? She tells me that of course he's not perfect, and his flaws will emerge eventually. But right now I can't imagine ever being angry or disappointed with him."

"Falling in love is always the same. Remember when you felt that way about Joe? Lonnie is right. Ben is not perfect. You'll see that eventually. You'll get angry, he'll get angry. You'll go out with your girlfriends and complain that he's too this or not enough that. But none of that matters if you truly love each other. You'll grow to love his quirks because they are part of him. You'll accept and embrace the bad along with the good, and so will he, if the fit is right. If you can bend when he stands firm and he can yield when it's important to you, then you have a fighting chance. Mutual respect, that's what it takes, as well as that little thrill you feel when you gaze into each other's eyes. Do you think this could be the one, Hallie?"

"I think he might be. You're right, Cora. I do remember seeing Joe in that same perfect way. But I really feel that Ben is different. Time will tell, I suppose."

Cora poured their tea. "I think Ben's wonderful. And so handsome! Reminds me a bit of Jack, actually. Oh, I remember the very first time I saw him. Jack, I mean. I attended a lecture he gave at my college. It was about keeping a professional distance from your patients. He was so young. It was his first and only lecture— it was a favor for a sick friend. Afterward, I approached him to ask a question. We started talking and couldn't seem to stop. Went for coffee, then dinner. We were married six months later. By then I knew most of his faults quite well, but I did discover a few more after the wedding. We argued now and then, but always had a genuine respect for each other. I adored him. I'm completely sure we would still be married if he hadn't died. That's the kind of love I want for you, sweetie. You'll have it too, I'm certain. I hope Ben is the one so that you don't have to wait any longer for it to come along. Here, have a cookie."

As always, time with Cora sped along. When Ben returned, Cora helped him put groceries away, then called for a taxi. Tom was busy, she said. "He's always off getting supplies for the yard or working on next year's planting budget. What would I do without him?"

After Cora was gone, Hallie sighed. "Why can't she be my mother?"

"She is incredible. But she loves you like family anyway, Hallie. I read somewhere that friends are the family we choose. Can't do much about who we're born to, so if they're not who we'd like to be with we can at least be picky about all the other people in our lives. And create a better family for our kids."

"Our kids?"

"I meant the generic 'we'. As in, we, as parents, can create better families for our children. But 'our kids' sounds kind of nice, doesn't it? Not that I'm in a hurry, I just…"

"I love you too."

That night, Ben once again tucked Hallie in bed. "Comfortable?"

She nodded. "Ben, I need one more thing. You. I know it's not exactly ideal. We won't be able to make love and I have this big belly right now, but I really want you to sleep here with me. Would that be all right?"

"Are you sure? What if I roll over and hurt you?"

"I'll yell and wake you up. Okay?"

"Yes." He took his clothes off, all except his boxers, folded them and piled them neatly on Hallie's dresser. She smiled, watching him. He turned off the light and crawled in beside her, feeling her warmth. He found her mouth, kissed it softly, touched her face, her hair, her neck.

They found a comfortable position, on their sides with Ben facing Hallie's back, her body curled into him, their fingers laced together. "We're a perfect fit," Hallie whispered, thinking of Cora's words earlier that day.

15

Ben and Hallie enjoyed playing house for the rest of the weekend. Gradually, Hallie's pain diminished; now Sunday was drifting toward evening, and she hadn't taken a pain pill all day.

Cora had called to advise that Tom was not available to transport Hallie to the house after all, so Ben volunteered to bring Hallie over.

"Do you have everything you need? Pain pills, pajamas, clothes for a couple of days?"

"Yeah, I'm all set. Did you give Cleo some extra food and water?"

"Yep. Cleaned the litter box, too. Anything else you need?"

"No, I think I've got everything. But I miss you already."

Ben pulled her close. "It's not going to feel right without you tonight. But I'll call you at Cora's."

"Thank you for taking such good care of me. I feel completely spoiled."

"I loved spoiling you. Hope I get to do some more of it."

"Maybe I'll spoil you for a while."

"Well, there is one thing I need you to do for me when you're back on your feet. I want you to meet my family. They keep asking about you."

"They want to check me out, huh?"

"They know I'm serious about you and yeah, they want to check you out. Would you be okay with that?"

"Ben, I'd love to meet your family."

"Great! I know they'll love you. I'll let them know when you're up to it. So— are you ready to go? Let me help you with your jacket."

When they pulled into Cora's driveway, the front door opened. "Do you need help?" Marion asked.

Ben called back, "No thanks, we're okay." He helped Hallie out of the car, picked up her bag with one hand and put his other arm around her shoulder. Marion took the bag from him as they walked into the house. "You must be Ben," she said. "Nice to meet you. I'll take this up to your room, Hallie."

Cora stood in the hall and held out her arms to both of them. "I'm so glad you agreed to come. Now, don't you worry, Ben. I promise we'll take good care of her. Let's go into the kitchen."

The kitchen was warm and bright. Cora motioned toward a rattan chair with a soft red cushion. "That one is for you, sweetie. Thought it might be a bit more comfortable than the hard old wooden ones. Now, what would you like? Cocoa, tea, a glass of wine?"

"No wine for me. I think I may have a pain pill before I go to bed. But hot cocoa sounds wonderful. Thanks, Cora."

"You're very welcome. Ben?"

"I'll take some cocoa too."

"Marion! Cocoa?" Cora yelled.

"No thanks. I'm going to bed!" came the response from the top of the stairs. And then: "Good-night everybody!"

Cora spoke of the weather, the beach, the birds that had visited that day, while she heated milk, measured cocoa and sugar and took out three large mugs from a cupboard. Glancing over at her guests, she saw they were holding hands. She poured the hot chocolate and Ben walked over to help her stir and carry the cups to the table. "Thank you, dear. Here you are, Hallie. Careful, I think it's pretty hot."

They sipped the rich chocolate. "Mmm, it's so good Cora. Thanks."

"It's a nice treat, isn't it? Well, have you two had a nice weekend? I would imagine you'll be missing each other after being together so much these past few days."

Automatically, Hallie and Ben glanced at each other and smiled. "Yes," Cora continued. "That's what I thought." Her eyes twinkled and her grin was so contagious that in a moment their smiles bubbled into laughter.

When they'd finished their cocoa, Ben reached over and squeezed Hallie's hand. "I hate to leave, but I should let you get settled in for the night. Sleep well. I'll call you tomorrow." He kissed her forehead. "Cora, thank you for the hospitality. Let me know if I can do anything to help with our patient."

"Of course. And don't worry, she'll be just fine."

Hallie stood and slipped her arms around Ben. "Thanks again for everything."

"I'll talk to you tomorrow." He kissed her softly and walked away. They heard the door close a moment later.

" 'Parting is such sweet sorrow.' Shakespeare really knew about love, didn't he sweetheart?"

"Cora, I feel so lucky. Ben treats me like a queen. But before I met you I never would have given him a chance. You've changed my life!"

"Nonsense. You changed your life, Hallie. Maybe I prodded a little, but no one else could have taken these steps for you. Now, what's next? A new career? Marriage? What do you see in your future?"

Hallie laughed. "All of the above, maybe? It's too soon to talk about marriage, but I'm not closing the door on it anymore. A new career, yes. That would be wonderful. I don't want to work with numbers for the rest of my life. I'm just not sure what I want to do exactly."

"Well, you have time to sort it out. Now, how are you feeling? Do you need a pain pill?"

"I think I will take one now and go to bed. I'm pretty tired."

Cora led Hallie upstairs to the room she and Marion had prepared. "I'm sorry about all these stairs, dear. I hope they're not too difficult for you."

"A couple of days ago it would have been a lot tougher. It's not bad now."

"Well, the stairs seem to be getting a bit harder for me to climb as the years roll by, but I keep climbing them. It's good for me, I know. Here we are." At the top of the stairs Cora turned a glass doorknob and opened the door to a huge gold and burgundy bedroom. An enormous four-poster bed stood against one wall; it was so high there was a wooden step stool to climb up. Extra blankets lay on the end of the bed. Bath and hand towels were stacked neatly on the cherry dresser. The far end of the room was rounded into a bay window with its own seat. Before it, two-dozen peach roses sat in a pitcher on a table. Another cushioned rattan chair had been placed beside the table. On the wall opposite the bed, a fireplace glowed, warm and inviting.

"Cora, it's so beautiful!"

"I'm glad you like it. This used to be my bedroom. It's still my favorite room in the house. Feel free to keep the fireplace on as long as you like. We had it converted to gas several years ago. Much more convenient than hauling wood up here. The switch is on the wall to the right of the fireplace. I've put a bell on the nightstand beside the bed. Please ring it anytime you need anything. Marion's room is down the hall, and mine is right next to hers. One of us will hear the bell and come running. The bathroom is directly across the hall. Make yourself at home, Hallie. It's so nice to have you here." Cora kissed Hallie's cheek and closed the door behind her.

Slowly, Hallie walked around the room, drinking in the details: a built-in bookcase filled with books beside the fireplace, a Tiffany-style stained glass lamp on the small bedside table. The cushions on the rattan chair and the window seat were in matching burgundy velvet; the accent pillows were burgundy-flecked gold.

Hallie curled up on the window seat, tucking a pillow behind her back. The windowpanes, placed carefully long ago to create the improbable glass curve through which Hallie now peered, revealed little in the darkness. She couldn't wait to see the view in the morning. *Cora's room,* she thought. *Cora's and Jack's.* She imagined the two of them sitting there, looking out at the Sound, planning their too few days together. Through closed eyes, Hallie saw their children, Barry and Christina, bursting through the door, impatient for attention. When she opened them again, her eyes were moist with both grief and envy for Cora's life. A life that must have seemed charmed, nearly perfect. Jack's early death was so painful, so cruel, yet Cora had not become bitter. She had continued to embrace life and be grateful for the love they had shared.

A generous soul. Hallie remembered reading that phrase somewhere; she marveled now at how well it described Cora.

Drowsy from the pain pill and the fire's warmth, Hallie flipped the switch off, changed into her pajamas and climbed the miniature staircase onto the bed. The sheets and blankets all smelled fresh and clean and she could not remember lying on a more comfortable bed. Drifting close to sleep, Hallie resolved to find a way to thank Cora for her generosity. She just had to think of some perfect way to show Cora how much she was loved and appreciated.

16

It was the morning light that woke Hallie. Sunbeams streamed through the windows and across the room. Hallie's first thought was that Cleo would love to bathe herself in the pool of warm light on the floor. Hallie's watch on the nightstand read 8:24. She could hear voices downstairs; the morning activities had begun.

Hallie stepped to the floor and crossed immediately to the window. Now the view was breathtaking, as she had expected: calm, deep blue water lined by mountains, and not a single cloud in sight. Monday morning had dawned bright and warm after a rainy weekend.

She touched her belly. The swelling was down a little, and the pain had eased considerably. In the bathroom, she brushed her teeth, put on a clean sweat suit and pulled her hair into a ponytail.

Downstairs, she found Cora and Marion in the kitchen. "Hallie! Awake already? I hope we weren't making too much noise?"

"No, not at all. I don't usually sleep late. I woke up and saw what a beautiful day it is and just had to get up. I feel so much better this morning!"

"I'm glad. That doesn't mean you should overdo, though. Sit down and I'll get you a nice cup of tea. Breakfast is almost ready. Marion is making her famous blueberry pancakes."

"I'll make the tea, Cora. You sit down, too," Marion said.

"Thank you, dear." Cora sat next to Hallie. "How did you sleep, sweetie pie?"

"Like a rock. Didn't wake up once. That bed is so comfortable! And the room is so lovely, Cora. You're spoiling me."

"That's the whole idea."

Marion brought their tea, then finished making breakfast and sat down at the table. They feasted on pancakes and fresh squeezed orange juice, chatting between bites.

"Marion knows someone else with endometriosis, Hallie."

"Really? When was she diagnosed?"

Marion took a sip of juice before she spoke. "A few years ago. She was a friend's daughter. Had the same surgery you did. She felt better, at least for a while. Her doctor told her she should get pregnant. Said that's the best thing for it."

"You're kidding!"

"Nope. That's what she told me. I don't know if she tried that. I don't talk to her anymore."

Marion stared at her plate, silent again. Hallie glanced at Cora, who shrugged slightly.

"That's interesting. My doctor hasn't said anything about pregnancy. Of course I'm single, so she probably wouldn't recommend it for me," Hallie said.

"When will you be seeing Sarah again?" Cora asked.

"Wednesday morning at 9. Then I'll go back to work after my appointment. I'm sure I'll be fine by then. So I'll stay here again tonight if that's okay, and go home tomorrow afternoon."

"We'll see how you're feeling tomorrow. If you need to change your plans and stay longer, that's perfectly fine."

"Here's a cozy little scene." Tom had appeared at the archway separating the kitchen from the living room. He scowled at Hallie.

"Hi, Tom," Cora said. "Would you like some pancakes?"

"No, thank you, ma'am. Made myself some breakfast at home this morning. Is there anything special you'd like me to do today?"

"Yes, I would like you to clean and refill the hummingbird feeders. Remember to do that twice a week when the weather is warm, Tom."

"Yes, ma'am. Uh, Cora? I would like to speak with you today about the summer budget."

"I thought we'd settled that last week."

"Well, I neglected to include a few more expenses. Could we discuss it later, alone please?" He jerked his head toward Hallie. "Wouldn't want to impose on your visiting time."

"We will discuss the budget after lunch. In the meantime, I would appreciate a more cordial tone."

Tom grunted his good-byes and left, closing the door a little too hard behind him. "Honestly," Cora said. "I don't know what's wrong with him lately."

"He doesn't like me for some reason. I think he suspects I'm taking advantage of your generosity, Cora."

"Well, it's really none of his business who my friends are. He's worked for me for so long, I guess he's become a little too protective. You don't have that problem, do you, Maid Marion?"

"Are you kidding? I know how hard it is to say no to you, once you've made up your mind to help. Seems to me you force people to take advantage of you. So whose fault is that?"

"By the way, old woman, what do you want for your birthday?"

Hallie, giggling at Marion's candor, stopped now and listened intently.

"Not a thing, Marion. Don't you spend your money on me."

"It's the same thing every year. She won't give me any ideas, and she's not exactly the easiest person to buy for."

"When is your birthday, Cora?" Hallie asked.

"It's July third, dear. My mother, proud first generation American that she was, was so disappointed— I was mere hours away from being born on the fourth."

"This is a big one, though. You have to help me out this year, Cora!" Marion pleaded.

"Nonsense. I'm still just one year older. Eighty is simply one more than 79."

"You're impossible! Hallie, maybe you can worm something out of her."

"I'll try!" *That's how I can thank Cora! I'll do something really special for her birthday. Maybe something she'd like to do, somewhere she'd like to go?* Hallie tucked the question away for later.

Cora waved the subject away with a flick of her wrist. "Back to something more important. Hallie, do you feel up to that tour of the house I promised so long ago?"

"Absolutely! I was hoping you'd offer."

Once again Cora led the way upstairs cautiously, one at a time. On the second floor, Cora started down the hallway. "There's the room you're using, of course, and the bathroom across the hall. Then comes Marion's room. It's a nice-sized bedroom with a big window, and an overstuffed chair she likes to use for reading. Now this," she said, opening another door, "is my little room. Or at least it has been since Jack died. I just couldn't bear staying in that big bedroom without him."

Cora's room, in contrast to her wardrobe, was filled with subdued colors: sage green, pale peach, ivory. Her favorite scents floated on the air: sandalwood and vanilla. A large desk faced the one huge window in the room. The bay window in the master bedroom was spectacular, but Cora's room boasted an even better view of the Sound. "Your room is just beautiful, Cora," Hallie said.

Outside her window hung one of the hummingbird feeders Tom was to re-fill today, and one of the little birds appeared as they watched, hovering beside the feeder and dipping his long, thin beak into the homemade nectar.

"Look! See his green head, and that flash of red on his chest? That's a male, I think. Whenever another bird challenges him at the feeder, he flares his tiny tail out and chases it away. It's like a frightened cat, I suppose, arching her back and making her fur stand on end. When it senses danger, even the tiniest creature tries to make itself look bigger and fiercer than it really is. Fascinating, don't you think?" She sighed, as they watched the little bird disappear into the trees. "Well, shall we continue the tour?"

They walked back down the hallway and continued up the stairs another flight. "You'll have to excuse the dust, sweetie. I'm afraid it's been quite some time since this floor was inhabited. This was Christina's room when she was a teenager," Cora said, opening a door. "She loved blue."

Wallpaper, peeling slightly in the corners, covered the walls with pale blue hearts on what was once a white background. Now it was yellow, nearly brown in some areas. The hardwood floors still shone, but the windows needed a thorough cleaning. Except for a lone rocking chair, the room lay empty, abandoned. Hallie looked at the sloped ceiling, the built-in cabinet, the walk-in closet. She wondered what Christina had studied in this room, what dreams she'd had, what she and her friends had giggled about. "What a lovely room, Cora."

"Well, it used to be. I know I have too much space here. I don't feel right about asking Marion to keep up the areas we don't use. I could hire someone else, I suppose, but why bother? I have plenty of room for guests on the lower floors. And I rarely have guests, anyway. Once or twice a year when the kids come for a visit, that's all.

"Now, down the hall here is another bathroom. Look at the claw-foot tub, isn't it beautiful? And this room..." she tapped on a closed door, "was a study. I used to come up here to catch up on my documentation. You know, my client files. I would take notes during my sessions, then later record more detailed observations in the files. This was my room to do that undisturbed." Cora once again turned a glass doorknob and entered her past. Another room of quiet beauty. Framed prints covered the walls, some instantly recognizable, some not familiar to Hallie at all. Built-in shelves covered an entire wall, floor to ceiling, and were packed with dusty books. Cora's desk and chair remained, tucked into a recess in the wall, facing the beach and her beloved Puget Sound. "If I bought the house today I would remodel this room first, I think. Brighten it up a bit. I'd get rid of this dark cherry and bring in light oak, or teak maybe. I'd lighten the floors, too. You see," she said, turning to

Hallie, "this house was really meant for a young family, not a silly old sentimental lady who can't let it go."

"Oh, Cora. It's your home. There's so much of you here. I would hate to see you move out."

"It's bound to happen eventually. Unless I die suddenly and they take me out feet first, which is a possibility I suppose. Anyway, there's one more room I want to show you."

Cora trudged back down the hall and started up the staircase again. "One more flight, it's not far now. I used to spend a lot of time here."

At the top of the final flight of stairs, the house narrowed into one small, round room. This was the turret visible from the beach. Long before she'd met Cora, Hallie had often looked up at this house while walking on the sand. She had gazed up at "the tower," as she had silently named it, with its pointed roof, its rows of windows, built to see far into the distance. Hallie had admired the entire house, but she had fallen in love with the turret's romance and imagined the room inside. Now she was about to see it.

As expected, the room was perfectly round. A bench had been built along most of its perimeter, its cushions covered in lighthouse-print fabric. A small table and four chairs occupied the room's center, and a large telescope mounted on a tripod stood beside the door. The windows were screened and each could be opened with its own crank handle. From the ceiling hung a planter with a huge Boston fern. "Marion insists on climbing up here to water this thing. She says it wouldn't look right anywhere else, and I suppose she's right. Sometimes I still sit up here and watch the fishing boats, sketch the mountains, or do a little writing. But I don't come up here as much as I used to, and I miss this room. I fancy it misses me a bit as well."

Hallie turned around, looking out the windows at the miles of water, sand, boats and beachcombers. "Oh, Cora! This is an amazing room. I'm so sorry you can't use it more."

Cora smiled. "You look just as enchanted as I did the first time I saw it. This is where Jack proposed to me. It's true! He didn't surprise me with a diamond ring; no, he brought me to this house and told me he had bought it for us, for the family we would create together. Did he know how to sweep a girl off her feet!"

"No wonder you can't give it up. How could you possibly walk away from this place?"

"I keep thinking that Barry or Christina might move back to the area and want the house. But they've settled elsewhere. If I asked, one of them would move in. But I simply won't disrupt their lives for my sake."

"Maybe they don't know it's even an option, Cora. I mean, how could they not love this house as much as you do? Maybe they'd really want it if they knew they could have it."

"No, I don't think so. Barry isn't married and has no children. He says the house is too big for one person, and he loves his life in New York. Christina and her husband own a business, so they can't relocate. No, I'm going to have to come up with another option. Hey, Hallie, since we're up here already, what if we ask Marion to bring us some tea and cookies?"

Marion joined them and brought an early lunch with the tea; she said after lugging the tray of goodies up the stairs she needed a break anyway. "Hallie, Ben called. I told him I'd have you call him right back. Here's the cordless phone. Oh, and remember Tom wants to talk to you after lunch, Cora."

"Oh that's right. Marion, tell him I won't be available after all. I want to spend the afternoon with Hallie. I'll talk to him after she leaves tomorrow."

"Sure, give me the dirty work. Oh, don't give me those puppy dog eyes. I'll tell him. He won't like it, though."

Hallie stepped into the hallway to call Ben. His voice mail picked up, so she left a quick message and returned to Cora and Marion.

They spent hours looking out at the water and chatting idly. When Marion finally returned to the kitchen to prepare their dinner, Cora and Hallie stayed behind and watched the sun set behind the mountains. Hallie wished with a sudden pang that Ben could be there, but otherwise she felt completely at peace.

Tom left early that day; he was already gone when Cora and Hallie joined Marion in the kitchen. "He was about as red as that cushion when I told him you were postponing your little chat, Cora. And you were right, Hallie, he's sure got some kind of problem with you. He grumbled something like 'she's up to no good, Cora's falling for some kind of scam,' blah, blah, blah. That kind of thing."

"Oh, no! I'm so sorry he feels that way. Cora, do you think it would do any good if I talk to him?"

"No, sweetie, I don't. He's made up his own story about you and he's not going to be confused by any evidence to the contrary. But I'm going to talk to him, by God. Anyway, let's not let grouchy old Tom ruin our dinner. What is it, Marion? It smells wonderful."

Hallie did not take a pain pill that night, and Tuesday morning she woke up feeling so much better she felt almost guilty for not working. Still, she was tender and a bit swollen, so she was grateful not to have to squeeze into her work clothes.

She and Cora had another marvelous day together, chatting and exploring the house. All day, simmering in the back of Hallie's mind was the question of Cora's eightieth birthday gift. She listened, waiting for Cora to exclaim that she had always wanted this, or had often thought of doing that. But Cora, as always, was preoccupied with Hallie's needs and desires: "Another cup of tea, sweetie? Or would you prefer some nice hot cocoa?" And: "Here's a shawl for your shoulders, Hallie. Don't want you to catch a chill."

But finally, a possibility: "Have you ever been up to Victoria, Hallie? It's a lovely trip by boat. I'd love to take you up there for high tea this summer. What do you think?"

High tea in Victoria? Maybe I could do that for her birthday, Hallie thought. But when Cora decided to go for a quick walk that afternoon, Hallie went to the kitchen to get Marion's opinion. "Have you come up with any ideas for Cora's birthday?" she ventured.

"Hmm? Oh, actually, that was all a cover. I've been planning something for months. I'm taking her up to Victoria for a day. She loves it up there and can't really go by herself anymore. Why? She doesn't suspect anything does she?"

"No, not that I know of. That's a great gift, Marion. She was just talking about how much she'd like to go up there for high tea."

"I've already got that scheduled at some big hotel up there. I don't know what it's all about, but she seems to like that sort of thing."

"She'll love it. Uh, do you have any suggestions for me? For Cora's birthday, I mean."

Marion scowled as she thought it over. "No, not right off. I was so relieved to come up with something that I just shut my brain down on the subject. But if something occurs to me I'll let you know, how's that?"

"Thanks, Marion."

"Sure thing. Oh, Hallie? Whatever you decide, you should know that Barry and Christina are planning a surprise visit for the week of her birthday. So you might want to think about having your celebration either early or late. They're helping me with the trip, and surprising her by showing up and tagging along. We're going the day of her birthday, the third, but they'll be here the whole week."

"What a wonderful surprise! She'll be thrilled. I hope I can come up with something special. She's done so much for me. I can't even tell you how she's changed my life. I just think the world of her."

Marion smiled. "Hard not to like Cora, that's for sure. She thinks you're pretty special, too, Hallie. That's clear."

"Thanks. Is it all right if I use the phone?"

"Of course. There's one in the living room."

Hallie hadn't heard from Ben yet; she thought she would use Cora's absence to check in with him. This time, he answered on the first ring. "Hey! Is it a good time?"

"I was just going to call you. How're ya feeling?"

"Pretty good. I'm just a little sore now. I'm not taking the pain pills anymore at all. So I'm on track to see the doctor in the morning and then head back to work. I don't even want to think about the pile on my desk."

"Can I take you to lunch tomorrow?"

"I'd love that."

"Are you going home tonight?"

"Yeah, I need to see my cat, decide on my clothes for tomorrow, maybe do laundry."

"Do you want some company?"

"That's tempting, but I'm not leaving until after dinner. I'm going to need a good night's sleep if I'm going to get through the day without a nap."

"Okay, but come see me when you get to the office. All right?"

"I promise. Can't wait to see you."

"Me too. I'm glad you're feeling better. I'll see you in the morning. I love you."

"I love you, too. 'Bye."

She smiled as she returned the receiver to its cradle. Saying 'I love you' had become routine for them. Glowing, she went back to the kitchen to wait for Cora.

That night, Hallie was happy to go home. She had enjoyed staying in Cora's house and having her near, but there was something comforting about being surrounded by her own belongings. She popped a movie in the VCR, grabbed Cleo and curled up on the couch, completely content. Crawling into bed later she smiled, remembering Ben there beside her. Soon, she was sure, he would be back.

17

Wednesday morning came too quickly. Hallie dreaded the pile of work, which, she was sure, sat waiting on her desk. First, though, she had to keep her doctor's appointment. It would be interesting to hear more about the surgery.

Dr. Shaw didn't keep her waiting long. She walked into the exam room, reading Hallie's chart, then looked up. "Hi, Hallie. How are you feeling?"

"I'm still a little sore, but the incisions seem to be healing quickly."

"Let's see." Dr. Shaw instructed Hallie to lie back on the exam table, and unzip her pants. "No swelling, no redness. Looks good! Go ahead and sit up.

"Now, about the surgery. As I mentioned in recovery, I was able to cauterize all the endometriosis cells I found. There was a lot of it, Hallie. There's an area behind the uterus called the cul-de-sac. The endometriosis had really built up heavily in that area. There was some on your ovaries and fallopian tubes; there was a lot of scar tissue there as well. A few cells had adhered to your abdominal wall."

"So what happens now?"

"Well, you can go on birth control pills. If we start them right away there's a chance the endometriosis won't build up again, but there are no guarantees. This tends to be a chronic disease. And Hallie, there's something else: there is already some damage to your ovaries and fallopian tubes. Because of the scar tissue in those areas, it's unlikely that you will be able to conceive a child. It's not impossible, but the odds are against you. I'm sorry."

Dr. Shaw's voice suddenly seemed distant. Hallie's mind replayed the news, waiting for her heart to grasp its meaning. *It's unlikely that you will be able to conceive a child. Unlikely. Against the odds.*

Hallie took the prescription for birth control pills. She tried to speak, but her throat hurt. She did not want to cry in Dr. Shaw's presence again, so she closed her mouth, nodded and swallowed.

"Hallie? Are you all right?"

Hallie smiled and shrugged. She swallowed again and tried out her voice. "I'm not sure," she whispered.

"I'm so sorry. I know this is a shock. But you may end up proving me wrong, you never know." Sarah Shaw put her arm around Hallie's shoulders and walked her to the waiting room door. "Please call if your symptoms come back or if anything changes at all. Okay? And say hi to Cora for me."

Later, Hallie would not remember the drive to the office. She had been so eager to see Ben, but now she couldn't bring herself to look for him. Instead, she walked directly to her office, nodding absently as people greeted her along the way. She closed the door and sat behind her desk. As expected, a large pile had accumulated in her in-box. She stared at the memo on top of the pile, reading the subject line over and over and not understanding it; it might well have been written in a foreign language.

She picked up the phone and began to retrieve her messages. Most were wishes for a speedy recovery; a few were clients who wished to speak only with her. She wrote down names and numbers, but found it difficult to concentrate. She had to listen to some of the messages two or three times.

Hallie returned the more urgent phone calls and began to go through the contents of her in-box. She tried to lose herself in the work, to shut out all other thoughts. But Dr. Shaw's voice was relentless, repeating over and over what could not be ignored or denied. Hallie felt cold and hollow, empty.

Inevitably, Ben appeared at her office door. "Hey! I thought you were going to come see me!"

"Sorry. I just wanted to… I just…I can't talk right now."

"Hallie? What is it? Listen, it's almost lunchtime. Why don't we take off, get a bite and talk. Hallie?"

She looked up at him. How could she tell him? She knew he had been thinking about their future. They *both* had. Children were part of the picture for Ben, no question. Their relationship was still so new; this could mean the end for him. Why would he waste any more time, risk getting more serious with someone who could never give him what he wants? She had to tell him and accept his decision.

"Okay. Lunch sounds good."

At Ben's suggestion, they drove to a restaurant out of the immediate area, hoping to avoid co-workers. Hallie was silent, staring out the window. "We could talk now, get it out of the way so we can digest our food better," Ben said, smiling gently.

"Let's wait until we sit down."

They sat, looked over the menus quickly and ordered their lunches. Ben waited, watching Hallie examine the tablecloth. "Hallie? Whatever it is, you can tell me." He reached out and took her hand in both of his. "Just say it."

Meeting his eyes was so hard. Once again, Hallie did not trust her voice. She cleared her throat, sipped water and opened her mouth to speak. "Ben. You know how I feel about you. I know you love me too. But this is all pretty new and I want you to know that you don't owe me anything. You're not obligated to me for anything."

"Hallie, what's this about? I want to be obligated to you."

"Please, just let me get through this. I found out something today. Something bad."

"From your doctor?" He swallowed. "Hallie, are you all right?"

"It's the endometriosis. It's caused a lot of scarring. It looks like I probably won't be able to have children."

She looked steadily at his eyes as she said the words. Kept watching them afterward, waiting for his response. It took a moment for the words to settle, for their meaning to be absorbed. When they took their full effect, Hallie saw what she had hoped she wouldn't. There was a flicker, just for a moment, and Hallie saw pain, disappointment, a sense of finality. She watched as he pushed those emotions away before he spoke.

"Probably? So it's not definite?"

"No, she said I could prove her wrong, but the odds are against me. That's pretty much exactly what she said."

"Well, there you go! You'll prove her wrong. All the new technology, fertility drugs and all that, it won't be a problem. And Hallie, we could always adopt. I don't want to blow this great thing we've got going because you may or may not have trouble getting pregnant someday. Do you?"

But Hallie wasn't listening anymore. All she could think about was Ben's first reaction, the involuntary flash of sad resignation that registered on his face before he could stop it. *That's my answer. It's over.*

Hallie nodded and smiled at his attempts at conversation over lunch. They drove back to the office in silence. When they parked, he reached over and squeezed her hand. "God, I'm such an idiot. I should have been thinking about how this is making you feel. I'm so sorry, Hallie. This must seem so unfair. You must be hurting." He reached out to hold her.

"Thanks, but I'm okay. I've got to get back to work though. Thank you for lunch and everything. I'll see you later." She was out of the car and almost to the building before he could even wonder what was wrong.

He called to her as she walked through the door, but she didn't look back.

Hallie spent the next two weeks working and avoiding Ben. He would appear at her office, only to find her chair empty. He couldn't seem to find her in time for lunch. He left notes on her desk and messages on her voice mail. He sent e-mails.

At home, Hallie would listen to message after message of apology. Ben's voice would greet her, pleading for a live conversation, another chance. "Please tell me what to say or do. You don't have to go through this alone. I miss you." Two or three hours would pass and he would call again, convinced he finally understood what crime he had committed. "Hallie, it's Ben. I should have thought about you first, considered your feelings before telling you I was okay about the baby thing. It was completely self-centered. I realize that now. When it finally occurred to me that you were feeling bad, it must have seemed like an after-thought. I'm such an ass. Please forgive me, Hallie." And then: "Hallie, I was such a jerk to suggest we adopt a baby someday when I had no idea how you feel about that. I should have asked you first. Please give me another chance. I love you."

Hallie's resolve nearly crumbled several times. She began to erase the messages without listening to them. With all of her being, she missed Ben, mourned the life together they had just begun. Sometimes she wished they had made love; then she would shake the thought from her mind and tell herself it would have made things so much more difficult now.

Fortunately, she had the perfect preoccupation. Cora's birthday was approaching quickly, and she had to come up with a really special gift. One evening she resorted to flipping through the yellow pages, desperate for ideas. When the phone rang, she didn't move. The answering machine beeped and she waited for Ben's voice. "Hi Hallie, it's Lonnie. Just wondering how you're feeling and when we can get together for a karaoke night or whatever. Give me a call!"

"Lonnie?"

"Hey, you're there! How you doin'?"

"I'm fine. Sorry I haven't called. I've been going through something. I'm not seeing Ben anymore."

"What? Why?"

"It's a long story."

"Hallie, are you okay? Do you want me to come over?"

"I'd like that."

"I'm on my way."

Based on the distance between their homes, Hallie estimated Lonnie would arrive in forty-five minutes. She was at the door in just under thirty. She hugged Hallie, took her jacket off and sat at the kitchen table.

"What happened?"

"I'm making cocoa. Want some?"

"Sure, thanks. Hallie, what's going on?"

"Well, it looks like I'm not going to be able to have kids."

"Because of your endometriosis? Oh my God, Hallie, I'm so sorry. When did you find out?"

"The Wednesday after my surgery. I went in for my post-op appointment with Dr. Shaw? She said there was a lot of scarring and my chances of conceiving aren't good."

"And Ben dumped you when he found out? What a creep!"

"No, it wasn't like that. Do you want whipped cream or marshmallows?"

"Whipped cream. What *was* it like then?"

"He said it didn't matter. He said I could end up having a baby anyway. He said we could adopt. He said we had such a good thing going that he wouldn't let it go just because I might not be able to have a baby."

"Okay. I'm officially confused."

"I'm letting him go, Lonnie." Hallie sat down with two mugs and slid one across the table to Lonnie. "We haven't been together very long. I don't have the right to ask him to make this kind of sacrifice. He wants children. His own children. You should see his face when he talks about kids."

"Yeah, well, you should see his face when he looks at you!"

"We love each other, but that's not enough. I've been through this before: trying to get pregnant and not being able to. It ruined my marriage. I'm not going to repeat history. It wouldn't be fair to Ben. He would stay with me, he'd probably end up marrying me out of some sense of loyalty, because he loves me. But how long would it be before he started resenting me? He'd start missing the kids he might have had. He'd have them all dreamed up in his mind— their names, what they'd be good at, what they'd look like. And I would be the one standing between him and his dream. No. I won't do that to either of us."

"Uh, correct me if I'm wrong, but I thought it was Joe diddling his secretary that put a damper on your marriage."

"That's not the whole story. I lost a baby and couldn't get pregnant again. That's what drove Joe away."

"God! I had no idea! But Hallie, Ben's eyes are wide open. He knows going in that there's a problem, and he'd still choose to be with you, if you'd let him."

"You didn't see his face when I told him. He was devastated. He only let it show for a few seconds, but I saw it. And I knew I had to let him go."

"You should talk to him about it, Hallie. How did you break up with him? What did you say?"

"I didn't. I know if I talked to him he'd convince me to change my mind, and I can't let that happen."

"What? Hallie, you've got to be honest. Tell him why you're pushing him away. He'll tell you how he really feels about this whole thing. Give him a chance!"

"I can't talk about this anymore."

"Think about it. Just tell me you'll think about it!"

"Okay, I will. Now, tell me what's going on with you."

"Hey, I'm doing something really exciting this weekend! I'm going up in a hot air balloon! Doesn't that sound like fun? You just float around for a while and then they give you champagne and food. I hope it's clear so we have a good view. Apparently Steve has been planning this for a long time. Kind of romantic, isn't it?"

Hallie smiled. A hot air balloon ride. She closed her eyes and pictured a colorful balloon, floating above a green valley, mountains in the distance. The perfect place to celebrate someone's eightieth birthday.

19

Hallie woke with a start. The noise she'd heard must have been in a dream, that was all. She listened for a moment, heard nothing, and settled back into her pillow. *Pound Pound Pound!* "Hallie! Answer the door!" No. Not a dream. It was Ben, here, now, right outside.

Exhaling deeply, she considered her options. She could simply not open the door. She didn't think Ben would break it down; he would probably just get tired and leave— eventually. Or, she could go to the door and insist that he leave. More problematic: she would have to convince him to leave without discussion. Or, she could face him and tell him the truth. Break it off cleanly. Maybe Lonnie was right; maybe that was the fair thing to do.

Slipping into a bathrobe, she peeked through the peephole. There he was, head down, arm up, about to pound the door again. "Ben, it's midnight. Can we talk in the morning?" she called through the door.

"Hallie! I'm sorry, I know it's late, but you won't see me, you won't answer the phone. I'm going crazy! Tell me what I did wrong. I'll fix it, whatever it is."

"Ssh! You'd better come in." She opened the door and tried not to look at his face.

They sat at the table, each of them silently reflecting on the last time they'd been here together. How joyful, how hopeful they'd been. How long ago it all seemed now.

"Ben, you did nothing wrong. You've been wonderful, and I love you as much as ever. But that's not enough."

"Of course it's enough. You mean everything to me, Hallie. We fit, remember? We feel right together, don't we?"

"We do. But everything felt perfect with Joe in the beginning, too, and then he couldn't deal with losing the baby and not being able to get pregnant again. No, let me finish. I saw your face when I told you what the doctor said. That was your gut talking, your uncontrolled reaction. That was the truth. It would be too painful for you if you could never be a father. You want it too much. I want to have babies too. It's something I've always wanted, and I probably won't be able to. I'm stuck with this body, there's nothing I can do about it. But you're not stuck, Ben. Our relationship is still new. If we end it now, you'll look back someday and may not even think of it as a serious one. But if we stay together, get serious, make a permanent commitment, you'll be giving up something really important to you. You'll already be making a concession before we've even begun. I can't ask that of you, I won't. It would be so much more painful to lose you later, when you finally face that you want a child more than you want me. I know you don't think that would happen, but trust me. Passion fades. Boring routines take over and you have to work at staying in love. When you've already lost something so precious to you, how long would it be before the resentment kicks in?"

Ben leaned back in his chair, shaking his head. "I hear what you're saying. I do. And I'm sorry I responded the way I did. But I honestly don't feel I would be losing anything. Whatever happens, I want us to face it together. We might be years away from marriage and possible babies, but I see that happening for us, Hallie. Yes, it would be a shame if we can't make our own baby. But I've experienced a small taste of life without you and I know I don't want that. It's you I want, Hallie. If we ever have a baby, that would just be a bonus. Please…" He reached for her hand, squeezed hard. "Please don't push me away because it wouldn't be what's best for me. It would be the absolute worst thing that's ever happened to me. Please, Hallie. Please let me love you."

Tears. She saw tears in his eyes and his voice was breaking. *He really does love me,* she thought. *He's hurting as much as I am.* Words formed and crept to her tongue, eager, aching to be spoken: Yes. Hold me. Love me. Forget logic, forget reality. Just stay. She rose from her chair. Arms opened wide, Hallie drew him to her and held him close. Those unspoken words hurt when she swallowed them, leaving her throat raw so that she choked on the new ones she resolved to say in their place.

"I can't. This is so hard, but I have to end this now. I know that someday when you're watching your kids play this will all make sense. If you stay with me, eventually you will resent me, and that would be more than I could take. Please Ben, you have to promise not to call or try to see me. Let's not make this any more difficult than it has to be."

He released her and took a step backward, watching her face. She would not meet his eyes. "You're so wrong, Hallie. This is a mistake. I hope you figure that out before it's too late. In the meantime, I won't bother you. You can go back to being safe and alone. But remember what you told me about Cora? How she changed your life and brought you out of your little cocoon? Do you really want to crawl back in there? Jesus, Hallie! You're so afraid, you won't let yourself live. I know that bastard Joe did a real number on you. You keep thinking that any guy would respond the way he did to the same situation, but it's not true!"

"That's not what I think. I know…"

"Bullshit! If you don't think it, you sure do feel it. I am not Joe, and I never will be. And you think so little of yourself that in your mind I'm going to just move on and find a woman to plug into the space you left behind. That won't happen. Do you think people find this kind of connection every day? They don't. They live lonely lives and settle for something less. Something with just a few pieces of the puzzle missing. Maybe something with no passion, no spark. Or with nothing *but* passion that's gone in six months. Or they just keep looking forever. Some people never find what we have, Hallie. Not in their whole lives."

"Not being able to have children is a pretty big puzzle piece to miss, too. Besides, there are a lot of people out there, Ben. How do you know your Ms. Right isn't around the next corner?"

"Because she's right here in front of me! I've been dating a long time, Hallie, and I've never felt something even close to what I feel for you. I doubt that I ever will again. So don't tell me you're doing me a favor by dumping me, all right? You're not! Hallie, look at me!" Lifting her chin, he forced her to meet his eyes at last. "You're breaking my heart."

"I'm breaking both our hearts. I have to. No matter what you say today, you'll feel differently in five or ten years. If I lost you then, it would kill me."

Ben shook his head. "Life is risky, Hallie. But you can't guess how I'll feel about anything that far in the future. The only thing you can be sure of is that we love each other. That's the only sure bet. I know that I'll love you for the rest of my life, baby or no baby. You're acting as if you know me better than I know myself. But it's not me you know so well, Hallie. It's Joe. You're assuming I will feel, think and act exactly like him. I'm not Joe!"

"Ben, please. I'm not going to change my mind. I have to be strong. It's not what I want, but it's the right thing to do. I know you can't see that right now but you will someday."

Ben collapsed into a chair and covered his face with his hands, then sat back and looked up at Hallie's face, red and puffy from crying. "I guess I've said all I can. I'll let you get some sleep. I promise I'll leave you alone, if that's what you want. I was sure I'd be able to talk you out of this craziness. I believe we belong together, Hallie. I wish you could have enough faith to believe it too."

He stood, walked to her, held her head in his hands. When he kissed her forehead, he heard one sob escape. "You can change your mind, Hallie. Just call. I love you. Don't forget that." A moment ago she had been completely exhausted, but now she seemed more awake and aware than she'd ever been before, drinking in all the details of Ben's face, his smell, his warmth, even the color of his shirt— it was exactly the shade of the first wine they had shared at the Italian restaurant, she was sure.

A dull ache began to gnaw at her core, a newly-formed, physical presence: the longing for Ben, the missing of him. She would carry it as part of her being, first like a boulder on her back, then diminishing with time until someday, she hoped, it would become a precious souvenir of long ago. Hallie reached past her pain; she tried to imagine touching that place someday and finding only a sweet memory to cherish. She told herself, even while he still stood before her, that memories of Ben would always bring a smile to her face.

20

The Saturday before Cora's birthday was gloriously cloudless, glowing with summer warmth. To the west, the Olympic Mountains were fully revealed, proudly surveying their kingdom of islands and sea creatures dwelling in the cool waters of Puget Sound. Shielding her eyes from the brilliance of sun on water, Hallie watched a fishing boat bobbing gently in its serene, liquid cradle.

Hallie walked, breathing in the sweet smells from the flowers lining the streets of Cora's beloved Edmonds. *Life can still be good,* she thought. *I can be happy.* She missed Ben terribly and spent most of her waking hours trying to push him out of her mind, and, while at the office, avoiding him. But she would not grieve today, she told herself. Today was for Cora.

Cora did not know much about the plans for her birthday, only that Marion had something up her sleeve. So she had invited Hallie to lunch today, thinking it would be their private celebration. Hallie knew, however, the afternoon would turn out a little differently than Cora imagined. Barry and Christina would be arriving today; Christina was expected between 1:00 and 1:30, and Barry would follow shortly, no later than 3:00. Excited for Cora, and curious about her children, Hallie was thrilled to be involved with this creative little surprise party of Marion's. Not wishing to intrude, she resolved to leave as soon as gracefully possible after Barry's arrival.

Approaching Cora's beautiful house, Hallie immediately felt better, almost content. She sighed, walked around to the side door and knocked. Marion, opening the door, looked ten years younger, beaming with a sly grin. "Hello, Miss Hallie! How are you today?" Marion said loudly, trying hard to sound normal. Lowering her voice to a stage whisper she added, "She doesn't suspect a thing." And raising it again for Cora's benefit, "Lunch will be ready in a few minutes. Cora's waiting for you in the living room."

"Thanks," Hallie said, and saluted Marion with a conspiratorial OK sign.

"Hallie? In here, sweetie!" Cora called. "Look at you! You look so pretty in your yellow dress— as pretty as this glorious day."

"Well, you're looking pretty spiffy yourself!"

"Thank you, sugar pie. I thought we might go for a little walk after lunch. Breathe in some of this summery air. How does that sound?"

"Sounds like heaven, Cora. Listen— I don't have your birthday gift today. I'm afraid you'll have to wait a bit longer."

"No rush, dear. I'd like to stretch this one out as long as possible. It will give us another reason to see each other. Now,

I have something to tell you." She reached out and held Hallie's hands in her own. "Ben has called me a few times recently. He wants to know if you're all right. He asked me to tell you that he misses you terribly and wants another chance. Of course, I was shocked the first time he called. I realize this is none of my business, and that you may not want to tell a doddering old lady all your secrets, but I know you care for this man, Hallie. What happened?"

"Oh, Cora, I'm sorry you got dragged into this. It's not that I didn't want to tell you, but with your birthday coming up I just didn't have the heart to burden you with my problems."

Cora sat back. "What's your middle name?"

"What?"

"You heard me, your middle name."

"Jane. It's Jane."

"Hallie Jane McLaren, I'm disappointed in you! See, if I'm going to yell at you, I have to use your middle name. That's why we parents give our children middle names you know, so it's clear when we mean business. Anyway, you are never a burden, my dear girl. I love you to pieces. I don't live close to my grandchildren, and I fancy you have become an adopted granddaughter. I couldn't love you more if you were my real granddaughter— or daughter for that matter. As far as I'm concerned you are part of my family now and Hallie, that means we are here for each other no matter what. Right? Okay then. Never protect me again. Clear?"

"Yes. Oh, Cora. You are my best friend. I love you too. I'm so sorry. I've been wanting to tell you. Dr. Shaw told me that I probably won't be able to have children. Ever. Ben loves kids, he wants to be a father more than anything. When I broke the news to him, the look on his face was just heartbreaking. He saw us getting married, he saw me as the future mother of his children, and I had to tell him that it just isn't going to happen that way."

"Hallie. My darling girl. Of course Ben was devastated. You are, too. I'm so terribly sorry."

"Thank you."

"So. Your endometriosis has done some damage, and the odds are against your conceiving. But it's not impossible?"

"No, but it's not fair to ask Ben to play those odds with me."

"Okay. And which prospective father would find it fair? Someone who doesn't want children?"

"I guess I haven't thought ahead that far."

"No, I guess not. Hallie, you want children someday, correct? Or are you now completely giving up on that possibility?"

"No, I still hope I will."

"But not with Ben, because Ben wants them too much. Am I understanding this correctly?"

"It sounds so much more logical in my head, Cora."

"I know, sweetie. Listen. Life is not fair. We are all faced with challenges. This is one of yours. Don't turn away from someone who truly loves you because you want to spare him some pain. Anyone you end up with will go through the pain of whatever hurts you, whatever disappointments or trials you suffer. That's the point, actually. When you choose your mate, you'll have a partner for life. You share all the good *and* all the bad.

"Think about this: if my husband had been able to see into the future and told me that he would die young and leave me with two teenagers, do you think I would have chosen someone else? Not on your life, sugar pie. I wouldn't trade one minute of my time with him for a lifetime with someone else. That's the way Ben feels about you, Hallie Jane. Okay, that's it for now. Just some food for thought." She leaned over and touched Hallie's cheek. "Speaking of food: Marion, how's that lunch coming?"

The three women sat on the sun porch, one of Cora's favorite areas of the house, enjoying the special treats Marion had prepared: crab cakes, smoked salmon, warm spinach salad. Cora was in fine spirits, but when she began to speak wistfully about her children, Marion was barely able to maintain her poker face. When Cora gazed out the window, longing for her loved ones, Marion winked slyly at Hallie.

When lunch was over, Marion shooed them away from the table, refusing all offers to help. "You said you wanted to go for a walk, so you two go ahead while I clean up."

Hallie sneaked a peak at her watch: 12:15. Somehow, she had to get Cora back to the house by 1:00. They couldn't miss Christina's arrival. Hallie retrieved Cora's hat from the living room. "Do you want to wear a jacket?"

"Well, here's your hat, what's your hurry?" Cora laughed. "No, sugar, I think I'll be fine without a jacket."

"Don't you stay out there too long, Cora. You don't want to get too tired out," Marion said.

"Yes, Mother dear."

Hallie held one of Cora's arms as they navigated through the soft sand toward the water. In Cora's other hand was her favorite walking stick. Near the water's edge the sand moistened and firmed, and Cora picked up speed with the more solid footing. "Ah, Hallie, just breathe in all this beauty. Isn't it glorious? Look at Mt. Constance!"

"Which one is that, Cora?"

She pointed. "Just there, see? The one with the double peak. At first I thought it was a bit ironic: her name is Constance, but she is defined by her duality. But when I'd given it a little thought, it made complete sense. We are all a bit conflicted, you see. We all have good and evil streaks. Kindness and cruelty live inside us all. And even the most brilliant among us will occasionally act out of pure, raw emotion. All of those apparent contradictions are givens when it comes to human nature. We are meant to feel conflicted and confused sometimes. Over the years, Constance has reminded me of that. She's been such a comfort. The mountains are spectacular from here, but have you ever been over to the peninsula?"

"No, that's another thing I haven't gotten around to yet."

"Oh, you must go. Take the ferry over to Kingston and explore for a couple of days. You'll fall in love with Washington all over again, I promise.

"Hey, sweetie, I hope I wasn't stepping over the line with my little lecture earlier. I just hate to see you unhappy. Don't try to deny it, I know your face pretty well. Sad thing is, Ben's just as miserable. Seems like a waste of time to me. But I'm not going to rant on and on, tell you how time passes in a flash, how I'm about to turn 80 and the only thing I'd wish for is more time. No, no, I won't burden you with any of those tired old clichés."

Hallie laughed hard, tears forming in the corners of her eyes. "Cora, you are incorrigible!"

" 'I yam what I yam,' darlin'. Let's take a little break, shall we?"

Hallie turned to face the house and saw Marion, waving wildly from the fence line. "Uh, Cora, maybe we should go back now. You seem tired."

"I'm fine, just need a minute."

"Well, if it's all right, I'd like to go back and have a cup of tea. My throat's a little sore."

"Oh, sweetie. Are you getting sick? Well, I wouldn't wonder with all you've been through. Of course, let's go back and I'll have Marion make you some chamomile tea with a little lemon and honey. It works wonders."

Hallie smiled, pleased that her little ruse did the trick. Cora so loved to take care of people. From the gate, Marion saw them trudging back and retreated quickly into the house.

"You should have said something earlier, Hallie. We didn't have to go for a walk today. You shouldn't be out here in this breeze. And you probably felt you couldn't disappoint me because of my birthday coming up."

"Cora, it's all right! I'd just really like cup of that tea. I'm glad we got some fresh air." Hallie helped Cora onto the front walk and through the gate, then slipped ahead to reach the door first. Marion opened it, mouthed the words She's Here, and pointed toward the living room.

Cora, watching the ground as she made her way into the house, continued to fuss about Hallie's fictional sore throat. "Marion, please fix some tea for our girl. She's coming down with something. Don't forget the honey and lemon. I'll take some too. Well? What's wrong with you two?"

Marion and Hallie stood, grinning at Cora. "Oh, that's how you got her to turn around? Fibbed about feeling sick?" Marion asked.

"Just a sore throat," Hallie said, grinning even wider.

"What's going on here?" Cora asked, intrigued.

Marion looked toward the living room and nodded. Around the corner she came, a woman who could only be Cora's daughter.

"Chrissy!" Cora gasped. They embraced and laughed with the same voice. "You said you couldn't come!"

"I lied!"

"Oh, let me look at you." They stood, face to face. Christina was maybe four inches taller than her mother, but had the same round, pale blue eyes. Her hair was almost entirely white, cut elegantly to her collar and swept to one side. Their smiles were identical, wide and unselfconscious: pure joy. "You look terrific! Oh! I'm so excited I don't know what to do with myself!" Cora looked at Marion. "You knew about this? And Hallie, you too?"

"Marion filled me in. That's why I had to get you back up here so quickly. Marion waved us back early."

"Yes, I got here a little earlier than expected."

"I'm so sorry you weren't here when she arrived," Hallie said.

"Nonsense! It was perfect, just the way it happened. Oh, where are my manners? Christina, this is my dear friend Hallie McLaren."

Christina held Hallie's hand, squeezed it tightly. "Hallie, I've heard so much about you. Mom is lucky to have such a good friend."

"I couldn't ask for a better friend than your mom. She means a lot to me."

Marion moved the group into the living room, then did bring in tea, along with a tray of cookies and other treats. As they all caught up on each other's news, the rest of Cora's surprises were gradually revealed. Barry arrived to complete the reunion, and Marion shared their plans for the trip to Victoria. Surprised and delighted, Cora was actually speechless.

Hallie sat, watching Cora with her children, both warm, kind people like their mother. Both seemed fully aware of exactly how wonderful Cora was. Laughing and chatting, Hallie was once again filled with gratitude for Cora's presence in her life. But gradually, pangs of longing, of envy, of utter loneliness distanced Hallie from the happy scene; finally she stood to announce her departure.

"Oh, Hallie, must you leave? It's gotten so late. Please stay and have dinner with us."

"No, Cora, I really should go. You three need to catch up."

"But there are so many stories to tell you! So much to tell Barry and Christina about you!"

"No, really, this is their first night here. You should have them all to yourself."

"All right, then. But you must promise me you'll come back while they're here. Promise?"

"Of course. I'd love to! It was so nice to meet both of you. Have a wonderful visit!"

Cora saw her to the door, hugged her tight and whispered, "I love you, sugar pie. Please take care of yourself, or you really will get sick. Now we're not going to Victoria until Wednesday, so please come back before then. If I don't hear from you, I'll call. Good-night, sweetie."

Walking up the hill to her apartment, Hallie considered the events of the day: meeting Cora's children, both as wonderful as she; the warm, loving family they were; Cora's wisdom and inarguable logic; her affection for Hallie, unchanging and unbound; Marion's delight in arranging this surprise for her employer.

Tom, Hallie thought suddenly. *Where was he today?* No one had even mentioned him. She shrugged. *Must have taken the day off.*

Finally, inevitably, Hallie allowed her mind to replay Cora's loving reprimand; Hallie found she could no longer defend her actions toward Ben. Cora was absolutely right. What was she waiting for? Someone who wouldn't love her as much? Would that make things easier? What if she was able to have a child someday, by some miracle? Would it make sense to marry someone who didn't want one?

She had told herself that her longing for Ben would ease over time, but her emptiness had grown with each thought of him, each memory of their time together. Why had she pushed him away when he was all she wanted? She couldn't think of a single defensible reason for them to be apart. Hallie found herself running, running toward her apartment, toward her phone, not thinking about what she'd say, just hoping it wasn't too late, hoping he would understand, hoping he still loved her. Hallie ran up the stairs to her door, shaking now, fumbling for her keys.

"Hallie?" His voice was behind her. *He* was behind her. "Hallie, I'm sorry for ambushing you like this, I just had to make sure you're all right."

She turned toward him slowly, afraid he might disappear. A sound escaped her throat that might have been the beginning of laughter or of tears, and she opened her arms. Ben, also afraid to believe this reality, moved toward her carefully, watching her eyes. There he saw a new understanding, deep trust and love above all, love so powerful between them it was terrifying, so perfect it hurt. He moved to her, accepting her arms, folding her into his own. He smelled her hair, kissed her neck and listened as she spoke of love and regret. "Please forgive me. I've been so stupid, I love you so much. I'll never push you away again, I promise."

Neither one would remember later which of them had unlocked the door, nor how they had found their way to the bedroom, only the sweetness of their gentle exploring, their passion, their abandon. There was simply this night, this perfect dance of tingling skin and hungry kisses, their senses filled with the sights, smells and tastes of each other, only each other.

21

"Can't I open my eyes yet?" Cora was getting impatient.

"Just a few more minutes. Behave yourself!" Hallie laughed. The two women were in Hallie's car, about to share an adventure in honor of Cora's birthday.

On the first leg of the trip, Cora described her visit with Barry and Christina and the trip to Victoria. Down to the finger sandwiches and petit fours served for high tea, Cora shared every detail. "Oh, I wish you'd been there, sweetie pie. We missed you. Next time, you'll just have to come along. The kids loved you, just as I knew they would."

Hallie had, at Cora's insistence, been over for one more visit with "the kids" before they returned to their respective lives. Again, she had been struck by their warmth, humor, and the strength of their connection: finishing each other's sentences and giggling at private jokes merely hinted at with a word or two. The gears of their brains simply worked in perfect synchronization. At their second gathering, Hallie felt only admiration for Cora and the family she and Jack had created. Reconnecting with Ben had somehow pushed envy and longing out of Hallie's consciousness. It was as if the bond between them had brought all of her blessings into sharper focus. The world seemed miraculous.

Not wanting to steal the spotlight, Hallie had not yet shared her good news with Cora. She intended to do so later today, over a champagne toast. Glancing over, she laughed out loud at the childlike grin on Cora's face; her manicured hands with their blazing nails covered her eyes so that she wouldn't be tempted to peek. Today she wore Capri pants and a matching tunic in orange, red and yellow. Cora was never one to wear subdued colors. Hallie bit her lip. A champagne toast would be a nice way to make her announcement, but suddenly she simply couldn't wait that long. "Cora, I have something wonderful to tell you, and I just can't put it off any longer!"

"Well, go ahead, dear!"

"Ben and I are back together!"

"I was wondering when you were going to tell me! Honey, I'm just thrilled to pieces. You two belong together, I'm sure of it."

"How did you know?"

"Oh, don't be disappointed, Hallie. It was written all over your face. You were floating so high I thought I might have to tether you to the ground!"

"Hmm. Interesting choice of words."

"You might as well have been wearing a sandwich board declaring the news: 'I've finally come to my senses and all's well with the world!' Well, I'll have to have the two of you over for dinner sometime soon to celebrate. Maybe we could go watch you sing and have a couple of those wonderful margaritas. Marion mentioned she'd like to come along sometime. Wouldn't that be fun? Now can I open my eyes?"

"Not quite yet. I guess you're right. How could you not know? I'm giddy!"

"Yep. You sure are. Barry and Christina even commented on it. They're very happy for you as well. Oh, while I'm thinking about it, they asked for your phone number. They said it was in case they couldn't reach me. I suppose they're picturing me flailing on the floor, unable to get up, while by some strange chain of events Marion is traipsing off to some faraway secluded place where there are no telephones."

"That's fine, Cora. They can have me check up on you anytime. Okay, open your eyes!"

They were parked on gravel, facing a grassy field. From where they sat, they could see a small building, a huge gazebo, and two vans with decals of balloons on their doors. "A hot air balloon ride? Oh, Hallie, it's perfect!"

"Really? Have you done it before?"

"Never! It's a brand new adventure, and I can't think of anyone I'd rather share it with. Thank you, sweetie!" Cora kissed Hallie's cheek with a loud smack, then used her thumb to wipe off the orangey-red lips left behind.

They checked in, signed waivers, and were helped into one of the vans. Several people were already seated onboard. The driver climbed up and announced, "Good evening, everyone! We're heading out to the launch site for your sunset flight this evening. I'll be coming to get you when you touch down. You'll be taking off from a field a couple of miles away, so just sit back and enjoy the ride. We'll be there shortly."

Scattered across the field were several baskets, lying on their sides. Long ropes reached out from several positions on the top of the baskets and connected with huge, brightly colored canvases. People were working at various ends of the contraptions, some tying lines, others checking off lists of required equipment.

The passengers were led from the van to their assigned balloon and pilot. At the pilot's request, some of the passengers stepped forward to help inflate the balloon. Cora and Hallie stood out of the way and watched as flames shot out, sending the necessary heat inside the balloon. The balloon expanded quickly and at last began to lift off the ground. Cora giggled and threw her arms around Hallie. "Look, sweetie pie! Ours is the prettiest!" Hallie took out the camera she had stashed in her purse and snapped a picture of Cora standing in front of the basket and swelling balloon.

Ten minutes later the balloon hovered directly above the basket, now standing upright itself. The late afternoon was clear and warm, a day seemingly made for this purpose alone. First the pilot, then the six other passengers climbed into the basket using footholds cut into the basket. At last Hallie, too, swung her legs over one at a time and stood inside the basket with the rest of the passengers. Only Cora remained. A crew member brought out a two-step wooden staircase— like the one Hallie had used to climb into bed at Cora's house— and slid the steps on the grass toward the balloon.

"Is that for me?" Cora asked.

The pilot answered, "Yeah, we thought we'd give you a little extra help."

"Humbug! At least let me try on my own," Cora said.

Holding the side of the basket, she stepped into a foothold with one foot and swung her other leg over the side of the basket. Hallie took her hand, and Cora brought her other leg inside, landing gently on the floor of the basket.

"Very graceful!" the pilot said. He stood at one end of the basket, beside some gauges and the propane tanks tucked in cubbyholes and asked, "Is everyone ready?"

The group cheered in response. When the pilot had given last minute instructions— keep hands inside the basket when landing, listen to the pilot, don't toss anything out of the balloon— the ground crew let go of the ropes holding the balloon down. The passengers grinned at each other as the balloon floated slowly upward.

Looking down, the ground seemed to move further and further away. Other balloons were taking off too, and Cora and Hallie waved at other passengers.

Floating and bobbing gently, they moved in a breeze they could not feel.

Periodically, the pilot pulled a lever that sent hot, loud flames high into the mouth of the balloon; otherwise they rose silently. Conversations began as they pointed out details on the landscape below: deer among the trees, horses trotting excitedly in the meadows, dogs barking at the sound of the propane flame. A swallow darted and swooped under the basket.

"We're at about a thousand feet above the ground now, folks," the pilot said. Far above the green earth, they could see mountains all around, framing the entire Puget Sound region: Cora's beloved home. Hallie watched as Cora wiped a tear away, overwhelmed by the beauty surrounding them.

"What's the highest you've flown?" Cora asked the pilot.

"I've had it up to about 12,000 feet above sea level. We won't get quite that high tonight, though. We want to touch down in time to drink some champagne."

"Hear, hear!" Cora said.

"We are now one mile above sea level, everybody," the pilot announced.

"This is what the world looks like from a mile above the ocean. What a gorgeous planet we live on," Cora murmured.

When the weather is good, sunsets on Puget Sound are breathtaking. Tonight, a few clouds hovered over the western horizon; just enough to glow orange and pink with the sun's farewell. "It just doesn't get much better than this, huh folks?" the pilot said.

Cora looked over at a young couple, cuddled up in each other's arms. "You should be here with Ben," she whispered to Hallie. "But I'm so glad you brought me!"

"I've been looking forward to doing this with you! Besides, I can always make him bring me again."

Shortly after sunset, the pilot brought the balloon down in a field a few miles from their starting point, and the vans took them back to the office and post-flight gathering place. Champagne was uncorked and poured for each passenger, and a toast made in honor of the safe and beautiful flight. "This is a long held French tradition," the pilot said. "Now, the buffet is open. Help yourselves to all you can eat!"

Cora turned to face Hallie. "French! How perfect! Now, I have a toast of my own. To Hallie: the best friend I could ever hope for! I wish you all the happiness and love in the world!"

"Thank you, Cora, but this is your birthday present, so I have to make a toast too. To Cora: the youngest eighty-year-old known to humankind! Thank you for being so wonderful!"

"I love you too, sugar pie! Now one more: To this marvelous day!" She finished her champagne, looked toward the buffet, nudged Hallie and exclaimed, "Look at the desserts!"

22

Late night phone calls tend to bring life-changing news: births, deaths, accidents. The courtesy not to call at a discourteous hour is normally tossed aside only when urgency requires it. So when Hallie's phone rang at 3:45 on a Tuesday morning, a rush of adrenaline woke her abruptly and completely.

"Hallie? It's Marion. Something's happened. It's bad, honey, real bad. Cora's been taken to the hospital. The paramedics said it's probably a stroke. I'm on my way down there now. Do you want to come along?"

"Of course. Will you come get me?"

"Be there in two shakes. Cora's pointed out your place to me, I think I remember. Oh, and I've already called Christina and Barry. Christina will be here later this morning, and Barry is going to wait to hear back from us. See you in a minute."

On the way to the hospital, Marion described the evening's events. Cora was tired, and said she had a headache. She decided to go to bed early and read for a while. She mentioned that it was probably all the excitement of her birthday finally catching up with her. "She asked me to bring a dinner tray to her room. When I did, she seemed fine, just a little sleepy. I went back to the kitchen, ate my own dinner, cleaned up and went to bed with a book. It's a good book, and I was still reading at 1:42 when I heard the big thump. I know it was 1:42 because I looked right at my clock radio sitting on my dresser. THUMP! You never heard such a horrible sound. I ran down that hallway and into her room just as fast as my legs would go, and there she was, lying there on the floor. 'Did you fall out of bed, Cora?' I asked her. Nothing. She didn't say anything, Hallie. Just lay there. I went to her and, oh Hallie, her eyes were just sort of glazed over. I knew she couldn't see me. She wouldn't answer any of my questions, wouldn't even look at me. It looks like she tried to get out of bed and just collapsed. Thank heaven she has a phone in her room. I called for an ambulance, and bless 'em, they got there in just a minute or two. They looked her over, asked some questions, and took her away. They said it looks like a stroke, but of course the doctors at the hospital will be the ones to figure that out for sure.

"Hallie," Marion said, and reached out to squeeze her hand. "What if she…"

"No, don't even think it. Cora will fight through this. She's going to be fine. I know she will."

At the hospital, the admitting clerk advised that Cora was in urgent care. Tests were being run; they would have to wait for the results. Only family members were permitted to visit.

"Well, I'm her sister, and this is her granddaughter!" Marion said, almost convincingly. "We had a big family. She was the oldest and I was the youngest. I'm older than I look!"

"Uh-huh." The nurse looked slightly amused, then sighed. She looked at Hallie. "Are you really her granddaughter?"

"I'm the closest to a granddaughter she has in the area. Please let us see her."

"Maybe just for a few minutes. But you should know that she hasn't spoken. Also, she appears to have some paralysis on her right side."

"But she can recover, right? The damage isn't necessarily permanent?"

"It's too soon to tell. We need to wait for the test results. Has, uh, the rest of her family been notified?"

"Yes, I called her two kids after the ambulance left the house," Marion said. "Her daughter will be here sometime today. Hallie, let me sit and collect myself a bit before we go in."

"The waiting room for her section is at the end of this hall. Feel free to sit as long as you want. Mrs. Rouget is in room five-forty-seven. But you can only be in there for a few minutes. When her daughter comes, she can give me written permission for you to see her."

"Thanks."

"You're welcome. I'm Cathy, by the way. I'll be here until noon."

Hallie walked Marion to the lounge where other haggard looking people sat or stood in huddles, comforting each other. Marion sat heavily in an available chair. "Hallie, I honestly never thought anything would happen to Cora. I thought she'd outlive me! She's always seemed so…"

"Indestructible, I know. That's why I think she's going to be okay this time. She's going to come back to us, Marion. I'm sure of it. You have to be sure, too. We're going to go in there and help her find the way. Okay?"

Marion looked up at the ceiling, just for a moment, took a deep breath, let it go with a sigh, and stood. "Okay." Gripping Hallie's hand almost painfully, she took the first step toward Cora's room.

The dimly lit room held four beds, but three were empty. The fourth, Cora's, was closest to the door, with only its foot visible from the doorway. Still holding hands, Hallie and Marion walked slowly around the corner until Cora's face came into view.

But it wasn't Cora's face at all. Her hair was a white jumble, flattened on one side. There was no smile, no twinkle in those dead eyes. Hallie swallowed once, nodded at Marion, squeezed her hand and let it go. They went to opposite sides of Cora's bed.

"Cora honey? It's Marion. What's this all about? Can you tell me? Can you see me, Cora?"

Cora's eyes shifted first, then her head turned, catching up. She tried to smile, but the right side of her mouth opted out.

"Hey, you! I knew you were in there! Cora, Hallie's here too."

Hallie took her hand carefully, working around the IV needle held in place with tape. "Hi, Cora. I wanted to make sure you're okay." Cora turned her head once again, this time in Hallie's direction. Her eyes filled, and a tear escaped from each one. Hallie took a tissue from the bedside table and dabbed at Cora's tears with one hand, while the other still held Cora's right hand.

Cora glanced down at that hand and grimaced a little. From the other side of the bed, her left hand set off on a journey; up it lifted, hovered for a moment, then sailed through the air and back down, onto Hallie's hand; slowly, Cora's fingers curled around Hallie's.

Voices drifted in from the doorway; low tones and medical terms impeded their understanding, but a few key phrases rose to the surface. "probable CVA...severe impairment...80-year-old Caucasian female...poor prognosis."

Marion and Hallie glanced sharply at each other across the bed, and Hallie shook her head. *They don't know her! They can't reduce her to a one-line description, a statistic. This is Cora Rouget we're talking about, not some generic 80-year-old woman.* The voices faded, moving down the corridor to discuss other patients.

Hallie smiled at Cora. "Did you hear any of that nonsense?"

One nod. "Bunja boojhid."

Hallie gasped and looked up at Marion, who had stood straight up, eyes wide. "Did you hear that?"

Hallie nodded. "Cora, you're absolutely right. It *was* a bunch of bullshit. You're going to be just fine."

Cathy appeared in the doorway to advise that the attending doctor would be seeing Cora in a few minutes and bringing in the test results. "He'll probably want to speak with you both, since you're her family, so go ahead and wait for him right here." She winked broadly.

"She spoke! She's been looking at both of us, she squeezed Hallie's hand, and she spoke just now! Made sense, too!" Marion nearly danced as she relayed the good news.

"That's a very good sign," Cathy said softly. "Very encouraging. Be sure to tell the doctor when he gets here, and I'll make a note on her file."

The updated file was the entire focus of the doctor's attention as he entered Cora's room moments later. Cora, Marion and Hallie waited silently, watching him read. Abruptly, he snapped the file shut and looked up. "Well, Mrs. Rodgit, is it? I'm Dr. Werner."

"It's Rouget. It's French," Marion said.

"Ah yes, Rojay." Marion glanced at Cora, who, ever so slightly, shook her head. "Now then, I'm going to examine Mrs. Rojay for a few minutes. Afterward, I'd like to speak to one or both of you about her condition."

Hallie and Marion relinquished their posts and waited by the door as Dr. Werner (*Dr. Wiener,* as Hallie had already silently dubbed him) pulled the curtain around Cora's bed. Just before he made Cora disappear, Hallie was sure she winked at them.

Moments later, the hurried, harried little doctor pulled the curtain back briskly. "All right then. Shall we go to the waiting room for a bit?" And he was out the door without a backward glance.

"Cora, we'll be right back," Marion said. Hallie blew her a kiss; Cora smiled with the left side of her mouth.

"Mrs. Rouget has had a CVA, a cerebo-vascular accident, commonly called a stroke. There's some paralysis on her right side, as I'm sure you noticed, and clearly her speech is affected. The good news is she's responding to questions appropriately, and she is able to feel pain and pressure in her right foot and leg. It looks like we were able to treat her fairly soon after the stroke occurred, and that's definitely in her favor. We've given her medication to remove clots and improve blood flow in her brain. This may prevent further damage. The damage that took place initially, when the stroke hit, could be permanent. We just don't know yet how severe that damage is. As far as the length and degree of her recovery, it's just too early to speculate. Any questions?"

Hallie swallowed. "Why did this happen? Cora is active, she walks every day. She—"

"Risk factors include family history, high blood pressure, poor diet, smoking and of course age. Part of the recovery process should include an analysis of lifestyle and personal habits. Anything else?"

Hallie and Marion sat, staring at the floor, trying to sift through their thoughts, to uncover one coherent question. An exhausting effort that would take more time than Dr. Wiener could spare from his busy schedule.

He nodded, satisfied by their silence. "All right. We'll be watching her closely over the next few days to see how she progresses, then we'll reevaluate. She'll be moved shortly to her own room— she's probably on her way now. You can ask at the nurse's station where to find her."

The two women watched his shoes turn— *About Face!* Hallie thought— and move quickly, squeak, squeak, squeak toward the door. There they stopped and turned again. Hallie and Marion looked up at the doctor's face.

He sighed. "It's good that she walks everyday. Those muscles will help her through rehab. It improves her chances for recovery." He nodded, then turned once more and disappeared.

"It's all those damn cookies she eats with her tea, I just know it. They've clogged up her arteries. I should have cut her off years ago! I should refuse to bake for her. Make her eat vegetables. Oh, Jesus, Hallie, it's my fault!"

"Don't do this, Marion! Hey, no one force-fed Cora all those goodies. These were her choices to make. Besides, she eats well; she just treats herself to dessert now and then. It gives her such pleasure. I think this must be heredity at work. And, she lived eighty completely healthy years before this happened, so that must mean she's taken pretty good care of herself. Plus, you heard him, she's in good shape and that will help her get well. But don't start blaming yourself, or Cora will kick your butt as soon as she's on her feet."

Marion coughed out something between a chuckle and a sob. "I'm gonna look forward to that. Okay. Let's go track her down."

Glancing at her watch Hallie said, "You go ahead. I need to make a couple of phone calls first."

Ben answered on the first ring, half a step from dreaming. "Hello?" He sounded confused.

"Hi. I'm sorry to wake you."

A smile entered his voice. "Told you I should have spent the night."

"Well, I thought I needed sleep, but it turned out not to be a good night for that." She took a deep breath, then echoed Marion's words from the phone call that had woken her up roughly a year ago. "Listen, Ben, something's happened."

The second phone call was to Hallie's supervisor at his home number. He was an early riser, she knew; hopefully 5 o'clock wasn't too early. "Art? It's Hallie. Sorry to bother you at home, but I'm not going to make it in today. I'm at the hospital with a close friend. She's had a stroke."

"Sorry to hear that, Hallie. Will you be back tomorrow?"

"Yes. Her daughter is flying in today. I just want to be here until her daughter gets here, and then I'll need to go home to bed. I didn't get a lot of sleep."

"Yeah, well, that's fine. But I would like to talk to you when you get in. Stop by my office, would you kid?"

"Sure. See you then. Thanks."

Stop by my office? Wonder what that's about. Hallie shook off the thought. *Sorry, the worry quota has been filled for today,* she decided, heading back to the nurse's station.

23

Christina swooped into the room, raincoat flaring out like a superhero's cape. "Mama?" she asked Cora. *Are you still my mama?*

"She's sleeping. She's okay. Let's go to the lounge and Marion and I can fill you in on what we know," Hallie said.

Marion retold the story of finding Cora on the floor beside her bed and calling 911. Then Hallie took over and related the events since she and Marion had arrived at the hospital, including Dr. Werner's little chat. "So everything's been done that can be, and now we have to wait and see what happens over the next few days. Christina, trust me, she's all there. Sharp as ever. It's just a bit of a shock to see her struggling to talk and unable to move her right side, especially when she smiles. But she's going to recover, I can feel it."

Christina smiled and touched Hallie's hand. "Thanks. And you, Marion. Thank you for acting so quickly. You probably saved her life. I spoke with Cathy on my way in, the nurse at the admissions desk. She said she bent the rules a little, letting you two stay with Mom. I signed a statement allowing you both to see her anytime. Now, is there anyone we need to call? Does Tom know yet?"

"Tom completely slipped my mind." Marion looked at her watch. He's probably getting to the house right about now. I'll call his mobile phone."

"Thanks, Marion. We'll meet you back in Mom's room."

Hallie and Marion had dragged three chairs into Cora's room and now Christina and Hallie occupied two of them. When Cora woke, she saw the two of them watching her and smiled in her new lopsided way. "Sawee aboud dis, Cwis."

"Well, you should be sorry! Scaring us all like this." Christina stroked her mother's hand gently. "How ya feelin', Mama?"

Another half grin, a one-shoulder shrug. "Ah be okay."

"I know, Mama. I know you'll be just fine."

Hallie decided to drive Marion's car back to Cora's house and walk to her apartment. Christina had rented a car at the airport, so she and Marion would drive to Cora's together. Before leaving the hospital, Hallie had leaned over and kissed Cora's cheek—her left cheek— and whispered, "I love you, Cora. I'll see you tomorrow after work."

Christina had walked her to the door. "Thanks, Hallie. I am so glad she has you here. I'll call you with any news."

Hallie fished a business card out of her wallet and gave it to Christina. "It has my office and cell phone numbers. Call my cell today if you need to reach me. I'll keep it with me all day."

The solitary drive to Cora's house seemed agonizingly long. Hallie parked Marion's car in front of Cora's house, locked it and went to the front door. She was about to knock when the door flew open and Tom appeared, looming tall and looking angry as ever. "Hi, Tom. Here are Marion's keys. She's coming home later with Christina."

"I suppose you want a ride home?"

"No thanks, I'll walk. Cora's doing better already. I think she's going to be okay."

"Well, you'd know I guess. Guess you've gotten real tight with Cora and her family."

Exhaustion, stress, and concern for her friend had taken their toll at last. Tom's timing couldn't have been worse. Hallie had had enough of Tom's hostility and vague accusations. She was going to end this, now.

"What the hell is your problem exactly? You keep insinuating that I'm some kind of con artist, after what? After Cora's money? You claim to care about her, but instead of asking me how she was, you just couldn't wait to insult me again. All I've done is spend time with Cora. I've been lucky enough to become friends with her. She's the most wonderful woman I've ever known or could ever hope to know. She deserves better than your miserable face around here, that's for sure. Just leave me alone. You'd better be good to Cora, too, because if you're not, if *you* take advantage of her in any way, you'll have me to answer to! Is that clear?"

Hallie turned around and started walking. Angry adrenaline quickened her pace, even up the long hill, and she was inside her apartment holding Cleo before she'd stopped shaking.

When she was again breathing normally, Hallie felt foolish and slightly guilty. True, Tom had always been rude to her, but did he really deserve that blast today? He was probably worried about Cora, too. *But why did he have to take it out on me?* Hallie sighed. *I should have risen above it. I should have shown him a little compassion. Maybe it would teach him something, make him stop and think. Now he just has one more reason to hate me.*

"You don't hate me, do you, sweet girl?" Hallie rubbed Cleo's neck. In response, Cleo lifted her head and closed her eyes, nodding with the movement of Hallie's hand. Hallie smiled as the cat's purr revved up. When Hallie's stomach began to growl too, she realized she hadn't eaten anything yet. She stood, still petting Cleo, then lowered her to the floor.

Foraging in the kitchen, Hallie nibbled on crackers and peanut butter, a granola bar, an apple. Supplies were low; grocery shopping had not been given a high priority lately. She returned to the couch, crunching on the apple, and thought about the very eventful last two weeks.

Flashes of making love with Ben brought aches of desire to the pit of her stomach, a smile to her lips. The fourth of July: Ben took her to a friend's party in downtown Seattle. From the roof they watched the fireworks over Puget Sound, Ben standing behind her, his warm arms around her, his soft whispers punctuated by the sounds of the colorbursts in the sky. Promises of more skyrockets to come.

Hallie's thoughts shifted back to Cora: the balloon ride— floating in the deep blue sky of almost-evening, Cora's shining child's eyes drinking it all in. Cora took nothing for granted. She took the time to stop and smell not only the roses, but the lilacs, peonies and dahlias. She drank it all in and exclaimed at their beauty so that others would be reminded to do the same. Once in awhile, Hallie was certain, one of those blooms stood a little prouder, believing in its beauty because Cora had noticed it.

Cora, please be all right. The world needs you. I need you. Hallie stood once more, tossing the apple core into the garbage before finally collapsing in her bed.

Hours later, Hallie woke to a shadowy room and a ringing phone. "Hullo?"

"Hey, beautiful. Sorry for waking you up. I didn't think you'd be napping this late."

"It's okay." She yawned, looking at the clock on her dresser: 5:30. "I didn't think I would be either."

"How's Cora?"

"I haven't heard anything since I left the hospital. They were going to call if anything changed."

"That's good then, she must be stable. Hey, want to go get some dinner? Might do you some good to get out. Plus, I'm dying to see you. I missed you today."

"I missed you, too. Dinner sounds great, especially since I have no food here. Just give me a little time to put myself together a bit."

"Deal. See you in an hour. Love you."

Over dinner, Hallie shared the story of her encounter with Tom. "I mean, I really let him have it. I was so angry! Now I feel bad. I'm sure he's just trying to protect Cora. As off-base as he is, I have to remind myself that he loves her too."

"No, don't beat yourself up about this. The guy was rude to you; he's been a jerk since you met him. There's no excuse for that. It's not like you have a history of running scams against sweet old ladies. Maybe I should go beat him up. I think I will."

"Silly. Well, I just hope he doesn't complain about me to Christina. Marion knows how he treats me; she shrugs it off. But Christina doesn't know me very well. She's known Tom for a long time."

"Then you don't have anything to worry about. Anyone who knows him would have to realize what a creep he can be. Hey, Christina knows how much her mom loves you. I'm sure that matters more to her."

Hallie smiled. "Thanks. God, I wish I didn't have to work tomorrow. It's going to be hard to wait until after work to go see her. And my boss wants to see me first thing tomorrow, why I have no idea."

"Art? I saw him a couple of times today and he did not look like his jolly old self. He probably pissed a client off and wants you to bail him out."

"Maybe."

Later, Ben kissed Hallie softly at her door. "See you tomorrow." He turned and walked slowly down the stairs, sighing loudly, then looked back up at her when he reached the sidewalk.

Hallie grinned at him standing there, waiting for an invitation. "Wanna sleep over?" she asked at last.

He bounded up the stairs two and three at a time, lifted her and kissed her neck.

Giggling, she joked, "I'll take that as a yes." But when she wrapped her arms around him she held on with all her strength.

24

"I should really keep a change of clothes over here," Ben said when he opened the bathroom door after his shower.

Hallie sat at the kitchen table, reading the headlines from the morning paper. Cora's face had dominated Hallie's dreams and followed her to consciousness. Waking early, too early, she'd watched Ben sleep for a while, then slid quietly out of bed. She had already showered and was getting dressed when Ben opened his eyes.

"You still have time to run home before work."

"I'd rather drive in with you today."

"That's a nice thought, but I'm going straight to the hospital after work."

"That's okay, I'll come too. I want to see how Cora is. I don't think my clothes will smell too bad."

"Will anyone notice you're wearing the same thing you wore yesterday?"

"Hmmm. I hope so."

"Wicked man. Well, I want to go in early, so hurry and get ready."

"Okay. I'll spring for coffee at Starbucks!" he called over his shoulder as he went into the bathroom.

The previous day's events seemed far away, even fictional— a movie she'd seen years ago. One that had made her cry. *But this is real. This is Cora.* Sitting in Ben's car, she sighed and looked out the window. Ben's fingers curled around hers, and she met his eyes. "She's going to be fine, Hallie."

"I know."

"How about you? Are you okay?"

Hallie was about to say Sure, I'm okay, I'm fine— but it wouldn't quite come out that way. Instead, a painful lump rose in her throat and her chin quivered.

"No, don't cry. It's going to be okay," Ben said.

"I'm so scared! And angry! How could this happen to her? She's so kind and generous and thoughtful. She is always there, whenever I need her, even when I don't know that I do. She pokes around until she finds out who you are and then tells you why you're so wonderful. All my parents ever do is tell me what I'm doing wrong, how it should be done, and what steps I need to take to please them, but it's never enough! To them, I'm one big disappointment, and to Cora, I'm a miracle to be treasured. I just want her to be all right. It makes me so angry that she's suffering. It's so completely unfair!"

"So you're mad at God?"

"Yes! God, fate, the universe, or whoever was sleeping on the job to allow this to happen!"

Ben pulled into the parking lot, turned the car off and faced Hallie. "I'm sorry about Cora, and I'm sorry that you're hurting. I know you love her. Come here."

Hallie unfastened her seat belt and wrapped her arms around his back, hugged him tight. "I'm scared she's going to leave me, Ben."

"I know. And Hallie? She will, eventually. You have to hang on to the time you've had with her, the time you still have ahead, and let go of the rest. None of us knows how long we've got, but we know it's not forever. We just have to do the best we can."

"I'll be okay. It just hurts right now."

Holding her close, breathing her in, Ben wished he could snap his fingers and take the pain away. He leaned back to look at her face. "Is there anything I can do?"

She took a deep breath. "You're doing it. I'm okay now." She pulled down the vanity mirror and dabbed away straying eyeliner with a tissue. Her eyes were a little red, but passable.

"You look beautiful," Ben told her, rubbing her back. "Ready? Oh, don't you have to meet with Art this morning?"

"Shit! I completely forgot. Thanks for reminding me."

"At lunch you can tell me what he wanted."

"Can't wait."

They kissed softly, then scrambled out of the car. Co-workers smiled at them and whispered to each other, no doubt about Ben's unchanged clothes. He shrugged, grinning, and kissed Hallie's cheek before heading toward his office.

"Good morning, Art. You wanted to see me?"

"Hallie. Nice to see you! How is your friend?"

"We're hoping for the best."

"Stroke, right? Uh, have a seat."

"Thanks. Yeah, it was a stroke. But we, well, we're hoping for the best."

"Uh huh. Hallie, I'll get right to the point. You are a fine accountant, and a great employee."

"Thank you, Art."

"But I've noticed some changes lately. You used to work late every day, put everyone else in the department to shame. Your clients came first, no matter what. You usually didn't even take your breaks. I worried about you, to be honest. Now, I see you taking all your breaks, everyday."

"We're entitled to our breaks, aren't we?"

"Of course. It's not just that. You never work late anymore, Hallie. Now I see you scooting out of here at 4:30 sharp every day. With Ben Lawson. Don't get me wrong, your personal life is your business. But I used to be able to count on you to go the extra mile. I could give you extra assignments, drop you into some sticky situations and you'd always produce. That's why you got promoted, and that's why you've been getting raises every year. Honestly, kid, I don't think you're heart's in it anymore. You went and got yourself a life and your job performance is suffering because of it."

"You're telling me my job performance is suffering because I'm only meeting all the requirements of the job, rather than going above and beyond all the time?"

"You've changed, Hallie. Your priorities are different now."

"Is this about my day off yesterday? I'll be caught up by the end of the day, Art."

"All I'm saying is that you're not the go-getter you used to be, and go-getters are the ones that get the big rewards. I thought you were on track for upper management and now I don't see you going there. That's all. It's time for you to decide what you want to do here. If you want to be a drone like those other clock-watchers, that's okay. It's wasted talent, but it's your decision. If you want to go all the way to the executive level, you can do that, Hallie. It's up to you. Just think about it, all right?"

There was nothing more to be said. Hallie rose, walked to her desk and sat, staring straight ahead, waiting for her emotions to settle. Unable to beat back the bramble of her wild, conflicted thoughts, she turned to her numbers, safe and orderly, and resolved to get through her in-pile before lunch.

Anger rose, hot and pulsing as she began to work, but gradually ebbed as the hours passed. By the time Ben appeared in her doorway, Hallie's thoughts and emotions had untangled themselves completely.

Ben, however, was not so calm when Hallie recounted her meeting with Art. "That son-of-a-bitch. He's telling you to dump me and sell your soul to the firm!"

"No, I really don't think so. He's saying that it's the really ambitious people that make it to the top there. I had raised his expectations and now I've disappointed him. Simple as that. He's telling me that the choice is mine. He's giving me an opportunity."

"Yeah, an opportunity to give up everything but work."

"Or, to think about what kind of career I really want."

"What?"

"Well, I've never been crazy about my job. I was never as ambitious as Art thought I was. I worked late a lot, but only because I had no personal life. The past couple of years I spent more time singing than working after hours. Maybe it's time to reassess things."

"Think about what you want to be when you grow up?"

"Exactly."

"Hmm. Lumberjack? Astronaut? Florist? Rock star!"

"I'm just going to think about it for awhile. What about you? Do you see yourself climbing the corporate ladder? Becoming a CFO or something?"

"Yeah, that's the plan I guess. Actually, I've started looking around. Couple of years ago, a headhunter approached me about an upper level position, but I wanted to get a little more experience behind me. I think I'm about ready to move on now. But working so close to you has been great; it's been hard to think about being somewhere else. If you decide to make a change, it'll be easier to move forward with that."

"You do what's right for your career. We can still meet for lunch. We don't get to see each other during the day much anyway."

"You're right, I know. It's just been nice having you close by."

"Yes, it has. But I think we'll be fine working at different places. If anything, it'll just give us more to talk about, right?"

"I'm behind you, Hallie, whatever you want to do. Hey— after we go to the hospital and get a bite to eat, we should go to my place."

"Why?"

"To get a change of clothes. Maybe we can grab a few extras, too."

"I like that idea."

"I hoped you would."

They walked back to Hallie's office. "See you soon." Ben kissed her cheek.

"Come get me at 4:30, on the dot!" Hallie called after him.

25

Over the next few weeks, Cora's speech improved dramatically. Now she only slurred a bit once in a while. "Shound a bit tipshy, don' I?" she joked. Her right hand was still very weak; she could not trust it to hold her water glass. But it was her right leg that most concerned her.

After a week in the hospital, she was sent to a nursing home/rehabilitation center. There she labored to retrain her body to function as before. Standing between parallel bars, she held on tight and took her first tentative steps. At first she could manage only two or three before begging her physical therapist, Bethany, to bring the wheelchair to her. Nine days later, Cora had graduated from the wheelchair altogether, using a walker she dubbed Fred, her dance partner.

Once, Bethany dared to suggest that Cora may be "dancing" with a partner permanently. She suggested Cora look into buying a fancy new walker from a catalogue. "Look Cora, it has wheels, a basket to carry groceries, and a bench to sit on when you're tired. You can get it in pretty colors."

Cora was furious. "No! This is not open for discussion, little girl. Pretty colors? Who the hell do you think you're talking to? Walkers are for frail old codgers, something I will never be! Look, I'll work harder. I'll do whatever it takes. Get your whip out! Just don't say that this is it for me. That I'll be dependent on one of these damn things for the rest of my life. I will not accept that."

Bethany took a deep breath. She had heard all this before, but not from Cora. Anger seemed ill fitting, out of place coming from Cora. "Okay. I'll work you harder. I promise, Cora, if you do the work, your muscle tone will improve and your right side will function as fully as possible when you leave here. But you can't count on complete recovery. Your post-stroke life will be different. I'm sorry."

Bethany left Cora in her room, and the catalogue on the table. Cora picked it up with her good hand and threw it at the closing door.

Hallie visited Cora each day after work, and most Saturday and Sunday afternoons at the Death and Torture Center, as Cora called it. Christina was still in town, staying at Cora's house. Each evening, she would get Hallie caught up on Cora's progress before leaving for the day, and Hallie would stay on for an hour or two. Weekends, they all ate lunch together, Marion included.

Cora's walker dance had become almost graceful; she was careful with her posture and moved in a smooth, quick, one-way fox trot: slide, step-step, slide, step-step. When Hallie was watching, Cora would wiggle her behind, turn and wink. Hallie laughed every time, thrilled to see a glimpse of the old Cora.

But Hallie was concerned. After rapid improvement in the first few weeks, Cora had hit a plateau. The nurses at the center euphemistically said she had "stabilized," but it broke Hallie's heart to watch Cora work so hard, sweating through physical therapy and painful exercises, with no visible improvement for over two weeks now.

One evening, a ringing phone greeted Hallie as she arrived at home after seeing Cora. "Hello?" she asked, trying to catch her breath.

"Hallie, it's Christina. Have you had dinner?"

"No, actually, I just got home. But I think Ben is on his way over."

"Well, I want to talk to you about Mom, and thank you for all you're doing. Could I buy dinner for you and Ben? There's a great new restaurant right down the street."

"That's sweet, Christina, but you don't have to treat us. I'd love to have dinner with you. I'll call you as soon as Ben gets here."

They met Christina at the restaurant; she was already seated when they arrived. She rose when they reached the table. "Hello, Ben. So nice to see you again. Please sit. And I do insist on paying, so please order whatever you'd like."

"Is everything all right, Christina? You look worried."

"I am, Hallie. No, no, Mom's fine. It's something else. I really want your take on this. It's about Tom."

Hallie flushed. "Oh, Christina. I'm sorry. I swear I was planning on apologizing. I realize Tom's been working for your mom for a long time, and I had no right…"

"Apologize? Hallie, what are you talking about?"

"I'm talking about my little run-in with Tom. What are you talking about?"

"Run-in?"

"Yeah, the day your mom went to the hospital. I drove Marion's car to the house and gave Tom the keys. Tom's never liked me. He thinks I'm taking advantage of your mom or trying to con her somehow. Anyway, he made one of his snide remarks about me and I lost it. I was just really tired; normally it wouldn't have bothered me that much."

"Interesting. Yeah, he would guard Mom's stash pretty carefully. Hallie, I've been looking at Mom's household budgets. She's very organized. There are notebooks with records of each year's budget and expenditures. There's a set for the kitchen expenses, Marion's responsibility, and another set for the garden, lawn, and household maintenance: Tom's. Mom keeps them for five years, so I can't go back any further than that. But Hallie, it looks to me like Tom has been overcharging for years and pocketing the change."

"Are you sure?"

"I've been researching local prices, and yes, I'm sure. Tom's annual budget runs from June 15 of one year to June 14 the next. He presents a proposed budget and Mom either approves it or adjusts it, and puts it into place. Just hands him the money for the entire year, and he makes the necessary purchases. They share a separate bank account strictly for Mom's expenses."

"I remember them talking about the budget when I stayed at your mom's place in June. Tom was irritated because he'd been trying to pin her down about it. My surgery was on the twelfth, so it was the Sunday the fifteenth when I went to stay with her. He tried to set up an appointment with her the second day I was there. That would have been the second day of the new budget, and he wanted to talk to her about some additional expenses."

"Well, I saw this year's budget, and Mom was more than generous, believe me. This guy recorded flower bulb purchases at five times the price they charge at either of the two closest nurseries. Of course they're even cheaper at the big department stores. And it's that way for everything: grass seed, bedding plants. The trees and shrubs are way out of line— by a hundred dollars apiece in some cases! Twice in the last five years he's purchased a tractor lawnmower. I'm sure he made a pretty penny on those! I don't think Mom even looks at his entries. Once the budget is decided on, it's completely in Tom's hands."

"So he must plan ahead and ask for an overblown budget to begin with," Ben said.

"Exactly. And Mom trusts him. She believes what he tells her about his budget needs, because he's been taking care of this stuff for so long. The past three years, the bastard has even asked for extra money before the year is over, and she's given it to him!"

"What are you going to do?" Hallie asked.

"I want to nail him, but I need your help. I have to be really sure about this. Hallie, you're an accountant. Would you go through the records, just to be sure? I'll provide you with a list of prices and you can compare them with what he claimed he spent on each item. I know it's a lot to ask, but…"

"Of course. I'd be happy to."

"Thank you. I can get you the older records right away. When you finish with the previous years I'll bring the new one to you on one of Tom's days off. If you come to the same conclusion, I could use your help breaking the news to Mom. I think she'll take our word for it if we're both convinced he's guilty."

"Well, I'll do anything to help stop this creep from stealing any more of her money. I feel so bad! All this time I've been cutting him slack because I thought he was being protective of Cora. I guess he's really been protecting his personal line of credit."

"That's not all. Mom has included both Marion and Tom in her will. They don't know what she's earmarked for them, but she's dropped hints. He knows he's getting something. If he thinks your name has been added to the list of her beneficiaries, he might be concerned that it would reduce the amount she leaves him."

"I suppose he would think that way. He probably does think I'm after her money! It's pretty easy to suspect someone else of having ulterior motives if you have them yourself!"

"So Hallie," Ben said. "Are you still going to apologize for yelling at him?"

"Hmm. Maybe I should. Might help to create a little smokescreen while we're checking out his handiwork."

Christina laughed. "I knew I could count on your help!"

"Hey, count me in, too," Ben said. "Anything I can do, just let me know."

"All for one, one for all?" Christina smiled.

"A crusade for Cora," Hallie said. "Definitely a worthy cause."

26

Two weeks passed, and Hallie spent most of her spare time looking at Tom's expense records while Christina and Ben continued to research and add prices to the list Christina had already collected. It was all there in stark black and white: Tom was a thief. He was taking advantage of the kindest woman imaginable.

"How can he live with himself? How can he look in the mirror each day?" Hallie asked Christina and Ben.

"I'm sure he justifies it to himself somehow," Christina responded, shaking her head. "Most thieves do. They've had a hard life, they deserve to get ahead. That sort of thing."

The three of them were meeting over dinner again, to go over Hallie's findings and exchange the older notebooks for the latest one. "Without looking at the current year, I would estimate that Tom has pocketed $15,000 over the last five years. That's conservative, though, because prices have risen during that time, and we're comparing with current prices. But, he seems to have gotten more aggressive in recent years."

"And of course, all this is a bonus in addition to his salary, which is very generous, as you can imagine," Christina said.

"When I figure out how much he's skimmed from the new budget so far, we'll bring all of this to your mom. Then what? The police?"

"You're damn right. I want to see the look on his face when they haul him away."

"Your poor mom. This is going to be a huge blow for her. She trusted him. She invited him into her home, fed him dinner regularly, put him in her will for heaven's sake! It's going to break her heart that someone she considered family has been deceiving her all this time."

Christina nodded. "It's going to be a shock. But she's been having some doubts about Tom lately. She's made comments here and there, mostly about the way he treats you. When we were here for her birthday she even said she was going to give him an ultimatum. I remember exactly: she said, 'I'm just going to tell Tom that he has to start treating Hallie cordially or he can bloody well start looking for another job.'

That was up in Victoria, where she says 'bloody' all the time. She thinks it makes her sound Canadian." Christina laughed.

"She was going to fire him because of me?"

"She loves you, Hallie. As far as she's concerned, *you're* one of the family, not Tom. She thought, still thinks, Tom is a loyal employee and does a good job for her. But she's never been as close to him as she is to Marion. She'll be upset at first, but I think she'll be okay."

"I hope you're right. It won't take me long to go through the new expenditures, since we're only six weeks or so into the new budget. I'll call you when I'm finished."

"Thanks again for all your help, Hallie. Oh, and thanks for helping me with those price lists, Ben. That was a lot of information to gather."

"Hey, I'm happy to help. Let me know if I can do anything else. You, too," he said, nudging Hallie. "It's kind of exciting, actually. I feel like some kind of undercover cop! The secret dinner meetings are definitely a bonus."

Hallie nodded. "Yeah, it's been great getting to know you, Christina." She cleared her throat. "But, uh, could I ask you something?"

"Of course, sweetie. Anything."

"Are you okay with your mom's feelings about me? I mean, is it weird for you that this stranger has come into her life?"

Christina laughed briefly, but loudly, and touched Hallie's arm. "Of course not. This is my mom we're talking about, Hallie. When she loves someone, she loves them fiercely and forever. She takes people under her wing and adopts them. There have been many, but you are special to her. It's sweet of you to be concerned, but no, I stopped being threatened by Mom's friends when I was about 12. I realized then that there's something magical about her. She draws people to her because she truly cares about them, and her heart is big enough to hold all of us. Believe me, I am fully aware how lucky I am to be her daughter. I regret not living closer, not allowing my kids a better opportunity to see her on a daily basis, but Kurt, my husband, had the chance to buy the business in southern California. I was against it at first, I knew it would keep us down there, but Mom herself talked me into it. She said that this was our big chance and that I should jump on it. She said we would talk on the phone all the time, fly back and forth. And we have, we do. I miss her, we all miss her, but I also love her even more for insisting on letting me go. Now that my kids are in their late teens, I understand how difficult that sacrifice is; and she made it so graciously. She is an amazing woman."

"Hear, hear. To Cora: Long may she amaze us," Ben said, raising his glass of wine.

"To Cora," Hallie and Christina repeated. Their three glasses, meeting in a decisive clang, sounded like victory.

27

"Mom, we have something to tell you. We waited until we were completely sure, but this is something we have to act on now."

Cora, Christina, Hallie and Ben sat in the visiting lounge of the nursing home; Cora's walker was parked close by.

"What on earth is it? I knew something was amiss when you all showed up together. You look as if someone has died. It's not me, is it?"

"Mom, this is serious. It's about Tom."

"Tom? Is he all right?"

"Well, it turns out that Tom is not quite the man we all thought he was."

"You mean he turned out to be nice?"

Christina smiled. "Mom, he's been stealing from you. He's been asking for much bigger household budgets than he needed, then recording inflated prices for nearly all of his expenditures, and pocketing the difference. I had Hallie look at the records to be sure. Ben helped as well. We're sure about this, Mom."

Cora looked from one to the other, each one nodding in response. "Christina, I need to speak with my lawyer. Tom will be taken out of my will immediately. I'm assuming you have proof of all this?"

"We have some very compelling evidence, Cora," Hallie said.

"All right. Then we will be taking the matter to the police. And of course Tom must be fired. My lawyer first though. His name is Morris Sparks. Please call Marion and have her get the number from my address book. I want to call him now."

"Okay, Mom. Are you all right?"

"No, I am certainly not all right. I am furious! How dare he pass himself off as a human being all these years? Shame on me for not seeing through that façade. Shame on us all for putting up with his shabby treatment of anyone who might threaten his little scam. Hallie, I'm so sorry I didn't defend you more strongly against that horrible man."

"It's not your fault, Cora. You didn't know this was going on. You trusted him."

"I did indeed. Why, I'll never know. I thought he had a charming, crusty shell that only I could see beyond. What a fool I've been. Thank you, all of you, for opening my eyes. Now, Chrissy, would you call Marion, or bring me the phone so I can?"

Cora called her attorney, interrupting a meeting to instruct him on changing her will: the advantage of being a long-time client. He agreed to meet with her at the nursing home the following day to sign the papers. When the phone was back on the corner table, Cora turned back to the group. "Christina, I would appreciate it if you would contact the police, and Hallie, would you please be there when they arrive? I'd like you both to present the evidence to them. Then I want you to tell me what action they expect to take. Is that all right with everyone?"

Christina nodded, then touched Cora's arm. "Mom, there's one more thing. We need to get what's left of this year's budget out of that bank account you share with Tom, and we need to get all the records of withdrawal for the last five years. Those will tell us when he's been taking his little bonuses. We'll need that added proof for the police. Do you feel up to a little outing?"

"Of course."

Cora's silence on the way to the bank was solid and thick, a fortress not to be challenged by idle chatter.

The bank teller greeted her warmly, until the changes in Cora's face and demeanor quickly transformed her own. Mrs. Rouget had never used a walker before; she had always seemed so sturdy. She always smiled, really smiled, and called her 'dear.' Today, however, her glow was gone. Today, Mrs. Rouget was all business.

And what strange business it was. The teller shifted into the more formal presentation she usually reserved for her less cordial customers, and followed Mrs. Rouget's requests; she issued a cashier's check for the entire balance of her account, and printed out records of withdrawal for the last two years, and ordered three more years' worth from their microfiche files. "There will be a fee for this," she said.

"Fine. Let me know when they're ready."

"Of course. Thank you, Mrs. Rouget."

Back at the nursing home, Christina parked the car. She had suggested they immediately open an account at another bank with the cashier's check, but Cora had postponed it. "I'm afraid I'm all tuckered out from my morning romp with Bethany," she said. Now, Christina told Hallie and Ben that she would walk Cora to her room and come right back.

"Good-bye my darlings. Thank you."

"'Bye, Cora! Have a good rest. See you soon!" Hallie and Ben watched Cora and Christina walk slowly into the building.

Once in her room, Cora sat on the bed, sighing deeply. "Are you okay, Mom?" Christina asked.

"I will be, dear. I just need a nap. I'll see you tomorrow. Call me later if anything else comes up."

"Okay. See you tomorrow then. I love you."

As she walked down the corridor, Christina felt an ache, a physical pain. Something was wrong, terribly wrong. She stopped in her tracks, turned, and retraced her steps back to Cora's room. She didn't know what she expected to find, but she couldn't get there fast enough. From the doorway, she called "Mom?"

In the dark room, Cora lay on her side, fully clothed, facing away from the door. She was crying, sobbing, bent in a fetal curl. "Mom?" Christina whispered, stepping softly toward the strange sound.

"Chrissy, just go home. I'm tired, I told you, I just want to be left alone."

"Mama, I'm sorry that Tom hurt you like this. Please, is there anything I can do?"

Cora turned onto her back and stared at the ceiling with her wet blue eyes. "You can tell me who I am. Tell me, because it's clear I don't know. I thought I was quite brilliant when it came to judging character."

"You are! You've always had an amazing ability to size people up within the first five minutes of meeting them. You were always proven right! Remember that boy I dated in high school? Brad? He was on the varsity basketball team, a straight A student, everyone thought he was so wonderful? But you knew right away what he really was. You told me, 'Chrissy, that boy is no good. I don't know how I know that, but mark my words, he's going nowhere fast.' Oh, I was so angry with you! He was the most popular boy in school, and he wanted to date me! Well, do you remember what happened?"

"Yes, I remember."

Christina ignored her. "He was working at a jewelry store part-time and stealing loose diamonds. Taking them out of the store in his socks. When they caught him he had half a million dollars' worth wrapped in foil under his bed. See? Only you knew he wasn't what he seemed. And you had serious doubts about Tom, too, didn't you? But you had a soft spot for him, and you thought he had one for you too. Right?"

"That's what hurts, Christina. That I could be taken in by someone simply because I thought he cared about me. Why *doesn't* he care about me? Did he ever, or did he start plotting the day I hired him? Have I made him angry, treated him unfairly, to make him turn on me suddenly? Or did his anger rise slowly, bringing him to this decision gradually? I turn over these possibilities in my mind and none of them makes sense. How could this happen?"

"It happened because you are a generous, loving soul, Mom. It happened because you are always willing to look beyond the surface and see the best in people. As for when it started and how he justified it to himself, only Tom can answer those questions. Personally, I don't think his answers would change anything. Tom was simply capable of great deception for the purpose of lining his pockets, same as any thief. One person managed to fool you in your eighty years, and even then you had concerns about him. That's not such a bad track record, is it?"

Cora sat up and opened a drawer next to her bed, brought out a lace-edged handkerchief and blew her nose, then motioned for Christina to sit beside her. "Thank you, shweetheart. Oh, there I go again. My new accent makes me sound a little like Bogie!" She sighed. "I s'pose I don't have much to feel sorry for myself about, do I? He didn't take me to the cleaners so much that I'd notice it, hasn't wiped out my bank accounts or held Marion and me hostage. Okay. I'm finished blubbering."

"Sure you're all right?"

"Positive."

"All right. I love you, Mom. We'll be calling the police when we get back to the house. They may need to speak with you, I don't know. Would that be okay?"

"Yes, it's fine. And if they don't want to talk to me, let me know what they say."

"I will, I promise." Christina stood, then bent down to kiss her mother's forehead, smooth her hair. "I'll see you soon."

Around the corner from Cora's room, Christina leaned against the wall, eyes closed, hands balled in tight fists. Never before had she been called upon to comfort her mother. Only when her father died had Christina seen her mother crying this way, but even then Cora had been strong, had comforted her children. True, Cora had tried to keep her emotional state a secret this time, but something in her voice or her face had tipped Christina off. Something had told her that the world had changed, just slightly; a tiny mutation had caused an evolution to the next stage of their relationship. Was it the stroke? Was that the genesis of this change? Was it the shock of Tom's betrayal? Or was it a more complicated recipe, subtle dashes of this and that tossed together, adding up to an inevitable, new reality? At what precise moment does a person become old?

Christina took a deep breath, squared her shoulders and walked briskly back to the car.

28

"Doesn't surprise me in the least. I always thought he might be up to no good," Marion said. Christina, Hallie and Ben had gone straight to Cora's house to contact the police and to bring Marion up to date. Now, she shook her head. "Cora treated that man like family. How could someone be so greedy, so... foul? So ungrateful?"

Christina shook her head. "It's a mystery, I guess, but he's going to be punished. The police are coming over to take our statements and the evidence we've put together. Unfortunately, we only have records…"

"For the last five years. I know, I help with the shredding. Damn! That's only a penny plunk in the bucket if he's been stealing for almost twenty-four years. Oh, Christina, I'm sorry. I should have watched him closer. I should have watched those records myself. Cora, once she puts her trust in you, it's there all the way. But I knew, something in my gut told me he was a bad one."

"Marion, it's not your fault. Please don't blame yourself. None of us thought he was a prince, but that didn't mean he was a thief. I never would have known if I hadn't felt the need to look at the year's budget. If Mom hadn't had the stroke, there wouldn't have been the extra expenses of her care, and I never would have opened those books. I guess there always is a silver lining, isn't there?"

"Yes, ma'am, there sure is. Well, anything I can do, you just ask, understand?"

"Thanks, Marion. One thing you can do is call a locksmith to come change all the locks on the house."

"I'll call someone right away. Thank you for figuring all this out. Thank you, too, Hallie. It's pretty handy having our own little accountant around." Marion smiled, wiping her dry hands on her apron. "After I make that phone call, how about some tea and cookies?" Without waiting for an answer, she disappeared into the kitchen.

The bank statements had provided the most compelling evidence of all. Near the end of each of the budget years, the end of May, Tom had withdrawn whatever was left in the account, which then remained empty until Cora's check was deposited in mid-June for the new budget. Hallie quickly estimated the total windfall for the entire five years: a whopping $16,457.12. "I wonder if he's stashed it away somewhere, or if he just blows it when he gets it."

"At least he won't be getting anything this year," Ben said.

Today was Monday, Tom's day off; they had planned it that way. When the police officers arrived, Hallie, Christina and Ben presented them with the evidence they had collected. Christina had painstakingly made copies of all the budget and bank records and price lists she and Ben had gathered, so the police could have the originals.

"What happens now?" Christina asked.

"Well, ma'am, we'll have to get a statement from your mother that she didn't authorize those bank withdrawals. His name is on the bank account, which may be a problem, but clearly you can demonstrate that the account was used strictly for household expenses relating to his job, and that what he claimed to be spending was way out of line, I think we'll have a good case against him. This is first-degree theft and possession of stolen property. He may serve some time; more likely he'll probably have to repay what he's taken, and I would imagine he'll be doing some community service. Would it be all right if we go see your mother tonight?"

"Of course." Christina gave him a slip of paper with Cora's name, room and phone numbers and the address of the nursing home. "Will you contact us after you arrest him, Officer Brandt?"

"Yes, ma'am, we'll be in touch."

The locksmith arrived as the police were leaving. Christina game them instructions, then collapsed into a chair. "Hallie, Ben, we did it!"

"First degree theft!" Hallie said.

"We really are the three musketeers!"

They laughed, but Hallie stopped suddenly. "Wait. The police have to get their statement from Cora, so Tom won't be arrested until when? Tomorrow? He'll be here in the morning, won't he?"

"You're right. We have to call him and tell him he's been fired. I'd better do it. I think Mom's had enough for today."

Hallie brought her the phone, followed by Marion with the number. They all watched Christina dial. "Hello, Tom? This is Christina, Cora's daughter? I'm fine, thank you. I'm calling to tell you that your services are no longer required here. Your final paycheck will be mailed to you. Good-bye." She pushed a button, ending the call.

"Did he say anything?" Hallie asked.

"I didn't let him say much, but I did hear 'What the hell...' before I hung up. I'd bet dollars to doughnuts he's making a beeline to the bank right now. He's in for quite a surprise, isn't he?" Christina shrugged. A shiver passed through her, and she shook her head.

"Marion, I will not let you cook tonight. You are coming out with us. We have to celebrate!"

"You want the house empty when he sees the money's gone?" Marion asked.

Christina smiled. "Never could fool you, Maid Marion. We might as well give him some time to cool down and think a bit. If he wants a confrontation I'll be happy to give him one, but I'd rather wait until he's had a chance to blow off some steam somewhere else. Besides, we really do need a celebration, don't you think?"

"Absolutely!" Hallie said. "And it wouldn't be complete without you, Marion."

"Thank you. I'd like that. Sure don't want to be here by myself if he decides to show up."

Suddenly Hallie felt a strong urge to leave quickly. Tom's angry face was not a pleasant thought. She was not afraid, not with Ben nearby, but she felt a little uneasy, even so.

Christina caught her eye, nodded. "Let's get out of here, shall we?"

29

Relief and wine made them giddy. Relief that they had saved Cora from any further losses; relief that her stroke had not damaged her more drastically. They toasted each other's brilliant investigative talents and devotion to Cora. They toasted Cora herself.

"And finally," Ben said, "to Cora's imminent homecoming, when we will all be together to celebrate once again."

"That's the best toast we've had all night. Amen to that, Ben," said Marion. She finished her wine in one large gulp and put her glass down on the table with a loud clang.

They had walked to a nearby restaurant, and now, hours later, they all walked back to Cora's house together, breathing in the warm salty air. Out on the Sound, they could see the Edmonds-Kingston ferry leaving for the Olympic peninsula, its lights glowing above the smooth black water.

Christina and Marion led the little procession; Hallie and Ben walked behind them, holding hands.

"I forget sometimes how beautiful it is here," Christina sighed.

"I love it. It's really starting to feel like home now," Hallie said. "Your mom helped with that. I've learned so much about the area from her. And, just having her so close makes me feel more— settled, I guess."

Christina laughed. "She loves Edmonds so much, it's impossible not to get caught up in her enthusiasm. Of course she might just be trying to sell you on the area. I'm sure she wants to keep *you* close by."

"Well, moving away would be really difficult now."

"It was excruciating for me."

Approaching the house, they grew quiet. The apprehension they had felt before dinner had not disappeared; it had simply been hovering, waiting for their return to the house. "I think we should have had more wine," Christina whispered.

Something was wrong. Christina's instincts had served them well; now they were all even more grateful that she had insisted they leave the house.

Tom had been here, all right. They stood, looking at the side door, dangling now by one hinge. Three panes in the large bay window were broken; shards of glass shone reflected moonlight on the finely trimmed shrubs.

"Fat lot of good the new locks did," Marion whispered.

"Stay here. I'll go inside and make sure he's gone," said Ben.

"Be careful!" Hallie called after him. Christina drew Hallie and Marion close, squeezing their hands.

Ben was out of sight just a few long, painful minutes before pushing the door aside and calling, "He's gone. But it's a mess."

Hallie followed the other two women into the house. Tables were overturned, chairs sliced open. The pictures of Cora's family that had lined the hallway lay on the floor on beds of broken glass. Straight ahead, the kitchen floor was covered with pieces of Cora's china. Crystal wine glasses and vases, once proudly displayed in Cora's sideboard were now thousands of tiny shards on the floors and counters.

Perhaps worst of all, Cora's beloved artwork, peaceful scenes of summer days, children playing, fields of flowers, mountain lakes, had been savagely torn from their frames, ripped and shredded, and piled in the center of the floor.

It appeared that nothing had been stolen, nothing obvious anyway— the TV, with its shattered screen, had not been moved, and the stereo remained untouched.

Marion stood, turning slowly, tears filling her eyes. "Poor Cora. How could he…?" Her faced changed, hardened. "I'm going upstairs to see what else he's done."

"No, Marion! Wait!" Ben called, running up the stairs behind her, but Marion had gotten a head start. She went directly to Cora's room, opened the door, and caught her breath. Ben appeared in the doorway and found Marion facing Cora's bed, her hand over her mouth. "I'm sorry, Marion. I'd hoped you wouldn't have to see this."

In the center of Cora's bed, a large knife had been plunged through the quilt and into the mattress.

Marion's shoulders began to shake, and Ben put an arm around her to guide her out of the room.

"No one touch anything. Let's call the police, and we'll wait for them outside," Ben said as they walked back down the stairs.

"Ben? What is it? What's upstairs? Marion? Are you all right?"

"Chrissy, we need to call the police right away. Tom has lost every last one of his marbles. He's stabbed your mother's bed, left the knife in there right up to the handle. He's twisted things in his mind so that he can actually hate Cora. No sane person could ever hate her, you know that. We've got to report all this to the police, and we need to warn Cora," Marion said, still leaning on Ben.

Hallie looked at Christina. "She's right. One of us should be with Cora until Tom is in jail. That knife upstairs is a threat. I'll go talk to her and stay until one of you can get there."

Marion shook her head. "No, I'll go, Hallie. Ben should stay here with you two in case Tom decides to come back."

"Thanks, Marion. I'll see you there as soon as we talk to the police," Christina said.

"Yes, ma'am. I'll see you at the nursing home. Oh, and sorry I called you Chrissy. I get a little upset and my manners just leave me."

"Marion, you've known me longer than most of my close friends. Chrissy is just fine."

"Please give Cora a big hug from me, Marion."

"I will, Hallie. I'll give her one from all of us."

For the second time that day, Christina called the police. When they arrived and listened to Christina describe the day's events, they took down a few notes and looked through the house. "He sure made a mess," one officer said when they'd finished searching the upper floors. "Did anyone see this guy hanging around today?"

"No. I called to tell him he was fired, and we went out to dinner. The house was in this condition when we came back."

"Okay. First thing we'll do is go talk to your neighbors, find out if they saw anything."

"What if they didn't?"

"Then we'll try to get a search warrant, look through his home, his vehicle, for something to tie him to this. We could check for fingerprints, especially where he knocked that door off its hinges, but it's not like on TV. It's pretty tough to get a good set of prints. Let's see what your neighbors have to say first."

As the police officers began to step over the debris of Cora's belongings toward the door, someone knocked on it. Hallie, Ben and Christina looked to each other, instinctively moving closer together. The talkative cop looked back once at them, then opened the door. "Yes?" he asked the visitor.

"Uh, hello, Officer. I'm George Garvin. I live right next door here? Thought I'd come see if everything's all right." George, the other long-time resident on Cora's block, was inching toward ninety. After Cora was widowed, he had developed a slight crush on her that gradually passed as he realized her friendliness was not encouragement. He had long ago forgotten his once amorous intentions, and been content with friendship and a sort of surrogate uncle status with Cora's children.

"George?" Christina called. The police officer opened the door wider.

"Chrissy, is that you honey? How's your mother?"

"Much better, thank you. But right now we've got a bit of a problem on our hands, George."

"Yes, yes I can see that. Why on earth would Tom do this?"

"How do you know it was Tom, George?"

"I saw him, honey, plain as day through my kitchen window. He tried to use his key, had some trouble with it, then completely lost his temper. Kicked the door down, well, almost down I guess. Then he went inside and did Lord knows what. I heard quite a commotion in there for a good half hour or more. I watched for you to come home, Chrissy, but I guess I nodded off in my chair. When I woke up the police were here, so I decided I should come over here and tell you what I saw."

"Why didn't you call 911 when you first saw him causing a disturbance?" one of the officers asked.

"I thought about it, but the truth is Tom's been working for Mrs. Rouget for twenty some odd years now, and I figured maybe he was just having a bad day. He'd be the one to fix anything he broke, that is if he's still working here after this. No, I thought my best bet would be to wait until I could speak to Chrissy here, or Marion. But when I saw the police car outside, I decided things were more serious than I thought and I came right over."

Both police officers, looking back at Christina, Hallie and Ben, smiled.

30

Over the next few weeks, Hallie and Ben helped Christina and Marion clean and repair Cora's house and replace her belongings. Tom was arrested and remained in jail pending his trial, having been deemed a threat to Cora, her family and property at his arraignment. The change of locks had been fortunate after all, since breaking and entering was added to the long list of charges against him.

When Cora was at last sent home, it was to a lovely but different version of the home she had left behind five weeks earlier. Christina had taken great care to replace every work of art that she could; the originals of course were lost forever. Some of the photographs had been damaged beyond repair. Christina had found others from the same general era, enlarged, framed and hung them in the hallway. Like the photos they replaced, these too captured moments of the family's life, but they were different moments, different poses from those chosen by Cora herself.

Hallie, Christina and Marion had gone shopping to replace Cora's china and crystal. Rather than buy an entire set of new china— Cora's pattern had long since been discontinued— they opted to collect pieces from different patterns. With great care, they created a new collection they hoped would reflect Cora's taste and style.

They held their breath as Cora pushed her walker over the threshold. She moved through the living room slowly, looking at the new art, the new vases of flowers and plants. In the kitchen, she inspected the hutch full of unfamiliar dishes. Entering the hallway, she snapped on the lights and stepped slowly, looking deeply into each new photograph as though it were hanging in a museum: something lovely but distant, disconnected from her.

When she had viewed the last picture, she stood with her back toward her waiting audience, clutching the walker. Her head drooped, just for a moment; then she breathed deeply and turned slowly around. "Thank you, all of you, so much. I can see how much you've done for me. I wouldn't have believed there was so much violence inside that man."

"Mom, come into the kitchen and sit down. I'll fix you some tea."

"Yes, that would be nice."

Hallie's throat hurt. Cora was so sad! The world felt wrong, somehow.

Not wanting Cora to see her own pain, Hallie looked away. Through the kitchen window, she saw a seagull. Its wings were wide and ruffled in the breeze as it rose up and, amazingly, backward, directed only by the whims of the wind. Hallie thought about the balloon flight she and Cora had shared; the smile on Cora's face had glowed brighter than the sunset. Hallie would do anything to bring that smile back.

Christina and Marion served tea at the kitchen table. "No cookies for me, Marion. I have to start eating a little better now," Cora said.

"How about some fruit? I've got some ripe Bartlett pears waiting for you."

"Not just now, dear. Christina, I would imagine the police took pictures of the mess Tom made in here?"

"Yes, they took a lot of pictures, Mom. They took away some of the damaged items, also. Some of the art. They took the knife he left behind as evidence, too."

"Do we have copies of the photographs?"

Christina had lifted her cup to sip some tea, and now lowered it back to its saucer. "No, but I took some myself, Mom. Do you want to see them?"

Cora nodded, eyes closed at first. She opened them and looked first at Christina, then at Marion and Hallie. "I think it's just something I need to do."

Marion started to speak, but stopped herself. Christina rose, walked into the living room and returned with a stack of photographs. As Cora took them from her, Christina glanced at the other two. They had all worked so hard to spare Cora this pain, but she was not one to abide being so sheltered.

They watched her face as she looked at the pictures: the door, hanging from one hinge, the sliced paintings, broken windows. She seemed strong and steady until she came to the last photo. One shaky hand went to her mouth; her eyes grew wide, then closed. Hallie looked at the picture in Cora's hand. At first, she didn't understand its impact on Cora. It showed yet another pile of Tom's handiwork: objects destroyed and thrown in a heap. Looking closer, Hallie saw it: a dandelion puff, flattened and torn. Cora's magical wish, mortal after all.

Cora tapped the photographs on the table like a deck of cards and lay them down in a neat, even pile. Sighing, she spread her arms wide, one hand reaching for Christina, the other grasping Hallie's hand. She brought Christina's hand to her mouth, kissed it with a loud smack. "Things. Just things.

None of you was hurt, thank the heavens above. What would he have done if any of you had been here? That son-of-a-bitch would have had to answer to me if he'd hurt any of you, I can tell you that. As it is, he's going to prison for quite a long time if I have anything to say about it."

The others responded noisily, thrilled to catch a glimpse of Cora's fire. When the room was silent once more, Hallie took a deep breath. "Cora? I've brought you a nice Cabernet for later. To celebrate your homecoming. What do you think?"

With great effort, Cora's eyes found Hallie's. Hallie watched her try to smile, a smile of almost frightening sorrow. Slowly, Cora released Hallie's hand and said, "I don't think I'm up to a celebration tonight. I'm a bit tired. I appreciate all you've done, Hallie, all the time you've taken off from your job. Go home to Ben and have some fun. You've put your lives on hold for me long enough. Christina, that goes for you, too. I want you to go home to your family as soon as you can arrange it. I'm going to be just fine. I'll move to the spare room down here so I don't have to go up and down the stairs until I'm ready. Marion takes care of the housekeeping and cooking. I just need a new gardener and handyman, or –woman."

"I thought I'd stay long enough to help you find someone."

"Thanks, but it's not necessary, Chrissy. I can take care of it."

"I may need to testify against Tom."

"Probably not for a few months. These things get dragged out, you know. You can certainly go home in the meantime."

"I just want to make sure you're settled and comfortable before I go back."

"Honestly, Christina! I am not a child! Stop treating me like one!" Cora rose, leaning on her walker. "I'm tired. I'm tired of pushing this damn thing around. Tired of thinking about this business with Tom. Tired of not being myself, and of all of you walking on eggshells and babying me! I'm going to go lie down for awhile."

Marion, drumming her fingers on the table, tilted her head and watched Cora slide-step toward the hallway. "Hey! Old lady! When you're finished feeling sorry for yourself, let me know what you want for dinner!"

Cora stopped under the arch that divided the rooms and twisted slowly around. She smiled gently, her eyes sad once more. "Nice try, Maid Marion. Anything you want to cook is fine with me."

She disappeared around the corner, pushing the walker toward her new bedroom.

31

Hallie's morning had been productive, her in-box nearly empty by eleven. When her phone rang, she smiled, anticipating Ben's voice, probably inviting her to lunch. "Hello, this is Hallie McLaren."

"Hallie? Hey, stranger!"

"Lonnie! God, I'm so sorry I haven't called you back yet." Lonnie had left messages at work and home, but Hallie just hadn't found the time to call.

"I've been trying to reach you for weeks, woman. Where have you been?"

"I'm really sorry. I know I've been incommunicado. Cora had a stroke, and then some other crazy things have been happening, but it's settling down now. We should get together."

"Is she all right?"

"I think so. Turns out it was a fairly minor stroke. But she's using a walker now, and she seems pretty depressed. Her daughter has been here since it happened, but she's going home in a few days. Anyway, when can we get together? Maybe we can get all of us together, you, Steve, Kim and Jeff and Ben and me?"

"Hallie, I have a couple of things to tell you. Kim broke up with Jeff. She's seeing a new guy, Andy something. He's an engineer."

"Wow, I have been out of touch. What else?"

"Steve and I are still together, but we have a bit of a problem."

"What is it? Can I help?"

"Don't think so, not this time. I'm pregnant, Hallie. Hal? You still there?"

"Say it again."

"I'm having a baby in April. Steve wants to get married, but I'm not sure about that yet. I've told my parents, Steve's told his parents, but I had to tell you before we went public completely."

"Lonnie, I can't believe it! How…"

"How did I get pregnant in this day and age? You tell me! Diaphragm and a condom, you'd think I'd be safe. No such thing, I guess. But I'm going to be thirty in a couple of months. I love Steve, can't really see myself with anyone else at this point, and here's the weird part: I am already in love with this kid! Be happy for me, Hallie."

"I am happy for you. I'm happy you're happy! You're really okay with this?"

"Uh-huh. Took awhile, but I'm really excited about it now. But I can't do this without you, Hal. Promise me you'll go through this with me? Help me pick out baby furniture that's not all pastels and bunnies? Let me cry on your shoulder when my body blows up beyond recognition?"

"Of course! Hey, I'll throw you a baby shower!"

"Cool! Free stuff!"

"Lonnie? I'm really sorry I wasn't there when you got the news."

"No sweat. Glad you resurfaced, though."

"When can we get together?"

"Can you meet me for lunch today? I really want to run the pros and cons of marriage past you."

When she said good-bye to Lonnie, Hallie rang Ben's line. "Hey, how's your day?" he said.

"It's good so far. Listen, I can't have lunch with you today. I'm meeting Lonnie. I've been out of the loop way too long, and she wants to talk to me."

"Girl talk, huh? No boys allowed?"

"Not this time. Want to come over for dinner?"

"Dinner and dessert?"

"Sounds yummy. You can follow me home."

Meeting Lonnie for lunch usually entailed anything but eating: a power walk through the park while solving age-old philosophical and political puzzles. Hallie would then hastily buy yogurt and fruit to eat at her desk.

Today, Lonnie had actually suggested a restaurant and was devouring her third piece of bread when Hallie arrived. "Try the bread, it's really good. Hurry, before I eat it all!"

Hallie took a piece from the breadbasket on the table. "How are you feeling?"

"I get sick most mornings, and sometimes in the afternoons if I eat or smell something that Clancy here doesn't like."

"Clancy?"

"Yeah. You know how everyone hates her own name? I'm calling the baby every outrageous name I can think of. I figure I'll keep calling it all these crazy things, and when I come up with a good name, he or she will be born loving it."

"Good theory! So, you don't know if it's a boy or girl?"

"I find out this Thursday. They said I could choose not to be told, but I really want to know who's in there. Anyway, I do get sick a lot. I mean _a lot_. I have to eat crackers before I get out of bed, and pretty much all day long. I can't eat butter, that sends me on a quick trip to the toilet. When I don't feel sick, I'm starving. And Hallie, I've been so tired. Just dragging my butt around. It's like an alien has invaded my body and totally taken over!" She looked down at her flat belly, her tiny intruder as yet undetectable. "You have total control, don't you,

Melba?" Laughing, she shook her head. "Hallie, I can't believe it sometimes. I wake up in the morning and think: Am I really pregnant, or was it a dream? Then: the nausea hits, the package of crackers beside the bed comes into focus, and it's real again.

"Listen, there's something I want to ask you, but first I have to ask something else. Is this going to be painful for you? I mean, you may not be able to have children and you've always known you wanted them, and here I got myself knocked up by accident, and I've never been all that sure I even wanted kids. Will this bother you? Will you end up hating me and not wanting to be close to the kid?"

Hallie smiled. Lonnie was never one to sugar coat an issue. "I appreciate the question, but Lonnie, I will never hate you and I could never distance myself from your baby. I'm excited about this! Of course I want to be part of your baby's life."

"That's good, because here comes question number two: Would you consider being my baby's godmother? If Steve and I died or became horribly mangled or something, you are the person I would want to take care of my baby. You would make such a great mother, Hal, you're so kind and patient. I don't have any sisters, my brother's a lost cause, my dad's gone and my mom is too controlling and too old. So would you? Please? Think about it, anyway, all right?"

"I'm so honored that you would ask! I don't need to think about it, Lonnie, of course I'll do it! Does this mean I can be Aunt Hallie? Then if Ben and I end up together he'll be Uncle Ben!"

"Ooh, lots of rice in your house. Hey, what about Ben? Will he have a problem with this?"

"No way. He's so crazy about his nephews. I know he'll be just as thrilled as I am about this. What's your due date in April?"

"The 23rd, but that will be confirmed on Thursday, too."
Lonnie reached across the table and squeezed Hallie's hand.

"Thank you. For everything. You're going to be a great auntie. Hallie? I owe you an apology."

"What for?"

"Taking you for granted. I know I neglected you horribly when Steve and I were in our euphoric stage. Let's never do that again, okay? No matter how busy our lives get, let's always make time for each other. Best friends forever, right? Promise?"

"I promise. But I have to tell you something. You know I love you, Lonnie. Always have. I've thought of you as one of my best friends for a long time. But I didn't really know how you felt about me. So asking me to be your baby's godmother— well, there's no better way to share your opinion of me. Thanks for that."

"Oh, Hal! We've been through so much together, but I know what you mean. I used to wonder how close you really felt to me, too. There was always something a little closed off about you, you know? But you've changed a lot in the past few months. Ever since you came out of the singing closet, you've just been more... what? More accessible, I guess, more genuine maybe."

Hallie nodded. "I know, I held back from you. From everyone. I'm sorry about that. I feel like I wasted a lot of time. Cora made me see that."

"Thank God for Cora. But I feel so much closer to you now. Plus, we've both found our perfect guys, right? So no more getting caught up in the throes of the honeymoon stage. I know we'll be spending a lot of time with our men and our careers and all, but our time together is important. We'll just have to set a date at least once a month for a girls' night out. I'll need a break anyway, and I'll need to see you. Okay?"

"You'll see me more than once a month because I'm going to have to see that baby, too. But I agree, once a month for just you and me, and Kim too sometimes. We'll make it happen.

"Speaking of careers, how long are you going to be able to work at the gym?"

"Well, I can keep teaching the low-impact aerobics class for a few months, but I'll need to start modifying my more strenuous activities pretty soon. We actually have a class that's specifically for pregnant women; I'm going to ask if I can take over that one."

"And after the baby comes?"

"Yeah, hold on to your seat. I think I'm going to take some time off. Steve's medical practice is fairly well established now, and I think I'm going to stay home for a while."

"You? Not work? How long a while?"

"I'm thinkin' three, four years. I know, never thought I'd think this way either. Just a few weeks ago, Jodi told me that I could take over as general manager when she's ready to retire, which will be in two years or so. Me, running the whole gym! I was so excited about that. But suddenly I really like the idea of pushing a stroller through the park and witnessing first words and steps and, I don't know, teaching the baby Chinese or something."

"You don't speak Chinese."

"I'll learn. And we might decide to have another baby, who knows?"

"Wow. You really are smitten, aren't you? So why are you hesitating about marriage?"

"Susan Sarandon and Tim Robbins. They seem to have their act so together: great relationship with mutual respect and— one can only speculate— fabulous sex, more than adequate finances, beautiful kids, and no marriage certificate. Why is marriage necessary?"

"Well, there's the wedding itself. That would be fun."

"True, but I'm not crazy about the idea of a maternity wedding gown."

"So get married now, before you start showing."

"You sound like Steve. The thing is, I don't want him to end up feeling stuck and hating me. I don't want him to marry me just because I'm pregnant with Hypatia here."

"Have you told him that?"

"And look like a pathetic, needy, high maintenance wimp?"

"Lonnie, listen to me. You are a beautiful, intelligent woman. Steve is in love with you. Maybe this wasn't planned, but look at you! You're ecstatic about this baby, and I'm sure Steve is, too. He wants to marry you because he wants you to be officially a family. If Tim Robbins felt the way Steve does and begged Susan Sarandon to marry him, don't you think she would?"

"Hmm, good point. Okay, I'll think about it. If I do decide to take the leap, will you be my maid of honor?"

"Of course! First a bridal shower, then a baby shower."

"But I won't be able to have a bachelorette party: no booze."

"Don't sound so sad. We'll just have the party after you stop breastfeeding."

"Deal!"

Hallie hugged Lonnie good-bye outside the restaurant and drove back to the office. A glimpse of her own eyes in the rearview mirror surprised her. She was *happy* for Lonnie, *thrilled* about the baby. She was going to be a godmother! A baby was coming that would be part of her life forever. *This is good news,* she told herself, but she blinked back tears.

It hurt, the idea that there would be no child of her own to grow up with Lonnie's. No nursery to set up, no names to choose. The busy-ness of Hallie's life since reuniting with Ben, Cora's stroke and Tom's crimes had eclipsed the baby issue. Now, Lonnie's news had forced Hallie to take another peek at the glaring truth.

She shook her head. ***Stop it!*** *Talk about pathetic! This is about Lonnie, not you.* Hallie inhaled deeply, let one small sob escape, and silently began to consider shower gifts.

By the time she reached her office, she was full of ideas for both bridal and baby showers, as well as for simply making a new mother's life a bit easier. Thoughts of helping Lonnie eased her own pain somewhat; her sense of loss diminished as her shopping and task lists grew.

Excited now about her plans for Lonnie, Hallie's thoughts turned to Cora. What would cheer *her* up?

And then it came to her: an idea so simple and sweet and obvious that she couldn't believe it hadn't come to her before. She scribbled a few notes down before she noticed Ben standing in the doorway.

"Hi, gorgeous. How was lunch?"

She smiled, rose and kissed him. "It was good. Lots of developments in Lonnie's life."

"Yeah?"

"How would you feel about being a godfather?"

"Lonnie's pregnant?"

"Yep. She's due in April. She's asked me to be the baby's godmother. Isn't that great?"

He pulled back from her, looked at her face. "It is great. You'll be a wonderful godmother. But are you really okay about all this?"

She nodded. "I had a bad moment or two on the way back, but I'm okay. Life goes on. People are going to have babies. This one will be part of my life, and I feel good about that."

He pulled her close. "I love you."

"Thank God. Hey, would you do something for me?"

"Anything."

"This weekend, I want to rent a karaoke machine. Would you help me transport it to Cora's house? I think a karaoke party is just the ticket to liven her up a bit."

32

"I'm worried about her, Hallie," Marion said. Hallie had arrived home to a ringing phone after having dinner with Ben, who now sat on the couch petting Cleo. "Ever since Christina left, Cora just sits in her room all day. She says she's catching up on her reading, but every time I go in there she's just staring out the window. There must be something that'll lift her out of this funk, but I haven't come up with anything."

"You've got great timing, Marion. I've been thinking about this. I'd like to give her a little surprise party this weekend. But I need your help."

"Anything. What can I do?"

Over the next thirty minutes, Hallie and Marion brainstormed on arrangements for Cora's "coming out party," as Marion had christened it. Hallie contacted Lonnie, Kim, and Sarah Shaw; Marion would call a few others she had in mind.

"I hope Cora doesn't feel overwhelmed by all this," Hallie said as she plopped down beside Ben.

"Well, she's not happy now. She probably just needs a little push. And even if she's not thrilled about the party, she will appreciate the intent."

Hallie drew her legs up in front of her, hugged them. "I hope so. You know, before her stroke she said she wanted to bring Marion to karaoke night. It was the day of our balloon flight. I told her you and I were back together; she said she already knew because I was so happy. She said she wanted to see us together, and that Marion had been wanting to hear me sing. She was so… so Cora that day. So exuberant. God, I miss her."

Ben reached over, rubbed the back of her neck. "I'll bet she misses herself, too. Hey, if this party doesn't do the trick we'll just keep trying until we find something that does." He leaned toward her and kissed her cheek. "I've got a question for you. I've been catching a lot of shit from my sisters lately. I guess I talk about you quite a bit, and they've been nagging at me again to bring you around."

"Great! I'd love to meet them."

"There's something else. My parents will be going back to Arizona for the winter next month. I really want you to meet them before they go."

Hallie smiled, remembering their conversation the first night Ben took her to dinner. "Won't your mom start planning our wedding if you introduce me to her?"

"No doubt. She'll be hoarding cases of champagne and getting you subscriptions to bridal magazines. Actually, she's probably already working on that, since I've mentioned you to her once or twice, or I don't know, a thousand times maybe. So anyway, the family has conspired to create an opportunity for you to meet them all at once: dinner, this Sunday, at my parents' house. How does that sound?"

"Fabulous. What should I wear?"

"It'll be informal. We downgraded the dress code last year. I'm kidding! No, really, it will just be the family. Rachel's bringing the kids, so it's going to be loud and crazy. Wear whatever you want. They're going to love you, I promise. Almost as much as I do."

The phone rang again. "Maybe Marion hit a snag." But when Hallie answered it, no one spoke at all. Hanging up, she frowned. "Nobody there. That's been happening a lot lately."

"If it rings again I'll pick it up."

"You'll scare off my obscene caller? My hero."

"Or maybe we just won't answer it at all. Come back over here."

Hallie felt his lips on her neck, kisses of soft suggestion. They stretched out side by side, kissing, touching, whispering.

Cleo, miffed at the strange activity and sudden lack of space on the couch, stretched slowly, yawned, and walked to the bedroom to wait for her companions.

Saturday morning, Cora lay in bed and waited for the sun to light her room. Marion, she knew, would bring her breakfast, though she would try to talk her into coming to the kitchen table. It seemed so far away, the kitchen table.

Cora knew she was depressed. It was a diagnosis she had arrived at countless times for other people; how could she not recognize the symptoms in herself? She knew she should get help. How many times had she lectured her patients that depression was not a character flaw but a real condition requiring medical attention? Sometimes depression was a rational response to a difficult life experience, she would say. Medication isn't always the answer, but it can be a useful tool to help you get back on your feet. How can you deal effectively with an issue if you don't have the energy to get out of bed?

Physician, heal thyself, she thought. "Maybe tomorrow," she whispered. *You will die, you know, if you lie here too long. Pneumonia will set in and you will die.* The response came to her immediately, hanging heavily in the air; she opened her mouth to say them, make them real. "So be it." *Is that really what you want, old girl?* She shook the thought away.

Eyes closed, she leaned back against the pillow. *What would you like to do today, Cora?* she asked herself. *I'd like to throw away that damn walker. I'd like to step into a time machine and go back ten years. I'd like to pick up my walking stick and head down the beach.* She sighed. *Okay then, I'd like to hear Hallie sing. That's still within the realm of possibility.*

She imagined Hallie's face, conjured up her beautiful voice. Would she ever sit in that karaoke bar again, watching Hallie on stage? Cora thought of all the steps she would have to take, all the battles she would have to fight and win to get there. Too much. It was all just too much to think about, let alone actually accomplish. *The longest journey begins with a single step, old woman. There will never be an easier time to get started.* She tried to will herself to move, to put her feet on the floor, but her body felt so utterly heavy. She sighed, settling further into her pillow. *Another time,* Cora told herself. *Another day.*

Light had begun to creep into her room at last. Cora glanced at the clock: almost six. She had been awake since 2:30.

The tap on the door came at six sharp, as it had every morning since Cora's return. "Come in, Marion."

"I didn't wake you, did I?"

"You know you didn't. Amazing the way you bring my breakfast the moment my stomach starts asking for it."

"Well, maybe you'll eat something this time."

"Yes, Mother."

"You'll think I really am your mother before I'm through with you. You are going to eat your breakfast today. Every bite. I'm going to sit here and watch you do it. Then, you are heading for the shower. You're going to put some clothes on and we are going grocery shopping."

"Marion, I know you're trying to help, but trust me when I tell you that I simply can't do that."

"Cora, I have been trying to help. Today's the day I actually *will* help. You're getting up and out of here. Today!" Marion sat in the wicker rocker across from Cora's bed. "Start eating! Come on, that's an egg white omelet, and those strawberries are straight from the farmers' market."

Cora's stomach rumbled again. She was hungry, her body knew that; she just had no desire to eat. *Okay, so I start getting better today, not tomorrow. Start working, Cora.* "You big bully, ruining my lovely little pity party," she told Marion, and she picked up her fork. Marion grinned at Cora's choice of words.

"What's so funny?"

"You are, as always. Keep eating."

Marion's plan worked perfectly. After Cora's shower, she dressed in lime green, threw on her yellow jacket, pushed on her straw hat and said, "All right, Adolf. Put your whip away and take me shopping."

"Well don't you look sunny," Marion said.

"I don't have any gloomy clothes. Remind me to get some. Are you ready?"

"The car's running. Go ahead, I'm right behind you."

With Cora and her walker out the door, Marion quickly dialed Hallie's number, let it ring twice and hung up. She scribbled a quick note and hustled out the door.

"That's the signal! Cora's out of the house!" Hallie pulled Ben toward the door. Ben's car had already been loaded with balloons, streamers, a banner and a very large karaoke machine.

As planned, Hallie got the house key from Cora's neighbor George, and she and Ben got to work.

"How long do we have?"

"Marion promised we'd have at least an hour. Help me with the banner!"

"When will the guests arrive?"

"Oh! I need to call Lonnie! We've got a phone tree set up." She glanced at her watch. "If Marion gets Cora back here by 11:30, we can give her a little time to adjust to the decorations and having us here, then have people arrive about noon." She dialed Lonnie's number and set the day in motion.

Just shy of an hour later, the main floor of Cora's house was dressed in royal purple, hot pink, and sunflower yellow: Cora's favorites. Balloons hovered in every corner, crepe paper streamers floated from the ceiling, and, the *pièce de resistance*, made on the computer by Ben (according to Hallie's specifications): the banner. Fifteen 8" by 11" sheets of paper, lined up and taped precisely in place, the banner stretched above the arch that framed the kitchen. In the same bright colors, it read **Welcome to Cora's Coming Out Party!**

"I hope she appreciates the humor," Hallie said. She looked around at the room, satisfied. "It's perfect! I think we're ready!" They heard Marion's car in the driveway, car doors open and close. "And not a moment too soon!"

Giggling, they dove behind the far end of the couch and waited for the door to open.

Voices drifted closer, growing louder until they were just outside the front door.

"I tell you, I can open the door myself! Stop treating me like an invalid, Marion!"

"You are a stubborn old thing. Would you just let me open the door for you?"

"I will open my own damn door! You go get the groceries out of the car."

"Fine!"

Hallie and Ben heard a click as the doorknob turned. "She doesn't seem to be in a very festive mood," Hallie whispered.

"We'll just pretend we don't know that. Ready?"

Hallie nodded. With her fingers, she motioned 1—2—3 and they leaped into Cora's vision as she stepped inside. "Surprise!"

"What's this about?" Cora asked. Looking beyond them, she saw the decorations. She turned, taking it all in, her mouth wide open. Spotting the banner, she shot a glance back in Marion's direction— and smiled.

Ben had set up the karaoke machine at one end of the kitchen, and now Hallie led Cora there. Two microphones were plugged in and waiting. Cora shook her head, but she was still smiling. "You're going to sing for me? I get my own private little show?"

"Well, not quite. We've invited a few people over. It really is going to be a party. I hope that's okay."

Marion came bustling through the door, loaded with bags of groceries. "It better be okay!" she called. "We've gone to a lot of trouble for you, old woman!"

Ben went in to Marion and took the grocery bags from her arms, then followed her back into the kitchen where she started to put things away.

"You certainly have," Cora said. "Thank you for that. All of you." She breathed deeply. "How long before the troops arrive?"

Quickly, Hallie helped Marion prepare platters of food. "Looks like we're expecting an army, Marion," Cora said.

"Better too much than too little, I always say."

"You do indeed. Well, I suppose I should make myself a little more presentable." Cora, with Fred, disappeared down the hallway and emerged twenty minutes later, lipstick bright, ponytail tidied. She had changed into her purple and yellow tunic and Capri pants: the outfit she had been wearing when Hallie saw her for the first time. "Bring it on! I'm ready to party!" she said, a bit too loudly.

Looking up, Hallie recognized the clothes; she smiled. "You look wonderful, Cora."

"Do I? You know, I thought I recognized myself in the mirror just now. Think I might be coming 'round."

Coming 'round. Hallie saw a glimpse of Cora's old twinkle, and thought it just might be true.

Everyone they had invited came to the party, and most of them sang at least one song. Kim and her new boyfriend, Andy, joined up on "Wild Thing," and the good Dr. Shaw, prodded to the microphone by Cora, warned everyone before singing "Leader of the Pack" rather badly. George Garvin sang Dean Martin's signature song, "Everybody Loves Somebody Sometime," surprisingly well. Hallie sang all of Cora's favorites, to thundering applause.

Lonnie, who steadfastly refused to sing, motioned for Hallie and Kim to join her in the living room while Cora's florist friend sang "Close to You." She grinned.

"Did you find out? Is it a boy or a girl?" Kim asked.

"I've been so excited to tell you, but I wanted you both together. It's a girl! I'm having a girl!"

The three women embraced, each thinking about the little girl who was on her way to their lives. Hallie looked at her friend: her hair, nearly black, pulled back into a short ponytail, her eyes impossibly green. "I hope she looks just like you, Lonnie," she said.

Lonnie grinned. "Yeah? Thanks! Wish I could give her your voice, Hal. And your shoe collection, Kimmie." They laughed, and rejoined the party.

Hours sped by unnoticed. Hallie took center stage once again. "I have an announcement. Well, maybe a request. Cora has a secret, and she doesn't know that I've figured it out. Cora, I've heard you humming to yourself in the kitchen, even singing once in a while. That's right, you'd be making tea or cocoa and just start singing softly, absent-mindedly, hardly noticing. But I noticed! You have a great voice! So— I think it's high time you shared it with your friends. I am finally returning the favor you granted me. I think I have the perfect song for you— will you sing for us?"

Cora objected, shaking her head; but her friends and admirers clapped, stomped and whistled until she slid the walker forward and took the microphone from Hallie. Hallie pointed at the monitor, where Cora read the song's title. She smiled. "It is perfect. Thank you, sweetie." And she began to sing. It was an old song, a wartime melody with lyrics of longing, of loss. Of love made temporary by circumstance.

Cora's voice caressed each word, loving the song like an old friend. Her audience was silent, listening with pleasure and surprise at discovering yet another talent possessed by this remarkable woman. As she held the final note, they burst into applause and lined up to embrace her, one at a time.

When Cora turned at last to Hallie, the two women hugged tightly. "You're wonderful, Cora!"

"Thank you, darling girl. That was really fun. And thank you for this wonderful party." She reached for the microphone once more. "Now I have an announcement. I want to thank the three people who made this day possible. Marion, Ben and Hallie, I'd like to thank each of you for giving me a swift kick in the behind. I can't promise I'll feel this good every day, but I give you my word I will not give up and take to my bed like Greta Garbo in some old melodrama. Thank you, my dear friends. And thank you all for coming to my extremely overdue coming out party! I promise I will try to oblige by coming out of this bristly shell I seem to have crawled into recently. "

Marion, standing at the back of the crowd, was closest to the phone when it started ringing. "Rouget residence. What?" She walked into the hallway, away from the party. "That's great news! Thank you!" She raced back, clicked the phone back into place and yelled: "Hey! Cora! That was Morris Sparks on the phone! He got some news late yesterday, but didn't have time to call until now. Tom's confessed! He's pleading guilty! To everything!"

33

After Cora's attorney called, she sat, considering the news. It seemed that either Tom did have a conscience after all or, more likely, his lawyer convinced him he did not have a viable defense. Cora let this new reality settle down on her gently, like dust made suddenly visible by a sunbeam. There would be no trial, no testimony. She would not have to face Tom in court.

To her surprise, hidden under her tremendous relief was a tiny shard of disappointment. A part of her had still wanted to see him, to look into his eyes and try to find some answers. *Nonsense,* she told herself. *There are no answers. The man simply has no scruples. Some people don't. Just be grateful that he's out of your life and off the streets.*

When Marion announced the good news, most of the guests cheered and applauded; those few still in the dark about

Tom were quickly enlightened, and then they too joined in. But the phone call broke the momentum of the party. Everyone realized how late it had become, and took the cue to say good-bye.

As Ben packed up the karaoke machine and loaded it in the car, Hallie and Cora embraced. "I'm going to leave the decorations up for you, at least for the rest of the day. I can come back and take them down tomorrow if you want."

"Oh, let's leave them up the whole weekend. I love the festive look."

"That's great news about Tom. I'm so glad it's all over. Looks like he'll be in jail for a while."

"Probably for two or three years, anyway. Yes, that is very good news."

"Cora? Are you okay? Your eyes haven't quite caught up with your words."

Cora moved to the couch and sat heavily behind her walker. "Darling girl, I just don't know what's wrong with me. I've had this wonderful party given to me by people who truly love me. And, I've just found out that I won't have to testify against the man who stole from me and vandalized my property. The man who plunged a knife into my bed! I should be relieved. And I am, really, I'm enormously relieved! But there's this nagging little voice telling me that if only I could see his face I could find some reason, some explanation for his behavior. I know that's probably not possible, I tell myself I'm crazy to even think this way. But that voice is a stubborn one."

Hallie sat beside her, squeezed her hand. "Tom was in your life for over twenty years. This is a huge shock for you. It's just going to take some time for it all to sink in, but you'll get past this. Maybe there is no way to explain what happened. Maybe he is just a bad person. Really, is there anything he could say that would make any of it feel better?"

"I suppose not. I'm just going to feel sad and stupid for a while. Nothing will change that. Meanwhile, I still owe you and Ben dinner. Would you like to stay?"

Marion called in from the kitchen. "You'd better stay! I've got to get rid of some of this food somehow!"

When Ben returned from the car, he and Hallie headed for the kitchen to help Marion; Cora lagged behind, standing still with Fred a moment before she led their dance toward the others. Exhausted and blue as she was, the resigned despair of that morning seemed a lifetime ago. She would not surrender, not yet.

34

The next morning, Ben woke up first and watched Hallie until her eyes opened. "Good morning," he whispered.

"Mm-hmm, it sure is." She pulled him close.

"Let's go get some breakfast. My treat."

"That sounds great. I woke up ravenous, for some reason."

"Funny, so did I." He grinned, leaned in, nuzzled her neck. "After breakfast, I have to go home for a while. My laundry basket is piled to the ceiling. I'll have no clean clothes for work tomorrow if I don't go take care of it. Want to come with me?"

"Actually, I need to get some groceries and pay bills. Do you want me to meet you at your place, or will you come pick me up? We're still on for tonight, right? You still want me to meet your family?" Hallie said, drawing circles on his back with her fingertip.

"Hey, there's no backing out now. One of them calls me everyday: 'You're still coming, right? Does Hallie like salad? Does she like lemon meringue pie? Will she be offended if we offer her a drink?' I'm actually looking forward to getting it over with so there's no big mystery anymore."

"I hope they won't be offended if I have two or three drinks. I'm nervous about this!"

"No need to be. I have a really great family. You're going to feel right at home." He kissed her. "Anyway, I'll come get you about five. I told them we'd be there between 5:30 and six."

"That's fine. I'll be ready."

"Hey, Hallie. How hungry are you, exactly? Can breakfast wait just a little while?"

Laughing, she nodded. "Not too little a while, I hope!"

When their hunger, first for each other and then for breakfast had been satisfied, Ben kissed her good-bye. "I'll be back no later than five. Love you!"

At the grocery store, Hallie found herself smiling again and again. The world felt so bright and promising. Yesterday's party had been a roaring success; Cora seemed to be almost her old self again by the time Hallie and Ben had left. Hallie was closer to Ben than ever, and she would soon be a godmother to a brand new baby girl.

The thought of Lonnie's baby reminded Hallie of the shower she needed to plan. Maybe later she'd check out some of the local boutiques for gift and party items.

Deep in thought as she was, at first she didn't hear the voice calling her name. When she finally did, the sound of her name did not call her back to the present; this was a voice from her past.

"Hallie!" came the call again, louder this time, closer. "Hallie!" The voice was right behind her now. She turned.

"Joe." She stated it simply. It was not a question; she had known before she turned around that it was Joe tossing her name out as casually as if he owned it.

He stood, hands dropped to his sides, catching his breath from running after her, grinning. "Hallie! My God, you look incredible."

She looked at her shoe. Her mouth was dry; her face felt hot. Joe's presence here was all wrong. This was *her* grocery store, *her* neighborhood. She had banished this man to her memory. How dare he appear here, in her present?

He cleared his throat. "I don't blame you for not wanting to talk to me, Hal. Last time I saw you I was a total ass. I know I can't take any of that back. But would it help, just a little, if I told you I'd change it all if I could? I'm sorry, Hallie. For everything."

Hallie looked up, into his face for the first time in almost seven years. "What are you doing here, Joe?"

"I saw Ted and Sally a couple of months ago, they invited me over for dinner. They said they'd bumped into you going to a movie not too long ago. Said you were living in downtown Edmonds now. I looked you up, actually called a few times, but I couldn't bring myself to talk to you."

"Oh, so you're my obscene phone caller? That was getting scary, you creep! What makes you think you have the right to…"

"Sorry. I didn't intend to hang up. I really wanted to talk to you, I just didn't know where to start. So I've been hanging around quite a bit, hoping to bump into you. I knew it was a long shot, but I kept trying anyway. I was walking down the street just now and saw you getting out of your car. I couldn't believe it! I just wanted to see you, that's all."

"Why?"

"I know I hurt you, Hallie. Back then, I didn't care. I wanted to hurt you. Took a while to knock some sense into this thick head of mine. I told myself we had drifted apart, that losing the baby had changed you, and you weren't the person I'd fallen in love with. But I was just running away, Hal. Trying to make myself feel better any way I could. After we split up, I ran from one woman to another. It took a couple of years, but I realized that I couldn't find the right person because I'd already found her. I found the love of my life and I pushed her away. Pushed you away, Hallie"

Hallie shivered, thinking of Cora's words the day they met: *I'd bet my bottom dollar that young Joe has gone through a string of relationships and just can't understand why he can't find the right girl.*

I don't want to hear this, Joe. Not now." She turned and walked away from him, but he caught up quickly and spun her around.

"Listen, I know I don't have any right to ask for forgiveness. But can't we just go have coffee somewhere and talk?"

She shook his hand off her arm. "Coffee? Are you crazy?" She took a deep breath, let it go, and lowered her voice. "You were my husband, Joe. And when the first crisis of our marriage hit, you left me to deal with it alone. You didn't just abandon me, you turned to someone else while we were still trying for a baby! Yeah, I'd say it's a little late to talk forgiveness."

"I know, I blew it. I was a stupid kid, Hallie. It took a long time for me to realize what I lost. But think about it. Think about how happy we were, how right we were. Have you found someone else? Are you married?"

"I'm sure Ted and Sally told you I'm not married. But I'll bet they told you I was with someone at that movie."

Joe opened his mouth to speak, then closed it and looked at the floor, nodding. "Are you serious about this guy? They said you looked happy."

"I am happy. Happier than I've been in a long time. I almost blew this relationship because of the scars you left. I'm not going to let you ruin this for me."

"I just wanted you to know how I feel, Hallie. I thought you should have all the information before you make a decision."

"This decision was made a long time ago, Joe. We have nothing more to say to each other."

"Okay, I'll leave you alone. But here," he said, digging in his jacket pocket. He brought out his wallet, opened it, took out a business card. "Take this. I've written my home and cell phone numbers on the back. If you think about it and change your mind, call me. Or, if you just want to yell at me some more, call me. Hallie, I love you. I always will. If there's the tiniest little doubt in there somewhere, just the smallest part of you that misses me? Call me. It would be·stupid and senseless for both of us to lose our soul mates, don't you think?" Joe leaned forward and kissed Hallie softly on the cheek. "Please think about it."

He looked at her a moment longer, smiled gently, then turned and walked down the aisle and out of the store.

When he was gone, Hallie turned around and faced her shopping cart. She pushed it, too hard, then trotted a few steps to catch up to it; she took a deep breath. Her hands were shaking; her grip tightened on the cart's push-bar. *Focus!* she told herself. *Artichokes, tuna, olive oil.* But a louder voice surfaced. *How dare he? Who the hell does he think he is?* She looked at Joe's business card, still in her hand, now curved from her grip around the bar.

Tears stung her eyes, blurring her vision; she blinked. How many hours had she spent wishing Joe would suddenly come to his senses? How many times had she wished to hear the words that had seemed to come so easily to him today? *Soul mate.* Now her tears escaped, and she wiped them away with the back of her hand. When she closed her eyes again, it was her wedding day she saw, in snapshots like those she'd left behind in the home she'd shared with Joe. The two of them on the courthouse steps grinning, staring hungrily into each other's eyes. The electric rush she'd felt every time his fingers brushed against hers. *The happiest day of my life.* How completely sure she'd been that they would always be that close. No questions, no doubts in her mind. He was her home, solid, impermeable.

Then it had all collapsed, crumbled into a thousand questions that had been cluttering her mind ever since. Now here he was again, generating new questions just when she had begun to feel some certainty about someone else.

What if? What if he really just had a momentary lapse in judgment because of the stress we were under, and because he was so young? What if he really never stopped loving me?

What if he really is my soul mate?

But what about Ben? Ben, who would pick her up no later than five, introduce her to his family, and share her bed this very night.

She needed a friend, someone who understood the situation and could help her sort through it all.

She needed Cora.

But should I bother her with this right now? Maybe not. But wouldn't she feel worse if I didn't?

Abandoning the cart, Hallie walked through the automatic door and into the cool early September sunshine.

Cora, sitting at the window, saw Hallie's car pull up in front of the fence and watched her walk to the side door. "Marion, Hallie's here! Would you get the door?"

The door opened as Hallie brought her fist up to knock. "Hi, Hallie! Hey, what's wrong with you?"

"I'm not sure yet. Is Cora…"

"In here, sugar pie!"

"I'm making lunch," Marion said. "Are you hungry?"

"What? Oh, no, thanks. I had a big breakfast this morning." *With Ben, about a thousand years ago.*

In the living room, Hallie sat on the couch beside Cora, whose smile faded when she saw Hallie's face. "What is it, Hallie? You look like you've seen a particularly nasty ghost."

"That's exactly right, Cora. I have seen a ghost. The ghost of marriages past. I saw Joe."

"Joe? Oh, Hallie, how did that feel?"

"Horrible. I'm so angry— look, I'm still shaking!"

"Angry? What did he do?"

"Cora, he found out I was living in the area, and he started wandering around the neighborhood until he found me today at the grocery store."

"But why? What does he want?"

"You were right. Remember, you said that he's probably gone through a million relationships and couldn't figure out why he was still alone? That's exactly what's happened, at least that's what he said. Cora, he said he realizes that he still loves me, always has, he made the worst mistake of his life, blah, blah, blah. All the things I wanted to hear from him seven years ago, I heard today."

"Well. Maybe he's truly had some kind of epiphany. Or, maybe he's lonely and thinking it might be fun to have a romp with his lovely ex-wife. How did he find out where you live?"

"These people we used to do couple things with. I ran into them one night and they were oh-so-pleased to see me. They're Joe's friends now; he got sole custody of the friends."

"Ah. Did these friends know about Ben?"

"Yeah, they saw me with him. Joe said he wanted me to have all the information I needed to make the right decision."

"So he thought he'd lay his cards out and see which one you'd choose."

"I guess so."

"And you're here to sort out this tangle of emotions you're feeling, is that right?"

"Exactly! I hate him, Cora! I've hated him for such a long time. Joe was my best friend, and he abandoned me during the worst time of my life. He hurt me so badly I don't see how I could ever trust him again. But,"

"But, he was your first love and you've always secretly wondered if he was off somewhere kicking himself and pining away for you?"

"Yes. I have, it's true. And it was so much easier to hate him before I heard those words from him today."

"If you can't hate him anymore, does that mean you have to love him?"

"I don't know. I once vowed to love him for the rest of my life, and I meant it. I didn't have a single doubt about marrying him. He made a mess of it and pushed me out the door, but now... Cora, do I owe him another chance?"

"Sweetie pie, you owe him nothing. Look. It's been seven years since you were together. You have both changed a lot, I'm sure. You've gone in different directions and lived different lives. You've grown and learned, formed opinions and collected friends. If you choose to reconcile with your ex-husband, it will be a brand new relationship between two people who really don't know each other anymore. Maybe the foundation is so strong that you're still right for each other. Maybe not. Seems to me there are a lot of 'ifs' involved there.

"But let me tell you something, Hallie. When I see you with Ben, I see a connection so strong it's almost humming with electricity. He loves you, almost unconditionally. And I don't believe it's one-sided. The two of you look at each other and everyone ducks to avoid the sparks. What you and Ben have is not easy to find, Hallie. I know that it's been hard to let yourself get close to Ben, but you're there now, you made it! If you decide that Joe is the love of your life, remember that you still won't fully trust him for a long time. I know that you and Ben have been together for only a few months, but you trust him already, don't you?"

"Completely. He's been so patient with me. He's always there when I need him. When I had my surgery, he took such good care of me. He always makes me feel so special."

"What are the good things you remember about Joe?"

Hallie thought. Images came: Joe watching football on TV, Joe reaching for a beer instead of Hallie after work, Joe leaving her sick on the couch and meeting friends for dinner. *Something good. There has to be something!* "Yes. I remember. He always told me I was smart, smarter than he was. We used to have fun together, hiking, camping, playing backgammon. He could be really funny sometimes; we laughed a lot in the beginning. You know, it was hard coming up with the good stuff at first. There was a lot of bad, too. He wasn't very good at taking care of me. He spent a lot of time with his friends. I remember asking him to stay home with me just one night a week, and he resented it. He spent the weekends with me, usually, but Monday to Friday he was off playing basketball or poker with his buddies. God, I got so tired of watching him leave."

"You say you had no doubts about marrying this man, Hallie, but you were very young. I think it's only the very young who can experience that kind of love. Even the kind of love that starts out that way ends up tempered a bit over time. When you're young and in love for the first time you see your beloved as perfection itself. You believe he will never hurt you, or even slightly annoy you. The reality of love is very different. Falling in love for the second time, or staying in love for decades, you understand that nothing— and no one— is perfect. Having doubts may be an absolutely healthy response to committing yourself to another human being for life. Doubts may simply be proof that you're not so swept away that you can't make an intelligent decision.

"Knowing what you know now, do you think you would make the same choice? If you met Joe for the first time today, would you end up marrying him? Or would you have different priorities in choosing a mate?"

Hallie had been pacing in front of the window. Now, she sat heavily beside Cora. "Oh my God. I have no idea why I was confused. I see everything so clearly now. How could I have even considered Joe as a possibility? He was never half the man Ben is. Not even in the beginning! Cora, he never even tried to be. What on earth possessed me?"

Cora smiled and patted her hand. "Joe left a scar, Hallie, a deep one. When that happens, we all wonder a little bit: Was it me? Was it because I am not lovable? Well, now here was Joe, live and in person, answering 'No, it wasn't your fault, Hallie, it was mine and I love you.' Of course you would respond to that, if only for a moment. It's quite a lovely gift he's given you today. Now you can finally put all that ugliness away. Tuck it away on a dusty little shelf where it can't hurt you anymore."

"I have to call him and tell him to leave me alone. And I have to get my shopping done. I am going to Ben's parents' house tonight to meet his entire family. Thank you, Cora. I love you!"

"I love you too, sweetie pie. Would you like to use my phone?"

"I would love to. Oh, no, Cora, don't leave. I'd like you to be here for this." Hallie took out the card Joe had given her. Should she call him at home or leave a message at work? No, not a message. He could always say he didn't get it. She dialed his home number, wondering if he'd had enough time to get there.

He had. "Hello?" It was Joe's voice, and not on a machine.

"Joe? It's Hallie."

"Hallie, my God! I hoped you'd call, but I didn't think it would be this soon!"

"I won't keep you long." And Hallie's words came easily, without hesitation or second thoughts. She spoke of new and better lives, gratitude for pain endured and lessons learned. Of not glancing backward any longer, in anger or uncertainty. Of forgiveness and finality. When he seemed to accept her words at last, she was grateful for something else: she could say good-bye to Joe, knowing it was for the last time, with no regrets and, amazingly, no pain. Their time was simply over; it had ended seven years ago.

Hallie hung up and faced Cora.

"Well done, my dear. I'm proud of you. Now, what time is Ben picking you up?"

35

Ben carried a bottle of wine in one hand, and held one of Hallie's in the other as they approached his parents' home. He squeezed her hand, grinning at her, then let it go to knock on the door. "Ready or not…"

"I'm ready!"

He knocked, then opened the door into the kitchen. "Hello!" he called.

Voices, growing louder, called "They're here! Rachel, Ben and Hallie are here!"

Ben ushered Hallie into the house and closed the door behind them. His mother was the first to appear in the kitchen, and she closed the distance between them quickly, hand outstretched.

"Hallie! So wonderful to meet you. I'm Stevie. Oh, here comes everyone! Hallie, this is Ben's dad, Alex."

"Nice to meet you," Hallie said, her hand released by Stevie and caught immediately by Alex.

"So you really do exist," came a voice from the doorway. "I was beginning to wonder."

"Rach!" Ben called, and as his parents turned toward their daughter, Hallie caught sight of her for the first time. Stunning was the only word in Hallie's mind. Rachel was tall, close to six feet, Hallie estimated, and her hair was just a shade shy of black, even darker than Lonnie's. Hallie recognized those eyes, too, large, dark brown, widely spaced and endowed with those long, thick lashes usually seen only in mascara commercials. Ben's eyes were beautiful, but on Rachel they were simply miraculous. Clearly she worked at staying fit: she was slender, but her long sinewy limbs were toned, her muscles well defined. *And this is not the former model,* Hallie reminded herself. *This is the mother of twins.*

Seeing Rachel close up and smiling, Hallie literally caught her breath. "It's so nice to meet you, Rachel. I've heard so much about you."

Rachel beamed. "Ben never stops talking about you. It's about time he brought you around! My husband Sam's in the bedroom, trying to get the boys to take a nap before dinner. You'll meet him in a minute."

"Where's Natalie? Is she still coming?" Ben asked.

"Yes, she called. She's running late," his mother said. "Just a little, she said. I should have told her dinner was at four."

Rachel touched Hallie's arm. "Nat is always late. She tries, she really does, but she just can't seem to get out the door at the right time. Last Christmas I told her to come over at nine just to get her here by eleven."

"Oh, she's not that bad," Alex said.

"No, she's worse sometimes!"

"Oh! Where are my manners? Hallie, would you like a drink? Glass of wine?" Stevie asked.

"We brought a bottle of wine, Mom. It's a pretty good Syrah. Do you want me to open that?"

"Sure, honey. You open and pour the wine, and we'll meet you in the living room. Hallie, come on in here and make yourself comfortable."

Stevie motioned for Hallie to sit on the couch, then sat beside her. Through the huge window, Hallie could see forever, it seemed. Trees covered the hillside below them, all the way down to Lake Washington. The Lawsons' house was small, but built to take full advantage of the view. "Your home is lovely, Stevie. How long have you lived here?"

"Thank you, Hallie. Oh, we used to have a great big old place on the lake. That's where we raised the kids, from the time Ben was eight or nine. We lived there for a few years after the kids had all moved out. Natalie came home for a little while, and once she was on her feet again we decided it was time for a change. We'd already bought our place in Scottsdale, and we felt it was time to let go of the homestead. So we had this place built. It's big enough for the two of us, and we designed it so there's no wasted space. I guess it was finished about six years ago now, wouldn't you say, Alex?"

"Mm-hmm, six years as of July 27th. Ben says you're from Michigan, Hallie?"

"Yes, but I've been out here for a little over seven years. This is home now."

Ben brought in the open bottle of wine and a bouquet of glasses, then poured for everyone. They were about to toast when they heard the kitchen door open and close, hard. "Hey! Where is everyone?"

"In the living room, hon!" Stevie called.

Natalie burst into the room, flushed and grinning. "I made it! Hallie!" She raced to the couch, leaned over and hugged Hallie tight. "My God, you're gorgeous! Well, what do you think of our crazy clan?"

"Speak for yourself, Nat! We're not all crazy, honest, Hallie," Rachel said.

Sam emerged from the hallway. "Ssh! I think they're asleep!" He crossed to the couch, held his hand out. "Hi, Hallie. Great to finally meet you. Rachel was willing to bet you were a figment of Ben's imagination, dreamed up to get us all off his back."

"We told him he either had to introduce us to you or admit he was gay," Natalie said.

"Well, the mystery is solved, once and for all I hope," Ben said. "I'm straight, and very choosy."

Hallie smiled, looking from face to face. Through dinner and dessert she marveled at the laughter, the good-natured teasing, the genuine appreciation they all felt for each other. *This is a happy family.*

When the twins woke up, Rachel and Sam led them into the kitchen for their own dinner. Hallie followed, watching the sleepy boys gradually re-energize and begin to chatter as they ate. "They're beautiful, Rachel."

Rachel smiled. "Thanks. Yeah, they're something. Twins have been a challenge, that's for sure. Diapers, breast-feeding, trying to synchronize their schedules. What a nightmare. But now that they're getting a bit less dependent I can breathe again, and they're getting to be more fun. But be warned, Hallie: twins run in the family!"

"Don't say that, you'll scare her away!" Ben said from the doorway.

"I don't scare that easily. Twins wouldn't be the worst thing in the world, right?" Hallie smiled at him, then looked at the floor. He caught her eye, blew her a kiss.

Rachel looked from Ben to Hallie as she retrieved the two-handled cup Jonah had tossed to the floor. "Everything okay? Did I say something wrong?"

Hallie shook her head. "No, no everything's fine. I've had some physical problems. I'm not completely sure I can have children. It's a wait-and-see kind of thing. I'm fine, really. It's been an adjustment, but I'm okay with it now. If it happens, great, but if not, well, that'll be okay too."

Rachel's eyes had grown wide, and her hand covered her mouth. Sam, wiping Nate's face, glanced up. When Hallie stopped speaking, Rachel went to her, arms open wide, and they hugged. "Hallie, honey, I'm so sorry. I didn't know."

"It's okay. Really. It stings now and then, but I'm all right. I have a really close friend who's pregnant now, and I'm going to be the baby's godmother. I'm excited about that. I know there will be children in my life, one way or another."

Rachel stepped back and held Hallie's hands. "You're right. But by the time you're ready to try, there will probably be new options available. I'm sure it will all work out, Hallie."

"Thank you, Rachel. I appreciate that."

One by one, the other members of Ben's family filed into the kitchen and sat around the table watching Nate and Jonah finish their dinners. "I don't know why we always end up in here," Stevie said.

"Because this is where your famous lemon meringue pie is! Who wants a piece?" Alex asked, pulling it out of the fridge.

"I'll take the biggest one!" said Natalie.

"I'd love one," Hallie said. *What a year,* she thought. First Cora, then Ben, and now his wonderful family had entered her life in just a few short months. Taking her first bite of Stevie's 'famous' pie, she wondered briefly how many occasions she would be a part of in this kitchen, with this family. Grinning at each of them, she was filled with wonder, with hope. "Stevie, this pie is so delicious!"

Ben caught her eye, smiled, and squeezed her hand. He leaned over and whispered, "Told you they'd love you." He kissed her ear, to a chorus of "Aah," and "Isn't that sweet?" and from Natalie: "Looks like love to me!"

Hallie, glowing and grinning, felt a wave of admiration. Clearly, Ben was a product of his upbringing. Somewhere recently, Hallie had read the phrase: It's never too late to have a happy childhood. The first step, she'd thought at the time, would be to create your own family. A family of choice. *This is a family I could be happy with,* she thought now.

If someone had mentioned Joe at this moment, it would have taken Hallie several moments to imagine his face.

36

Brewing at the back of Hallie's mind for weeks now was an idea. If she didn't want to be an accountant, what *did* she want to be? Once she found the answer to that question, she realized, she could set a new goal for her career and achieve it. She could make it happen. Her parents were too far away to dissuade her, and everyone around her now simply wanted her to be happy. She could afford night school or a training program, or whatever it would take, within reason.

So what did she want? What kind of work would energize her, excite her? A few ideas occurred to her, and she began to turn them over in her mind, examining them and searching for flaws each night as she waited for sleep to silence her questions.

Did she want to pursue a singing career? People seemed to think this was an option for her. But she knew it could be a rough road. The odds were against becoming rich and famous, and she wasn't at all sure she wanted that kind of life anyway. She was just now digging in, planting roots that she hoped would grow strong and sturdy. Late nights, weekends in bars, and long months on the road away from home did not appeal to her, not now.

But was there a way to sneak music into a new career? Singing truly fed her soul, replenished every cell in her body. It made her feel authentically, wholly herself. But how could she make a living as a singer without all the ugliness that went along with it?

One night as she lay beside Ben, a possible answer came to her, a whisper in the dark.

She could teach. Not as a music teacher in a school, but as a private singing instructor with her own business. Hallie's Harmonies: Personal Singing Lessons. She imagined teaching children, beautiful little budding divas and rock stars hungry for encouragement and validation, strolling up the walk to a charming little house, wooden sign pointing the way.

Now that she had the idea, it was time for research. Hallie formed a list of questions to explore. Would a business license be necessary, and what would that entail? What does a typical singing instructor charge? What kind of advertising would be needed and how much would it cost? What exactly does an instructor teach? (She had some idea about this, having taken lessons herself, but she would need a detailed description.) Was there a certification program she could enroll in? If not, how would she acquire all the skills needed to become Super Singing Teacher? How long would it take to build the business to the point where she could quit her "day job?" And, was there something she could do, other than accounting, to supplement her income if necessary?

Hallie's own singing teacher had never really known how valuable the lessons had been. While Hallie had been hesitant and withdrawn during the lessons, in private she had blossomed. Using her new skills, her range had expanded, and she had greater control and resonance. So Hallie decided that a visit to her own teacher would be a good place to start; she could get some answers, and it would give Hallie a chance to thank her as well. So Hallie arranged a lunchtime visit.

Emily Klausen, as always, was coolly polite. Everything about her was neatly pressed; everything except her hair, that is, which was prematurely gray and a little wild, sticking out in every direction from the French twist she attempted each day. The woman herself was in her mid-forties. Her hair had aged far beyond that.

"Please, sit down. Would you like some coffee?"

"No, thank you, Emily, I don't want to take up too much of your time."

"No hurry, dear. My first appointment isn't until three. What is it I can do for you?"

"Well, I'd like to ask a few questions. I'm thinking about becoming a singing teacher myself."

"I see. So you'd like to know about the practicality of the profession, is that it?" Emily's mouth tightened, an expression Hallie recognized from her less-than-stellar performances during her lessons. "Frankly, I'm surprised, Hallie. You have a lovely voice, dear, but you hold back. I don't think that's something you'd want to pass on to your students."

"You're absolutely right. I was holding back in my lessons. It's just where I was at the time. My life is completely different now, and I think I am too. I'm not a secret singer anymore. I belt it out! In front of people! And I wanted to thank you, Emily, because I'm really using the techniques you taught me. They make a huge difference!" Hallie saw Emily's face soften, her shoulders relax. "I wish I would have put in the effort here. I should have. But please know that I did benefit, I really did."

Emily smiled. "I'm so glad, Hallie, because honestly, you were the most frustrating student I think I've ever had! I mean, clearly you are so talented. So talented! But you just wouldn't cooperate. I could see that you simply weren't comfortable singing in front of anyone, not even me. Ridiculous for a singer of your caliber. After a while, I stopped trying to draw you out and just went through the motions. Where do you perform?"

"Oh, no, I don't perform, not really. Just karaoke with friends. But people really applaud for me! It's wonderful. And I really love it. So I've been thinking about creating a new career for myself. Remember, I'm an accountant, and I thought those skills would be handy for running my own business. But what else do I need to think about?"

"Do you play an instrument? Your students need accompaniment."

Hallie had been thinking about that. She'd taken piano lessons for years— her mother had insisted it was a ladylike skill Hallie needed— but hadn't played since moving to Washington. "I was considering getting an electronic keyboard, and maybe a small karaoke set-up so that students could choose the kind of music they'd like to sing."

"Hmm. That's not a bad idea. Of course, you need to be familiar with different styles of music, and it goes without saying that you must be completely comfortable with actually teaching the techniques. You should probably think about taking more lessons yourself."

"Absolutely. I'd planned on asking about more lessons with you. Another question: I don't want to be too nosy, but how financially viable is this? Could I make a decent living doing this full time?"

"Well, generally people charge anywhere from twenty to fifty dollars per lesson, depending on experience. You could have people sign up for six- or eight-week courses, or allow them to pay for one lesson at a time. It's difficult to schedule enough students on weekdays because most people work or attend school. You're looking at weekend and evening work. There are people who return for tune-ups now and then, but you're usually seeing students for a few weeks and then never again. Word of mouth must be positive, because advertising is very expensive. I keep a little ad in the yellow pages, and post my name and number in local music stores, and I stay pretty busy. I usually work four afternoons and evenings a week, and all day Saturdays, during the day, of course. I make forty to fifty thousand a year teaching. Not bad, but not enough on its own, not with a mortgage. But I also sing with a jazz group most Friday and Saturday nights, and that supplements my income fairly well. I also design greeting cards and sell them to gift shops in the area. I like to have little pockets of income filtering in from different places."

"Wow! You are busy. Do you like what you do?"

"I love it. Every day is new and fresh and MINE. I do not work for anyone else. If I need to take a day off, I clear a day and take it. On the downside, if I take do a vacation, my income dips. But it's worth it for me, Hallie.

"I heard someone say once that singing is a dime a dozen talent. So many people can sing. Okay, that's true. A lot of people have the ability to sing. But what's truly miraculous is that every single voice is unique. And once in a while, someone very special comes along who not only hits the notes, but has an extraordinary range and a spark you can't define. To find a student like that, give her the tools she needs and watch her bloom? Oh, it's a tremendous feeling! And, I still have my own creative outlets for balance. I have a great life, Hallie. I do recommend more than one source of income, but if this appeals to you, go for it.

"One more thing. Do you still live in an apartment?"

"Yeah, I do. I know, I'm thinking I'll need to rent a house. I don't think I could get away with that much noise, especially evenings and weekends."

"A house is a good idea. I was in an apartment when I started teaching, and it didn't work very well. There was a lack of music lovers in my building, I'm afraid. The police were called so often, I just started making coffee for them before each lesson. Not every student is gifted, you'll see.

"Now, I'm going to make some coffee for myself. Please join me. We can plan your next lesson, if you like. Cream and sugar?"

37

Hallie came from Emily's visit with a lot of information, and a lot more questions. No job would ever be perfect; Hallie understood that, but she was not at all thrilled about the prospect of working evenings and weekends, when Ben was free. But now that she'd identified a possible new career goal, she was impatient to give up accounting forever. That was going to take some time, even if she did decide to teach; in order to rent a house, buy a keyboard and advertising, and have time to hone her skills and learn more singing techniques, she needed a good, steady income. Besides, Emily had recommended other income sources anyway.

Well, she could always provide tax or private accounting services part-time. But she wanted another option. One that would allow her to remain above the poverty line, continue to have some leisure time, and get started on her new life quickly. But what?

This was the question, running through her mind like a ticker tape when Ben appeared at her office door. "Hey! Almost 4:30. Wanna do something tonight?"

"What do you have in mind?"

"Well, it's karaoke night, isn't it? It's been a while. Why don't we head down early and have some dinner. Want to invite Lonnie or Cora maybe?"

"Let's invite both. Kim too. What about your sisters? Would they be interested?"

"Maybe Nat. Rachel needs more notice to arrange a sitter. I'll call Natalie. You call the others, and we'll head out."

"Okay. See you in a minute!"

Hallie was making her last call when Ben returned, grinning. "It's ringing," she said. "Just a sec. Kim? Hey, it's Hallie. Want to come out for karaoke night? Lonnie and Steve are coming, and Cora and Marion."

Ben waved, getting her attention, and whispered, "And Natalie. Oh, and Rachel."

"Really? Sorry, Kim, I was talking to Ben. Looks like his sisters are coming, too. Do you want to call Andy? Okay! See you there!" She hung up. "Kim said she'll come for sure, and she'll bring her boyfriend if he's free. So, Rachel's coming?"

"Yeah. I thought I'd ask just in case, and she was so excited that she volunteered Sam to look after the kids. She called him at work and got the official okay. Sounds like we're gathering quite a crowd."

"Should be fun! Cora and Marion are meeting us there for dinner. Lonnie, Steve and Kim are coming later."

"Rachel and Nat are coming after dinner. They're really psyched about hearing you sing. Natalie might even get up there if we nudge her a little."

"Cool! Okay, let me just clear off my desk."

They met Cora and Marion in front of the restaurant. "Cora! You look wonderful! Where's your friend?"

Conspicuously missing was Cora's nemesis, the dreaded walker. "Fred? I've cast him aside. Meet my new dance partner." She lifted the cane in her hand: metal, four-pronged. "Not quite as pretty as my walking stick, but it keeps me a bit steadier. I'm pleased with my progress, though. Funny, since I got pushed out of bed and back into my life, it's amazing how much better I feel." She grinned at the three of them.

"Okay, now tell them the bad news," said Marion, scowling.

"Oh, let's go inside and sit down first, shall we?"

Hallie looked at Marion as they went through the door; she frowned, but said nothing.

The hostess showed them to a table, and they settled in. Hallie and Ben looked from Cora to Marion and back again. "Well?" Hallie asked. "What's the bad news?"

"Oh, it's nothing, really. I just have to have a little surgery."

"Surgery?"

"It's minor, absolutely routine. They just need to clean out a few veins, that's all."

"Angioplasty?" Ben asked.

"Yes. I'll be out of the hospital in a day. Amazing what doctors can do now, isn't it? They're going to make sure I don't have another stroke. So that's *good* news, isn't it? Marion's just being a little dramatic."

"An operation is always bad news, if you ask me. There's always a risk to it. Especially at your age."

"Ouch! No need to get nasty about it. I'm going to go have this little procedure, be a bit more careful about what I eat, and hopefully I'll have another ten good years in the company of my dear friends. Then you'll be obligated to throw me a wild bash for my ninetieth birthday."

"Hmm. Ten years. I wonder what marvelous changes I'll see?" Cora grinned at Hallie and Ben.

"There she goes, changing the subject again," Marion grumbled.

"Marion, I think you're worrying enough for all of us, don't you? Look, this is my best bet. My doctor thinks I'm healthy enough to sail through the surgery. I have you to take care of me, and Barry or Chrissy will come if I need them. You don't want to find me crumpled on the floor again, I know that. So, I'm doing what I need to do to make sure that doesn't happen. My little stroke was a warning, and now I need to heed that warning. Fretting about it won't make it easier for any of us. No, I'm here tonight to have fun and listen to our Hallie sing. I intend to enjoy every minute."

"When is the surgery, Cora?" Hallie asked.

"Monday morning. Marion is taking me to the hospital. She should be able to pick me up the next day. End of discussion. Who wants a margarita?" She pointed at Marion. "Don't tell me I shouldn't. I said I'm going to be a bit more careful, but I'm not going to stop living. One drink is not going to hurt, and it might actually help. I suggest you have one, too."

When dinner was over, they moved into the bar, pushed three tables together and waited for the rest of the group to arrive. Lonnie and Steve came first, then Kim and Andy, and finally Natalie and Rachel, arriving together and ignoring the eyes of everyone in the bar watching as they walked to the table.

Karaoke Kyle was back, resplendent in his trademark green polyester, and clearly thrilled to see Hallie. His smile faded somewhat when he noticed how cozy Ben and Hallie were.

Ben was proven right; with a little encouragement, Natalie took the stage and belted out an old Pat Benatar song. "She's really good!" Hallie said.

"Yeah, and believe it or not she used to refuse to sing outside the shower," Rachel said.

"Oh, I can believe it," Cora said. "Sometimes it's the most talented people of all who don't believe in their own gifts."

Rachel smiled. "I suppose that's true. It's so great to see Natalie bloom like this. It's strange that her time as a professional model and actress was when she was most insecure."

It was hard to imagine Natalie as timid or troubled, but Hallie knew she had been. Watching her now, radiant on the stage, Hallie smiled. Natalie had made a decision to change, had worked hard to become healthy and whole. Amazing what was possible with a little love and support.

When Hallie's name was called, she bounced up to the stage, smiled at Kyle, and launched into one of her favorite songs.

At the table, everyone watched and listened with pleasure, but no one more so than Ben and Cora, who tapped Ben's arm. "Just look at her! She's become so confident. Isn't it wonderful?"

Ben grinned back at her. "*She's* wonderful."

"Yes, she certainly is. I'm so glad you noticed," Cora said.

Lonnie was the first to leave. "I'm so tired these days I can't stand it. This baby is just draining my energy," she yawned. Steve stood up and said his good-byes, taking Lonnie's hand as they left. Kim and Andy made their apologies soon afterward.

Rachel was exhausted, as well. "I didn't want to say anything to Lonnie, but I don't think I've caught up on my sleep yet. I can't wait until the boys are teenagers."

"No, then you'll be losing sleep for a whole new set of reasons," Natalie said with a smile. "But I'll take you home if you like. I have an early morning anyway. Hallie, you're amazing. Cora, Marion, nice to meet you both. See you guys soon!"

When they were gone, Cora leaned over to Ben. "Your sisters are lovely. I'll bet Rachel's twins are just gorgeous!"

"Well I think so, but I'm not exactly objective. Yeah, Rachel and Nat have always been beautiful. Sometimes people are too intimidated to talk to them, but they're so outgoing and friendly that they've always been able to put everyone at ease pretty quickly.

"Natalie had some trouble for a while. She entered a couple of pageants, started modeling, made a couple of commercials. She had an agent, the whole bit. You see how beautiful she is; but it was never good enough. She was under all this pressure to enhance her cheekbones, her chin, change her hair color, and always, always, lose a few pounds. She was young, and she started to believe it all. She started dieting, and before long food was all she thought about. Avoiding food. Estimating the calories in a slice of cucumber and a cherry tomato. Once I begged her to have dinner with me and I literally watched her eat three pieces of lettuce out of her salad and tell me she was full. We saw her losing weight, looking emaciated and pale, like a strong wind could have knocked her over. Finally, my parents, Rachel and I had an intervention with her. It took a while to convince her that she had a problem, but she saw the light eventually. She decided that she couldn't pursue modeling and acting and stay healthy. Some people can manage it, but Nat just couldn't. So, she started eating, went back to school and became a pediatric nurse. She seems really happy now; no more nonsense about cheeks and chins."

Cora drummed her fingers on the table, deep in thought. "Beauty is a strange thing. It is prized and rewarded in our culture as if it were a virtue. We judge people based on outward appearance, especially women. Poor Natalie; to be so beautiful, and to be told to change this or fix that, or lose ten pounds you can't afford to lose, all to feed the public some predetermined notion of beauty that no one could, or should attain. Small wonder so many teenaged girls starve themselves to death. Oh, it makes me so angry I want to shake someone!"

Hallie looked at Marion, who sat staring into her drink during Cora's speech. "Marion? You all right?"

She looked up slowly, her eyes meeting only Hallie's. "It's just a little hard for me to think that beauty could ever be a burden. Ben's sisters, and you, Hallie. You're all as sweet and kind as anyone I've ever met. But I can't help but hate you just a tiny bit. Life had to have been easier for you. When I went through school, bug-ugly as I was, the kids laughed at me, made fun of my old dresses, called me names like 'fatso.' The pretty girls were all friends, and of course the boys wanted to date them. But no one gave me the time of day, except to be mean. I had one friend, Susan, whose vision was so bad she wore those awful Coke-bottle glasses. No one wanted to be around her, either. We got pretty close, but after high school she went off to college and I didn't, so we lost touch. I was all alone in the world and thought I always would be. And why? I couldn't help the way I looked. I just never had pretty features. I didn't eat any more than any other kid, but my mother was fat and I grew up fat, too."

"But you're not fat, Marion. I've never seen you gain an ounce," Cora said.

"No, I'm not fat now. After high school I had to make a living, and once I started working I lost weight and never gained it back. Stopped eating my mother's cooking, too, I guess." She wrinkled her nose. "Too much starch. Now, I don't think much about it one way or another. I keep busy and I stay pretty thin. But the homely part I can't change."

Hallie frowned. "Marion, I don't know if life has been any easier for me. It's true that kids didn't pick on me about my looks, but they whispered and pointed if I wore something they didn't like, or didn't get the ball over the net playing volleyball. I think it's just a difficult time, when kids are trying to figure out where they fit, and sometimes they only feel okay if they make others feel they're not. I had friends, but my parents weren't loving or supportive. They didn't encourage me and didn't praise me much when I excelled. I didn't have a lot of confidence in any of my abilities. I became an accountant because it was the only thing my parents believed I could do.

"I think a lot of people just aren't wise or worldly enough to seek beauty where it really counts. You've always struck me as a beautiful, strong woman. I can count on your honesty and trust you with my life. And I can't be the only person who feels this way, Marion. You just need to get out there and show the world how gorgeous you are!"

Marion sat, mouth open, staring at Hallie. Tilting her head to one side, she said slowly, "You're just being nice. Aren't you?"

Cora interjected. "She most certainly is not being nice. She's being honest. And you should be able to recognize that. You silly woman! Why haven't you ever come clean with me before this? I had no idea you were harboring this outrageous self-image! It is simply astonishing what people put themselves through!"

"Marion," Ben said. She looked at him, startled. Scared, almost. "Marion, I have never thought of you as homely.

Never. Tough and no nonsense, yes, but definitely pretty. Honest."

"There. You see?" Cora asked, exasperated. She scribbled something quickly on a slip of paper. "Ben, please submit this to Kyle. Thank you, dear."

"Cora? What did you do?" Marion asked as Ben followed Cora's orders.

"This is *your* coming out party, Marion!" Cora said. "You are going to do something fun and crazy and completely out of character. Tonight. No, you will not argue with me! This is not negotiable!"

Moments later, Karaoke Kyle announced: "We have a couple of new singers tonight! Please put your hands together to welcome Cora and Marion!"

Cora took Marion's arm, leaving her cane behind at the table. "It's going to be fun. Loosen up!" Cora said, laughing at Marion's stiff posture.

The title flashed on the monitor's screen. "I know you know this song. I've heard you sing along to it on the radio. Here. Have a microphone." She handed it to Marion, and picked up the second mic for herself.

Marion, looking terrified, raised the microphone to her lips and began to sing.

The song was "When Will I Be Loved," made famous by one of Hallie's favorite singers, Linda Ronstadt. Cora had never sung a rock and roll song before, and Marion could barely carry a tune. Halfway through, Marion began to giggle. They sang only half the lyrics, laughing and clinging to each other through the rest. The audience laughed with them, clapping in time to the music.

As the song ended, Hallie leaped to her feet, cheered and applauded them back to the table. Marion, grinning wider than Hallie had ever thought possible, helped Cora into her chair and then collapsed into her own. "My God that was fun! Thank you for dragging me up there, Cora. I was awful, and they loved me!"

Hallie was still laughing when Karaoke Kyle began speaking again. "Well, we're nearing the end of the night. It's been a slow one, tonight, folks, not a lot of volunteers coming up. So, I'd like to make a request. Could we get Hallie to come up for one more song? What do you say, Hallie?"

And, to Hallie's amazement, the audience began chanting her name: "Hallie! Hallie! Hallie!"

She looked around. There were a lot of familiar faces: Wednesday night regulars. But there were people she had never seen before, too. They were all looking her way, clapping and calling her name. They all wanted to hear her sing again.

Ben squeezed her hand. "Your fans are waiting!"

She stood up and headed toward the stage. The audience began to cheer and applaud. "Thank you, Hallie!" Kyle said into the microphone. He lowered it then and asked, "What song would you like?"

She chose a favorite Beatles' song, "In My Life." She loved its message of honoring past loves while celebrating a commitment of soul mates. It was sweet and lovely in Hallie's voice.

As she held the last note, the audience once again burst into applause. "Thank you," she said, and gave the microphone back to Kyle. "We missed you last time we were here," she told him.

"Thanks. Yeah, I had another gig that ran long, so I had a friend fill in for a while."

"Well, it's nice to have you back." Hallie stepped off the stage, and the applause continued as she returned to her seat.

Her three biggest fans stood at the table, clapping. Ben greeted her with a hug. When the applause at last died down, the four of them put on their coats and prepared to leave. Hallie was talking to Cora when she felt a presence behind her.

She began to turn at the same time someone reached between her and Ben to tap her on the shoulder. Behind her was a man she had never seen before. He looked to be approaching sixty; his suit, tie and raincoat stood out in the casually dressed crowd. "I'm sorry to intrude," he said. "I was wondering— have you ever sung professionally?"

"No, I haven't. I'm not all that interested, actually."

"Listen, here's my card. My name is Jim Schultz. I was just wondering if you've ever considered singing commercial jingles or doing voiceovers."

"Uh, no, I haven't even thought about that."

"I work for an agency that recruits people for that kind of work. Some of the recording is done in my studio, and for some I send people somewhere else. I'd like you to come down and audition, if you're interested. I think I can find work for you. You have a good range; you can sing different styles of music. We're always looking for someone like you. The pay is pretty good. What do you think?"

Bells were ringing loudly in Hallie's head. *This may be the answer!* "When and where do I audition?"

38

The next morning, Hallie sat in her office staring at Jim Schultz's business card for the twentieth time. Last night he had patiently answered her questions, described the entire process of recording professional jingles. All she had to do now was call for an appointment to audition.

Butterflies danced inside her as she put the card down and tried to concentrate on work. She had promised herself she would make the call on her lunch break; now she was impatient for the morning to be over, and even more impatient for her accounting career to be over.

Until Mr. Schultz approached her, she had not shared her career plans with anyone. She had wanted to wait until she'd cleared the path of all obstacles. Then a stranger had appeared and offered to plow a huge one right out of the way. So, when he had given his card and spoken to her before blending back into the crowd, Hallie told Ben, Cora and Marion a little about her new aspirations.

She hesitated telling them everything, especially Ben. Setting up shop as a singing teacher would mean moving into a house. She would rent if necessary, but with a little help she might be able to pull off a mortgage. That would be an enormous commitment, however, and considering her relationship with Ben, she had thought that perhaps her next move would be with him. She knew he was thinking about that, too, but she didn't want to rush the decision simply for the convenience of a new career. So, she'd been thinking about talking to Ben about it all, mulling over word choices. And, considering carefully whether she was really ready to live with him. She thought she was, in fact she longed for the time when they would spend all their nights together. But she would not push him into it if he wasn't ready for that particular leap.

Now, here was a possible way to make a decent living outside of number crunching. What if she could earn enough just by singing jingles and narrating commercials? Maybe she wouldn't need another income as a teacher. Maybe it wouldn't be necessary to move…at least not yet.

That's it. I'll do my best at the audition and see how much money I can make through Mr. Schultz. No need to make any other decisions yet.

She looked at the clock on her desk: 11:42. Her in-box was empty. *Close enough*, she thought, and she picked up the phone.

Ben appeared at her door as she was hanging up. "Hey!" she said. "I have an appointment tomorrow at five to audition for Mr. Schultz!"

"Good for you, Hallie."

"Want to help me decide on a song tonight?"

"Sure. Ready for lunch?"

"Yeah, I'm famished." She slipped on her jacket and closed the door behind her. "Everything okay?" she asked, catching Ben's eye.

"Yeah, fine. Uh, I was thinking about something kind of special for lunch, if that's all right."

"Special? What's the occasion?"

"Nothin'. Just wanted to have a nice romantic meal with you."

"Sounds wonderful. You're sure you're okay? You seem a bit distracted."

They had reached his car; he kissed her cheek, then opened the passenger door for her. "Nope. I'm all yours."

But he didn't talk much on the way to the restaurant, and only nodded or grunted acknowledgements to everything she said. Hallie smiled, though, when she realized they were pulling into the parking lot at the Italian restaurant where they'd had their first real date.

"This *is* special. Thank you for being so thoughtful," Hallie said, touching his hand as he parked the car. He grinned at her.

But sitting across from him inside the restaurant, it was clear to Hallie that Ben had something on his mind. His eyes wandered from hers, he scowled, and fidgeted with his fork. "Ben, what is it?" she asked.

He looked at her at last. "Sorry. It's that obvious, huh?"

"Yes. You're completely transparent. What's going on?"

"Okay, here goes. Hallie, I've been thinking. About us. A lot. I mean, a lot. You're all I think about, actually. I love you more than I ever thought I'd love anyone. More than I ever could love anyone else. I know, for certain, deep down to my soul, that you are perfect for me. We are perfect for each other. I am so grateful, every day, that we found each other. And I know you feel the same way. Tell me you feel the same way."

"I do, Ben. I really do."

"Okay. Then tell me one more thing. I know we haven't really known each other a long time, but it doesn't matter. I'm ready to take the next step. I hope you are too."

"Next step?"

"Hallie, I'm tired of spending nights apart. Every night I spend at my place I toss and turn, wishing you were beside me. I want to wake up to your face every morning for the rest of my life. I want us to live together. You know, we've been together almost six months. What else do we need to know about each other? Well, a lot, I know, but we won't learn anything more until we live together. What do you think?"

"I think you have the most amazing timing. I've been thinking about this, too. I was going to talk to you about it, but I didn't want to rush you."

"Really?"

"Yeah. And I think we should get a house."

And Ben smiled, ear-to-ear, pure joy radiating from his face. Hallie smiled back, thinking that in that moment she knew exactly how he'd looked as a little boy.

The following day, Hallie went directly to the studio from work. She walked to the receptionist's desk, checked in, and was shown the way to the recording area. An entire band was setting up in a corner of the room. Jim Schultz crossed the room to greet her. "Nervous?" he asked.

"Oh, I'm just quaking in my boots, that's all. I've never sung with a live band before."

"Hey, you'll be fine. Just do what you did the other night. Knock 'em dead."

They discussed the song Hallie had chosen, and Jim gave the band a few instructions. Hallie stepped behind a large microphone hanging from the ceiling, and waited for her cue.

It was over quickly. Suddenly Jim was beside her again, shaking her hand. "You were great! I'm going to be able to keep you busy, Hallie, no question. I'll be in touch."

"I'll look forward to it. Thank you!"

Driving home, Hallie sang along with the songs on the radio, drumming on the steering wheel. Raindrops hit softly on the windshield, a perfect syncopated rhythm. Tiny miracles were everywhere, she thought, showing off, daring to be noticed; today, the world seemed to be bursting with them. When her cell phone rang, she smiled, sure it would be Ben checking in with her and asking about the audition. But when she answered it was a woman's voice, a troubled voice, speaking her name.

"Hallie. It's Cora. Please, can you come? Something terrible's happened."

39

On the day of Hallie's audition, Cora had risen early and shuffled into the kitchen to make tea. It was dark, the early October day covered with steel-gray clouds. She'd flicked on the light, filled the kettle and turned on the stove, popped a teabag into a cup, set out another cup for Marion, and sat at the table with a book to wait for the kettle to whistle her into action.

When Marion appeared, yawning, Cora had barely looked up. "Tea, dear?" she'd asked.

"I'll get it. What's up for today?"

"Not much. I'd like you to go to the store. I'll make a list. I'm a little sore today, damned arthritis, so I think I'll stay home if that's okay."

"Fine. You know, there's some yard work that needs to be done. Want me to get going on it, or do you plan on hiring someone?"

"I think I'll ask about that at the flower shop or the nursery. Surely they know of someone who can do odd jobs around the house. I don't want you to be doing that heavy work."

"I'm not all that old, you know. I can plant bulbs and prune trees."

"Of course you can. I just don't think you should have to do that and everything else. Wouldn't be right."

"Cora, I'd do it if it were my own home. And I kind of think of this place as partly mine."

Cora had smiled at her. "As well you should, Marion."

The kettle had begun to whistle then, and Marion took it from the stove to the two cups that Cora had set out for them. "If you feel guilty for overworking me, you could always pay me a little extra," Marion had said, and they'd laughed.

After breakfast, Marion had showered, dressed and left for the store. Pausing at the door, she'd asked Cora for any last minute additions to the grocery list.

"I can't think of anything, but if you see something interesting, feel free."

"Okey dokey."

"Maybe we can play a round of Scrabble when you get back."

"If you insist."

"Come on! It'll keep my mind sharp."

"Cora, you win every time. I think it's working too well."

The rain had begun while Marion was shopping; it was pouring as she packed the groceries into the car's trunk.

Always a careful driver, Marion made sure the road was clear before turning left from the store's parking lot and heading back toward Cora's house. She stopped at a four-way stop sign and waited two full seconds before proceeding.

But others are not so careful. She saw the car coming from her left, just as she put her foot back on the gas pedal, but her mind registered no danger. *He has to stop at the stop sign,* she thought simply.

He didn't. The driver of that souped-up old car had just come from a liquid brunch and was enjoying the rush of speeding on wet streets. His cell phone rang, and he looked down at the screen to see who was calling and so he did not see the stop sign, felt no need to slow down. When he looked up at last he saw Marion's car in the intersection; he hesitated, then tried to stop, too late. Marion heard tires squealing and turned her head to see a young man's frightened face.

She had time to think: *Uh-oh.* Just a momentary sense of dread, of finality. Then, she imagined Cora's smile, and in Marion's last moments she felt only gratitude.

Cora, writing letters in the living room, had just glanced at the clock. She was wondering why Marion had not returned when she heard the sirens. She told herself that there was no connection; but she was not a worrier by nature and she could not argue with the cold terror creeping through her body. She stood and walked to the hall; pacing, she watched the door, trying to will Marion to stumble through it, carrying too many bags of groceries as she always did.

But somewhere, in the pit of her stomach, Cora knew Marion would not be coming home. And, when at last the knock came at the door, she would not allow herself even one moment of false hope.

"Is this the home of Marion Bauer?" the police officer asked.

Cora smiled gently. Could it be only a couple of hours that she and Marion had settled that question once and for all? "Yes, Officer. It most certainly is."

"Are you her mother?"

Tears blurred her vision now, and she blinked. "I am the closest to family she has." Cora, allowing a little hope through the open door after all, refused to speak of Marion in the past tense. Not yet. She would make these men say the words she so dreaded hearing.

"May we come in, ma'am?"

The police officers informed Cora that Marion had been in an accident; she was pronounced dead at the scene. The driver of the other car was alive, but in critical condition. The police believed that alcohol was a factor in the accident, but this would be confirmed with a blood test later. The survivor had been transported to the nearest hospital. Marion had probably died instantly, they told her.

Cora sat, very erect, watching their eyes and nodding, feeling the numbness of shock setting in. When she showed the policemen to the door and closed it behind them, she stood, staring at it. She wanted to bring the officers back in and scream until they took it all back.

"Are you all right, ma'am?" they'd asked. And she had responded that she was fine.

But how could she be fine without Marion? They had known each other so long they could finish each other's thoughts. Marion had saved her life the night of her stroke. Just this morning she had offered to take on the yard work; she had seemed almost eager to solve that dilemma for Cora. And was it just two nights ago that Cora had coaxed her onto a stage? Cora remembered Marion's face that night, shining with a childlike joy Cora had never seen before. *Why didn't we have more fun together, Marion? Why did I bury you in the mundane?*

Marion's body would be taken to the funeral home of Cora's choice, the police had said. Would the closest one be all right? Cora had nodded. She knew that one well: Memory Lane. She hated the name, trite and saccharine as it was, but she was connected to the place just the same. It was where her husband's body had been sent so many years ago.

She had to make the arrangements. That is what one does in these situations. Make decisions, give directions. Cremation or burial? Urn or casket? *This is why sudden death feels so surreal. How can I go from grocery lists to funeral arrangements in the space of three hours?*

And yet she was grateful for the behavioral guidance of obligation. Step one: pick up the phone. Step two: dial the number of the funeral home. Step three: identify yourself and make an appointment.

Marion had often expressed her wish to be cremated. "There's only so much land on this planet. Why in the world do we take up so much space with dead bodies?" Cora could almost hear her voice now.

Yes. She would have Marion's body cremated, and she would have her ashes put into an appropriate receptacle. Later, there would be time to decide what to do with them. She would plan a memorial service, maybe have it here, at the house.

But she was jumping too far ahead. *One step at a time,* she reminded herself, and she picked up the phone.

When she hung up from the funeral director, Cora sat, back straight, facing the window. Puget Sound looked busy, steel gray water churning up white peaks, seemingly angry that the universe had irreversibly changed once again. Fate had pointed its finger at Cora's world and decided that today there would be a cruel collision of two paths.

Cora sat, outwardly still and silent, and allowed her mind to ask the unanswerable. *Why? Why Marion, who wasn't even sixty, yet here I sit, eighty years old and useless without her?* Inevitably, the whys were followed by the what-ifs: *What if I had gone shopping with her? Would I have slowed her down just enough to prevent this? Or, what if I hadn't sent her today at all? What was so urgent about shopping today?*

But no one had tapped Cora's shoulder and whispered the options: Go without groceries today, or be without Marion for the rest of your life. No one had offered her that choice.

Ridiculous. Cora thought, shaking her head. *No point to this at all. Marion was killed by a drunk driver. It was a terrible, senseless accident. Stop feeling so picked on and get on with life, old woman.* It was just what Marion would have told her.

She looked at the clock. How did it get so late? There were more calls to place, more decisions to make. But she need not do this alone. She lifted the receiver once more and dialed another number.

"Hallie? It's Cora. Please, can you come? Something terrible's happened."

40

"Ben, it's Hallie."

"Hey! How did the audition…"

"Listen, I'm on my way to Cora's. There was an accident today. Ben, Marion's dead."

"What? What happened?"

"I don't have a lot of details yet, but obviously Cora's upset, and she's asked me to come over. I don't know what she'll need me to do or how long she'll want me to stay, but I need to be there."

"Of course. God, Hallie, I'm so sorry."

"Thanks. I'll call you later."

When Hallie hung up, she pondered Ben's condolences. But she was not sad, not yet anyway. Instead, she nearly shook with rage. She was angry at whoever had caused this to happen. She was furious that Marion's death would leave a huge hole in Cora's life and that Cora had to feel this grief and sorrow. And, perhaps most of all, Hallie was angry with herself.

Why had she known so little about someone she saw so often? Marion was important to Cora, part of her family, really, and Hallie didn't even know her last name. How old was she? Fifty-five, maybe? Fifty-eight? Had she ever been in love? Did she have any friends, other than Cora? Any hobbies?

Hallie had been curious about Marion, had come close to asking all the questions now floating through her mind. But something had held her back, and now there would be no more chances.

Cora opened the door and smiled. But as the two women embraced, she surrendered to her grief at last and wept, rocking in Hallie's arms.

That evening, Hallie went to her apartment, collected Cleo and a suitcase of clothes, and returned to stay at Cora's house; this time, Hallie would be taking care of Cora.

Hallie accompanied Cora to the funeral home the following day and sat beside her while the arrangements were made. The funeral director's questions seemed to Cora as though they were being transmitted in a garbled code or from a great distance, or both. Hallie helped to translate, repeating his words softly until their meaning became clear to Cora.

Back at Cora's house, Hallie made them lunch. Cora ate very little; she pushed the food around on her plate and spoke of Marion.

Marion had no living relatives. To Hallie's surprise, Cora revealed that Marion had been married once, briefly, when she was barely twenty. Her husband beat her on their wedding night, but convinced her to give him one more chance. She did, and when the second beating came three months later, she moved back home with her mother. (Her father had died two years earlier. Her only sibling, a younger sister, had died shortly after birth.) Marion filed for divorce; her husband did not appear in court and the marriage was dissolved in his absence. She never saw him again. Marion renounced her married name and changed all of her identification back to Bauer.

She took some typing and shorthand classes and landed a job as a secretary at a small marketing company. She had been thinking of moving out on her own when her mother was diagnosed with breast cancer. A double mastectomy and radiation therapy would not save her; the cancer was aggressive, colonizing quietly throughout her body, invading even into her bones. Marion stayed and cared for her mother until she died, an agonizing six months later.

The Bauer home was paid for in full, but it was a large house on more than six acres of land, and Marion could not afford to pay the utility bills and property tax; nor could she comfortably manage that much property. So, she sold the house and tucked the money away in a savings account— she called it her emergency fund. She had sacrificed her job to care for her mother, so during her last months in the house, she looked for places to live and to work.

She found both when she answered an advertisement in the newspaper: Wanted: live-in caregiver for elderly woman. It had been difficult watching her mother die, but Marion had learned something about herself: she was a natural caregiver. She could always earn a decent living as a secretary, but she hated the work. In caregiving, she'd found her passion.

She applied for the position, interviewing with the woman's daughter. The daughter lived in a different city, and the mother, while alert, was unable to stand for more than a few minutes and therefore needed someone to cook, clean and help her bathe and dress. Marion was twenty-two and completely alone. The daughter doubted Marion's ability to care for her mother, but she took pity on the poor girl— she had, after all, just lost *her* mother— and hired her on the spot. Within a month, all doubts were gone as Marion worked day and night to keep the house and her new "mother" spotless.

Ten years later, Marion's employer died, and her daughter recommended Marion's services to a friend whose mother had been diagnosed with Parkinson's Disease. Marion loved her new home, but this one lasted only four years. Her client's tremors grew steadily worse until she could not walk, feed herself or even speak coherently. The family admired Marion's efforts, but in the end decided their mother should be in a nursing home where she could be watched around the clock.

At thirty-six, Marion was untethered once again, this time without a handy referral. But, at the grocery store one day, she happened upon a little note on the community bulletin board: 'Help! Widow living alone in a house too big for one person needs live-in housekeeper. Not particularly fond of cooking; if you are, so much the better. Must be a non-smoker with a good sense of humor. Most important of all, be willing to put up with a few eccentricities. Call number below to set up interview. Let's chat and see if we hit it off.'

Hallie smiled. "You remember exactly what you wrote?"

"Well, it may not be verbatim, but that was the general gist of it."

Marion of course made the phone call, met Cora and lived in her house for twenty-three years.

"So she was fifty-nine?"

Cora sighed. "Not quite. Her birthday was less then two weeks away. I wanted to do something special for her this year."

"Cora, did she ever date while she lived with you?"

"Briefly. She used to play Bingo now and then, and once she met a man there. Frank, I believe was his name. They saw each other for, oh, close to a year, I'd say. And then suddenly he was just gone. Never called, never came around again. I asked what had happened about a dozen times, and got about a dozen different answers, none of them completely true, I'm sure. I think he wanted to marry her, and she wanted things to go on as they were. Her husband, if you can call him that, turned into such a monster after they married that Marion was terrified it might happen again. And I think," Cora continued, putting her fork down once and for all, "she didn't want to leave me. She felt obligated to me by then. Taking care of people was her whole life; it was what she did. The last thing in the world she wanted was a man to take care of her. Remember the friend she told you about, the one who also had endometriosis? That was Frank's daughter. I think Marion was quite close to her once."

Cora and Hallie sat in silence, both staring at their plates. When their eyes met at last, Hallie reached for Cora's hand. "Thank you for telling me about her. I'd wanted to ask her about her life so many times, but I was afraid I'd offend her. She seemed so private, so…"

"Closed. I know. She kept herself to herself, as she liked to say. She had to know someone a long time before she'd start to open up. I was just nosy and relentless, so eventually she broke down. But she liked you, Hallie. Remember the other night when she told you about being picked on by other kids in school? I hadn't heard those stories. She was just starting to trust your friendship." Cora shook her head. Her chin trembled as she spoke again, so softly Hallie could barely hear her: "What a terrible goddamn shame."

Fresh tears showed in Cora's eyes when she looked back at Hallie and squeezed her hand. "Well, I have some phone calls to make. I've been putting it off long enough. Would you help, sweetie pie?"

Cora and Hallie took turns making calls, breaking the news. Finally, Cora called Barry, then Christina. She hung up and looked at Hallie. "They both said they'd come to help with the memorial service."

"That's great, Cora," Hallie said, but the two women communicated a great deal more than they spoke aloud. They both knew, and would not say, that Cora's kids were coming to find a replacement for Marion.

41

Hallie took a couple of vacation days to spend more time helping Cora plan and shop for the memorial service. They decided that Marion's birthday would be the perfect day; that gave them ten days to prepare.

There were so many details to consider. Who to invite? Who would speak? What should be said? What food should be served— main courses, or just hors d'ouvres and desserts? Should there be one large picture of Marion, or many, depicting different periods of her life?

During a shopping trip, Hallie and Cora were discussing these many options when Cora suddenly turned to face Hallie.

"What is it, Cora?" Hallie was a little afraid, seeing the look on her face. "Are you all right?"

"Yes, sugar, I'm fine. But I want you to do something for me. Today. While you're staying with me and before anyone else can come along and object to it."

"Of course. But what could be so objectionable?"

"I want you to take me to the jail so I can see Tom."

"You do?"

"I do. I've been thinking about it a lot, and I need to see that man's face and ask him why he did it. Did he steal from everyone or just me? I have to confront him. Do you understand?"

"Yes, I think so. He worked for you for a long time. I guess I'd want to ask those questions too."

"I asked Marion to take me and she flat out refused. She said that a man like that has no reasons that would make sense to decent people. She was afraid that I'd get him all riled up and he'd come after us again first chance he got. I was going to take a taxi and go by myself, but I'd rather have you with me for moral support. What do you say?"

Hallie considered Marion's words. "If it's really what you want, but you know Marion may have been right. We've talked about this before, too. Seeing Tom probably won't answer any questions for you. And it might just make him angry again."

"I know, but I still have to do it. Besides, he's likely to have plenty of time to cool off in there. My lawyer found out that he's going to be moved to the prison in Monroe soon, so if we go now we won't have to travel that far."

"Okay. Let's go."

Hallie sat beside Cora at the table in the tiny room set aside for visits at the municipal jail. The bench was hard and uncomfortable; its resemblance to a picnic table was a bit unnerving in this atmosphere so far removed from such a happy event. Windows near the top of the high ceilings were reinforced with bars; most of the work of lighting the room was left to the dim fluorescent bulbs hidden in a line of cone-shaped fixtures.

The single door to the room also held one high window. When a visit was in progress, a guard stood outside, watching the prisoner's interaction with his guests. The guard was there now, watching the two women who were the first to visit Tom Hosking.

Another guard brought Tom down the hall to the visiting room. The first guard opened the door for them. Cora and Hallie looked up and saw Tom coming through the door. He wore a bright orange jumpsuit and handcuffs, and ankle shackles bound his feet together. *Just like in* The Fugitive, Hallie thought. She cleared her throat to suppress a nervous giggle.

Cora glanced at her briefly, squeezed her hand under the table, and, taking a deep breath, looked back up at Tom.

He stopped in the doorway, looking from Cora to Hallie and back again. Looking at the floor, he seemed to be considering something. His visitors waited. Finally, he looked up again and moved forward to the table. Hallie saw Cora wince at each clunk of the chain between his feet.

Tom sat at the table facing the women and swung his legs around the bench. "Well. What a surprise. The dynamic duo."

"Hello, Tom," Cora said. "I've come here to ask a few questions. I'd like you to be brutally honest. We know you can be brutal, we're just not sure of the honesty part. Do you think you could give it a try?"

He looked at her with cold eyes. Angry eyes. "Sure, Cora, I'll be honest. What have I got to lose?"

"Good point. All right then. I want to know when you started stealing from me. We only had records going back five years. Did you start before that?"

"I wasn't stealing from you, Cora. I was giving myself a little annual bonus. And yes, it was for more then five years. I started my creative budgeting about two, maybe three years after I started working for you."

"That long. Had you stolen from anyone else you worked for?"

"Yep. It's easy when they trust you. I'd take little trinkets here and there and pawn them for cash. When something was missed, they just thought it would turn up eventually. Then they'd forget all about it. People who have too much just can't keep track of everything. But you, Cora, you were the first person who trusted me with a whole budget and bank account. You made it easier than it'd ever been."

"I see. So it wasn't a personal vendetta. You've always been a thief."

"Hey, I was just making sure I got paid what I deserved. The world is too lopsided. I was tired of getting the short end of the stick, so I started evening things out a bit, that's all."

"And trashing my house. Was that just a bonus?"

"That was a message not to cross me."

"But it was too late. The damage was done. You'd already been caught."

"I was angry, that's all."

"*You* were angry. How extraordinary. You probably don't know this, Tom, but I've been poor. I know what it's like to go to bed hungry. I grew up at a time when people worked dawn to dusk and still couldn't feed their families properly. When the town doctor couldn't collect payment from his patients because they simply didn't have it to give, and yet he kept treating them because it was the right thing to do. A scholarship and full-time job got me through college, not wealthy parents. My husband and I worked hard for everything I have now. But even if I were poor today I would be wanting for nothing because I like the person I've become and I love the people in my life. And if you had managed to embezzle an endless fortune, you would still have nothing: no integrity, no values, nothing worthy of pride, of a sense of accomplishment. I should hate you, Tom, but I can only pity you. You are bitter and empty. You could have had so much, and you squandered it all."

"What? What could I have had in my measly little dead end handyman job?"

"You foolish man. You could have had my friendship, my loyalty, my..." Cora watched as Tom rolled his eyes toward the ceiling.

"You know you were in my will, you idiot."

"Great. A few thousand dollars thrown my way for spending my life planting flowers and fixing toilets?"

"No, I thought twenty some odd years of service deserved a more substantial reward. I was leaving my house to you and Marion. It's paid off completely. You and Marion would have sold it and split the entire windfall. You also could have had a Goddamn raise any time you asked. Instead, you thought it was wiser to betray my trust and vandalize my home. Surprised? Well, I'm just a sentimental, silly old woman I suppose. Not so sentimental that I didn't have you cut out of my will immediately, of course."

"You expect me to believe that? Your house must be worth..."

"Nearly three million dollars. That's right. Half would have been yours."

Tom sat up straighter and put his hands in his lap. "I'll be damned. Now I guess it'll all be Marion's?"

Cora looked down at her lap and spoke softly, "Not anymore. I have to do something thinking about that."

"Why? Did Marion rip you off too?"

She closed her eyes tight for a moment, then looked into his face. "Marion was killed in a car accident a few days ago, Tom. I realize you don't care about any of us, so I don't expect, or want, any expression of sympathy from you.

"I do have one more question, though, and then we'll go. What if one of us had been home when you went there to tear it apart? Would you have hurt us? Killed us?"

Tom looked Cora directly in the eye. "I wouldn't have killed anyone. I swear. But I might have knocked you out so I could have gotten the hell out of there."

Cora stared back for a moment or two. "I believe you. Thank you for your honesty. Hallie, shall we?" She motioned to the guard.

"Cora, wait a minute." Tom said. "I had no idea you were so... decent. Guess I didn't believe anyone could be. I've been looking out for myself for so long it never occurred to me there was another way. I wish I could be like you. And I am sorry about Marion."

He turned and allowed the guard to lead him out of the room.

42

After the menu and other details had been planned for Marion's memorial service, Hallie returned to work. But Cora seemed so small and alone in that big house; Hallie couldn't bring herself leave her alone at night yet, at least not until Christina and Barry arrived.

She missed Ben. He had been joining them for dinner most evenings, but Hallie wasn't comfortable approaching Cora about having him spend the night. Hallie enjoyed her time with Cora, but lying in bed alone each night made her ache for Ben. At least now they could have lunch together again. She glanced at the clock, then looked up to see him approaching.

"Hey, gorgeous! Ready to go?"

She grinned, hugging him tight.

Between bites, Hallie asked, "You don't mind, do you? That I'm still staying with Cora?"

"Of course I do. I miss you. I want to go house hunting with you and pick out throw rugs and, I don't know— quilts. But I understand that she needs you right now. Her kids are coming soon, right?"

"Yeah, they'll be here the day after tomorrow."

"Do you think Cora will sell the house now?"

"I don't know. She really loves that place. Well, who wouldn't? I think she'd rather find a new housekeeper and stay there. Cora's so easy to please, and the house is so beautiful, surely there's someone out there who'd want to take care of her."

"Well, it's a big place, a lot of work. Marion had no ties, no family or home of her own. How many people are like that?"

"But Cora wouldn't mind if someone needed time off to visit friends or family. And there are a lot of people who rent homes their whole lives. I'd rather live in a beautiful house with Cora than in a tiny apartment alone. Wouldn't you?"

"I suppose. I hope you're right. I hope Cora finds the perfect person to take over. I just think she might have to consider other options. But I'm sure her kids will talk to her about all this."

"You think she should move into a nursing home or something?"

"I'm just saying that she's not getting around as well since the stroke, and her health could get worse. It's a lot to ask for a housekeeper to be a nurse too."

"Well, all they have to do is get to know her. Anyone who knows Cora would love to take care of her. I'd consider it a privilege."

"You're right. I'm sure she'll find someone. I just don't want it to be you. I'm selfish, I want you back home so we can start planning our life together."

She smiled. "I want that too. I can't wait to start looking for quilts."

Barry and Christina arrived late Sunday afternoon, within an hour of each other. Hallie greeted them, then quietly went to her room to start packing. She was emptying Cleo's litter box and jumped when Christina appeared suddenly in the doorway.

"Sorry! I didn't mean to startle you, Hallie. I wanted to thank you for taking such good care of Mom this past week. I don't know how she would have managed without you."

"It was my pleasure. She means the world to me."

"It's just— well, I need to ask a favor. Barry and I are going to be very busy looking for a new housekeeper and researching other possible living arrangements for Mom. I was wondering if you'd consider staying here just a bit longer. Just until the memorial service."

"But I work during the day; I can't be with Cora all the time."

"That's all right. You'll still be coming home at the same time every day, and our schedules will be less predictable. Please, I just think she needs the stability right now."

"Okay. I'll stay until after the memorial service. Uh, you said you'll be looking for other housing options for Cora?"

"Frankly, we just don't think it's going to be feasible for her to stay here without Marion. How are we going to find someone like her, someone who's willing to take care of this whole house, all the meals and Mom? Marion was one of a kind. I just think it's too much to ask of anyone else. But who knows? Maybe we'll find someone wonderful. We'll give it a shot."

Hallie wanted to argue with her, as she had with Ben, but somehow Christina's words seemed heavy with truth simply because she had spoken them.

Hallie re-filled Cleo's litter box and followed Christina downstairs to dinner. "I'll be right there," she called, ducking into the bathroom.

Looking in the mirror, she swallowed painfully. She could not, would not imagine this house with someone else in it. Or Cora, living in a nursing home, shuffling around with people who were her peers in age only. No, life simply could not be so cruel. Could it?

Hallie washed her hands, splashed water on her face. It was good that she was staying a bit longer. She had to help somehow. She had to make sure Cora would stay in this house.

After dinner, Hallie called Ben. He answered on the first ring. "You're not going home tonight? But I thought you were leaving as soon as Christina got there."

"I was going to, but Christina asked me to stay until the day of the memorial service. She and Barry have a lot to do in a short time, and they thought Cora would feel better with me around. It's just a few more days."

"I understand. I just miss you. You have no idea how much I was looking forward to seeing you tonight."

"Yeah, I think I have an inkling. I miss you, too, but I promise we can leave here together after the memorial service."

"Can I get that in writing? Preferably in blood?"

"I'm sorry."

"Oh, I'll be all right eventually. Say hi to Cora and Christina. I love you, Hallie."

After they'd said good-bye, Ben sat, deflated. He stared at the phone, daring it to ring again, re-connecting him to Hallie who would say she'd changed her mind and could he come over right away. He shrugged. *Stop being a selfish brat,* he thought. Standing slowly, he picked up the flowers he'd bought earlier and began looking for a jar or vase to put them in. He would keep them alive overnight and take them to Hallie at the office in the morning.

Hallie held the receiver a moment before she hung up; she sat down heavily. Ben was clearly disappointed; so was she, but Cora needed her here, more than even she realized. Ben would just have to understand that. Right now, Cora had to come first.

43

The next few mornings, Barry and Christina said their good-byes before Hallie had finished making Cora's breakfast. "Aren't you joining us?" Cora asked each time.

And one or the other would reply that they wanted to get an early start and that they would get something to eat on the run.

On the third morning, Barry added as they were leaving, "We'd like to take you two to dinner tonight as soon as Hallie gets home. How does that sound?"

"Love to, dear."

"Thank you, Barry," Hallie said.

Hallie served Cora her oatmeal as the door closed behind Barry and Christina. "What do you suppose they want to tell us tonight?" Cora asked.

Hallie took a deep breath. "I think they want to tell us that they don't think they'll be able find a new housekeeper. I think they'll tell you that it's time to look for another place to live."

"That's pretty much my take on it too. Well, my darling girl, do you think that's the solution?"

"No, Cora. I think they need to find a housekeeper for you, and I'll help pick up the slack."

"You can't do that, Hallie. You have a life, a young man, a job. How can you possibly take on the care and feeding of a doddering old woman?"

"It's no trouble, really. We'll find someone who can do the household chores and cooking, and I'll help with whatever you need: running errands, planting flowers in the yard. It will be fine. Besides, you don't know how to dodder."

"But Hallie, it's hard running one household, let alone two. No, we just need to find someone who can do it all. Or, we need to hire two people, like before."

"What if we can't find the right people?"

"Well then, I might just have to look at a nice retirement condo somewhere."

"You'd do that?"

"Only if I have to. Hallie, I love my home. I raised my kids in it and dreamed a thousand dreams looking out at that beautiful view. I'd miss it. But I'd rather die than be a burden to my kids. I will not have them worrying about me rattling around in this big old house. They're looking to the imminent future and wondering how self-sufficient I'm going to be in a year or two. And they're absolutely right. I may need a lot more help. So, maybe the best thing would be to sail out of here now. Gracefully."

"No. I just don't believe that would be best for you. It would break your heart, Cora."

"It might break a little piece off, sweetie pie. But there will be plenty left to keep me feisty. Now if I lost track of you, that would be tough."

"No chance of that."

"All right then, it's settled. I'll surprise the hell out of my kids tonight and tell them I'm ready to move. Oh, I can't wait to see the looks on their faces. Won't that be fun?"

Plodding through her workday, Hallie felt disoriented, as if the world had shifted slightly on its axis, not enough to say, sink California, but enough that things just felt wrong. Everyone seemed to think it was a jolly good idea for Cora to leave her beautiful home and move to some golden age community— even Cora herself! Cora, who could no more fit into that environment than fly to Mars; although she would be far more likely to sign up for space travel than Bingo in the game room. Hallie had resolved to prevent it, and now this move looked inevitable. She imagined Cora leaving the house for the last time, looking back sadly as the car pulled out of the driveway.

Hallie sat at her desk, work forgotten now as she tapped her pencil and tried desperately to come up with a solution.

And it came to her. It was so simple, so obvious, so… perfect. Why hadn't she thought of it before?

She, Hallie, would move in with Cora. She would quit her job here, and start her music lesson business at Cora's. With no rent to pay, she wouldn't need such a big income, so she would have time to continue her own lessons and prepare to take on students. And, if the voiceover work materialized Cora would be fine on her own for a few hours at a time. Hallie could start her new career *and* take care of Cora!

Now she was frantic. She had to tell Christina and Barry. She had to propose this to them before they made other arrangements. Maybe she should leave early, talk it over with them now, and then dinner could be a celebration! She stood, intending to tell her boss that she had to go attend to an emergency somewhere. That's when she noticed the flowers sitting in a vase on her filing cabinet. Ben had given them to her Monday morning.

Ben. They had begun to plan their life together. They were going to find a house and live together. Ben was impatient for it all to begin, and until Marion's death, Hallie had been too. Things were different now. How could she sacrifice Cora's happiness for her own?

But could she make Ben understand? Would he wait for her? Was it even fair to ask?

Hallie sat back down, sliding her wheeled chair a few inches backward. It all came down to one simple fact: Cora needed her. Hallie *had* to do this. She defined herself as a good person, a moral, just and kind person, but what had she really done to deserve those labels? Here and now, she could make a difference in someone's life. *And not just anyone's life: Cora's. Who deserves it more?*

Once again, Hallie rose to her feet. This time, she did not stop until she reached her boss and told a story about an emergency that had just called her away from the office.

She did not stop at Ben's office on the way out.

44

At Cora's house, Barry and Christina were just returning from their day's errands when Hallie arrived. "Hallie! You're early, is everything okay?" Christina asked.

"Fine. How was your day?"

"It was okay." Christina glanced at her brother.

"It was a waste of time, Hallie," Barry said. "A few people answered our ad for a new housekeeper. We interviewed three people this morning."

Christina interrupted. "We thought it made sense to see them in their own homes— you know, get a feel for who they are. Well, they were either too inexperienced or weren't willing to help Mom bathe or dress. She doesn't need a lot of help right now, but she probably will at some point."

"One person said all the right things," Barry continued, "but her own apartment was a complete disaster. We came up empty-handed."

"We don't have to talk about this right now. Let's go inside and see Mom," Christina said.

Cora greeted them at the door. "Well, here's the whole gang! Lovely to see you so early, Hallie. Barry, my dear, where are you going to take all these gorgeous women for dinner?"

"How about Paris, Mom? Rome, maybe?"

"I prefer Portofino this time of year."

Hallie cleared her throat. "Uh, could I... I need to talk to all of you. Could we sit down?"

"Sounds serious. Is everything okay?" Cora asked.

"Everything is wonderful, Cora. I have a proposition for you. I have to tell you all that the idea of Cora moving out of this house and in with a bunch of frail old folks has had me tied up in knots. You're very brave, Cora, but I know it would break your heart. So I've been doing a lot of thinking and I've come to a decision. I can't let you move out."

Cora started to speak, but Christina held up her hand. "Let's hear her out, Mom."

"This is what I propose. I will move in with you, Cora. I will take care of the housework, the grocery shopping and meals, and whatever other help you need. In exchange, I'll get free room and board, and your blessing to start a home-based singing lesson business. Of course Cleo will live here with us, and we may need to hire someone for the yard work; I think I may be a bit busy for that, too."

"Hallie, what about Ben?"

"He'll come visit. I'm sure he'll be here a lot, if that's okay."

"Of course. But is that enough? No, Hallie, I can't ask this of you. You'd be giving up too much. I told you, I'll be fine in a retirement condo somewhere. You know, there are some very nice ones now."

Christina shook her head. "Wait a minute. Hallie, why do you want to do this?"

"Because it's important. I love Cora, and I think I know her fairly well. If she leaves this house I'm afraid the grief will kill her. You're not going to find anyone like Marion. I'm the closest you've got. This way, I can quit my job and start a new career without being strapped for money. I can build it up over time while I'm here helping Cora."

"But sweetie pie, I could live another ten years. Maybe even twenty. What about your life?"

"Cora, I love you like family. Lots of people live with family, even married couples. I'm not sure how it would all iron itself out, but we'd make it work."

Christina looked at Barry and burst out laughing. "I can't believe you came up with this! We wanted to ask you, but we were sure you'd have to turn us down and we didn't want to make you feel bad. Oh, Hallie, are you absolutely sure you want to do this?"

"Yes. Absolutely, positively. So, problem solved. You've found someone. I'll give my two week's notice at work tomorrow."

"Hallie, what does Ben think about this decision?" Cora asked, her eyes narrowed.

"He... he'll understand."

"You haven't told him?"

"Not quite yet."

"You haven't told him because you know he'll be upset. Hallie Jane, what are you thinking?"

"I'm thinking that this is something I have to do, and Ben will understand."

"What if he doesn't?"

"He will."

"Well, there's one thing I need to make clear right now. If you think I'm going to allow myself to come between you and Ben, you're crazy. If you can't convince him this is a good idea, then we'll go back to Plan A. I'll move out."

"Cora..."

"Sorry, sugar, this is not negotiable. I will not be the reason you two didn't work out. Period. So get on the phone and invite him to dinner."

45

Ben agreed to meet them at the restaurant, and was waiting for them outside when they arrived. He greeted them, and kissed Hallie on the forehead. "I went to see you this afternoon and you were gone. I was worried about you. I was about to call when you called me."

"Sorry, I just had some things to take care of."

All eyes were on Ben when they were seated at the table, menus in hand. He looked from one conspirator to the next. "Everything okay?" he asked.

"Not quite," Cora said. She put her menu down. "You know, Ben, it's a real bitch getting old. Here's the deal. There is no one to replace Marion, and my options aren't all that peachy. There are plenty of nice assisted living condos with nice views and a nice gas fireplace, but the truth is that I want to live in my home until I die. I said I would be all right moving out, but I was lying and Hallie knew it. She knows how I feel about that old house of mine. I want it to be mine until I'm floating around in the clouds and smiling down on it with my husband. Then I want it to belong to someone else who loves it the way I do. So Hallie here, bless her heart, has offered to move in with me and take over Marion's job, including the care and feeding of one old woman. She's planning on quitting her job and starting to teach singing in my house. She's got it all figured out, you see, except for one thing."

"Me. Except for me. I see. What about our plans, Hallie? I mean, I'm sorry, Cora, I understand this would be a big help for you. But... when were you going to tell me this, Hallie?"

"Ben, try to understand. This wouldn't just be helping Cora out, I believe it would be saving her life. I just feel I have to do this. I still want to live with you, but Cora needs me now."

"Wait. You were going to live together?" Cora asked.

"Yes. We just decided, well, right before Marion died. We were going to buy a house together. I've already been looking, Hallie," Ben said. "I've picked out houses for us to look at together."

"I'm sorry. I just wouldn't feel good about making a home together if it meant that Cora would have to leave hers."

"But you feel fine about not considering me in all of this? I'm not sure how I'm supposed to feel about this, Hallie. I understand that Cora is important to you, but she's not family. She is not your responsibility. Sorry, Cora."

"She's more family to me than my own parents, Ben. Listen: I know you've got a wonderful, close knit family, but here's a news flash: not everyone does! Cora is more important to me than almost anyone in my life. I guess I just trusted that you would understand that!"

"Let's just all take a deep breath. I'm sorry we ambushed you like this, Ben." Christina said.

"Maybe we should table the subject for now and enjoy our dinner," Barry added.

Cora glanced at her children, then looked back to Ben. "No need. I'm turning down Hallie's generous offer. I will not cause this rift between you. But think about this, Ben. She loves you very much. Don't doubt that. She didn't talk to you about this first because she didn't know how to explain it to you. She's a good person, so she felt strongly about helping her friend. That's all there was to it. Now, could we please order some wine and get this wonderful meal started?"

Cora watched Ben from behind her menu as he fidgeted and stared at the table. He looked at Hallie and met her eyes. They smiled. Cora, with a smile of her own, returned her attention to the wine list.

Later, Cora, Christina and Barry drove home, while Hallie and Ben opted to walk. "She let me off the hook," Hallie said.

"Hmm?"

"Cora. She made it her decision so that I wouldn't have to feel guilty about not moving in with her."

"Yeah, I caught that. But it's for the best, Hallie. Do you really want to put our lives on hold? Even for Cora?"

"It's just going to hurt so bad to see her move out of there, Ben. She loves that house so much. She belongs there."

"Well, it's a beautiful house. But it's just a house, Hallie. Cora has money. She'll find a nice place."

"I guess. I just wanted to make a difference."

"You do. You make a difference every day."

Holding hands, they breathed in the cool salty air and walked to Cora's house. Hallie looked at it from a distance, bright and warm, its glow flooding the yard. She sighed.

Cora heard them coming and opened the door before they'd reached it. She too was glowing. "Come in, you two. We have a proposition of our own. For both of you."

Barry brought in a tray of drinks. "This is a delicious tawny port I found in the pantry. Here, everyone." He handed out the five crystal glasses, took one for himself and put the tray on the table. "Here's to friends and family, and the few and precious situations in which they overlap."

"Friends and family," the others repeated, and they all sipped.

"Now sit, everyone, please," Barry said. "The three of us have come up with a solution to everyone's dilemma, I think. Here's what we're offering. Both of you move into the house with Mom. Hallie, you move forward with your career plans, and quit your accounting job so that you're here with Mom most of the time. Ben will continue to pursue his career of choice, and maybe do a little yard work, as you would with your own house. Occasionally, the two of you could paint, wallpaper, or remodel as you see fit. If time is limited, you can hire someone else to do whatever work is needed. In addition to room and board, Hallie will receive $1000 per month as salary. Mom will continue to pay the property taxes, utility bills and for all the groceries.

"If you stay with Mom as long as she is able to live here, and look after her day to day needs, you will inherit the house when she passes away. If Mom has to live elsewhere before her death, you can live here without her and pay only the property taxes and utilities."

"I realize it's not the same as having your own place and living alone together, but this is a big house. There's enough room for all of us to have some privacy when we need it. And of course you two can go out and enjoy yourselves on your own whenever you like," Cora said.

"As long as Mom is healthy enough to be left alone," Christina added. "Otherwise, you'll be responsible for finding someone to supervise her in your absence."

"If you two do not stay together and never get married, the offer will extend to Hallie only. If you get married eventually— no rush, of course— the house will belong to both of you; in the event you then divorce, state community property laws will apply," Cora said. "But I know that would never happen," she added quickly.

"What do you think?" Barry asked.

Hallie realized her mouth was open. She closed it, and swallowed hard. She turned to Ben, who was watching the floor intently. He began to shake his head.

"Ben?" Cora asked. "What's troubling you?"

"We can't do this," he said. "Your offer is too generous. This house must be worth millions. You can't just give it to us."

"It's been paid off for years, Ben. Yes, it is worth a lot; a lot more than we paid for it, let me tell you. But I've discussed this with Barry and Christina. I was planning on leaving the house to Marion. She deserved it, but now she's gone. I realize it's highly unlikely that you two will spend quite as much time here with me as Marion did, but the truth is I want you to move in here because I simply enjoy your company. If you do this, taking care of me might become quite a demanding job. It will mean making sacrifices. In return, I want to do something to give you two a boost, a head start. My kids are fine with it, and I want you to be as well."

"Barry and I are both pretty well set financially, Ben. We love the house, but neither of us would be able to live in it, and it would be worth giving up whatever money we could get from it to know that Mom is happy, loved and cared for, and here for as long as possible. And somehow it feels like the house will be staying in the family this way," Christina said, nodding toward Hallie.

Looking from one face to the next, Ben smiled at last. "Hallie, you're sure this is what you want?"

Biting her lip, she nodded, afraid to speak.

He reached over and touched her hand briefly, then turned to the others. "I'll talk to my landlord tomorrow. Hallie, we can just pay another month's rent and move out right away if you like. Okay?"

Cora put her glass down and started toward Ben, who met her in the middle. Cora squeezed him tight and whispered, "Thank you, darling boy. Welcome home!"

When Ben said goodnight, Hallie kissed him at the door. "You could stay if you want," she whispered.

"No, I'll go home tonight and pack up some clothes. But I'll miss you."

"Thank you, Ben. This means so much to me."

"It's the right thing to do. But I feel a little like I'm taking advantage of them. This is an amazing offer. We've found our home, Hallie."

Later, alone in the bed she would soon share with Ben, Hallie drew her knees up and hugged them to her chest. How did Cora do it? Ben had felt hurt and betrayed by Hallie's decision to live with Cora. He had been on the verge of ending their relationship, and Cora had waved her magic wand and made everything perfect. She looked at the window at the far end of the room, her eyes adjusting to the darkness.

This was their home now, like Ben had said. Whatever their future held, it would be based here, with Cora at its heart.

46

Black clouds, looming low all morning, finally burst with fat raindrops as the final guest arrived for Marion's memorial service. Inside the house, Hallie carried the last platter to the table.

"It looks great, Hallie!"

"Thanks, Christina. Do you think we have enough coffee?"

"Plenty. Let's go sit down. I think we're ready to start."

Hallie took her seat between Ben and Lonnie.

Marion had never been a churchgoer, so Cora had insisted they not have a minister preside. Instead, several friends had agreed to speak.

Christina began. "When Marion first began working for my mother, I wondered how in the world the two of them would get along. Two strong-willed, stubborn, opinionated women living in the same household? How would this work?

"But it did work. It worked because my mother is an infinitely patient and understanding person. She understood that Marion had to have her own way." She waited for the laughter to fade. "It worked because my mother respected Marion's knowledge and never questioned it. But most of all it worked because my mother knew intuitively that Marion had been hurt. Her prickly shell was her protection from life's cruelty. My mother's kindness eventually penetrated that thick skin, and those two tough broads became lifelong friends. Friends who were parted by death much too early.

"I remember meeting Marion for the first time. I'd brought my family home for the holidays. My older daughter was a baby, just over a year old at the time, barely walking, and she reached out to touch an ornament on the tree. Marion came running into the room, appearing out of thin air, I swear, and yelling, 'Don't touch anything or I'll tan your hide!'

"Needless to say, I wasn't pleased. 'Marion,' I said, 'do not speak to my baby that way! It's Christmas; let her have fun. The tree does not have to be perfect.' 'Well, it sure won't be if your little urchin doesn't leave it alone,' she said, haughty as hell. 'Marion,' I tried again, 'let her be a child. This holiday is as much about children's joy as anything else.' That stopped her. She stood, head down, saying nothing for a long time. Finally, I asked if she understood. 'No, ma'am, I don't. I guess I've never been a child.' And she turned around and went back to the kitchen.

"Well, I'll tell you, nothing could have made me sadder. I thought about my Norman Rockwell childhood, growing up in this beautiful house with the beach as my front yard. Making Christmas cookies with Mom and picking out the perfect tree with Dad. Leaping out of bed at dawn on Christmas morning and waiting happily for the cocoa Mom always made for us to sip while we emptied our stockings. I wondered about Marion, then, really wondered where she'd lived, and what life had been like for her. Clearly she had missed out on the magic. There had been no Christmas joy for Marion.

"So, that Christmas Eve, I stayed up later than everyone else and made cookies. Old-fashioned sugar cookies in the shape of bells, Santas and candy canes, with red and green sugar on top. When they had cooled, I put them on a platter and ate most of one cookie, leaving only Santa's belt and legs. Beside the platter, I left a note: Dear Marion, These cookies are for you. Sorry, I couldn't resist eating some. Please find time to have fun this Christmas. If you don't, I'm afraid I may have to take these cookies back. I'm glad I finally found you. Love, Santa." Christina paused, listening to the rain plunking against the window behind her.

"In the morning, I knew Marion would be the first one up, making tea and cocoa so that Mom wouldn't do it herself. I listened for her footsteps in the kitchen below our room, then I tiptoed down the stairs and peeked in. There she was, sitting on the floor with the note in her hand. She was crying. I went in, knelt down and put my arms around her. I didn't ask any questions, and she didn't offer any explanation.

"Every Christmas after that, there were gifts for my kids under the tree from Marion."

Christina's girls, Robin and Laurel, had flown in from college for the day, and now they cried with their mother as she rejoined them in the audience.

There were many other stories: some brief, others long and detailed. Accounts of Marion as strong and wise, others describing her sometimes surprising wit, her fierce loyalty, especially to Cora.

Finally, it was Cora's turn. She stood, leaning heavily on her cane; listening seemed to have tired her profoundly. When she stood before the group, her eyes shone. She smiled. "Thank you, everyone. Those stories revealed bits and pieces of Marion, and I'm sure that, in listening to each other, you learned a lot about her. But I suppose I knew her better than anyone. I knew the whole Marion, so none of these little tidbits surprised me at all. I can place them, you see, in the context of her life. They make sense to me.

"It wasn't always that way, of course. In the beginning Marion was pretty unfathomable. She often said that she kept her self to herself, that she was a private person. But I knew the truth and I called her on it. You're a coward, Marion Bauer, I told her. You're scared of life, and that's why you hide yourself away. Why don't you just open the window a crack and see what blows in? It's not all bad out here, you know. She got so angry with me she just wanted to spit, but eventually the message got into that thick skull of hers and she opened up a little. Just a little, here and there, but only to me. Then there came a day when she ventured out of her safe little world. Got herself a boyfriend. I saw her actually giggly and giddy! Can you imagine that? It was a joy to see, I can tell you. But, as someone mentioned, Marion was nothing if not loyal, and she sacrificed her own happiness for mine. I knew it and she knew it, but we never talked about it. I tried once, but she shut me down with a look that almost frightened me. She didn't date much after that, but she did see a couple of friends now and then. I see those friends here today, missing her.

"In the end, I think it's safe to say we were best friends; like an old married couple we had grown into each other's empty spaces. We were good for each other. I miss her, everyone knows that. I'm angry that she died so young and so senselessly. But she wouldn't want us feeling sorry for her or ourselves. She would want us to drink a toast to her and move on. She'd be pleased and surprised that so many of you remember her fondly. And, she'd be dancing a jig that Hallie and Ben will be moving in to help take care of the house and this crazy old woman. Marion's whole life was about taking care of people, and that is something to be praised and honored.

"So, everyone please raise your glass..." Christina and Hallie had just finished passing out champagne in flutes. "...and join me in a toast. To Maid Marion."

"Maid Marion," answered the chorus.

"Thank you, everyone. Now, let's eat!"

Lonnie stood beside Hallie, munching on crackers. She and Steve were the last remaining guests. "Where's Kim?" she asked Hallie.

"She couldn't get away from work."

"Too bad. What's in that spread? It's delicious!"

"Oh, it's a smoked salmon-cream cheese thing that Cora just threw together. She said it was one of her old stand-bys."

"Well, it's great. I may eat the whole thing. Oh, and Hallie, before I forget to mention this? I'm married."

"What did you say?"

Lonnie nodded. "Steve and I eloped. Flew down to Vegas last weekend and got married in one of those really cheesy chapels. I think they had a drive through window. Anyway, it's done, we're married, I'm a wife. We are Dr. and Mrs. Wakefield. And I didn't even have to wear a maternity wedding gown."

"Did you buy a gown?"

"No, I rented one in Vegas. They actually had some nice ones. It was pretty, really it was! But look at this!" She held out her left hand. The ring was simple, but elegant, a large round diamond flanked by a row of baguettes on either side. "I have a matching wedding band, but we haven't had time to have them soldered together yet. Isn't it beautiful?"

"It is, Lonnie. And you seem so happy! Are you?"

"Yeah. I really am. I was scared to death at first, but I want our baby to have two married parents who love each other. Maybe this happened a little faster than we would have liked, but when I tried to come up with reasons not to marry Steve, I pretty much drew a blank, Susan Sarandon notwithstanding. I'd said no a few times, so I made up my mind to say yes the next time he asked. Damned if he didn't ask that night! And when I said yes, Hallie, he swooped me up in his arms and swung me around, he was so happy. Then he brought out the ring, and I actually cried. How sappy is that? I only wish you could have been there to catch my lilies."

"You had lilies?"

"Yeah, the chapel provides dusty old silk flowers and I'd have none of that; so we went to a florist before the ceremony and bought some dark coral calla lilies. The florist tied a burgundy ribbon around the stems for me. They were so beautiful. Calla lilies are so feminine, with their perfect curves. Almost erotic, actually."

"Erotic flowers? All I know is *she* was beautiful." Steve had joined them. "The most beautiful bride there ever was." He kissed her on the cheek.

"Yeah, you have to say that. You're my husband now." Lonnie pushed him away, laughing.

Hallie grinned. "You are positively glowing! Congratulations, you two!" She hugged them both.

"Oh, but hold on," Lonnie said. "You have news of your own. What's this about moving in here with Cora?"

"Yeah, we're moving in here to look after the house and Cora. I guess I'm adopting her. It just makes sense. I'm going to quit my job and figure out what I want to do when I grow up, and I'll do it here, so I can take care of Cora."

"And Ben?"

"Ben's moving in, too."

"With you?"

"What do you mean, in the same room? Yes, Lonnie, we're moving in together."

"Wow. That's big."

"We were actually talking about it before Marion died. This just seems like the best solution for everyone."

"It is," said Ben. He stood behind Hallie and slid his arms around her waist, clasping them together on her belly. "I get to live in this great house with two wonderful women. What more could anyone ask for?"

"More champagne?" The offer came from Cora, and she began pouring before anyone could answer. Only Lonnie did not have a glass. "Not for me, thanks. Want to keep my little girl sober."

"Oh, that's right! Let me get you some lemonade," Cora said, and she was off toward the fridge without another word.

"How are you feeling?" Hallie asked.

"I'm still feeling a tad woozy in the morning. I never realized how wonderful crackers are. Whoever invented them should be canonized, you know that?" She helped herself to another one. "Saint Shmo, cracker man and patron saint of pregnant women. But when the nausea wears off about mid-morning, my hunger is truly becoming a scary force to reckon with."

"Any weird cravings?"

"Yeah, basically anything edible. I just go through the fridge and graze. My mother says, 'You are going to lose that figure of yours, you know. This is the time to be more careful about what you eat, not less.' But getting back to you: are you really okay about moving in here with Cora?"

"Absolutely. She's done so much for me, Lonnie. She's so generous and giving. This is the least I can do."

"Well, this place wouldn't be too tough to take. Can't blame Cora for not wanting to leave it."

"Exactly. But getting back to you, can I throw a belated bridal shower for you?"

"Oh, hell why not? I'll look at my schedule and call you. Will there be champagne at my shower?"

"There doesn't have to be. I can make it a non-alcoholic shower."

"No, go ahead and let them drink toasts to me. I'll just smell it— feel that little tickle up my nose. That won't hurt little Hagatha, will it?"

"Snorting champagne bubbles? No, I haven't heard anything about the dangers of smelling alcohol while pregnant."

"It'll probably be the next exposé on some news show. 'The catastrophic effects of champagne inhalation on unborn babies: Why you may be guilty of damaging your fetus without drinking a drop.' I can just hear Mike Wallace's accusing voice."

"I wouldn't worry about it. There'll be another study next year that raises doubts about the whole inhalation danger issue."

"Good point. Okay. Champagne sniffing is approved."

Cora reappeared with Lonnie's lemonade. "Hear, hear," she said. I'm all for a little champagne sniffing. After my surgery I even plan to indulge in a little sipping."

Cora's surgery, postponed after Marion's death, was now rescheduled for the following week.

"Hallie told me you were having surgery. Good luck with that."

"Thank you, Lonnie. I'll be just fine. I'm planning to stick around for a while. I've just got to see this baby girl of yours, for one thing."

Lonnie sat on a kitchen chair with a sigh. "Why am I so tired all the time?"

"Because your body is very busy, Lonnie. You're housing a growing baby. Be sure to stay well-nourished and rested," Cora said.

"Yeah, everyone says that, but it's hard to eat right when I spend part of every day with my head in the toilet. My mother says I'm tired because I exercise for a living. She's never understood the 'exercise craze' as she calls it. But she still thinks she's a nutrition expert."

"The nausea won't last long, I promise. And the prenatal vitamins work wonders, too."

"Yes, but they don't taste good on crackers." Lonnie scooped up another cracker full of Cora's dip. "Mmm. Steve, you should take me home or I'm going to eat this whole thing. Thanks, everybody. This was nice. Hallie, I will call you next week about the shower."

"I'll get your coat," Christina said.

At the door, Lonnie kissed Hallie on the cheek. "I've already told Druscilla about you. I told her she has an Aunt Hallie who sings like an angel."

"Thanks. I can't wait to meet her. By the way, are you ever going to come up with a real name for her?"

"My mom has been lobbying hard for her name to be in there somewhere. Steve has some strong opinions, too. It's under negotiation right now," Lonnie stage-whispered. "Bye, everyone!"

She walked up the driveway, arm in arm with Steve, who looked back once, grinning and waving. The sun, just peeking through a break in the clouds, made his wedding ring glow.

Hallie re-joined the others in the kitchen. "I like Lonnie," Cora announced. "She helped today. She actually made me laugh. I'm so glad she was here. Please tell her that when you see her, Hallie. She reminds me a little of Marion, you know. If Marion had been a little less guarded, a little more joyful, she could have been like Lonnie. She was that quick, and that funny when she wanted to be."

"That crossed my mind today, too, Cora," Hallie said. "It makes me sad for Marion, but I'm so grateful for Lonnie's friendship."

"I'm sure she's grateful for yours, too. Now, how about we stack up the dishes, put the food away and leave the rest until tomorrow?"

"Barry and I will do this, Mom. You three go relax for a bit," Christina said.

"No way. I'm helping. We'll be finished a lot faster with three people working," said Hallie.

Cora and Ben looked at each other and stood at the same time. "Make that five. 'Many hands make light work,' after all. We'll all relax together when we're done," Cora said.

They worked efficiently and quickly, speaking only as the tasks required. Sorrow still hovered in the air, but it no longer felt quite so heavy. Joy would return soon, they were sure.

When the kitchen was clean, Cora sighed deeply. "There's just one more item on my list today, and I need your help, everyone."

"What is it, Mom?" Christina asked.

"Sweetheart, go get the big flashlight from the hall closet, would you please? Hallie, would you go get the box for me?"

"Of course," Hallie said.

From the mantel over the fireplace in the living room, Hallie lifted a shiny wooden box, and carried it into the kitchen. Barry was on his way out the back door, and now Cora directed the rest of them to follow him.

Barry brought a shovel from the tool shed, and Cora led the way to spot in a corner of the flower garden, close to the sun porch. "Chrissy, shine that light right here, where my foot is. Barry, would you dig the hole, please?"

The rest of them stood in silence as Barry pushed the shovel into the soft dirt. When he was finished, Barry leaned the shovel against the house.

"I've been trying to think of a special place to put Marion's ashes," Cora said. "But all her life, Marion really only wanted a home, a real home and a real family. I think she found that here, with us. We spoke about that the day she died. So I want this to be her home forever. Hallie, Ben, I know this will be your house eventually. I hope you don't mind."

Ben glanced at Hallie before answering. "Not at all, Cora. Marion is where she should be."

So Barry placed the box in the hole he had dug and covered it with soil.

"'Night, Marion," Cora whispered.

47

Barry flew home the day after Marion's memorial service, but Christina decided to stay until after Cora's surgery. Hallie had given her two week's notice at work, and felt she could not take any more vacation time.

There was so much to be done. Hallie felt obligated to leave her office tidy and organized, so she was putting in long hours there. And moving was always more work than she remembered.

After work, she spent hours at the apartment packing her belongings into boxes labeled according to their destinations: Kitchen, Bathroom, Bedroom, Storage. Standing up to stretch her back, she noticed her answering machine blinking. With a start, she realized she hadn't checked her messages there in over a week.

Beep: "Hallie, it's your mother. I don't understand why you're never home. I hate this machine. Call me, *if* you're not too busy." *Love the sarcasm, Mom.* Beep: "Hallie, it's your mother. Why are you avoiding me? Is it too much to ask for you to just call once in a while? I have friends whose kids call every day, just to check on them. 'Not my ungrateful daughter,' I tell them. 'We're lucky to hear from her at Christmas!'" *Gee, I wonder why!* Another beep, and Hallie's finger hovered, ready to push the delete button.

But this was a different voice. A male voice. "Hallie, this is Jim Schultz. I have some projects coming up I think you'd be really good for, so give me a call and let me know your status. Thanks."

Jim had called already! She'd forgotten to call him with her new number— Cora's number. Hallie glanced at the fridge and saw that number now, on the note she'd scribbled and tucked under a magnet so long ago.

She fished out Jim's card from her purse and dialed his number. It was after hours, so his voice mail picked up. She waited impatiently for the beep. "Hi, Jim. This is Hallie McLaren. Sorry I've been a little out of touch. I've been helping a friend through a crisis. I need to give you my new phone number..."

New phone number, new home, new career. Tonight she and Ben would be crawling into the same bed at Cora's house for the first time. Hallie smiled, thinking of Ben coming home to her every night. Life could be so exciting, so strangely sweet.

She looked around at the apartment being stripped bare of her possessions. On the wall was the framed print Cora had given Hallie for her birthday. Climbing onto the sofa, she lifted it from its hook and leaned it against the coffee table. Cora had given her this after knowing her what, two weeks? And seven months later, Hallie's entire life was changing. *Cora is my fairy godmother,* she thought. *She waved her magic wand and transformed a hermit into a princess.*

But in this story, Cinderella goes to live with Prince Charming in the fairy godmother's beautiful house. *Happily ever after? It's certainly shaping up that way.*

Smiling again, Hallie began rolling glasses in newspaper, humming along with songs drifting through her mind.

She worked until Ben knocked on her door, having decided to drop by and help load her car. When they were done, he held her close. "No more work for now. Let's go home, and I'll fix us something to eat."

Hallie backed her car out onto the street, and Ben followed her home in his.

Cora joined them in the kitchen while they ate a late dinner, but Christina excused herself to call home.

"Now I want you two to consider this your house. We are a family, and we all have free run of the place. You don't have to ask what you can eat, where you can put your feet, or how late you can stay up. We have equal status here. Any objections?" Cora sat back and crossed her arms over her chest.

"No objections. I think we'll all be pretty easy to live with. I promise not to use the last of the milk without buying a new carton in time for breakfast. And if we start redecorating, we'll run the colors by you first. How does that sound?" Hallie asked.

"Fine by me," Ben agreed.

"All right then. We are officially roommates. Cheers!" Cora raised her teacup and sipped.

Soon after, she excused herself and went to bed earlier than usual, Hallie noted. Christina too said goodnight early, and Hallie and Ben were suddenly alone.

They passed the rest of the evening in unexciting tasks: cleaning the kitchen, unpacking. Finally, they took sheets and blankets from the linen closet— Cora's sheets, of course, Hallie's would have been far too small for the enormous bed in the master bedroom. Together, they made their new bed.

It was the first time Ben had seen the room, and Hallie enjoyed watching him explore, wide-eyed as a child on Christmas morning. "Are you cold? I'll build a fire," he joked, and flipped the switch for the gas fireplace. "Wow. This place is incredible!"

"I know. When I stayed here after my surgery I felt like Oliver Twist with his new family."

"The details are amazing: look at all the carved wood trim around the ceiling."

"I love the window seat, too. And we have our own little table over there."

"I can bring you coffee in the morning and we can watch the waves rolling in."

"Sounds like the perfect way to start the day. So you're really okay with this?"

"I'm way past okay, Hallie. It's not like Cora is going to be difficult to live with. And you were right. She needs your help. I love you even more that you feel so strongly about giving it."

"I was wrong to leap into such a big a decision without talking to you first, though. I'm sorry about that. From now on, you'll be the first to know every one of my little schemes."

"Deal. Hey— I think I have a little scheme of my own right now."

"Oh yeah?" Hallie giggled at his obvious intent.

"Uh-huh. I think we have a bed to break in." He lifted her onto the newly made bed and stood in front of her. Leaning down, he kissed her, so softly at first that their lips barely touched. In an instant she felt her desire rise, a physical presence in the pit of her stomach, the tips of her fingers, her tingling toes. She slid back, pulling him toward her, breathing him in. Still fully clothed, she wrapped her legs around his back and smiled, savoring the details of his smell, his skin, his tongue on her neck. Anticipating all the adventures they would have in this room. Their room.

48

Life was busy over the next few months. Cora's surgery went smoothly; Christina stayed until her mother was back on her feet, then returned home to California at last. "Thank you, Hallie. I know I'm old enough to be your mother, really, but I kind of think of you as a little sister. Welcome to the family," she'd said as she was leaving for the airport.

With all her heart, Hallie wished she had been born into the Rouget family.

After she had completely vacated her apartment, a couple of days passed before she realized she still had not returned her mother's phone call. She hadn't shared her plans or given her new number or address to her parents. For the moment, they had no possible way of reaching her. It was a delicious feeling of absolute freedom, and she savored it for a few moments, along with the wild thoughts it inspired: *I could disappear forever, cut all ties with my parents. They'd never find me! I'd never have to listen to the litany of my faults and mistakes, never have to hear why whatever I'm doing or thinking is wrong.*

"What wonderful thoughts are you entertaining?" Cora asked, entering the room. "You look like the proverbial canary-eating cat."

"Oh! No, I'm just dreaming an impossible dream. Fantasizing about never calling my parents again. But I need to call them today. I just remembered they don't know where I am. It's not going to be a pleasant conversation."

"You don't talk about your parents much."

"Exactly. Let's just say they've given me really good negative examples of parenting. I know everything I would never do with my own children, if by some miracle I ever have any."

"I'm sorry. Parenting is a difficult job, God knows, but it amazes me when I see people doing it haphazardly. It seemed to me with both my children that the better I was at mothering, the easier it got. Did your parents hit you, Hallie?"

Hallie closed her eyes, remembering.

Her mother, towering over her, screaming in her face: "*...goddamn ungrateful little good-for-nothing-bitch!*" while Hallie tried not to cry. Waiting for the anger to peak, she held her breath until finally, finally, her mother's hand hit her face once, twice, three times, until Hallie was knocked backward or sideways, into a wall or a chair or onto the floor. Lying there wherever she'd landed, she would sob at last, knowing it was over for now, all over until the next time she failed her mother.

Less frequently, it was her father's belt— a few lashes across her behind or her legs— that served as punishment for such infractions as 'talking back,' putting off her chores, breaking a dish, spilling her milk at the dinner table. Her father hit hard, but without the accompanying list of Hallie's sins and epithets. And it was only in her mother's eyes that Hallie saw the utter disgust, the seething hatred she seemed to inspire. By far, Hallie had preferred her father's belt.

She nodded now, answering Cora's question. "Every now and then. But they did worse than that. They— mostly Mom— called me worthless. They laughed at my ideas. I sang for them once, and they acted like I was making a total fool of myself. They pushed me into accounting, and now that I'm leaving it behind I'm suddenly angry with them. They didn't believe in me! How could I believe in myself? But they're the only parents I have. And, I really have to call them."

Cora touched Hallie's hand. "They don't deserve you, sweetie."

She turned to leave, but Hallie stopped her. "I'd like you to stay, if you don't mind. I could use the moral support."

So Hallie made the dreaded call and listened to the angry voice speaking of her lack of gratitude once again. The voice went on to speculate on what might have happened during Hallie's lack of contact: horrors of heart attacks, strokes, sudden deaths. Hallie focused on Cora's gentle smile, tuning out some of the tirade, but hearing the last 'what if' she simply couldn't help herself. "Well if one of you had died I wouldn't have been able to do anything anyway."

"Very funny. As usual you are missing the point. Now who is this woman you're living with?"

"Her name is Cora Rouget and she is the most wonderful person I have ever known." Cora flashed a grin at her.

"What's so wonderful about her? She obviously hasn't been a very good influence on you. It's not like you're a great judge of character, Hallie, you must know that by now. Does this Cora person think it's all right for a daughter to cut off all ties with her family?"

"Mom, I'm sorry it took me a while to call you, but I've been really busy. It wasn't Cora's fault. Besides, I'm talking to you now, aren't I? Clearly I haven't cut you off completely, have I?"

"What in the world has gotten into you, Hallie?"

"There's more. I am living in Cora's house with Cora and one other person. His name is Ben."

"You're living with a man."

"Yes. He's my boyfriend and I love him."

"You're living with a man. Hallie, I thought you'd learned something from the Joe fiasco."

"I learned a lot, Mom. Enough to know when someone loves me. One more thing: I'm changing careers."

"You're what?"

"I've had an offer to sing jingles and do voiceovers for commercials. I'm quitting my accounting job."

"Jingles? Don't they use professional singers for that kind of thing?"

"Yeah. That's what I'm going to be, Mom. A professional singer."

"Really. Well, judging by the new music I've heard lately it seems just about anyone can be a singer these days. But it's your life, I guess. Mess it up if you want to."

"Yes! You're right! It is my life! Now, if you have a pen I'll give you my new number and address."

When she hung up, Cora gave her a high five. "My little champion. You did great, sweetheart! You're a brave girl. Need a hug?"

Nodding gratefully, Hallie rested her head on Cora's shoulder, comforted in the cocoon of her soft embrace.

Hallie's last day as an accountant arrived quickly. There was a lunchtime party: a Good Luck banner, a few balloons, a huge cake. Art delivered a brief and rather trite speech about following one's heart's desire. He thanked Hallie for her contribution and led the group in a round of applause. Hallie watched everyone eating cake and talking in well-established cliques. Each person gradually made his or her way toward Hallie, wished her well, and returned to work.

When they had all gone, Hallie and Ben remained behind, packing up the remains of the cake. "There's some Tupperware in the cupboard. We'll borrow that, and you can bring it back on Monday," Hallie said.

"Hey. You okay?"

She shrugged. "Yeah. This was just so…"

"Superficial? They always are, Hallie."

"I know, but… No, it's more than that. *I* was superficial here. No one knew me. No one cared about me, and it was my fault. I never let anyone get close."

"You let me get close."

"You know what I mean."

"Yeah, I guess I do. You're right, you were quiet. You kept to yourself. Most people are too busy with their own lives to put in much effort making friends. So, they gravitate toward people that make it easy for them. But you've changed a lot, Hallie. If you were staying, you would end up making friends here."

"Do you think so?"

"Of course. Who wouldn't love you, given the chance? Besides, you have friends and you'll keep making more. And you have me."

"I have a lot, don't I? It just hit me that my absence here won't really impact anyone. I worked here for years, and I didn't leave a mark." She shrugged again. "It doesn't matter. I'm going on to do what I really want to do. I have great people in my life. I'm going to stop whining now. Sorry."

Ben kissed her, briefly. "That's my girl. I'm going back to work. You're really okay?"

"I'm fine. I still have some work to do, too. I'll see you at 4:30."

But Ben's face appeared at her door early, not quite 4 o'clock. He grinned. "Are you finished?"

"Actually, I have one more thing I want to get done. Can you give me a few minutes? Why are you leaving early, anyway?"

"We're not leaving yet. And you do have one more thing to do, but not in here. Come on."

"What? But I really have something I don't want to leave undone."

"Leave a note with instructions. Go on, I'll wait."

"What are you up to?"

"Go on, leave a note. Hurry!"

"Okay!" She'd been scribbling notes for her successor all day; she added a few lines now. "All right. What do you have hidden up that sleeve of yours?"

"Follow me, Ms. McLaren. It's time to leave your mark."

"Ben, what...?" But he raised one finger to his lips, ending her questions.

They rounded the corner to the main reception area. All the lights were off, except one: the one directly above Stella's desk, which had been completely cleared. Ben raised his hand and motioned toward Hallie. "As you all know by now, our little diva here has denied all but a lucky few the experience of hearing her sing. And no one has been invited to attend one of her private little concerts, so often performed right here, on Stella's desk. Stella, did you ever suspect?"

"Not once. Hallie, thanks for putting everything back the way you found it!"

They were all there, sitting around desks or standing beside the partitions separating the cubicles. "Well, we can't let her leave without performing one more time. This time, to a full house. What do you say, Hallie?"

Hallie's co-workers applauded their encouragement. Ben turned back to Hallie. "Your stage awaits, darlin'." He held his hand out and helped her onto the desk.

Hallie stood, looking out at the now silent figures in the shadows. How many times had she stood here, wishing she could sing in front of a living, breathing audience?

"Oh, one more little surprise!" Ben handed her a microphone, then ran to the back of the room. "Remember that karaoke machine we rented?" he called. "Got it right here. What would you like to sing?"

How long had he been planning this? Now, unable to see his face, Hallie still knew he was grinning his widest. "How about 'Something to Talk About'?" Considering the gossip they'd inspired in this office, it seemed a fitting choice.

It was a fun song to sing, loud and sexy. People clapped, some sang along. A few danced. When it ended, Hallie bowed low as the crowd burst into applause.

Standing straight again, she looked at the faces she had seen so often; faces she wouldn't be seeing again soon, if ever. They had hardly known her, and now they were clapping, cheering, whistling and calling for more. They were surprised and elated that, with Ben's help, she had revealed a little more of herself. When the show was over, the crowd gathered around Hallie for their final good-byes and good wishes; this time, those wishes felt genuine.

The following week, Jim Schultz called to schedule a recording session, and Hallie found herself singing about cat food. A few days later she sang a jazzy little scat as background for a cleaning product. Soon she was reading copy extolling the virtues of frozen entrees.

When a commercial aired nationally featuring Hallie's voice singing lines from West Side Story's 'Somewhere,' phone calls started coming in to Jim, asking who she was. "You may end up with a recording contract in spite of yourself," he told her.

"Just tell them I'm not available."

"That'll only create a mystery and make them want you even more."

"That's okay. They can want me. I just don't want to go in that direction."

"You're either crazy or really smart. Lotta people would kill to be in your shoes."

"I have obligations here. I can't be traveling from town to town to sell a CD. Besides, this is fun! I like singing about pizza."

"Well, you're doing a great job. Let's see. Come in next Thursday, about 2 o'clock, and we'll put a schedule together for the next few weeks."

"Sure. See you then, Jim!"

Within five months, Hallie was already earning a livable wage working for Jim. He was calling with more and more offers; Hallie could work as much as she wanted.

At home, she, Cora and Ben had eased into a routine. Ben did indeed bring her coffee each morning, which they drank at the little table beside one of the huge windows in their room. Hallie then made breakfast for the three of them; afterward Ben got ready for work while Hallie cleaned up.

When he was gone, Hallie and Cora went walking; slowly at first, as Cora recovered from her surgery, then picking up speed and distance as she grew stronger.

After Cora's bath— during which Hallie simply stayed close by, just in case— Hallie took her grocery shopping, clothes shopping or to art galleries or an afternoon movie. When Hallie worked, Cora occupied herself with books, writing letters, or seeing friends.

Time flew, as only happy time can. Winter weather blew into town, wet and blustery, bringing an early snowfall to the Cascade Mountains. One weekend, Ben took Hallie and Cora up to Steven's Pass. Cora sat in the cozy bar, reading and watching the skiers zigzag down the slopes, while Ben gave Hallie a refresher course on the hill. Hallie recited his instructions to herself: *weight forward, feet together, plant my poles, quiet upper body.* It wasn't long before she was almost able to keep up with Ben.

Soon they were making plans for Thanksgiving. Christina sent Cora a plane ticket, so Ben and Hallie decided to spend the holiday with his family, a loud, chaotic, joyful gathering. Hallie contributed dessert; it had been years since she'd made apple pies for Thanksgiving, her one culinary specialty, and she waited nervously until the first bites produced a round of "Mmm" and "It's delicious, Hallie!" She blushed a little, but beamed as she thanked them.

Cora enjoyed her Thanksgiving with Christina's family, especially spending time with her granddaughters. But traveling alone had become difficult for her, and she resolved to stay home for Christmas. Christina's family decided to do the same and Barry said he couldn't get away, so Hallie, Ben and Cora spent Christmas together, "creating new traditions," as Cora put it. Ben brought home a huge tree and they decorated it, combining the ornaments the three of them had each collected separately. "They complement each other perfectly!" Cora exclaimed. Christmas Eve, they sat beside the glowing tree sipping eggnog and spiced cider. Cora led them in a few carols, and they topped the evening off with popcorn and *It's a Wonderful Life* on TV.

In the morning, they ate cinnamon rolls and opened gifts, then bundled up with presents for Ben's family and drove to the Lawson's home. Ben's parents treated Cora like visiting royalty, and they, Rachel and Natalie all had gifts for her.

The twins played happily with their new toys while the adults toasted each other and the upcoming New Year, sharing stories of Christmases past and welcoming Cora and Hallie as the two newest editions to the family.

Hallie squeezed Ben's hand and blinked back happy, startled tears. *So this is the way holidays are supposed to feel. No arguing, no accusations, no insults. No drama at all.*

She watched Ben's face as he listened to his father recounting the year Natalie insisted on making a pie by herself, start to finish. The results were nearly inedible, but the rest of the family bravely ate their assigned wedges, praising Natalie's efforts and smiling as they forced down each bite.

"I was the only one who refused to eat it," Natalie said. "I still can't make a pie to save my life."

"No, she really can't," Rachel agreed.

The room filled yet again with laughter, but Ben sensed Hallie's gaze and turned to see her grinning at him with pure, childlike joy.

Over Cora's objections, Hallie and Ben decided to spend New Year's Eve at home. "You're too young to be babysitting an old woman!" she exclaimed.

"All our friends have plans already, and besides, who wants to be out driving with all the drunks on the road?"

"Yeah. Let's stay home and get drunk safely!" Ben said.

So Cora chilled the champagne while Hallie baked a salmon filet; at midnight they turned on the TV to watch the fireworks bursting around the Space Needle.

On Valentine's Day, Ben and Hallie exchanged suitably syrupy cards; that night Ben surprised Hallie with a dozen lavender roses. For Cora, he brought yellow ones.

But Hallie's birthday was perhaps the happiest occasion of all in those months. She woke early and caught her smile in the bathroom mirror. *What a difference a year makes,* she thought, remembering how lost and alone she'd felt that morning a year ago, until Cora's gifts had arrived and changed everything. There would be no angst for Hallie today. Turning thirty was a time for celebration; she was grateful to leave her twenties behind.

Hallie's new life was so busy that Lonnie was eight months pregnant when her bridal/baby shower was finally scheduled. Now it was arranged; RSVP's in hand, Hallie planned the menu, drinks and prizes. "Cora, do you want to go shopping today for the shower?"

"Love to! What do you have in mind?"

"I think we'll just do snacks— cheese and crackers, chips and dip, maybe a fruit plate. Last I heard, Lonnie's craving raspberries. But what about games? We should have something fun to do, but some of those shower games are so silly. What do you think?"

"Shopping always inspires me. We'll brainstorm along the way and something brilliant will come to us."

They had a wonderful day together, tossing around ideas and shopping for groceries and gifts. Cora had been to and given far more showers than Hallie, and her memory for detail was impressive.

"They've gotten so much more fun in the last twenty years or so, believe me. Women used to worry so about being prim and prissy, sitting with their ankles crossed, wearing their pearls and thinking 'pregnant' was a dirty word. I was born into the wrong era, Hallie."

"Were you a rebel, Cora?"

"Always. Still am, really. I've never been swayed by outside influences. I've always been my own person. If you want to convince me of something, you have to back it up with evidence and sound reasoning, not just 'because that's the way we've always done it.' I don't accept a lot of what we are expected to believe in because so much of it is purely cultural. Go to another country and you'll see a completely different reality. Different customs that are carried out simply because that's the way they've always done it. I do believe there are some objective rights and wrongs, I suppose, but very few. Don't kill people, unless they're about to kill you. Don't kill animals that you're not going to eat. Don't infringe on anyone else's personal freedoms or choices. I've always been fairly outspoken about those beliefs. I'll admit I've gone a little too far at times. But those showers I used to go to? Rooms full of those prissy women cringed when I arrived. I'd wear dungarees, as we called them, and use nasty words just to shock them.

"Of course my biggest sin was that I went to college and graduate school to pursue something other than a husband. There were a few that were so scared of me they scratched me off their invitation lists. Others were naughty enough themselves that they enjoyed my presence— I raised the bar on their own acceptable behavior. Whatever they did, they could never be as bad as Cora Duprés. But a few sad, voiceless women just envied me, I'm sure. I like to think maybe I nudged them into an independent thought or two."

"Your maiden name was Duprés?"

"Yes. My grandfather was from France. I loved it that my married name rhymed with Duprés. It didn't change the flavor of my name, you see what I mean? I loved Jack dearly, but I honestly didn't believe I should have to change my name in order to be married. It's symbolic of women being their husbands' property. I did it because it was important to Jack that we have a family name, and in our culture that means the man's name prevails. So I relented. But I use Duprés as my middle name."

"Cora, I don't think you weren't born into the wrong era. Your generation needed you to challenge the status quo, shake things up a bit."

"Every generation needs to challenge conventional wisdom. Even misguided attempts at enlightenment are admirable in my opinion. I suppose I would have had a lot of fun as a hippy, don't you think?"

Hallie laughed. "Why didn't you join the movement? I'm sure you would have looked beautiful in bell bottoms and peasant blouses."

"Uh huh. Flowers in my hair, stoned on some exotic drug…No, I was already in my forties back then. By the Summer of Love, I was far too firmly established with The Establishment. Ah, but the hippy movement didn't last, anyway. Comfort won out over rolling in mud *au naturel* and the joy of material possessions was rediscovered. But a lot of wonderful music and art came from that little journey."

"That's true. What other era do you think you would have liked?"

"Excellent question. Hmm… now that I think of it, the ones I'd most like to see are the ones that haven't happened yet. I'd love to peer into the future a few years, to see you as an old woman, Hallie. I'd love to see Lonnie's baby as an eighty-year-old. What wonders will we have invented by then? Eighty will probably be relatively young. Wouldn't that be something to see?"

"Maybe we will see it. Maybe we'll be floating around just watching the world go on without us, like a great TV show that never ends."

"Or maybe we'll keep coming back. Who knows? Some people believe we seek out the same souls in each life we live— same people, different relationships. So you might have been my brother in our last life, or a cousin. I kind of like that idea. It means we will see each other again and again."

"That's a nice thought. Maybe you'll be my mother next time."

"I'll plan on that. In the meantime, how about if I buy you some lunch?"

"Good idea. I'm starving."

"Me too."

Cora took Hallie's arm and pointed her in the right direction.

49

All the shower invitees, from a list supplied by Lonnie, made themselves available for the big event. Hallie wasn't surprised; Lonnie's popularity seemed as effortless for her as breathing.

The guests arrived on time, and Cora's living room quickly filled with women connected by Lonnie.

Ben headed out the door to play golf with friends. "Have fun, everyone! See you tonight, Hallie," he said, kissing her cheek before he headed out the door.

"So you're Hallie," Lonnie's mother said. There was no mistaking her: Lonnie had inherited her green eyes and dimpled chin. But her aristocratic air seemed as far from

Lonnie's earthbound frankness as earth itself was from Alpha Centauri. "I'm Marie. How nice of you to host this little get together. I tried to convince Lonnie to skip these little conventions and have a real wedding instead. We could have booked our club. They have a fabulous room, and the catering service is top notch. But I just couldn't talk sense into that girl. Oh well, at least she showed good taste in men. Steve's a doctor, you know. And you must be Mrs. Rouget? Lonnie's mentioned you as well."

"Please, call me Cora. You have a lovely daughter, Marie— beautiful, clever and approachable. It's a rare combination." Cora smiled broadly, sneaking a glance at Hallie.

Kim was there, as well as a few of Lonnie's friends from the gym, two cousins and Steve's sister, Kate. Finally, Lonnie herself arrived. Steve waved from the car door. "I'll call you when I'm ready to go, babe!" Lonnie called. "Hi, everyone! Oh, Hallie. Everything looks so beautiful!"

Hallie and Kim guided Lonnie to her chair— the most comfortable one in the room. "This is your throne for the day," Hallie said. "And, here is your crown." She placed a cardboard tiara on Lonnie's head.

"Look at me! I'm a pregnant princess!" Lonnie said. "Where's my scepter?"

"A scepter: I knew I'd forgotten something," Hallie said.

"Where does one buy a scepter, I wonder?" Lonnie mused.

Everyone sat, and Cora helped Hallie serve drinks while the women chatted. Hallie brought Lonnie a bowl piled high with raspberries and whipped cream. "You're an angel! For some reason, this little girl just loves her berries."

"Well, enjoy them, and then I have some games planned."

"Can't we just skip straight to the presents?"

"We can do whatever you want. Presents first?"

Lonnie looked at the pile of gifts on the coffee table. I'll open a few, then we'll play games and I'll open the rest. Is that okay?"

"Of course. This is your day!"

The guests had brought two gifts each: bridal and baby. Lonnie's face lit up with anticipation and joy as she tore open each package: a candelabra, silver picture frame, pink and yellow sleepers, and from her mother, a gift certificate generous enough to cover a nursery full of baby furniture. Hallie volunteered to write down the list of gifts and givers as Lonnie opened them.

"Someone hand me one more, then we can do something else," Lonnie said.

They passed a gift bag from one to another, until it reached Lonnie. "Oh!" she said. Slowly, she lowered the bag to the floor beside her. And then, "Uh oh."

"Lonnie, are you all right?" Kim asked.

Hallie reached over and touched Lonnie's arm. "Lonnie?"

"I'm afraid we're going to have to pass on the games, Hal. I think my water just broke."

Marie screamed. "Call 911!"

"Mom, calm down. Hallie, bring me a phone so I can call Steve."

Lonnie called Steve's cell phone first. "No answer. He must be home already. Oh boy!"

"Lonnie?" Hallie asked.

"So that's what a contraction feels like. That was a good one, too!"

"Do you want me to call Steve at home?"

"Just dial it for me, I'll talk to him."

Hallie dialed, then handed the phone to Lonnie. "It's ringing."

"Hey, Daddy! Actually, no, it's not really over, but we're cutting it short."

"Lonnie, please! Tell the man you're in labor!" Marie yelled.

"Steve, it looks like this baby is going to be a little early. I don't want to wait for you to come all the way back over here and then have to drive to the hospital, so why don't I catch a ride and meet you there? Would you call the doctor? Yes, I know you're a doctor, but you don't really want to deliver our daughter in the car, do you? Okay. I'll see you at the hospital. I'm fine. I love you, too." She pushed the 'off' button and gave the phone back to Hallie. Lowering her voice, she said, "Hal, would you take me to the hospital, please? I don't think I'd trust my mother behind the wheel right now."

"Of course, I'd be happy to."

Cora appeared with Lonnie's coat and purse. "Could I ride along, too?"

"Yes, thanks. Mom? You'd better come along with us, too."

"But my car…"

"It'll be fine here, Marie. You can pick it up later," Cora said.

Everyone hustled out the door, with shouts of "Good luck!" and "Call me when it's all over!"

The four women ran to Hallie's car. There was a brief debate about seating arrangements until Lonnie screamed, "Mom! Cora is a doctor! Let her sit back here with me! Silenced, Marie sat in front beside Hallie.

"You're doing just great, sweetie," Cora said, putting her arm around Lonnie.

"It's a good thing I opened presents first, huh? Oh, God, here comes another one!"

"Remember to breathe," Cora said.

"Cora, is it really supposed to hurt this much?"

"I'm afraid so, sweetheart. The only consolation is that it won't last forever. And you do get a baby out of the deal."

"I was in labor for three days with you, Lonnie. It was pure agony."

"Maybe we can compare labor stories after the baby comes, Marie," Cora said.

"Good idea!" Lonnie shouted.

Hallie's cell phone rang. "Would you get that, Cora?"

"Hello, Hallie's phone. Oh, Steve! We're almost there. Where are you? Okay, we'll watch for you. She's fine, dear, she's quite a trouper. You're a very lucky man."

"Let me talk to him," Lonnie said, grabbing the phone. "You'd better get there soon. You wouldn't believe what this feels like, and I am not going through this without you! Okay! I love you too, just get to the damn hospital!"

"Lonnie, your language!"

"Mother, shut the fuck up!"

"Thatta girl," Cora whispered. "The contractions are about thirteen minutes apart now. I think this baby's in a bit of a hurry."

"Cora, am I too early? Do you think she's healthy?"

"Don't you worry, Lonnie. Chances are your baby is just fine. Some babies just have their own timetable right from the beginning."

Hallie glanced in the rear view mirror and saw that Lonnie relaxed a bit; the contraction had passed, and Cora's comforting arm held her close. "Lonnie? How you doin'?"

"I'm fine right now. As much as I want Steve with me, I'm really glad you're all here."

"Me too. Hey, have you decided on a name? Other than Myrtle or Gladys?"

"I think we have: Lily Jane. Steve and I both love 'Lily,' and the Jane is for you, Hallie. What do you think?"

"It's beautiful, Lonnie. A beautiful name for a beautiful little girl."

Marie coughed.

"What, Mom? You don't like the name?"

"Well, I thought you might have given some consideration to a family name. My name also belonged to my grandmother, you know. I'm not fond of the name 'Lily.' It sounds like a disreputable woman's name to me. But if it must be so, at least it could be 'Lily Marie.'"

"Disreputable? You mean like someone who'd get pregnant before she's married? Sorry, Mom. It's my baby, and Steve and I are naming her. Understand?" Halfway through Lonnie's response another contraction hit; the result was that her voice rose until she hit the last word in a shriek of amazing pitch. Hallie wondered in passing if such a scene had ever been dramatized as an opera.

When she saw the hospital rise over the horizon, Hallie let out a long, silent breath of relief. "We're here! Hang on! I'm going to drop you off at the emergency entrance. I'll go park and be right in."

"Marie and I will take good care of her, don't worry," Cora said.

Steve had already joined the group when Hallie reached them. Sitting in a wheelchair, Lonnie answered the admitting nurse's questions, with Steve taking over when contractions interfered with Lonnie's concentration. Finally, they were sent up five floors to the maternity wing, where another nurse showed them to Lonnie's room.

"I'm Linda," she said. "Here, let me help you onto the bed. There will be a doctor here shortly to examine you and then we'll have a better idea how soon your baby will be born. I understand you've contacted your doctor?"

"Yes. I left a message," Steve said. "Her service said she's on call and she should be here soon."

"Okay. Well I think you should be seen as soon as possible, so whichever doctor arrives first? Is that okay with you?"

"I want my doctor."

Linda looked to Steve. He shrugged. "Listen, I'm a doctor. I can examine her and find out how much she's dilated. If there's an emergency I can take care of her. If everything's okay, we'll wait for her doctor."

"Is that okay with you?" Linda asked Lonnie.

She nodded. "He's seen it all before."

"Lonnie! Must you be so crude?" Marie walked to one of the two chairs against the wall nearest Lonnie's bed and sat, immediately crossing her legs.

Linda smiled. "Okay. I'll be at the station. Just push the button if you need anything, and I'll let you know when your doctor arrives."

Steve drew the curtain around the bed. They could hear his voice, soft and soothing. "Here. I brought your favorite nightshirt. I'll help you put it on if you like."

"Oh no, no, no. It's another contraction!"

"All right, just hold my hand. Squeeze as hard as you want. Breathe, nice and steady. That's it. Okay? Raise your arms. Hold on to my shoulders, I'm going to raise you up a bit and take off these pants. Arms up again. Good. Comfortable?"

"Much better."

"Okay, I'm going to take a peek. Tell me if anything hurts, all right?" There was a pause.

And then: "Steve? STEVE? I'm having another Goddamn contraction and it FUCKING HURTS!"

"Wow, that was only three minutes between. Hold on, babe. Okay. Lonnie? Our daughter is apparently really eager to see her beautiful mother. She's on her way. You're almost fully dilated. We're going to have our baby today. Lonnie? You're so strong, and you're going to be fine. We're going to get through this just fine. Right?"

"Promise?"

"Promise. Now you just lie back and relax. Here's a blanket. Is the position of the bed okay? Are you warm?"

"I'm fine. NO, NO, I'M NOT FINE! IT'S ANOTHER ONE! I can't do this! Why did I ever think I could do this? How can anyone do this? How did my mother get through this much pain? She can't even handle a hangnail!"

Outside the curtain, Marie snorted. Cora went to her, touched her hand. "Women say crazy things when they're in labor, Marie, you know that," she whispered. "Do you remember anything you said?"

Marie studied the air above Cora's head. "I remember telling my husband to take his thingy, go straight to hell and never come near me again. I suppose you're right, Dr. Rouget."

"It's Cora, please. Of course I'm right. Soon you'll have a beautiful granddaughter and Lonnie will be her old self again."

"I've never quite understood my daughter's old self, Cora. She's not exactly the daughter I imagined I would have."

"She's lovely, and a joy to be with. And she's going to be a wonderful mother, you just wait and see. She'll make you proud."

"Want to know a secret? She already does."

Cora returned Marie's smile and sat down on the chair beside her.

The noise behind the curtain eased, and Steve opened it at last, revealing Lonnie sitting up in the bed, wearing a buttoned down oversized shirt in a sage green just a shade lighter than her eyes. Seeing Lonnie flushed and a little frightened, Hallie thought she was probably the most beautiful woman in the world.

"I'm going to go page the doctor again. If she doesn't get here soon, I'm going to deliver this baby myself," Steve mumbled, half to himself, as he left the room.

"Can I get you anything? Ice chips? I've heard ice chips are a good thing," Hallie said.

"No, just stay with me until Steve gets back?"

"Of course. Don't worry, Lonnie. Everything's going to be fine."

"I really just WANT THIS TO BE OVER! Oh my God, Hallie, I had no idea it was going to be like this. Why didn't anyone tell me?"

"Well, I've never been through it, but I think it's because everyone feels differently about it when it's over. When it's over, you'll have a baby to love and take care of.

You'll be too busy to think about what it took to give birth. You'll be adjusting to life as a mother and watching your baby grow."

"Life as a mother. I'll be a mother for the rest of my life, Hallie. I'll be changed forever."

"Yes. You'll have a little girl. She's going to coo and cry and giggle. She'll learn to walk holding your hand, and hear stories read in your voice. When she can talk, she'll call you 'Mommy,' and when she's hurt no one else's lap will feel quite right. This is your baby girl, Lonnie. I can't wait to meet her."

"Me too. I love you, Hal. OH MY GOD!"

Steve returned, followed by Dr. Shaw. Cora's mouth dropped. "Sarah? I didn't know you were Lonnie's doctor."

"I met her through you, Cora. I liked having that connection," Lonnie said.

"Hi, everyone!" Dr. Shaw said. "Well, it looks like we have a baby to deliver! Lonnie? Are you ready? Sorry, stupid question. Let's get you down to delivery. Steve, you can go scrub. The nurses will get you a gown."

Sarah helped Lonnie back into the wheelchair, and Hallie, Cora and Marie stood at the doorway and watched as Lonnie was whisked away. Lonnie looked back once and waved. Then they rounded a corner and disappeared.

Nurse Linda hurried to them on her sensible white shoes. "Are you all waiting?"

Hallie and Cora hadn't really made that decision; now they looked at each other and nodded. "Yes, we'd like to stay."

"Of course I'm staying," said Marie.

"Oh! I should call Ben," Hallie said.

"I'll show you to the waiting room. We'll come find you when there's news."

Less than an hour later, nurse Linda herself brought the news to them. "Mrs. Wakefield had her baby girl a few minutes ago. The baby is a little more jaundiced than we'd like to see, so she's being treated in the neonatal intensive care unit. The

level of jaundice is not too extreme, though, and she seems
healthy otherwise, so don't worry. I'll let you know when Mrs.
Wakefield is back in her room."

"Is Lonnie all right?" Hallie asked Linda.

"She's just fine," Nurse Linda responded with a warm
smile. And the shoes carried her away again.

"Jaundice? Isn't that serious?" Marie asked.

"It can be. But it's very common. I'm sure Lily will be
just fine," Cora said.

"But she said Lily's in intensive care."

"Absolutely routine under the circumstances."

"You're sure?"

"I'd stake my life on it," Cora said. "Nothing at all to
worry about, Grandma."

"Grandma! Hmm. Grandma." Marie tasted the word
like wine, rolling it around on her tongue to test its worth. "No,
I think I prefer Nana. What do you think, Dr. Rouget?"

"Please, Marie, call me Cora. Well, I have a Grandma
kind of family. My own grandmother was from France, so I
grew up calling her *Grandmére*: Grandmother is the English
equivalent, so 'grandma' seemed natural to me. But if Nana
feels right to you, by all means use it."

"Perhaps Grandma is best. It's more traditional, after
all."

Now the minutes ticked by slowly. Despite Cora's
reassuring words, Hallie began to worry about the baby. Her
goddaughter's health was not perfect; less than perfect,
whatever the degree, was unacceptable. Suddenly, sitting still
was also an impossible option. Hallie stood and walked over to
a pile of magazines on a nearby table. She looked through
them, fighting an impulse to pace like a caged cat. After Cora
had worked so hard to calm Marie, Hallie didn't want to appear
nervous or worried, but occupying her thoughts was getting
difficult. She chose a trashy Hollywood gossip magazine and
was starting back toward her seat when Ben appeared in the
doorway.

Hallie dropped the magazine and ran to him. "I didn't think you were coming."

"I changed my mind. Took all kinds of crap about being 'whipped' but I don't care. I just thought you might like some company."

Shortly after Ben joined them, Sarah Shaw arrived. "Lonnie's in her room. She's a little tired, but she's fine. The delivery was very quick, as you know. Lily weighs six pounds four ounces and she's twenty inches long, so she's a good size. I think the nurse told you that she's a little jaundiced, so she's under a lamp in the neo-natal ICU. She looks like a little sunbather in there, with her eyes covered for protection. We'll see how quickly she improves over the next few hours, but I believe she'll be fine. Lonnie and Steve just came from seeing her and Lonnie is asking to see you all, but please don't stay too long. She needs to rest."

"Cora, you and Marie go ahead. I'm going to run down to the gift shop and get her some flowers," Hallie said.

"Good idea. Wait a minute!" Cora fished out her wallet and gave Hallie a fifty–dollar bill. "Make them from all of us."

Knowing better than to argue with Cora about money, Hallie put the bill in her own wallet and grabbed Ben's arm. "Will you go with me?"

The selection was limited in the hospital gift shop; there were several bouquets already arranged in glass vases with hearts and swans, and a few with pink or blue ribbons. Hallie chose the largest arrangement because it included a few calla lilies: Lonnie's favorite flower, and of course the inspiration for Lily's name.

"Let's get a balloon, too. I want it to be festive up there." They bought a pink It's A Girl! balloon, and headed back up to Lonnie's room.

But festive it wasn't when they walked into the room, flowers and balloon in hand. Lonnie sat, propped up in bed, and weeping into her hands. Marie stood on one side, Cora on the other, and Steve sat on the bed facing Lonnie. He looked up when Hallie and Ben walked in.

Hallie feared the worst: "Is Lily all right?"

He nodded. "I think she's going to be fine, but Lonnie doesn't believe me. She thinks she's done something wrong, something that caused Lily to be born early and sick."

"I'm already a terrible mother!" she sobbed from behind her hands. "I'm just going to keep making a mess of everything. Lily's going to hate me!" She looked up. "Hallie, you take her! Pretend she's yours and raise her for me. She'll love you. She'll know you're a good mother. But me? I don't know how to change diapers or comfort a crying child. I don't even know what I did to make her sick! A good mother would have avoided whatever it was I did!"

Steve stroked her hair. "Honey, you did nothing wrong. You took very good care of yourself. Sometimes things just happen. But Lily is going to be fine. I promise you."

Lonnie looked past Steve, ignoring him. "Hallie? Take her, okay?"

Hallie put the flowers down on the ledge beside the bed, and let the balloon float up to the ceiling. Cora shifted positions so that Hallie could move in close to Lonnie. Taking her hand, Hallie spoke softly, just for Lonnie. "Listen to me. You did nothing to hurt Lily. I know you're afraid of being a mother. It's a frightening thing to be responsible for another human being. But— no, look at me— you are going to be a good mother. I know this because you want to be a good mother. It's important to you. And Lonnie, I know you. When something is important, you move mountains to get it done. So when you need help, you'll seek it out. You'll read books, you'll ask for advice, you'll think things through. You'll never hurt your daughter with careless words. As for the rest, you'll learn. Diapers are easy. You'll tackle that one before you and Lily leave the hospital. Holding her, giving her a bath, comforting her, all that will come easily. Everything else will come with time. You don't have to feel comfortable right now with everything that will come over the next twenty years. You'll deal with every phase of Lily's life, one at a time. It's going to be all right. And you're not alone. You have Steve, Lily's grandparents and her godparents."

"She even has an extra grandma," Cora whispered loudly.

Lonnie smiled then, and took a tissue from the box Marie held out to her. She blew her nose and wiped the last tears from her face. Looking at her husband, she nodded. "I'm sorry. I just— I didn't expect anything to go wrong. And I hate hospitals. Bad things happen in hospitals."

"You're worried, you're scared and you're exhausted. You just gave birth: you're entitled. But I love you, babe, and that little girl is lucky to have you for her mom. I swear it," Steve said.

She looked back up at Hallie. "She has a pretty wonderful godmother, too."

"Are you okay?" Hallie asked.

Lonnie nodded again. "I will be."

"Okay!" Steve said. "Now can I pass out cigars?"

The day after Lily's birth, Ben answered the phone when it rang before dawn. Ben's voice drifted into Hallie's dreams, luring her toward consciousness. "Lonnie? That's great. Yeah, I think she's waking up. Hold on. Hallie? Are you awake enough to talk to Lonnie? It's good news."

Nodding, Hallie blinked and reached for the phone. "Lonnie?"

"She's okay, Hal. The nurse just told me that her bilirubin test came back normal. High normal, but normal. Isn't that great?"

"Billy Reuben?"

"Bilirubin— all one word. It's what measures the level of jaundice in her blood. Hallie, she's normal! I'm holding her right now! She just finished nursing! I just had to call. I'm sorry, I know it's early."

"It's okay, I'm glad you called. When can we come down? I want to see that baby girl."

"Come anytime. Not now, of course, it's only 5 o'clock."

"We'll be there in a few hours. And Lonnie? How are you feeling?"

"I'm a little sore, and I absolutely fucking hate hospitals, but you know what? I just nursed my baby for the first time and she seemed to love it. She burped and fell asleep just like I knew what I was doing. So how do I feel? I feel like the original Earth Mother. I am a goddess. See you in a while."

It was Sunday morning, so Ben, Hallie and Cora decided to go out for breakfast and then on to the hospital together. Walking into Lonnie's room, Hallie literally gasped.

There sat Lonnie, flushed and smiling wide, not a speck of makeup and absolutely radiant; Steve stood by her side, and they were both focused entirely on the bundle in her arms. Hearing their guests arrive, they looked up, their smiles growing even wider.

"Hey! Get over here and see this beautiful baby!" Lonnie said.

Hallie leaned over first, peering into Lily's brand new face. Hallie saw Steve's narrow nose, Lonnie's dimpled chin. As Hallie watched, Lily opened her eyes and actually cooed; Hallie fell completely, instantly in love. "Hello, Lily. I'm your godmother! I'm Hallie!" She touched Lily's tiny hand and watched in awe as the perfect little fingers closed around one of her own. "She's so strong!"

"I know, she's got quite a grip! Isn't she amazing?" Lonnie asked.

"She is perfect. Look at all that black hair!"

Cora and Ben closed in to have a look. "She's simply gorgeous!" said Cora. "I knew she would be."

Ben grinned and shook Steve's hand. "Congratulations, man. You've got a great family here."

"Hallie, do you want to hold her?" Lonnie asked.

"Silly question." They shifted Lily from Lonnie's arms to Hallie's; easily accomplished, with Lily wrapped so tightly in her blanket.

"The nurses swing her around like a little football sometimes. I guess they want us to see she's not as fragile as she seems," Steve said.

Hallie gazed into Lily's eyes and breathed in her clean baby smell. Lily, at first startled by the move, settled in quickly and closed her eyes, sleeping again in her warm cocoon. Hallie studied her little eyelashes, her shiny, miniature fingernails. *Someday I will paint these nails for you, Lily. I'll take you to the park and hold your hand. We'll play Candy Land and bake cookies.*

"She looks pretty comfortable with you, Hallie. Sorry, though, the offer I made yesterday isn't open anymore. You can't have her," Lonnie said. She laughed. "Sorry about my little outburst, you guys. I was pretty much out of my mind."

"Don't you worry about that for one minute," Cora said. "You'd just given birth for the first time and you were afraid for your baby. And every new mother has doubts about her own parenting abilities."

"Really?"

"Honestly. I had a wonderful mother: kind, gentle, so loving. I had a wonderful role model, but when I became a mother I panicked. I thought I'd never live up to her example; I was too independent, too ambitious. I thought I'd have to give up everything else I valued in order to be the kind of mother my baby deserved. But I took things as they came, trusted my instincts for the most part and thought things through carefully when I was unsure. Hallie was exactly right. You're going to be a wonderful mother because it's important to you. Trust yourself. You'll be just fine."

"Thanks, Cora. Can I call you guys when I panic again?"

"Anytime. I think our culture is so primitive when it comes to childbearing and –rearing. There should be a group of women ready to swoop in and help every new mother when she feels overwhelmed. So just think of us as your personal support group and call on us anytime you need us."

"My own little village? I'm going to take you up on that. Hi, Mom! Come in and see your granddaughter!"

Marie had appeared in the doorway. "Where is she?"

Hallie turned toward Marie, jostling Lily as she stirred. "Here she is, Grandma! Would you like to hold her?"

Marie took Lily from Hallie, smiling into her face. "She's beautiful, Lonnie. She has your nose, Steve. But that's her mother's stubborn chin. Isn't it, darling?" She rocked back and forth, shifting her weight from one foot to the other: the universal baby comfort sway.

"Oh! I almost forgot!" Lonnie said. "There's been a slight change in Lily's name. She is now officially Lily Jane Marie Wakefield."

Everyone smiled and nodded their approval, but when Marie looked up from her granddaughter's face at last, her eyes were moist and her chin, almost identical to the one she herself had so recently labeled stubborn, quivered.

50

In the ten months since her surgery, Hallie had been blissfully free of pain. Each month she had braced herself, preparing for the worst, and instead her periods had been... well, pretty normal: an occasional cramp, a relatively light flow, a reasonable four or five days. As each period had passed its heaviest time, she'd nearly danced with relief. Her energy seemed boundless. She only wished that she had found a doctor like Sarah Shaw years earlier.

It had been a busy ten months, as well, especially the last seven or so, and Hallie had been particularly grateful not to have to schedule around the screaming pain that had always accompanied her periods pre-surgery.

So, when the pain returned for her eleventh post-surgery period, Hallie tried to dismiss it as normal, and now rare, menstrual cramps. She kept her scheduled recording session, a two person commercial 'play' for a radio advertisement; she maintained an impressive poker face while performing, but when she returned home Cora met her at the door with concern very readable on her own face.

"Hallie, you're gray as a cloudy day. I watched you get out of the car. You're in pain. What's wrong?"

"It's my period. This is the first time since the surgery the pain has been this bad. I'm going to go change my clothes and relax. Maybe it'll get better if I rest for a while."

"I'll make some tea and meet you in the living room. Oh, here comes Cleo! She's been watching for you all morning." Cora smiled at the little black cat, scampering up the stairs behind Hallie.

After changing into her beloved sweatpants, Hallie joined Cora in the living room carrying Cleo in her arms.

"Now you curl up on the sofa and I'll pour some tea. You're sure this is the first time you've felt the pain return?"

Hallie nodded. "I've had some cramps, but I'm guessing those were normal. Mostly my periods have been a lot lighter and not painful at all. It's been absolute heaven. But this morning I had some fairly painful cramps, and now it's really bad. Not quite as bad as before the surgery, but almost."

"I'm so sorry, sweetheart. Endometriosis does tend to be a chronic disease, but maybe this is just a temporary setback."

"I hope so, Cora, because I'm supposed to be here to take care of you!"

"Hogwash. Let's just say we take care of each other. Whoever needs a little TLC at the time gets it from one of the others. That's what families do, after all."

"What if we both need TLC at the same time? I guess Ben will be a busy boy."

"I think it will all balance out in the end, don't you worry. By the way, how was work this morning?"

"It was fun. I felt lousy, but I really enjoyed it. I feel like an actor! I can't believe I'm getting paid for doing this stuff."

"I'm glad you're having fun. It's such a thrill to hear your voice behind all those TV commercials you've done. Now I suppose I'll have to listen to the radio more often, too. Remember that first Kitty Crunch commercial? What an exciting night! Your professional debut!"

Laughing, Hallie said, "I can't believe you made popcorn for a thirty-second commercial!"

"But what a wonderful thirty seconds it was! Your beautiful voice behind a dancing cat! Now that's entertainment! Oh, and the Shiny Bright commercial with that jazzy jingle and the smiling sponge?"

"That's actually my favorite commercial song so far. It was fun to sing."

"I like the one with that old Broadway tune for the camera ad. That one really showed off your voice. So what's next?"

"You'll never guess, Cora. After we finished today, Jim asked me if I'd like to appear in a TV commercial. Not just my voice, but me— in front of the camera! A friend of his directs commercials and contacts him when he needs actors, especially for musical spots. I think Jim waited until he was sure I could pull it off, but today he asked if I'd be interested. I said I'd give it a shot, mainly because I enjoyed the work so much today. This won't be much different, just with a TV camera. What do you think?"

"I think you should follow your heart. If this feels like it fits, wear it proudly. Have you ever acted before?"

"A little, in my high school drama class. I liked it, but of course it was on the forbidden career list at home. In my senior year, the drama club performed a musical: *Oklahoma*. I wanted to try out for it so badly I actually asked my parents."

"Don't tell me they said no."

"They said no."

"To a school play?"

"They said it would interfere with my homework time."

"They were afraid to let you shine, Hallie, afraid you'd choose a difficult path. They didn't want you to suffer, I appreciate that, but we all know where those good intentions lead. What a shame. I can just see you on stage under that spotlight, your voice filling the auditorium, all eyes on you, the audience forgetting to breathe, drinking in all that beauty. Your parents not only robbed you of that moment, they deprived themselves of it as well. Think how proud they would have been had they seen and fully appreciated how gifted you are." Cora shook her head. "You know something? It's about time someone told them that." She stood and marched quickly to the phone.

"Cora? What are you doing?"

"What's their number?"

"What are you going to say?"

"Trust me, Hallie. Give me the number."

Determination could be defined by Cora's expression at that moment, and Hallie of course trusted her completely, so Cora was soon dialing the number to Hallie's childhood home.

"Mrs. McLaren? This is Cora Rouget, Hallie's friend. So nice to speak with you at last. I'm sorry I haven't called sooner. I hope you and your husband are well? Good. And how is the weather over there? Actually, it doesn't rain here quite as much as you might think.

"I'm calling with some very good news. Our Hallie is becoming quite successful as a singer and actor. Actor, yes. In fact, we were just discussing some of her more high profile appearances. I don't know if you've seen any of her commercials? Well, you might not recognize her voice, since you've never heard her sing. We've recorded a few of them. Would you like me to send you a copy of the tape? I'd be happy to. You'll be thrilled to know that she's going to be

filming a TV commercial soon. That's right, not just her voice,
her beautiful face, too. The offers just keep rolling in; she can
hardly keep up with all of them. No, of course she's not
neglecting me. In fact, I have to push her not to neglect herself.
Sacrificing her own needs and desires is such a well-
established habit for Hallie.

"Most of all I want to tell you how wonderful your
daughter is. Her voice is exquisite, of course; her talent is
unquestionable. But what is even more extraordinary is her
kindness, her gentle soul. As lovely as she is, she is even more
beautiful because of her loving nature. Oh, you're very
welcome. I'll get that tape off to you in tomorrow's mail. Very
nice chatting with you. Give my best to your husband. I'll give
Hallie your love. Bye now."

Cora began giggling before she'd hung up the phone.
Now Hallie joined her. "You're the one who should be acting!
You're good!"

"Well, I *was* in a few plays in high school. But do you
think she got the message?"

"She won't have a clue what you were up to. I think
she'll be surprised that someone has such a high opinion of me.
And she may even watch the tape, just out of curiosity. Thank
you, Cora. No one's ever challenged my mother before, at least
not on my behalf."

"Well, someone needed to. Besides, it was fun! Now,
how about if I make dinner tonight?"

"No, I'll be fine."

"But I don't want you to stand on your feet to cook. I
know! I'll send Ben over to that little Italian place for take out.
Remember when I brought dinner to your apartment?"

"I'll never forget. That was my birthday."

"That's right! You were in such pain that day too, poor
thing. I just had to do something."

"You did something, all right. You spoiled me rotten."

"We all deserve a little spoiling now and then. You
more than most."

"Thanks, Cora."

"You're welcome, sugar. I'll go dig up the take-out menu from the restaurant so we can decide on what to order." She paused at the doorway and looked back at Hallie. "Sweetie pie? I love you very much. Every day I thank my lucky stars that you and Ben are here with me. I just wanted you to know that."

Hallie stopped petting Cleo and looked up. Smiling gratefully, she said, "I love you too, Cora. My life is so much better since you've been part of it."

Nodding once, Cora said, "Good. That's my motto—well, one of them anyway: Don't neglect to tell people how you feel about them. You never know what tomorrow will bring."

51

A few tomorrows later brought a miracle. It was the day Hallie filmed her on-camera commercial; the shooting went smoothly, in only a few takes, and Hallie, high on adrenaline, decided to drop in on Jim at the studio to share the good news and get her new schedule.

"Glad you stopped by. I just got off the phone from Stan, Hallie. He said you were a pro. Said he wished he could clone you. He asked if I'm your agent."

"Agent?"

"He thinks you could go to the top. I think so too. You really need an agent, Hallie."

"Well, do you do that? Are you an agent?"

He shrugged. "Used to be. I never really closed the door, just haven't seen anyone I wanted to represent for a while. Hey, I'm happy to keep things as they are. Most of your work is here with me. I just don't want to get in your way if other opportunities come along."

"But if you find those other opportunities for me, it's only fair that you benefit. If we call you my agent, you'll get a percentage of what I earn, right?"

"Yeah, that's right. I'll keep it low, especially to start out. If that's the way you want to go."

"I'm comfortable with you, Jim. I don't want to go looking for anyone else."

"Okay, you've got yourself an agent. But we'll draw up a contract, do it right. You need to get yourself a lawyer and make sure I'm not ripping you off."

"Okay, I will. Thanks, Jim! What have you got for me this week?"

They went over Hallie's schedule. "Are you free for all that?" Jim asked.

"Yeah, it's fine. Anything else?"

"One thing. You should probably take some acting lessons. You did great today, but you might want to be prepared for something a little more demanding."

"Okay. That sounds like fun!"

"I'll set up a meeting to sign the contract."

"Thanks, Jim."

"Hey, don't thank me. I plan on making a lot of money off you, kiddo. I'm going to have to send a thank you card to that karaoke guy."

"Karaoke guy?"

"That Kyle character, the karaoke host. He's the one who talked me in to checking you out."

"What?"

"He's done a little work for me on occasion, and he called me up one day, said 'there's a girl you've got to hear.' Bugged me about it two or three times until I finally agreed to come down on a night he figured you'd be there. He said you came about once a month, gave me a heads up that you were due to show up, so I showed up too. I got lucky; you were there that night. He was right. You are something special. I should really buy him dinner sometime."

Driving home, Hallie thought about Karaoke Kyle. It all made sense now: he had showcased Hallie several times that night, calling her up on stage when she hadn't even submitted her name. When no one had volunteered to sing, he could have had the stage to himself; instead, he often brought her up to sing with him or by herself. She had thought he was flirting, or perhaps responding to secret requests her friends had slipped through. Maybe she'd been partly right, but Kyle had also been promoting her talent, generating audience support and even working behind the scenes to help her begin a singing career. Clearly, Jim was not the only one who owed Kyle a thank you.

Later, Hallie was describing the day's events to Ben and Cora when the phone rang. Cora rose to answer it, saying, "Hold on, I don't want to miss anything!" She picked up the receiver. "Hello? Oh, hello there! Yes, she's right here. She's had quite an exciting day, but I'll let her tell you about it."

Covering the mouthpiece with her hand, Cora whispered, "It's your mother!" She and Ben looked at each other, then watched Hallie as she took the phone.

"Mom? Hi. I'm fine, how are you? She did? Did you watch it? What did you think?" There was a long pause, and Hallie's face turned first pink, then crimson. "Really?" Another long silence while Hallie illogically nodded at her mother's words. She looked up at her audience; tears shone in her eyes. She leaned against the back of the sofa. "Thanks. I appreciate that, Mom. Excitement? Oh, Cora just meant that I shot a commercial today where I'll actually be on screen instead of just singing in the background. I'll find out when it's being shown the first time, and let you know. Oh, that's too bad. Well, I hope she feels better soon. He does? Okay. I love you, too, Mom.

"Hi, Dad. Thanks. That doesn't matter now. Really. This means so much to me. I love you, too. Tell Mom good-bye. Thanks, Daddy."

Hallie pushed the off button on the phone and stared at it for a moment.

"Hallie? Are you okay?" Ben asked, touching her hand.

"Yeah. I'm in shock, but I'm okay. My fairy godmother over there just worked her magic again, that's all."

"What did they say, sweetie?" Cora asked.

"They watched the tape you sent. Mom said they should have believed in my talent. She said that because of their fear, I almost wasted my gift. She said they robbed me of the confidence I needed to pursue my dream. Cora, they both said they're proud of me and that they love me. Do you know how long it's been since they've said that?"

"Yes, I do. Too long."

"So where do you keep your magic wand?"

"It's disguised as a cane."

"I wouldn't be surprised. Thank you, Cora." Hallie closed her eyes as they embraced. A child's sorrow, so seemingly endless, began at last to dissipate as she rocked in Cora's arms. *They love me, they're proud of me*: these were the words her mind chanted, over and over until her heart began to believe them.

Behind Hallie, Ben caught Cora's eye. Smiling, he mouthed the words *Thank you*.

"Wait a minute," Cora said. "Who were you wishing a speedy recovery? A relative?"

"No, no, it's one of their endlessly ailing friends that I haven't seen since I was six. Someone's always being diagnosed with some horrible affliction and Mom seems to feel compelled to share all the grisly details. But you know, today it wasn't quite so tough to take."

"Funny how a few kind words can sweeten a whole barrel of bitterness."

Handing Hallie a tissue, Ben said, "One of these days we'll have to fly out there so I can meet your folks. Maybe I can be the bad guy and lay out a few ground rules."

"Like what?"

"Oh, like: for every negative news item they have to pay you one compliment. Every time they question your life choices, they have to follow up with a positive observation about your accomplishments. What do you think?"

"I think we shouldn't push our luck. We have to appreciate today's turnaround. I'm afraid to ask for more. I don't even want to ask for more. This is enough."

52

The day of Lily's christening was unseasonably warm, spring disguised momentarily as July. Lonnie was almost apologetic about the ceremony itself. "This is for my mother. Steve and I would have just added a provision to our wills, but Mother dear was shocked that we weren't going to have Lily christened in her church. 'Mom,' I said, 'I haven't been inside a church for ten years.' She didn't care. So we're having her christened, and pronouncing you and Ben formally her godparents. I hope that's okay," she told Hallie.

"Of course it is. Besides, she's going to look so pretty in a little white gown."

During the ceremony, Lily cried quite unceremoniously, but at Marie's party afterward, she was all gurgles and coos: "A girl after my own heart," Lonnie said.

"She is so beautiful, Lonnie!" Kim said. "I don't think I've ever seen such a gorgeous baby! Makes me almost want one of my own. Almost."

"Thanks. So who's the new guy, Kim?"

"Isn't he cute? His name is Joe. He's the CFO of some little company."

"What happened to Andy?"

"He turned into a jerk. Nothing unusual."

"Well, Joe is certainly cute."

"Joe who?" Hallie asked, joining them.

"My new guy. This one is really promising. I'll call him over so you can meet him. Joe!"

"He may be cute, but I don't like his name," Hallie said, laughing. She turned as Kim greeted the man behind her.

"Joe, this is…"

"Hello, Hallie."

"Joe. What a surprise."

Kim's jaw dropped. "You're kidding. You're Hallie's Joe?"

"Well, I haven't been Hallie's Joe for quite some time."

"Hallie, I'm so sorry, I had no idea. You never told me your married name was Chapman. What were the odds that I would meet the same Joe?"

"Astronomical, I'm sure."

"I didn't know you knew each other. Kim's mentioned her friends a few times, but no names," Joe said. "I swear, I didn't know."

"It's true, Hallie. I never mentioned your name. And Joe said he'd been married before, but never talked about his ex-wife. Wow. Ex-wife. This is so weird. Hallie, can I talk to you outside?"

"Of course." Ben had waved from a corner across the room where he stood talking to Steve. Hallie smiled in return and motioned that she would be right back. Outside, she touched Kim's arm. "Listen. I'm okay. Really."

"Are you sure?"

"Well, I don't think we'll be double dating anytime soon, but if you feel strongly about seeing Joe then you should."

"But Hallie, he cheated on you when you were trying to have a baby. Can I trust him?"

"I don't know. Last time I saw him, he'd said he'd thought about all that and felt bad about what he did. Maybe he's changed."

"But given that I seem to be a loser magnet, should I really take a chance on a guy that has a known loser past?"

"That's your decision. You have to ask yourself how you really feel about him. What does your heart tell you?"

"Well, I've been more excited about him than I have been about anyone for a long time. But it's very new— I've only been dating him a couple of weeks. He said he hasn't felt this way about anyone since his... well, since you. But Hallie? You're really important to me. I hate to think that we'll stop being close if I pursue this relationship."

"We can still be close, Kim. But if you end up with Joe, Ben and I will never come over for dinner or go out for drinks or anything like that. There's just too much history between us. I can't be his friend."

"I understand. Guess I've got some thinking to do, huh?"

"I'm sorry, Kim. I really want you to be happy."

"Me too. Think it's ever gonna happen?"

"I'm sure it will. Come here." They hugged, and Hallie looked up to see Lonnie peeking through the window. "Ready to go back in? I think Lonnie's worried about us."

"Why? Did she think we'd duke it out or something?"

"Yes!" she called from the porch. "I thought you'd be out here pulling each other's hair!"

Inside, Joe was waiting by the door. "I think I should leave. You can get a ride home, right? You stay and have fun," he said to Kim, and kissed her on the cheek. To Hallie, he said, "I hope I didn't cause any problems. Take care of yourself."

When the door closed behind him, Hallie said, "Well, that's not the Joe I used to know."

"Maybe he had a personality transplant," Lonnie mused.

"Oh, why can't I find a decent guy who's never been married to one of my best friends?"

"You don't have to stop seeing him, Kim. Honest," Hallie said, squeezing her shoulder.

"Yes, I do. I'm not going to give up your friendship. I need a Hallie-friendly relationship. There's got to be a guy out there for me somewhere. You haven't been married more than once, have you?"

"Nope, no more ex-husbands to worry about."

"That's a relief. But maybe I should get a complete list of your ex-boyfriends so I can check off the names as I meet them."

The three women were toasting Kim's new strategy when Ben joined them. "Everything okay?"

"Perfect," Hallie said. "Where have you been?

"I was talking to Steve for quite a while. He's so proud of that little girl he can barely stand it."

"Yeah, Lily's already got him wrapped around her tiny little finger. Imagine when she starts calling him Daddy," Lonnie said, rolling her eyes at the ceiling. "It always worked with my father."

"And then," Ben continued, "I was talking to your brother Aaron, Lonnie."

"Oh yeah? How's he doing? I hear he's held a job for six whole months."

"Actually, he seems really excited about his new career. He's building sets and props for one of the theatres downtown. In fact, he's started designing a few of them and his ideas are getting some attention."

"Really? That is exciting. Maybe I should start talking to him again."

"You're not talking to your brother?" Hallie asked.

"He owes me a lot of money," Lonnie whispered. "I got tired of asking, begging, pleading, screaming and threatening, so I just stopped talking altogether. My mother invited him today."

"He said he's going to come talk to you soon. He shared something else with me too," Ben said, grinning. "He's got quite a crush on you, Kim."

"What? He said that?"

"Only after I pointed out that he was staring at you. Look, there he goes again."

They all followed Ben's eyes to where Aaron stood, and caught him gazing in their general direction for a brief moment until his face reddened and he looked away.

"He might have just been looking at Lonnie, deciding whether to come talk to her," Kim said. Ben shook his head, still smiling. "What did he say exactly?"

"He said that he's always thought you're smart and cute and fun, and that he can't understand why you're still single. He'd love to ask you out but he's terrified you'll turn him down."

"He said all that? Wow, I had no idea. Usually I pick up on those vibes, but in all these years I've been clueless he felt that way."

"You asked me if he was single once, a long time ago, but I convinced you not to pursue him," Lonnie said, peeking over toward Aaron.

"You did? How?"

"I think I told you he was gay."

"That's right, I remember now! Why did you do that?"

"Well, I knew he had a thing for you and I didn't want it to ruin our friendship!"

"Would it?"

"Yeah, when it all goes to hell. You wouldn't want to be anywhere near him, and unfortunately, I am sometimes compelled to be near him."

"Lonnie, how often do I see anyone in your family? It's not like we have Christmas dinner together."

"We might someday!"

"Are you saying it would still bother you if I dated your brother?"

Lonnie pondered for a moment. "No, I suppose not. Maybe you'd be good for each other, I don't know."

"Great!" Ben said. "I'll go tell him."

"What is this, junior high?" Lonnie said.

"I think it's cute that he's too shy to approach me."

"Yeah, well, when he's too terrified to order dinner, then you tell me how cute he is." Seeing Kim's horror, Lonnie said, "I'm kidding! He's not quite that weird."

Watching Ben and Aaron approach the group, Hallie nudged Kim. "You've had quite an interesting day, haven't you?"

Later, Lonnie's mother Marie led the group in a toast to Lily, now asleep in Steve's arms. Everyone raised their glasses and sipped.

Marie had dominated Cora's attention for most of the party, but Cora had stolen quietly away during the toast and now stood beside Hallie and Ben. "Quite an eventful party, don't you think?" she whispered.

"Definitely," Hallie said.

"Are the rumors true? Was Joe really here?"

"He really was. Did you see the guy talking to Kim and me?"

"Yes. The fellow that spoke to both of you near the front door, and then left immediately? I thought so. Handsome boy, no doubt. Not as gorgeous as you, of course, Ben."

Ben shifted, looking at his feet. Cora continued. "Was he here as Kim's date?"

"Yeah, they've been seeing each other for a couple of weeks I guess. Kim didn't know it was the same Joe," Hallie said.

"No, I'm sure she didn't, poor thing. Oh well. If it's meant to be... She does seem open to other possibilities, however." Cora nodded toward Kim and Aaron, chatting quietly between bites of cake.

"Maybe you can send a little magic their way, Cora," said Hallie. "I think they could both use it."

"That kind of magic is either there already or it never will be. You just can't explain love."

Ben cleared his throat. "Still, it would be nice if Kim could find a guy other than Joe. I'm not sure I'd want him in our little circle of friends."

Hallie glanced at Cora and smiled. Ben was feeling a little insecure, maybe even slightly jealous! It hadn't even occurred to Hallie that Joe's presence might bother Ben. He knew how she felt—about both of them— didn't he?

As Ben, Hallie and Cora were getting ready to leave, Lonnie hugged each one and thanked them for coming. "I have to tell you something," she said. "Aaron gave me a gift for Lily a little while ago. A really cute little coral sleeper. I opened it, saw the sleeper and thanked him. Gave him a little peck on the cheek. He said 'you're welcome' and that was that. But just now, I opened the box to look at it again, and underneath the sleeper was an envelope filled with money. It was all the money I've ever loaned him, plus interest. I think my big brother's finally getting his act together."

Cora smiled. "For some people, growing up just takes a little longer. Looks like he's enjoying adulthood so far." They turned to look toward Aaron and Kim once more and found them grinning into each other's faces.

"Kim!" Lonnie called. "Hallie's leaving!"

Still beaming, Kim looked over, blew a kiss and turned back to Aaron.

"I'll see you soon," Lonnie said, and watched her friends walk across the porch, down the steps and the tulip-lined front walk.

Slowing her pace, Hallie breathed in the fresh spring smells, the sun's yellow warmth. Ben stopped and waited for her. Her smile answered his questions, unasked. Grinning himself, he opened his arms wide and drew her in. "It sure is a pretty day, isn't it?"

"It's perfect," Hallie agreed.

"Simply magical," said Cora.

53

"What did the doctor say?" Ben asked.

Hallie was returning from an appointment with Sarah Shaw; Cora had insisted that Hallie report her latest symptoms and discuss treatment options.

"Well, there are a few possibilities, but I'm only willing to try one of them. Right now my pain isn't incapacitating. It's usually bad for one or two days a month. So she suggested I start taking my birth control pills every day, without a break. That will stop my periods altogether."

"What are the other options?"

"There's a drug that would effectively throw my body into menopause, and that would stop my periods too. But then I may go through the symptoms of menopause: hot flashes, night sweats, irritability, weight gain, possibly even decreased bone mass. Doesn't that sound wonderful? There doesn't seem to be a lot of good choices. But Dr. Shaw said that there's some evidence that diet can make a difference. She recommended a book specifically about endometriosis and nutrition. So that's worth looking into. But I'll start taking the pill every day for a few months and see if that helps."

"Good idea. Hey, I was thinking that you and I could go out to dinner tonight. Something kind of special. What do you say?"

"That sounds wonderful. What are you doing home so early, anyway?"

"Well, I have some news. Hold on. Cora! Hallie's home!"

"Coming!" They heard Cora's steps approaching down the hall. In the past few months, those steps had become steadier and quicker than even before her stroke. The angioplasty had been a complete success. Now Hallie beamed at her. Cora wasn't even holding a cane. "How are things, sugar?"

Hallie laughed. "Things are grand, Cora."

"And your condition?"

"Manageable. Minor adjustments, just to see if I can improve things a little."

"Oh, that's good." She looked to Ben. "Have you told her?"

"I was just getting to that, but I wanted you here, too."

"What's the big secret?" Hallie asked, looking from one to the other.

"Come over here and sit down, both of you."

"Cora, do you know what this is about?"

"No, only that he has something big to tell you."

"To tell both of you," Ben said. "I have some good news. I've had a job offer. This is the one, Hallie, I feel it. It's what I've been waiting for."

"CFO?"

"No, not quite. Senior accounts manager for a major research company. The money's good, the benefits are great, but the most exciting thing is that the CFO is retiring in two years. I'd be groomed to replace her."

"Ben, that's wonderful!" Hallie said. "But how long has this been brewing?"

"A couple of weeks. They approached me and asked me to interview. I did, last Tuesday. It was almost too much to hope for, so I decided not to tell you about it until I knew for sure whether they wanted me. They called this morning and offered me the job. I felt like I had to negotiate on salary a bit, not look too eager, and we settled on a figure that's higher than I'd even imagined. This is my big shot, Hallie."

"Where will your office be?"

"Downtown Seattle. I'm not crazy about the idea of commuting downtown everyday; maybe I'll take the bus. But working downtown could be fun. You two can come down and have lunch with me, check out my new office. What do you think?"

"Congratulations, Ben. I'm just thrilled for you. When do you start?" Cora asked.

"I'm giving my two week's notice tomorrow. I just wanted to come home and tell you both first."

"I'm so happy for you, Ben. So that's why we're going out for dinner?" Hallie asked. There was a flicker of eye contact between Ben and Cora then, at least Hallie thought so for a moment.

"Yeah, of course! I want to celebrate!"

"Uh, I think I'll stay home. I'm a little tired. But you two go ahead and have a great time."

"Are you sure, Cora? Come on, you have enough energy to go have a nice dinner, don't you?"

"Not tonight, sweetie pie. I'm pooped. But really, I want you two to go out and paint the town. Okay?"

Something seemed a little strange, out of sync, but Hallie couldn't quite put her finger on it. "Only if you're really sure. But we'll miss you!"

"We'll do it another time, I promise. Now I'm going to make myself some tea. Do you want some before you get all gussied up?"

"Sure. Thank you, Cora."

When she was sure Cora was out of earshot, Hallie turned to Ben. "Does she seem okay to you?"

"Yeah, fine. Why?"

"I don't know. There's something she's not telling us. Some reason she doesn't want to come out to dinner with us. It's not that she's too tired, there's something else. I hope she doesn't think she'd be intruding. I should go talk to her."

"Hallie, I think she's fine, I really do. Maybe she'd like some time to herself."

"Do you think so?"

"Yeah. She probably enjoys being alone in her house, and it doesn't happen very often. She's not telling us that because she doesn't want to hurt our feelings, that's all."

"Maybe you're right."

"I'm sure that's all it is. Besides, I don't mind having you all to myself for one night."

Later, Ben caught his breath as Hallie came downstairs, ready for their evening. "Look at you!"

She grinned, navigating the stairs carefully. "I can't remember the last time I wore heels. Hope I don't fall on my face."

Cora walked in the room to say good-bye. "Hallie, you're absolutely stunning in that black dress. It looks like it was made for you."

"Thanks. I love getting all dressed up once in a while."

"You two have a lovely time. I doubt I'll be awake when you get home, so I'll just say good-night now."

"You have a nice evening too, Cora," Ben said.

Cora said nothing more, just blew a kiss from the doorway as they got into the car.

Ben had made reservations at a restaurant famous for its seafood and views of Puget Sound. They sat at a table for two by the glass wall, watching the fishing boats, seagulls and the first pink and orange tinges over the Olympic Mountains.

"I've always wanted to come here. It's so beautiful!"

"Wait till you taste the food. Would you like some wine?"

"I'd love some, thanks."

Ben ordered a bottle of wine; after the customary tasting ritual, when both glasses had been filled, Hallie raised hers. "To your new opportunity and continued success!" They sipped.

"Now I have one. To us. To the best year of my life."

Hallie gasped. A year? What was today's date? June 1st. It was exactly one year ago that she had invited Ben to karaoke night. Their first date. "I can't believe I didn't remember! It's gone by so fast, hasn't it?"

"Amazingly fast. And yet, doesn't it really seem like we've been together forever?"

Nodding, Hallie reached for Ben's hand. "I can't imagine my life without you."

"That's what I wanted to hear. Because I want to ask you something, Hallie."

Hallie would replay the next few minutes in her mind thousands of times over the years: Ben on one knee, the words of his perfect proposal, the opening of the tiny velvet box and her first glimpse of the beautiful ring. The applause of the restaurant patrons and staff when she said yes, and the feel of the ring sliding onto her finger. The deep warm colors of the evening sky reflected in Ben's eyes. His soft lips, sweet with wine as they kissed. Even as it happened, Hallie felt split in two: half in the moment, half seeing it happen, as though to someone else, drinking in the precious details. *Has anyone ever, in all of recorded history, been this happy?* she wondered. She didn't think it was possible.

Suddenly she remembered a long ago conversation with Cora. The day they met on the beach. *You just haven't found your Jack,* Cora had told her. Here it was, not quite fifteen months later, and not only had she found her 'Jack,' he had just put a ring on her finger. Cora's Jack had been gone a long time, but Cora still remembered the feelings: the euphoria, the passion, the excitement of starting a life with someone you love so completely it takes your breath away. Cora understood because she'd found Jack.

Hallie gasped. "Cora knew, didn't she? She was in on this! That's why she didn't come to dinner. Right?"

"Yeah, I had to tell her! I wanted her advice about the ring. She voted for the princess cut. Was that the right choice?"

"It's stunning. I love it! I knew there was something going on! I was worried about her! I thought she wasn't feeling well or something. How long has this been in the works?"

"Oh, a month or so I guess. You really didn't know what I was up to?"

"It was a complete surprise, I swear. The best surprise I've ever been given. I'm glad Cora knows. She must be pacing the floor at home waiting for us."

"Yeah, I think this was a tough secret for her to keep. She cried when I showed her the ring. Then she told me I'd won the love of a very special woman, and that I'd better remember that or else. She was laughing, but I know she was semi-serious. She loves you a lot."

"Well, it's mutual. I have to so much to thank her for. Living with her is really working out well, don't you think?"

"It is. I was a little apprehensive at first, but Cora worked hard to put me at ease. She makes sure we have our privacy, but she's so much fun that being with her is a real pleasure. I'm not uncomfortable there at all."

"I'm so glad. I just knew it was the right decision. I could feel it."

"That's exactly the way I felt about proposing. So tell me about your dream wedding, Hallie."

At home, Cora was waiting by the door. "I saw the headlights."

"Because you were sitting by the window?" Hallie laughed. "I knew you'd be up."

"She figured it out, Cora. She knows you were in on my little secret."

"Guilty as charged. Judging by the thousand-watt glow coming from the two of you, I think I know how it went. Congratulations! I've chilled some champagne. Could you stay up for one short toast, or are you too, uh, tired?"

"I think we could manage one toast," Ben said.

In Cora's favorite room facing her beloved Olympic Mountains, now barely visible in the moonlight, stood a tall silver champagne bucket filled with ice and a bottle of Dom Perrignon. "Cora! This must have cost a fortune!" Hallie said.

"Actually, I don't even remember what I paid for it. I've been saving it for a special occasion. This is as special as they come, wouldn't you say? I just need some help with the cork."

Ben opened and poured the amber bubbles and they stood, glasses up, facing each other. Cora cleared her throat.

"To Ben and Hallie, two extraordinary people who, extraordinarily enough, have found each other and decided to hold on tight, for better and for worse. I love you both and can wish you nothing greater than happiness equal to that my own marriage brought me. To long life and few bumps in the road before you. And most of all, to a love powerful enough to change the world."

Their glasses clinked in crystal tones, and they tasted the champagne, felt its fizz on their tongues. "My turn!" Hallie said. "To Cora and Ben, my two favorite people. I am so grateful for all your gifts, but especially for tonight. Thank you for conspiring to commit such a breathtaking act of love. And beauty! Look at this ring!"

Holding Hallie's hand up to the light, Cora watched the colors dance off the diamond's surface. "Sparkling rainbows. Isn't Mother Nature clever?"

"One more thing. To Cora, who has taught me the importance of a good toast!" Hallie exclaimed.

"Hear, hear!" Cora said, and they clinked once more.

Sipping the champagne, Hallie looked around the room and noticed some of the plants she had brought from her apartment, saw how they were thriving. She had always loved seeing new growth on her plants; it was as if they had agreed to an unspoken arrangement: she would take care of them, and they would reward her by sprouting tiny new leaves. She smiled at the thought, never fully formed until now. She nurtured the plants and they bloomed in gratitude.

Once again Cora seemed to read her thoughts. "Your plants are doing very well here, aren't they? They're thanking you for their new home."

Hallie simply nodded. For no apparent reason, she was dangerously close to tears.

Cora continued, "Cleo, too. She has so much fun roaming from room to room. I love to watch her, tail straight up like an antenna, nose wiggling into every corner, for all the world looking like the Queen of the Nile herself, exploring her vast empire. I don't know why I've gone so long without pets in this place. Cleo is an absolute joy. She, and the two of you of course, have brightened this place up, brought it back to life, really."

Hallie cleared her throat, regaining control over her voice. "Speaking of which, I want to ask you something, Cora. If it's all right with you, we'd love to get married right here. Have the wedding in the yard and the reception in the house. What do you think?"

"What do I think? I'm thrilled! I've always thought this would be the perfect place for a wedding! When? Have you set a date?"

"We're thinking next year, in July. So thirteen months from now. We want it to be small, just close friends and family."

"Whatever you want, darling girl. Oh, we're going to have a wonderful time planning this. I'd love to go along when you shop for your gown, may I?"

"Of course! I wouldn't have it any other way."

"It's such fun, Hallie. I wore a suit at my own wedding, but I've helped a few brides shop for gowns over the years: Christina, of course, and a number of friends. You stand on a pedestal, wearing one gorgeous creation after another while the salespeople and your friends 'ooh' and 'aah' over how stunning you look. In your case, they'll be completely honest.

"Well, I know you two must be tired, because I am weary to my old bones. I will see you in the morning." She kissed first Hallie, then Ben on the cheek, and walked out of the room, waving once from the doorway. Hallie smiled again at how sturdy she looked now.

Ben sat down, beckoning Hallie to join him. She did, leaning against him until he eased her head onto his lap, stroking her hair. "What is it? You seem so pensive all of a sudden."

"I was thinking about Cora and her husband, Jack. She once told me that if she had known how soon he was going to die, how long she'd be without him, she still would have made the same decisions all over again. She would change nothing about her life. Grief could have taken hold and made her angry and bitter, but instead she focuses on the time she had with him, the life they built together. She feels honored to be Jack's widow because it validates their love for each other. And she continues to live life to the fullest for the same reason. If she'd allowed anger to rule her, it would have been an expression of self-absorption, of railing at fate for not bending to her will. How arrogant that would have been! Of course she misses him, and his death was devastating at first, but losing him didn't destroy Cora's character. It might have even made her stronger, more determined to live well and become as kind and loving as she has. I admire that so much. Does any of this make sense, or am I a little too drunk for such a serious conversation?"

"Wow. I think I owe you a little more than a penny for those thoughts. But yeah, it makes sense. So are you saying that if I die before my time you'll carry on in grand style, following Cora's example?"

"Yes, and I would expect you to do the same. Never let yourself wallow in self-pity. Promise?"

"I promise. I'm sure it wouldn't be easy, but I promise."

"But you also have to promise that you'll eat fairly well and exercise, get your blood pressure checked regularly and never smoke."

"Cross my heart. Hey, I have a question for you. Will you change your name? Will you become Hallie Lawson?"

"Absolutely."

"No hesitation? You don't need to think about it?"

"No hesitation at all. Because of your family. From the first moment I walked into your parents' house, they made me feel at home. They've all gone out of their way to make me feel welcome. My parents would never be that kind to anyone before making him jump through hoops and slay a dragon or two first. I'm excited about joining your family."

"That's good, because I really want us to have the same family name. I wouldn't have had a huge problem if you'd chosen to keep your name, but I'm really glad you don't want to. Is that okay?"

"Yeah. A little tradition is just fine."

54

Hallie found herself smiling so much that her face hurt. Her days were busy, but not frantically so. She and Cora took time for their daily walks on the beach; time to relax and just be.

Working three or four days a week, along with the money she earned caring for Cora generated plenty of income, especially as Hallie was offered more and more commercials. Between her work schedule, her time with Cora and the singing and acting classes, she wasn't sure how to fit teaching in. It was a puzzle piece she turned over in her mind, wondering how it could complete a picture that already seemed finished.

Cora raised the teaching issue as they returned from their walk one day. The early summer sun had warmed them and the sand under their feet; the water reflected the sky's deep blue, and snow appeared only on the tallest peaks of the Olympics. Hallie, slightly drowsy from the sun and the mesmerizing rhythm of the waves, found her mind wandering until Cora's words began to drift into her consciousness.

"...start small, take on only one or two students, and see if you want to pursue it further. I hate to think of you missing out on something you'd like to do just because you think you're too busy."

"You're so sweet, Cora. I don't know. I'm just so happy right now, I sort of hate to change anything. Know what I mean?"

"I sure do. I see you wandering around here in a dream, grinning like a Cheshire cat. Of course there's no hurry, sweetheart. If it doesn't feel right to start something new now, then don't."

They had arrived back at the house; Cora tossed her straw hat onto the hook by the door.

The phone rang, startling both women. "Would you get that, Hallie? The bathroom beckons."

"Sure." Hallie shook her head, trying to clear the haze, and picked up the phone. "Hello?"

"Hallie?" She knew that voice; hadn't she just recently heard it somewhere? "It's Joe. We need to talk."

"Joe?" This day was feeling more surreal by the minute. "What is it?"

"It's about Kim. What did you say to her? Why won't she see me again?"

"Whoa. Hold on. I need a chair." She had answered the phone in the kitchen, the only non-cordless model in the house. Still holding the receiver, she pulled a chair over and sat. "Okay. Listen, Joe, I didn't tell Kim anything. She already knew our history, she just hadn't figured out you were the same Joe. When she did, she felt she couldn't see you anymore. Not to spare me, but for her own protection."

"Oh. So she's convinced that someday I'll have a fling with my assistant and kick her out? I suppose this is karma."

"It's not that she's sure history will repeat itself, Joe. It's that she's been burned so many times she thought it seemed well, not very wise to get involved with someone who has clearly burned someone else already. That's understandable, don't you think? But she likes you. It wasn't an easy decision for her."

"That's what she said. But Hal, can't you talk to her? You could convince her I've changed."

"I don't know that you've changed, Joe."

"Yes you do. You saw me, you know me. Please, Hallie. I never thought I'd feel this way about anyone again. Kim is really special. I think I could fall in love with her, Hallie. Won't you talk to her for me? Please?"

"Don't ask me to do this, Joe. Kim is my friend, one of my best friends. What if you get bored, or decide she isn't quite special enough? What if you do break her heart? I'd feel terrible if I was the one who convinced her to give you a chance."

"Just tell her that I care about her and that I admit I was a total louse in the old days. Tell her that I was young, that I didn't know how to handle my grief."

"She doesn't know about the baby."

"Well, tell her that I miss her, Hal. Listen: if I hadn't changed, why would it matter to me that someone I dated a few times doesn't want to see me anymore? Wouldn't I just move on to my next victim?"

"Okay, okay! I'll talk to her. But all I'm going to say is that you called to ask me this, and you seem genuinely distraught. That's all."

"Fair enough. Thank you, Hallie."

"I'm not doing it for you. Kim should have all the information before she makes a decision. And, would you do something for me, Joe?"

"Anything. Name it."

"Never ask me for another favor."

Hallie arranged to meet Kim for lunch; she hadn't had a chance to tell her about the engagement, anyway. So, she fixed something for Cora to eat and rushed to meet Kim.

She'd already been seated, but stood up as Hallie arrived. "You look gorgeous!"

Hallie beamed. "Thanks. I feel pretty good, too."

"No pain?"

"A little, but nothing I can't handle."

"I swear, if one man had to go through any of this crap we'd already have a cure for endometriosis. Menstrual cramps would have long since been eradicated. And, we'd have perfect, fool-proof birth control with no side effects except for a golden, sunless tan."

"Let me know if you find a genie in a lamp somewhere."

"Or a fairy godmother. So what's your news?"

"I have a couple of items, actually. Here's the first." Hallie held out her left hand, and the ring sparkled in the light on cue.

"HALLIE, OH MY GOD! Look at this thing! It's amazing. Okay, I want all the details. How'd he do it? Did he do the whole one knee thing?"

"He did! It was so wonderful. Best night of my life. He said that I am his family and his home. 'Marry me,' he said, 'and I will have the honor of growing old with my best friend, my partner, the only woman I could ever love.' I couldn't help it, I cried."

"No doubt! 'The only woman I could ever love?' He said that?"

Hallie nodded. "Do you think he rehearsed in front of a mirror? I can just picture him, holding up the ring and reciting those beautiful words." She sighed. "So now I'm walking around in a daze, just grinning and silly all the time."

"Well, Ben is a great guy. But he's lucky to have you, too."

"Thanks. So will you be my bridesmaid?"

"Of course! Lonnie too, right?"

"Yeah. I've already called her. She was so excited. It's going to be next summer, so we have lots of time."

"No you don't, Hallie. You have to book a place for the reception, and find a caterer, and…"

"No, we're keeping it low key. We're having it at Cora's house, and it's going to be fairly small."

"Wait a minute. Do your parents know yet? Because once they're involved, before you know it you'll be inviting Great Aunt Hildegard because she thought you were a cute baby. I'm telling you, my sister's wedding was a nightmare."

Hallie's daydream ended with a nearly audible *pop*. "No, I haven't told them. How could I not have told them? I've just been in this fog, I swear. Guess I need to call them, huh?"

"Yeah, I'd say so. Funny Cora hasn't said anything about that. She seems so organized and thorough."

"Yeah. It does seem funny, actually."

"We should look at the menus, because I unfortunately do have to go back to work this afternoon."

They ordered, and when the waiter had taken their menus away, Kim asked, "So what's item number two?"

For courage, Hallie took a deep breath, then dove in to her account of Joe's phone call. Kim sat, silent, until Hallie finished. "Well? What do you think?" she asked. "I mean, do you really believe that he's changed?"

Hallie shrugged. "I don't know. I've seen him twice in the last seven years, and just briefly both times."

"But what's your gut feeling?"

My gut feeling. Fighting her instincts had caused Hallie a lot of pain. It had been a while since she'd completely trusted herself. That was changing, and it felt wonderful. Maybe she could trust her feelings this time, too. "Okay, here it is. When Joe and I split up, part of what was so devastating was that I thought he'd been fooling me for years. I thought that he'd never been the person he seemed to be. I thought I'd never be able to trust anyone ever again, especially myself. And now Ben's come along and I've never been so completely happy. I believe that he will never become a different person and hurt me. I ask myself why it is that I believe that, and I realize it's because I think that Joe really *didn't* change that drastically. Maybe it was just that he reacted badly to a difficult situation. Now he says he's learned from that, he's grown. And if Joe really was the decent, loving, sweet person I fell in love with, I have to believe that his dive into deceit and cruelty was only temporary. Maybe he's an even better person than he was before; maybe hurting me has made him suffer more than I ever did. Maybe now he's really ready to love someone through all the ups and downs."

"That's a lot of maybes."

Hallie shrugged. "I have to believe it's possible. Now the question is, what do you think?"

"Oh, Hallie, I don't know! I've been seeing Aaron a little, and he's really sweet, too. I thought I'd put the Joe fiasco completely behind me. But I think we had something potentially big, I have to tell you. It was hard to walk away from that."

"So take a few steps in his direction. You're not serious with Aaron; date them both for a while and see what happens."

"It really won't bother you if I keep seeing Joe?"

"It really won't. I've thought about this carefully, Kim. Joe is part of my past. We got married too young and had too much pain to deal with. Our marriage didn't survive. They say the opposite of love is not hate, it's indifference. I wish him well, but I could never love him again."

"But could you socialize with him? I don't want to lose you."

"I'm sure it would be awkward at first, but over time I might be okay with it. Especially if you were happy with him."

Kim took a bite of her salad. "And what about Ben? Would he be okay with it?"

"I think so. It was a bit of a shock for him, running into Joe at the christening party, but it was clear that I have no residual feelings for him. I think Ben would be fine with it."

Kim shook her head. "Sure is a small goddamn world, isn't it? Thanks, Hallie. You really are amazing."

"You're welcome. But if Joe turns out to be a creep after all, you can't hold me responsible, right?"

"No, this is my decision, but I appreciate your honesty. I'm going to have to think about this one.

"So— when are we going shopping for my bridesmaid gown? You're not going to make me wear pouffy sleeves, are you? "

That afternoon, Hallie told Cora about her lunch with Kim. "Good for you, sugar pie," Cora said. "As Oprah says, forgiveness is something you do for yourself, not for the person who has wronged you."

"What do you mean?"

"Clearly you've forgiven Joe or you wouldn't have conveyed his message to Kim. You would have assumed he would abuse her too, that he was a monster incapable of human feelings, and you would have hung up on him without a second thought. Instead, you thought it through and gave Kim some gentle encouragement to see Joe again. You've let go of all that ugliness and accepted that Joe may be capable of great love, even if he made a terrible mistake in his past. So often, people can't forgive someone for hurting them. Of course, they'd like to be forgiven all their own nasty little trespasses, but somehow forgiveness doesn't seem to be such a virtue when they're licking their wounds from others. You're willing to grant Joe the benefit of the doubt for the sake of your friend's happiness. What a jewel you are! And I'll bet it feels better than carrying around all that anger."

Hallie nodded. "You helped. Remember the day we met? When I told you about Joe? You helped me put it all perspective. For the first time, I thought about what life might have been like for Joe since we broke up. I know how I feel when I hurt someone, even unintentionally, and you made me consider the possibility that Joe might have really suffered for hurting me. And it seems that, over time, his conscience did grow back. He has suffered, and I truly feel sad for him. I hope he can be happy. And if he and Kim are meant to be…"

"They'll figure it out. But it wouldn't have been the remotest possibility if you hadn't intervened. You did because you're a kind and loving friend. Those of us who know you are very fortunate indeed, Hallie."

"Thank you, Cora. But I'm the lucky one. I feel that this is exactly the place I am meant to be. Except for one thing."

"Your parents?"

"How do you do that? Yes, my parents. I haven't called them about the engagement yet."

"I was wondering when that would come up. As pleasant— and surprising— as that last phone call was, I know you must be a little uneasy about their reaction."

"Just a little. But, I'm not going to revert to my cowardly ways now. Full steam ahead, right?"

"Absolutely. But if you want, I'll be right here holding your hand. That's the real secret of courage: it's a lot easier to be brave when you have people backing you up."

"No doubt about that. Okay, here goes." She dialed the number and sat down. "It's ringing. Hi, Mom? Yes, it's me. How's everything? Good. Oh, that's too bad. I'm doing well, thanks, really well. In fact, I have some very exciting news for you. What? Oh, thanks, Mom!" She put her hand over the mouthpiece and whispered, "She saw my last commercial and she liked it!" To her mother, she continued, "No, that's not my good news. I'm engaged, Mom! Ben and I are getting married next year. In July. We're planning on having the wedding here, at Cora's house. It's going to be very small. Intimate. I hope you and Dad can make it. That's great, Mom, thanks. Yes, I'm very happy. Incredibly happy. He's a wonderful man, and you'll love his family, too. Thanks, Mom. Sorry about Mrs. Sugarman's diabetes. Okay, I will. I promise. I love you, too. Say hi to Dad. Bye."

"Well?"

"She said of course they're coming, that she's thrilled for me and she asked me to keep in touch with all the wedding plans. She said they'll help with the cost of the wedding. And of course, she told me Mary Sugarman was just diagnosed with diabetes."

"How tragically fitting. What else?"

"She said she loves me, Cora. She didn't balk when I said we were having the wedding here. She said almost nothing negative. How long can she possibly keep this up?"

Cora shrugged. "People change, Hallie, if they want to. Maybe your mother just needed someone to remind her how wonderful her daughter is."

"Well, I can't bring myself to believe this is a permanent change. But I'll take it as long as it lasts."

"Good girl. Now, come in here. I have something to show you."

Hallie followed Cora into the front room, where the three of them had toasted the engagement. In its center stood a black baby grand piano. "Cora! What in the world?"

"Call it an early wedding gift. Now, before you object, let me tell you my rationale."

"Rationalization, you mean?"

"Not at all. I've been listening to you lately. You think I don't hear you humming around here, but I do. I think you've been coming up with some melodies of your own. Am I right?"

"Once again you amaze me, Cora. Okay, it's true. I've had a couple of tunes running through my head. But I have my own electronic keyboard, remember?"

"Yes, I remember, but I really feel you need a decent piano to bring those songs of yours to the surface. You must nurture your talent, Hallie, pamper it. Such gifts are too easily quashed. I feel honored to help it along a little. Just promise me you'll play it."

Holding her friend close, Hallie swallowed painfully. Cora laughed. "Oh, don't go getting all weepy on me, sweetie. It's a piano. There'd be more to cry about if my money just sat useless in the bank, don't you think?"

"I love you, Cora. I want to be you when I grow up."

Now Cora looked into Hallie's face, touched her chin. "Don't you ever wish to be anyone else, Hallie Jane. You are too close to perfect as you are. Just be the best Hallie you can be, I'll be the best Cora I can be, and the world will spin as it should." She nodded toward the piano. "Go ahead, try it out! It's all tuned and ready for you."

"I think it may be the most beautiful thing I've ever seen, Cora."

"It will be much lovelier when you're sitting on its bench."

Hallie smiled, sat, and played the first melody that came to her. One of her favorites, it was a goal she'd set for herself while taking lessons: Debussy's *Clair de Lune*. She floated through it, slow and hesitant, the beauty of the notes sending shivers down her spine like moonlight itself, cool, brilliant, luminous.

Cora shone too, watching and listening.

Hallie basked.

55

The first signs were easy to dismiss; after all, everyone misplaces the occasional item, forgets an appointment now and then. It was unusual for Cora, but she *had* just turned eighty-one. She was allowed to forget things now and then, she said. But now and then became fairly often; finally, she was not simply forgetting where her sweater was, she was forgetting why she needed one.

Then she began to repeat herself; in a single conversation she would tell the same story, give the same information, twice. At first she would catch herself: "Oh, did I already tell you that?" Weeks later, she wouldn't catch herself at all. Hallie found herself counting: how many minutes before Cora would repeat herself? How many times in a single day? In an hour?

When Hallie found the milk carton in the stove one day, she tried to laugh it off; it should have been funny, a comical demonstration of stress or distraction. But Cora was not worried or preoccupied, except by her symptoms themselves. The truth began to permeate Hallie's very skin: something was horribly wrong.

Perhaps Cora had suffered another stroke, this time unnoticed. That could happen, Hallie knew, and with its possibility of improvement a stroke seemed to be one of the more hopeful explanations.

What frightened Hallie most now was *Cora's* fear, settling in somewhere behind her eyes, replacing their sparkle, their smile that had seemed so indelible just weeks before.

Yes. Something was wrong. Both women knew it, saw it in each other's faces before they finally spoke the words out loud. It was time for Cora to see a doctor.

Tests eliminated various possibilities; Cora had not had another stroke. There had been no heart attack; she was not dehydrated or suffering from potassium deprivation. Finally, there was little doubt; this was the worst-case scenario. This was Alzheimer's disease.

"The progression of Alzheimer's disease," the doctor explained rather robotically, "resembles a backward movement toward childhood, and finally infancy. Recent memories are erased first, and gradually those more deeply imbedded become fuzzy before they too fade away. Physical skills we have had the longest leave us last, including walking, speaking, even swallowing. In the final stages we return to our earliest states of helplessness, requiring complete physical care and supervision. Any questions?"

As Cora, Ben and Hallie walked away from the clinic toward Ben's car, no one spoke. Behind the wheel, Ben sat for a moment before he turned the key in the ignition. Beside him sat Cora, hands in her lap, eyes fixed toward the window. In the back, Hallie's eyes were wide, eyebrows raised, her mouth open as though she meant to object, to argue against this declaration so effectively that she would win and it would no longer be true.

They sat, each alone with their thoughts, their pain quiet for now.

At home, Cora squeezed Hallie's hand, patted Ben's arm and walked toward the piano room, as they now called it. "Cora, would you like some tea?" Hallie called after her. Her voice sounded hollow.

"No, thank you, dear. I'd just like a few moments to myself if that's all right."

Hallie watched Cora walk slowly away. At the archway, she swayed slightly and held onto the wall for a few seconds before continuing on.

Covering her mouth with one hand as though afraid to speak, Hallie reached for Ben with the other. His arms surrounded her, warm and solid, as if the world was a safe place. She buried her face against his chest and they rocked. Hallie's throat ached; she wanted to cry, but even more she wanted to scream, throw things, break windows. Howl at the moon. Ask the too obvious questions: *Why Cora? Why not some evil, angry person? What kind of God would allow this abomination?* But she just rocked, clinging to Ben, her thoughts ebbing to one simple word: *no, no, no.*

Finally Ben led her to the couch in the room Cora called the Formal Living Room, meaning the room they rarely used. They sat and waited. Hallie glanced at her watch: 3:20. It seemed so much later. "I'm so glad you came with us," she said.

"I wanted to go. Are you all right, Hallie?"

"I guess I should think about what to make for dinner."

"It can wait. Relax for a while."

"Maybe I should check on her? See if she'd like some tea now?"

"Hallie, she'll come out when she's ready."

"But maybe she needs me and she's too proud to ask."

In the piano room, Cora sat beside the window. Hallie was speaking in low tones, but Cora still heard her—*nothing wrong with my ears,* she thought—and smiled. She felt a pang of sorrow for all the people this awful disease would affect: all the people who loved her and would now have to care for her. Cora had seen this disease in action; client after client had contracted it themselves, and many more were dealing with an afflicted parent. And as a graduate student long ago, Cora had worked in a nursing home, had changed adult diapers and fed patients who could no longer lift a spoon to their own mouths.

Looking out at the water, she shuddered. In the other room, Ben was trying to reassure Hallie once again, trying to persuade her not to intrude on Cora's moment of privacy. He was a good man, Cora knew. Solid. Secure in his love for Hallie, committed to their life together. Cora knew their marriage would be a happy one, she just knew it in her bones. Hallie would be all right.

Christina, too, would be fine. She had a good life, a wonderful family. It wouldn't be long before her daughters themselves would marry and have children. Christina and Kurt would be wonderful grandparents; they would enjoy that role.

Barry had also carved out a life he enjoyed. If, in Cora's eyes it was a little lopsided—too much career, not enough personal fulfillment—well, it had been his choice to make, hadn't it? He loved New York, loved its hustle bustle excitement, its cutting edge atmosphere, its prideful air.

The sting of this hideous diagnosis eased a bit when Cora reminded herself that her job on this planet was pretty much done. She had lived her fair share of life, had lived it well.

Okay, then, old girl, you have exactly two minutes to feel sorry for yourself. And so she allowed all the predictable thoughts to invade her mind: *Why me? Why this cruel disease? Why not something quick, something that won't rob me so violently? Go ahead and take my life, but not my mind, my essence, my precious memories.*

And the memories came: seeing Jack for the first time, their first dance, first kiss, first clumsy groping in the dark. His proposal, here in this house. Having their babies, and all the millions of moments that made up their everyday lives. Saying good-bye as each child moved out, trying to hold back the tears but sobbing anyway, clinging to them as if she could make time stand still.

Cora remembered it all. She could even remember the last day that Jack looked and seemed completely healthy and robust, while inside his body, his clogged veins had been silently conspiring against him.

Are you out there, Jack? Cora wondered. *Are you waiting for me? Have you missed me all this time I've been missing you?* She sighed.

A gust of wind blew past, shaking the flowers in the yard. *Seasons, coming and going, that's all this is.*

Dying was not the issue at all, she decided. Of course not. She had never been one to hang on to life at all costs. No, it was about being fully alive as long as she was breathing. And most of all, it was about becoming helpless and forcing her loved ones into the terrible position of caring for an Alzheimer's patient. Feeding, dressing, changing diapers, answering endless questions and listening to the same stories countless times. Watching her slowly slipping away. Cora imagined their pained faces when she no longer remembered them. When she would be gone for good. That was what was so hard to bear: knowing that even when *she* became oblivious to her plight, her family would be continually traumatized by her condition. Some or all of her children (Hallie included) would be sacrificing their own lives until the disease finally, mercifully, set Cora's soul free.

She cried now, softly, hoping Hallie and Ben would not hear. It was all so unfair. The only thing that had ever worried Cora about growing older was the possibility of becoming a burden. Now that was the future to which she'd been sentenced. She buried her face in her hands.

And then a thought occurred to her, and she looked up again, through the window. The solution was simple, really. It was so obvious, and now Cora inwardly scolded herself for wasting one moment on tears and self-pity. Mother Nature had goofed, that was all, but She didn't have to have the last word. Cora still had full control of her destiny.

She was still wearing her jacket, and now she pulled a handkerchief out of her pocket. It was an old one, passed down from Cora's mother, a red embroidered 'D' for Duprés still there, in the corner. Normally Cora did not use any of her old linen handkerchiefs, but today, knowing that bad news was coming her way, she had wanted to feel it in her hand. Now she dabbed at her eyes with the soft fabric and tucked it back in her pocket. Then she stood, took a deep breath and went back into the living room.

She stood in the archway for a moment, arms folded in front of her, watching Hallie. "Sorry to worry you so, my love."

Cora walked across the carpet to a chair facing them. "All right. I've had some time to wallow in self-pity. Did me quite a lot of good, I must say. Tea is a lovely idea, sweetie pie, but I think instead I'd like something a little stronger. It's five o'clock somewhere, so they say. Would you care to join me?"

"Absolutely," Hallie said. "Would you like some mulled wine? It's so chilly today."

"Too much work. No, I think brandy is in order. Ben, would you do the honors? Brandy all around."

"Of course. Liquor cabinet in the dining room?"

"Yes. I'm afraid you'll have to rinse out the snifters. They're quite dusty."

Cora watched Ben turn the corner, and joined Hallie on the couch. She held Hallie's hand in both of her own. "Hallie, my darling girl, I want you to know right now that I love you very much. From the moment I scared you out of your wits that day on the beach, I've felt as if I've known you all your life. I wanted to draw you into my world, hold you there and protect you. I wanted to adopt you, I suppose, make you part of my family. And I've done it, haven't I? My biggest accomplishment in a very long time. Along the way, we became fast friends, didn't we?"

"Best friends, Cora. The best."

"Yes. Best friends. I wanted to be your benefactor, of sorts, and I suppose I am. But I never would have predicted how much you would do for me. There was that business with Tom, of course, and all your devotion when I had the stroke, but there was so much more. Because of you, Marion and I grew closer. It's true. Our closest moments ever all happened in the last few months of her life, and all because of opportunities you created. Your presence knocked down a wall in her somehow, opened her up in brand new ways. I've always prided myself on my ability to bring out the best in people, but I never quite had that gift with Marion. You did, and not because you were working at it, it just happened because you were there. Marion didn't even realize it. Neither did you, judging by the look on your face. It wasn't a dramatic transformation, no, it was subtle and gradual. But it happened. And I'm so grateful.

"But risking your relationship with Ben when you volunteered to move in here with me? Well, I finally understood then that you truly are part of my family. You know the difference between friends and family? Commitment. Permanence. Being related has nothing to do with it whatsoever."

"Speaking of family, Cora, do you think we should call Christina and Barry?"

"I'm getting to that, sugar pie. You may think this meandering is leading nowhere, but I'm going somewhere, I promise. Ah, here's the lovely lad now."

Ben leaned toward them, holding out a tray. They each took a snifter. Cora breathed in the syrupy fumes, eyes closed, smile wide. When Ben was seated— in the chair Cora had vacated— with a snifter of his own, Cora lifted hers high. "To life and its sweet pleasures," she nearly shouted, and sipped the brandy. "Delicious, isn't it?

"Now, onto important business. Both of you listen carefully, because I'm not going to say this again. Okay." She put her glass down on the coffee table, then looked up again, sighing loudly. "I can probably count on having a pretty good year or so. I'll start forgetting more, but I won't be completely incapacitated. I'll still know who I am, who you are, I'll recognize my family members and all that jazz. Of course I could still have many good years, but counting on one seems safe enough, almost a sure thing. This disease can pick up the pace as it sees fit.

"Here's the thing: I'd like to be at your wedding—I mean really be there—so I'm asking you to move it up a bit. How about this fall? I know it's a lot to ask, but I'm asking anyway. September is usually a lovely month, but if the weather is lousy we can have the ceremony inside. I have connections, so four months to prepare will be no problem at all; plus, it will give me— all of us— something wonderful to focus on. What do you say?"

Ben glanced at Hallie, then grinned. "The sooner the better, as far as I'm concerned, Cora. I don't want to give her time to change her mind."

"I want to see you dancing at my wedding, Cora. I think September sounds perfect. As long as you promise to help me find a gown and plan everything."

"I will be your personal wedding coordinator, sugar. So— we'll have a fabulous wedding in four months and I'll still be able to toast the happy couple. Agreed?"

"Absolutely!" Hallie said, raising her glass.

"First, though, you're right Hallie. I do need to share the bad news with my kids. Christina is an emotional creature like her mother, and she'll insist on racing up here. She'll talk to the doctor so she can hear his words directly. Possibly, she'll want a second opinion. Once she accepts the facts, she'll want to make decisions. I may need your help convincing her to take things as they come. There's no need to do anything drastic, not yet. And I have to be here to help with the wedding!"

"I'll talk to her if you want me to," Hallie said.

"Barry, on the other hand, won't be a problem; he'll be very calm and accepting, at least in front of me. He'll offer his help whenever and wherever it may be needed. He'll leave all the decision making to Christina and me."

Cora sat back, picked up her snifter, drained it, winked at Ben and squeezed Hallie's hand once more. "But you know what? I'm not going to make those phone calls until tomorrow. Let's just have a nice quiet evening, the three of us, what do you say? Hallie, I don't want you cooking tonight, so how about if we send Ben down the street to pick up some pizza? Yes, pizza sounds delicious. And I'll open one of those lovely Tuscan wines I've been saving for God knows what occasion. And," she said, holding Hallie's face in both hands, "there will be no more tears tonight. Promise me. This night is for the living, particularly those who live well! You go ahead, Ben. Get us a couple of big, cheesy, greasy, wonderful pizzas. Any kind you want, just no anchovies. I'll take care of our girl."

Hallie sighed heavily. "I only cried a little bit. I don't know if I'm finished yet."

"That's all right, sugar pie. You can cry a little more. Just not tonight. Tonight we celebrate life and your upcoming wedding. Happy thoughts, okay?" Cora brushed Hallie's hair away from her eyes.

"I can't believe you're comforting me. Well, to hell with that. Where's the wine?" Her voice broke slightly, but she would make— and keep— that promise to Cora. There would be no more tears tonight.

56

Cora's children responded to the news exactly as she'd predicted. Barry simply said, "Oh, Mom, no. Are you sure?"

"Yes, son."

"Damn. Okay, listen. I know this thing can progress pretty slowly. Just let me know what I can do. Call anytime, night or day. I don't think we need to make any changes yet, do you?"

"No, dear. Everything's under control."

"Okay. I promise I'll come out for a visit soon. Within a month, unless you want me to come sooner."

"A month will be fine. I'll look forward to seeing you then. Oh, and Barry? Hallie and Ben are getting married in September, here at the house. We'd love you to be here for it."

"Wouldn't miss it. Give them both my congratulations. I love you, Mom."

"I know, son. I love you, too. Always."

"I'll call soon."

But Christina listened to her mother's words and began to deny the truth even as a shiver traveled up her spine. Immediately, her mind went to another moment it could not comprehend, when she'd leaned against the wall in the nursing home after seeing her mother cry. How foreign Cora's frailty had seemed then, how wrong. Silently, unspoken, the words formed now: *That was just a preview. Here comes the main event.* But she said, "Have you gotten a second opinion, Mom? A number of other conditions can look like Alzheimer's. What tests did they run? You know what, I'm going to come up and we'll figure this out together. Don't panic. I'll call as soon as I know when I'll be arriving."

"Thank you, sweetheart. I look forward to seeing you."

And so Christina swooped in to try to save the day again, going numbly through the motions until she arrived at the inescapable, inevitable conclusion: her mother was dying.

"I know it's a shock, my sweet girl, but it shouldn't be, really. I'm eighty-one years old. Did you really think I'd live forever?"

"Yes! I did! And you've certainly never done anything to alter that perception, you know. You're larger than life! More powerful than death! Indestructible!"

"Not quite, it would seem."

"Why didn't you tell me you were human, Mama?" They were sitting in the piano room with Hallie. Late morning sunlight whispered promises of summer; beams like spotlights revealed a thick coating of dust on the piano.

"Go ahead, Chrissy. Cry all your tears now so that we can have a lovely visit before you go home."

"Home? No, we have to figure this out. You should come home with me, live with us. This is too much to ask of Hallie, and I won't put you in a nursing home, not permanently."

"Sweetheart, I'm not going anywhere, at least not right now. We don't have to make any decisions yet. The one good thing about this disease is that we have a little time before things get really rough. We'll know when it's time to make changes. For now, everything's under control, I promise you."

"I suppose you're right. But I want you to call me every day. I want to know about all your symptoms, every single change. And if you don't see them, then Hallie needs to call me. I'm going to come up once a month and make sure you're okay. No reflection on you, Hallie; I just have to see for myself. Plus I want to spend time with you. I'll bring the girls as often as possible."

"Sounds like we have a plan. Barry says he's coming out in a month. Maybe you can come at the same time. I'd like that. Now, what do you say we have a nice lunch and maybe see a movie? Just the three of us girls?"

"Why don't you two go and spend some time alone together? I'll make a nice dinner for all of us and be here to greet Ben when he gets home," Hallie said.

"Are you sure? We could go out for dinner."

"Yes, Hallie, please come with us," Christina said.

"No, really. I think I'd enjoy a little time alone. And I haven't cooked in a month of Sundays. It'll be fun. You two go ahead."

Alone. How long had it been? Weeks, Hallie was sure, since she'd had the house all to herself; Cora hadn't gone out with other friends for some time. And it had been a week since Hallie had even driven alone, a week since they'd gotten the news.

Some mornings, in the first moments of consciousness, Hallie had been utterly convinced that it had all been an ugly dream. Giddy relief had made her almost dizzy before the inevitable shift; the realization that landed on her, heavy and cold. But she'd held her emotions in check, smiled and laughed with Cora as always.

Cora had cried when she'd gone off by herself to the piano room the day they'd gotten the diagnosis; Hallie had seen how red her eyes were when she returned. But that was the only time, and Cora had been completely upbeat since then. Even when she thought no one was watching, Cora had remained calm; she even looked *happy*.

Now, Hallie waved good-bye, watching Cora leave with Christina. When the car had disappeared around the corner, she closed and locked the door, raced upstairs and ran water in the bathtub.

Immersed in the warm water, she closed her eyes and tried to quiet her mind.

She did not want to see Cora disappear, bit by bit, before her very eyes. Hallie's heart ached at the thought of a vacant stare from the eyes that now held so much spark. Yet Cora seemed so peaceful about it, so serene. Something seemed wrong about that, especially with this particular diagnosis. This was Cora's worst nightmare: dying slowly from a disease that imposed helplessness on its victim. That robbed her of her intellect. She may have accepted that her death was drawing near, but Alzheimer's? Hallie couldn't imagine Cora being at peace with that.

On the other hand, Hallie's mind argued, *Cora knows that there are many people who love her, people who could share the responsibility of caring for her as the need arises. Maybe she's accepted her decline as inevitable, and comforts herself with the thought that the burden won't fall on any one person.*

Maybe. Hallie tried to mold the idea into conviction, tried to make it fit. But somehow, a piece or two of the puzzle still seemed to be missing.

Let it go, she thought. *Maybe this is just one phase of Cora's grieving process.* Hallie knew that not everyone experienced those phases at the same time, in the same order, or in the same way. Perhaps Cora had arrived at acceptance too soon, and eventually would backtrack to another stage.

Stop borrowing trouble. Just be there if she needs you.

Hallie took a deep breath and slid down, allowing the warm water to cover her completely.

57

The day Christina flew home, Hallie and Cora went to lunch directly from the airport.

When their orders had been taken, Hallie cleared her throat. "Finally!" Cora said.

"What?"

"I was wondering if you were ever going to tell me whatever it is you want to tell me."

Hallie smiled. "Well, it's difficult."

Cora smiled. "Most worthwhile things are. What is it sweetheart?"

"It's just that, with everything you have to deal with, I was wondering if... well, if it might be a bad idea... I just don't want..."

"Let me guess. You're wondering if I'm up to the task of planning your wedding. You don't want me to take on such a daunting task if it will be too hard for me or—horror of horrors—even make me worse. You're guilting yourself into a little tizzy, aren't you, dear?" Cora laughed. "Well, let me assure you that I am perfectly capable of planning the best little wedding you've ever seen. I've already bought some notebooks so that I can keep track of every single detail. Christina will come up a few days early and help with the last minute stuff, and I have a lot of friends who probably feel they owe me a few favors. And, it's been scientifically proven that symptoms of Alzheimer's disease can be postponed or temporarily improved by putting your brain to work. Using it puts off losing it, you see. I want to do this for you, Hallie. And if I start having problems, I'll ask for help, I promise."

Their food had appeared, and Cora picked up her fork now. "Eat, Hallie, before it gets cold." She took a bite of her salmon and chewed, eyes closed. "Mmm, this is wonderful. I just love living where salmon is so fresh, don't you sweetie?"

"You're really sure that you want to take all this on?"

"Of course! Darling girl, it's going to be fun. I'll make it perfect for you, I promise."

Hallie's throat hurt; her eyes filled instantly. She stared at the window, trying in vain to hide her tears from Cora.

"Hallie?" Cora said gently. "Don't cry, my darling girl. I'm still here. You can cry for me when I'm gone. But only a little. Hallie, look at me. We're going to have a great time planning your wedding. It's something I'm excited about, honestly. It's not a burden, not in the least little bit. Are you hearing me?"

Hallie nodded, but couldn't seem to bring herself to look at Cora.

But Cora grinned, lifting Hallie's chin with one finger. "Hey, what do you say we go shopping? You could try on wedding gowns. We could call Lonnie and have her join us. What do you think?"

Every ounce of energy seemed to have evaporated from Hallie's body. Her limbs felt heavy, too heavy to move. Her temples throbbed. Cora was sick, mortally wounded by an unlucky roll of the cosmic dice. And yet here she was, effervescent as ever, wanting only to give and do more for Hallie. She had already done more for her than anyone, ever. What if the stress of being Hallie's wedding planner actually sped up the disease's progression? What if her condition deteriorated so fast that Cora wouldn't even be able to finish what she had begun?

What if she ended up not remembering the bride and groom at all?

And now she wanted to go shopping for wedding gowns? Nothing at this moment could seem more foreign to Hallie. "I don't think so, Cora. Thanks. I just— I think I just need some time..."

"Bullshit!"

"What?"

"You heard me. Stop wallowing! Damn it, Hallie. I'm not going to die tomorrow, or next week or next month. I'm here, right now, today, with you. I could be with either of my kids, or both of them if I crooked my little finger in the right direction. But I'm here with you, my dearest friend, to plan your wedding during the next few months of my life, and I want it to be a joyful time. So snap out of this little funk of yours and be a grown-up. You're getting married in four months, and I'm planning on being there to see it. Aren't we lucky?"

Like a cool breeze on a hot day, Cora's blast revived Hallie; her mind, sluggish with the effort of thinking sad thoughts, cleared instantly. *Okay. I don't have much time left with Cora. Is this how I want to spend it?*

She shook her head and dried her eyes with a paper napkin. "You're right. I'm sorry. This is over, I promise you. Let's call Lonnie and get going on these wedding plans. But first, do you want to share some dessert? I could use something really fattening."

Cora laughed loudly, her anger gone as quickly as it had appeared. "That's my girl! Something chocolatey and completely decadent?"

"I'd love to join you, but I'd have to bring the baby," Lonnie said. "She's been in a pretty good mood today, so I don't think she'd be much trouble. It's just that if she gets fussy I'll have to go for a walk with her, or even leave if she really starts screaming."

"That's fine! We'd love to see Lily. We're starting at Bridal Beauty. Do you need directions?"

"Nope, I've been there. I can be there in forty-five minutes, is that okay?"

"Perfect. See you then." Hallie pushed the end button on her cell phone.

"She's bringing Lily?" Cora asked. "Wonderful! Hallie, you still look a little sad for my liking, but trust me: trying on wedding gowns will lift your spirits. Euphoria will just sweep over you no matter how hard you fight it. Now I have a call to make. Could I borrow your phone?"

Hallie gave her the phone and watched as Cora walked away, turning back once, motioning with one hand for Hallie to stay behind. Moments later, Cora walked briskly toward her. A shiver crept up Hallie's spine, seeing Cora walk so solidly without even a cane. Her hard work in physical therapy and her daily walks had paid off, and for what? The irony hit Hallie in a sweeping wave, and she closed her eyes tight against the tears that threatened to surface yet again.

When she opened them, Cora was holding out the phone. Hallie swallowed hard and smiled. "What are you up to, Cora?"

"You'll see." Cora nearly sang the words.

Lonnie and Lily arrived at the bridal boutique as Cora and Hallie were getting out of the car. The women hugged and passed the baby around for kisses and smells. "She's so beautiful, Lonnie," Hallie said. "Her eyes are turning green, aren't they?"

"Yeah, they've gotten a little paler, and I see a green tint. But Steve thinks they're going to be light brown like his. We'll see."

Cora, holding Lily, said, "Let's get this show on the road, shall we ladies?" and headed toward the store's entrance.

Lonnie grabbed Hallie's sleeve and pulled her closer. "Are you okay?" she whispered.

"Damn, does it show? I'm trying to be cheerful."

"That's what shows. What's going on? Trouble with Ben?"

"No. Everything's great with him, thank God. It's a long story, and I can't really talk about it right now," she said, nodding toward Cora.

"Well, today's a happy day, right? So it's my solemn duty as Maid of Honor to make sure you have fun."

"Okay, okay. I'm trying. By the way, you're the Matron of Honor. You're married."

"What? Oh, my God, you're right. I'm married. I'm a matron. I've never been a matron before. I'm no longer a beautiful young maid, I'm an old hag of a matron."

"Hey, if you're a hag, sign me up."

"That's the whole idea. 'Come into my parlor,' said the matron to the bride. You too can be a hag! It all starts with a ring and a dress."

Cora was already in the store, and when Hallie and Lonnie burst through the door laughing, she turned toward them and smiled, still jostling Lily. "These are my friends Lonnie, who is the mother of this adorable baby, and Hallie, the bride-to-be. This," she said, nodding toward the woman behind the counter, "is my old friend Maureen and this is her store."

"Lonnie, how are you? So nice to meet you, Hallie. I've been expecting you. Cora was right, you're going to make a beautiful bride. I've taken the liberty of putting a few gowns in the fitting room for you to get started with, so let me show you the way."

"Normally, you see, an appointment is absolutely necessary here and generally customers are given only one hour at a time. Maureen has graciously agreed to clear her schedule for the entire afternoon, so we have the place all to ourselves. You can try on as many gowns as you like, Hallie. Plus, I've arranged for a few treats to make it really special," Cora said.

"Cora, you are amazing. Thank you." Hallie kissed her friend's cheek, so soft and warm.

They walked through a door— and into a fairy tale. The room was large and round. To their right as they entered were three huge dressing rooms, two with closed doors and one standing open, waiting for Hallie. Two burgundy overstuffed chairs stood at the edge of the room to their left, opposite three carpeted pedestals, each surrounded by three way mirrors. Windows took over where the mirrors ended, and behind the spectator seats were French doors leading to a small terrace. Between the chairs was a small table, upon which had been placed a silver tea service, a champagne bucket filled with ice and an open bottle of Veuve Cliquot, three flutes, strawberries and a vase full of lavender roses.

"Cora, how…?"

"You thought this was a spur of the moment decision, didn't you? Chrissy and I planned this whole thing, and I fully intended on bringing you here today. Maureen was just waiting for my call."

"You're so sneaky!"

"But that's why you love me, am I right?"

Hallie's chin trembled, just slightly, as the two women embraced.

Cora hugged her tight, then pulled back and held her at arm's length. "Now, I'll pour the bubbly while you go try on your first gown."

On her way to the dressing room, Hallie heard Cora behind her, complimenting Maureen on the room. "Everything is just perfect, dear. Thank you so much."

"My pleasure, Cora. Lonnie, I didn't know you knew Cora," Maureen said.

Hallie turned. "You two know each other?"

"Lonnie's a regular."

"How can you be a regular at a bridal store?"

Lonnie's face flushed. "Well…"

"Yes, and imagine my surprise to see her today, married and with a baby," Maureen said.

"Yeah, sorry about that, Maureen. I eloped."

"Well, that is a surprise. And your gown?"

"Rented."

"Really."

"Yep. We went to Vegas. I know, it's so tacky, isn't it? But getting married was a big step for me, and it just seemed right at the time."

"Well, maybe you'll renew your vows sometime and wear one of the gowns you've tried on here. There were many that looked so beautiful on you. Seems such a shame."

"We've actually talked about having another wedding in a year or so. I swear I'll come see you then."

"I'll look forward to it. Hallie, I think you'll find everything you need in there. When you run out of gowns, call me and I'll bring in the next load."

"Thank you, Maureen," Hallie called as Maureen briskly left the room. "Lonnie?"

"Okay, I have a guilty pleasure. A couple of years ago I came here with a friend who was getting married. I watched her try on dresses until I couldn't stand it anymore, and I finally asked if I could try one on too. Just for fun. And when I stood up there and twirled that skirt, suddenly I was a princess. It was magic! So, sometimes when I feel sad or angry or disappointed, I sneak away and try on wedding gowns. Just wait, Hallie, when you're standing on a pedestal in one of those gorgeous gowns, you'll understand. You feel so beautiful, so perfect. So, I don't know… powerful. You'll really march out of here a whole new person."

"Wow. This sounds like a serious addiction, Lonnie. No wonder poor Maureen was so confused."

"Oh, I don't just come here. I've been to stores all over the Seattle area, from here to Kent. But this is the best, really," Lonnie said loudly. "So go put one on and you'll understand."

"But you didn't even want to get married!"

"Just get in there!"

Inside the dressing room, Hallie looked around. A huge mirror filled one wall. Three pairs of beaded white shoes were lined up on the floor against it. On the other walls were hooks, placed so high that Hallie had to stand on her toes to reach them; one hanger on each hook held a huge gown in a zippered, clear plastic bag. On a small table was a white satin bustier.

Hallie hadn't even begun to consider what kind of gown she wanted: tank style, mermaid, strapless, long sleeves, huge train or no train, ornate or simple? She had no idea, so she wondered how Maureen had picked out these particular dresses. But even as the question was forming, she realized that it was Cora who had chosen these gowns, now hanging above her head.

She reached up and unzipped one of the plastic bags, then tucked the hanger through the opening. Dropping the bag to the floor, she hung the dress back up and stared at it. The fabric was so smooth, and it shimmered when it moved in the light. It had a low scoop neck and spaghetti straps, and just a little beading around the waist. The train was drawn up behind it, hung by its own little strap. This was the most beautiful gown she'd ever seen, and she was about to put it on. Suddenly she couldn't wait. She shrugged off her clothes and tossed them in a corner.

She slipped the dress over her head, made adjustments and reached back for the zipper. She had pulled it about halfway up when Lonnie called, "Need any help?"

"Yeah!"

Lonnie dashed across the room. Opening the dressing room door, Hallie grinned. She turned around, and Lonnie zipped her up. "Having fun?" Lonnie asked.

"God, yeah. Look at this dress!"

"It's a little big. Here." Lonnie picked up a small clip from a pile on the floor. Hallie hadn't even noticed them. "That's what these are for." Lonnie pulled the dress tight in the back, and clipped the extra material in place. "Now come on out here so we can all look at you!"

Lonnie helped put shoes on her feet, then led Hallie out. Stepping onto the center pedestal, Hallie faced the mirrors, and Lonnie spread the train out behind her.

"Oh, Hallie. Look at you! Maureen, come in here! Is this not the loveliest bride you've ever seen?"

Maureen appeared in the doorway and smiled. "Absolutely. Would you like to try on a veil?"

"Please!" Hallie stood, turning slightly from one side to another, looking at every angle offered by the mirrors. "Is this really how I look?"

"Mm-hmm. Stunning, aren't you?" Cora said, on her feet now and walking toward the pedestal. "Here, doll. Have some champagne."

Hallie took the glass and clinked it with Cora's. "Want some, Lonnie?"

"No, thanks. I'm still nursing. Cora, I want to ask you something. I am so exhausted. I thought pregnancy was tough! People tell me motherhood will get easier as Lily gets older. Will it?"

Cora's brow furrowed. "I don't think it gets easier. I think all those people are lying to you because they don't want you to despair so early in the game."

"What?"

"Really! In my opinion it doesn't get easier until they are living on their own with a good, steady income. That's when you get to relax."

"Oh my God. See, this is what I suspected all along. Tell me more," Lonnie said.

"It gets easier in some ways— no more late night feedings, no more sore nipples, no more milk leaking onto your favorite blouse. But then they're toddlers, getting into everything. You have to watch them constantly because they're so quick. They want to touch and taste everything, and it's a dangerous world out there. Then they figure out that they're actually little people, separate from you, and damned if they're going to do something just because you want them to! They develop opinions that make sense to no one but them, and defend them with unbending stubbornness. They start school, and they have to learn how to get along with other kids, other adults. Sometimes they think that Mom and Dad know nothing and their teachers or classmates know everything. They underachieve, they overachieve. They get sick. They become teenagers and stay out late. They get angry when you object to their behavior, but they come around, apologize and accept a warm hug from Mom, which feels much better than they would ever admit.

"And then they graduate from college and move out, start a career, fall in love. You wander through the house that suddenly feels hollow and huge and wonder where the years disappeared. You remember the first time your baby focused on a flying bird, the way her eyes lit up with an amazement so pure it made you cry. You remember her first laugh, her first 'I love you, Mommy.' And none of that other stuff, the hard stuff, matters one iota. You just want every minute of that time back, so you can do it all over again."

Lonnie smiled and looked down at Lily, sleeping now in her car seat. "Thanks, Cora."

Maureen returned with three veils for Hallie to compare. She chose one, and Maureen helped put it in place. "Of course you'll choose the headpiece for the veil— this one just has the comb to hold it on— but it will give you an idea of how you'll look."

"It looks great, Hal, but this is just the first gown. Go try on another one!" Lonnie said.

Hours sped by; when Lonnie fed the baby, Cora and Maureen helped Hallie dress and undress. As Hallie stepped onto the pedestal for the tenth time, they were all exhausted. But when Cora spread the train out behind her and Maureen slipped the veil back in place, Hallie caught her breath. This was it! This was her wedding gown.

"It's Italian silk. Don't you love the way it catches the light?" Maureen murmured.

"It's exquisite," Cora agreed. "What do you think, Hallie?"

"Perfect. It's just perfect." Hallie stared at the mirror, taking in every detail. The style was simple: spaghetti straps and another low scoop neck like the first gown she'd tried on, but this one flowed in a slightly-flared A line. A few crystal beads adorned the neckline and the hem, and the train barely brushed the ground. The back plunged very low, into a slightly rounded V.

"You don't have to make a decision today, you know. We can keep looking."

"This is my dress, Cora."

"Well it certainly looks like it was made for you. It doesn't even need much altering."

"Just a little tuck at the waist, it looks like," Maureen said. "If you're sure, I'll get some pins and mark it now."

"I'm sure. Oh, wait! I haven't even looked at the price."

"This is on me, Hallie. Price is not a factor," Cora said. "No objections, please. I would be hurt and offended if you turned me down."

"But…"

"No buts. Just say, 'Thank you, Cora, you're a doll.'"

"Thank you, Cora. You're a stubborn old doll."

"Close enough. Go ahead, Maureen, get the pins."

Lonnie said good-bye and took Lily home; shortly afterward Hallie was back to reality in her blue jeans and t-shirt. On the way home, she thanked Cora again. "You have no idea how much this means to me."

"Actually, I think I have an inkling. Wasn't it a wonderful afternoon? Your friend's baby is a beauty. What was her name again?"

"Lily?"

"Lily. And she's in great shape for someone who just had a baby."

Hallie swallowed hard. "No, it's Lonnie who had the baby. Lily is the baby's name."

Cora nodded. "Of course. I knew that. I'm just tired, that's all. Don't look so worried, damn you. I'm just tired."

Forcing herself to smile, Hallie nodded. "I know. I'm tired too. But happy. I felt like a bride today."

"Looked like one, too, sweetie pie. I can't wait to see Ben's face when you walk down the aisle in that gown. He's going to fall in love all over again. We all will, for that matter. That's a moment to look forward to." Cora sighed heavily, but the smile never left her face.

58

Cora was late getting up. It was a rare occurrence, but now she had slept so long that Hallie was beginning to worry. The tea she had made was lukewarm now, so Hallie poured it out and put the kettle on for a fresh pot. She was just about to go knock on Cora's door when the lady appeared at last.

"Sorry to keep you waiting so long, sweetheart," she said. "I had a rough night."

"Rough how?"

"I just couldn't get to sleep. It happens once in a while, when my arthritis kicks in—and this cool wet weather doesn't help with that—or when my mind is a little too busy. I usually take a sleeping pill when it's a problem, but I ran out a while ago and haven't been back to the doctor to get more. I'd like to make an appointment and have you take me as soon as possible."

"You take sleeping pills?"

"Don't look so shocked! Only once in a great while, and only a small dosage. I simply can't function without my eight hours."

"I understand. But I didn't know you had that much trouble sleeping."

"Well, I usually don't."

"You just take so little medication. This is a surprise to me, that's all."

"Hallie, it's perfectly fine that you don't know every single thing about me, isn't it?"

"I suppose so. I'll call the doctor's office now, while the tea is steeping."

"Thank you, dear."

Hallie was able to get an appointment for Cora that afternoon. Hallie had taken a book along to read while she waited for Cora in the doctor's waiting room. She had never brought Cora here before, to her family doctor, and Hallie had not been at all surprised to see the receptionists greet Cora like a long lost family member.

Now that Cora had been taken back to the examination room, Hallie tried to concentrate on her novel. But something seemed strange, out of place, that Cora even occasionally took medication to help her sleep. Granted, Cora would always be careful about taking anything, especially something as potentially addictive as a sleeping aid. Still, it seemed odd that the subject had never come up before.

Perhaps Cora was a little embarrassed by it? It was possible, Hallie thought.

At any rate, where's the harm? Certainly an occasional low dosage sleeping pill was a lesser evil for someone like Cora. Surely it was better for her than a sleepless night?

But now, with the Alzheimer's disease: how long would Cora be able to monitor her own medications? And who would decide when it was time for someone else to take over?

For now, of course, Cora was more than able to make her own decisions, but it would probably be wise to let Christina know about the sleeping pills, just to get her opinion.

Hallie began to reread the same paragraph for the fourth time, when Cora burst through the door into the waiting room. Beside her was the doctor's assistant. They were chatting like old friends.

"Thank you so much, Cora. I really appreciate your advice."

"You're so welcome, dear. Hallie!" She motioned for Hallie to join them.

"Sweetheart, this is Anna. She is a certified physician's assistant, isn't that wonderful? Hallie here is one of my dearest friends, and she has one of the most beautiful singing voices I've ever heard."

Anna held her hand out to shake Hallie's. "Nice to meet you, Hallie. Cora's been telling me all about you. Congratulations on your wedding!"

"Thank you. It was nice to meet you, too."

Leaving the clinic, Cora seemed reenergized. "All the people in that office are just lovely, aren't they? So warm and friendly. And my doctor is a wonderful young woman, too, very understanding and kind."

"You seem to bring out everyone's best, Cora."

"What a nice thing to say, sugar pie."

They stopped at a pharmacy to fill Cora's prescription, which she dropped into her purse, "for safekeeping," she said.

All the way home, Cora smiled to herself. She seemed so upbeat that Hallie was surprised when, before she'd even closed the door behind them, Cora excused herself to take a nap.

"I need to catch up a bit on my sleep, and then I'll be myself again. I'll see you in a little while."

"All right, Cora. I'll make tea for you when you wake up."

Hallie went to the kitchen, intending to start planning dinner, but Cleo appeared, looking for attention. So Hallie sat, and Cleo jumped to her lap. "I missed you, too," Hallie whispered, and Cleo purred even louder, leaning against Hallie and lifting her head as Hallie rubbed her neck.

Cleo had always had a calming affect on Hallie, but now it was her soothing presence that made Hallie realize that she was still…what? Troubled. There was something just slightly askew about the day's events. Nothing she could really put her finger on, though. Maybe it was merely a kind of generalized anxiety that had been lingering since the diagnosis. Hallie had not taken Cora to see a doctor since that dreadful day. It was probably tied into all the grief Hallie had been feeling…and anticipating.

Stop being so silly, she told herself. *There's nothing I can or should do right this minute. Let it go.*

She stood, forcing Cleo to jump down. Hallie washed her hands at the sink and started cooking, while Cleo sat, watching and waiting.

Alone in her room, Cora took out the pill bottle, opened it and dumped the capsules onto her bed. She opened a dresser drawer and found one of her favorite embroidered handkerchiefs that had once belonged to her mother. Placing it, too, on the bed, she unfolded it carefully, then scooped up all the pills—thirty of them—and put them in the center of the handkerchief. Then she tied the four corners together, forming a little pill pouch, which she tucked into a corner of the drawer. She covered it with a sweater and closed the drawer.

She was still smiling as she replaced the lid on the pill bottle, rolled it in tissues and buried it deep in her trashcan.

To convince Hallie that she had actually taken a nap, Cora would have to stay in her room a good hour. So she climbed onto her bed and picked up the book from her night table. Last night she'd been too sleepy to read much, anyway.

Cora opened her book to the place she'd marked, and for a moment she frowned slightly. She didn't like lying to Hallie, or anyone for that matter. But this business was no one else's; it was Cora's and Cora's alone.

The pills meant that she would never have to be anyone's burden, that she still had a choice.

The pills meant freedom.

59

Hallie had put everything on hold when Cora was diagnosed, but now life felt almost normal, and Cora insisted that she begin accepting work again and return to her acting classes. Still reluctant, yet undeniably relieved, Hallie obeyed. But between career obligations and wedding planning, time seemed to speed up. She climbed into bed exhausted each night, feeling a sense of precarious control— as though time were leaping away from her as she feebly tried to catch up.

Items on the Wedding List were steadily being checked off, however; Cora kept assuring her that they were ahead of schedule. It was early summer, and most of the decisions had been made. It would all fall into place, Cora insisted.

Christina, her entire family, and Barry arrived the day before Cora's birthday, with a plan to take her to her beloved Victoria. She refused to go.

"I can't go. I have too much to do here. Hallie's wedding is two months away."

"But you said we were ahead of schedule. You can take a few days, we still have plenty of time," Hallie said.

"No. I need to be here to answer the phone. What if there are questions only I can answer?"

"Then I can call you in Victoria; you can give me the answers we need, and I can communicate them to whoever is asking."

"No, damn it! I'm not going!"

A show of Cora's temper was always unsettling, but this time no one was prepared for such a sudden outburst; everyone stood in silence, listening and waiting. Speaking to no one in particular, Cora said: "The truth is I'm afraid. I have been to Victoria maybe half a dozen times in the last ten years. I know it, but not intimately. It's not home. I'm afraid of being in an unfamiliar place. I'm terrified, actually, that my symptoms will get worse, that new ones will surface." Now she looked at Christina. "I know you want to do something nice for me, something special for my birthday. This just isn't the right thing. I'm thrilled that you're all here. Let's just stay here and celebrate in style. Can we do that?"

"Of course, Mama," Christina whispered, and wrapped her arms around Cora's shoulders.

Cora broke from their embrace and wiped her eyes. "Okay! How shall we start? How about we all go out for a decadent dinner and a bit too much wine?"

"Sounds like a great idea," Barry said.

"Tonight's on me. Tomorrow night you can treat me all you like," Cora said.

So Cora's family stayed a few days and enjoyed the sights, smells and flavors of the area.

The afternoon of Cora's birthday, they, along with Hallie and Cora herself, went walking on the beach.

"Look!" Her granddaughter Laurel pointed excitedly toward the water, where a black figure slipped through the waves.

Cora stopped walking. "Oh! It's my old friend. They say there are several seals that live nearby and hunt for fish near this beach, but I'm convinced it's always the same handsome fellow coming to visit. See? He recognizes me!"

The seal had stopped moving and faced them now, only his head showing above the water.

"I've seen him, too. Before I met you, Cora. I was walking along one day and suddenly there he was, watching me," Hallie said.

"Take a picture, Dad!" the other granddaughter, Robin, said. Christina's husband, Kurt, was the undisputed photographer of the family; no one else even carried a camera when he was among them. But the seal disappeared under the water before Kurt could get the camera out.

"Keep watching. He may come back up," Christina said quietly.

The group stood, scanning the water for a glimpse of his shiny coat, but Cora shook her head firmly. "No. He's gone. He was saying good-bye," Cora said. When everyone turned to look at her, she continued. "I know him pretty well. That was his farewell dive." She dismissed the subject with a wiggle of her fingers, and turned back toward the house. "I'm famished. How about the rest of you?"

When Ben arrived from work, everyone piled into cars to head out for dinner. Cora had chosen an old favorite in downtown Seattle: fabulous seafood and an incredible view of Puget Sound. Laughter echoed in the rafters as Cora told her well-worn stories and elicited old favorites from the others.

Back home after dinner, Hallie carried out a huge cake, with candles circling the declaration written in purple icing: 'To Cora, Happy 82nd Birthday!' Below the words were two real champagne glasses, held in place by sugar roses. Everyone sang, then held their breath as Cora blew out all but one candle in her first attempt. Eyes shining, she looked at her family, laughing and clapping in her honor. In that moment, she believed with absolute certainty that no one in the world could be luckier. She felt utterly blessed.

It was a magical time, frozen frame by frame in their memories forever, while the slow, nearly audible hum of sadness and loss buzzed just underneath, ever present and never acknowledged.

60

Shortly after his return to California, Kurt had sent an entire album of photographs and Cora flipped through it at least three times a day. "Look at this one of you and Ben, Hallie. It's just beautiful! Why don't I send it to your parents?"

"That would be nice, Cora. They haven't seen a picture of Ben yet."

"They'll see him in person soon enough. Do they have their plane tickets yet?"

"Yes. Remember, I told you that they bought them as soon as we told them the date had changed." Hallie winced, as a flicker of pain passed through Cora's eyes.

"That's right. I remember. Well, good. I'm looking forward to meeting them. Look at this one of Robin and Laurel.

They're lovely, aren't they? They seem to be good girls, except for that horrible music they listen to. Honestly, Hallie, I try to be open to new ideas, new art especially, but I simply can't abide that... what do they call it?"

"Hip-hop."

"Yes. Terrible stuff. I wouldn't even call it music, really. I hate to be such an old fuddy duddy, but I can't help it."

"Well, I guess I'm an old fuddy duddy too. I can't stand the stuff either."

"Oh, thank goodness. I thought it was just me. Now, we have quite a few wedding errands today." She opened her notebook. "Let's see. Your gown is ready, so you need to go try it on. We need to decide on beer, wine and champagne, and meet with my friend about the cake. And we still need to meet with my other friend, the florist. That's a lot to do in one day, though. We'd better get started now!"

"Where do you get your energy, Cora?" Hallie smiled, but something felt... off–kilter somehow. There was something a little frenetic in Cora's boundless enthusiasm. Was she still recovering from Hallie's knee jerk reminder? In any event, she was right, these details did need to be attended to. Might as well get started.

"I miss our walks, Cora," she said as she drove them to the bridal boutique. "We need to fit them in somehow."

"Honey pie, we are planning a wedding. There's a lot to get done in a short time. Walking on the beach will just have to wait."

"I understand. I just miss it."

"So do I, doll. Anyway— do you think we need more than one case of champagne? Twelve bottles? Let me see... roughly fifty people, five glasses per bottle, that's sixty glasses. No, that won't do. That's not even two glasses per person. We'd better make it two cases." She scribbled on a notepad she now kept in her purse. "What about beer? Half as much?"

"I'm sure that would be fine."

"And do we need other wine?"

"Maybe a few bottles of red wine; I know a few people who don't like champagne."

Cora clicked her tongue. "Can you imagine? All right, then. And you'll trust me on the vineyards and vintages?"

"Of course. But don't spend a fortune."

"Ah, but I have a fortune, sweetheart. I might as well spend it!"

Hallie glanced at her friend, saw her wide grin, her white hair lit up by the morning sun, her eyes just a little wild. In that brief moment, all evidence of Cora's age vanished and Hallie saw the radiant, fearless young woman she had once been.

Hallie parked in a stall outside Bridal Beauty and looked at Cora once more. Now, in the shadows of a nearby cedar tree, Cora's face was softly creased once more. "What is it, sugar?" she asked.

"Nothing. You just look very pretty today, Cora."

"Do I? Isn't that wonderful! So do you. Let's go turn you into a bride again, shall we?"

Seemingly endless wedding arrangements kept Hallie too busy to think of anything else during the day. But at night, staring at the ceiling, messy emotions took control, their voices turned up to full volume.

Often, with Ben breathing softly beside her, Hallie cried silently, waiting for sleep to mercifully click off her mind. Each night, she came close to waking him up, longing to feel his warmth and comfort; but she knew he was growing impatient with her.

They didn't seem to agree on much these days, but each thought the other was irritable and distant. Ben felt excluded and unimportant in the wedding planning process. Hallie thought Ben was showing little support or empathy in a very difficult situation.

One morning, Ben asked about honeymoon ideas. "You and Cora haven't planned that yet, have you?" He had wanted it to sound lighthearted; now he winced at the edge in his voice, and continued quickly, "I think we should make it really special. A trip to remember: three weeks in Greece? Or Italy? How about Australia?" Silence. "Fiji?"

Hallie sat at the little table in their room, tapping her coffee cup. "I've been meaning to talk to you about this. I really think we should wait until... well, later."

"Christina already said she'd stay with Cora until we get back. Cora will be fine, Hallie. You know she'll be angry if we don't go because of her."

"I know, but I just don't feel good about leaving her right now."

"Okay, we'll make it a shorter one. How about ten days in Hawaii? Posh resort, rental car for exploring, Mai Tais, palm trees, you, me and a beach? Come on, Hallie. We'll regret it forever if we don't have a honeymoon."

"Won't we regret going if..."

"If what? If Cora dies while we're gone?"

"Ssh! She'll hear you!"

"Hallie, wouldn't we risk that even if she didn't have Alzheimer's? We can 'what if' ourselves to death. What if we leave the house and get killed in a car accident? That's what happened to Marion. Should Cora feel guilty for sending her to the store that day? Things happen, Hallie. We just have to keep living our lives. That's what Cora would want, with or without this diagnosis. Skipping our honeymoon won't change anything."

"Logic is not going to convince me, Ben. I can't shake this feeling. My heart, my gut is telling me my place is here right now." She held up her hand, stopping his next speech. "There's no way you can change my mind. Please try to understand."

"I understand, Hallie. I just know you're wrong." He kissed her forehead. "I'm tired of this, aren't you? I know you cry yourself to sleep every night. Don't you want a break from all this? Some time alone with me?"

"A break? A break from Cora? No! I want as much time with her as I can get! I don't know how I'm going to manage life without her! Don't you understand?"

"I gotta go to work. So you go spend time with Cora. That's your only priority, I guess. Sorry. I thought I might at least be number two on the list. See you later."

"Ben, wait," she called after him as he jogged down the stairs, but he didn't respond. She heard the door open, heard him say, "Have a nice day, Cora." Heard the door close behind him, a little harder than usual.

There was a pause, then: "Hallie Jane McLaren, soon to be Lawson, get your pretty little fanny down here. Pronto!"

Shit. How much had she heard? Descending the stairs slowly, Hallie was a child again, preparing to defend herself against her parents, judge and jury, verdict already reached.

But this was Cora about to reproach her, not her parents. And suddenly Hallie knew she deserved whatever Cora was about to say. Standing on the last step, Hallie waited for the words that had already formed in her own mind.

"Hallie, that is a wonderful man you're lucky enough to be marrying shortly, and if you dare deny him a honeymoon based on some misguided sense of duty to me... I will fire you. No caretaking duties, no dilemma, am I right? Unfortunately, I will also have to fire you as a friend, because I do not have fools as friends. Is that clearly understood? You will apologize to Ben. Today. You will marry him next month and fly away to Timbuktu or whatever exotic locale you choose and have your wildly romantic honeymoon. *Capice?*"

Hallie nodded at her shoes. Gently, Cora lifted her chin until their eyes met. "And then you will tell me all about it when you get back. Understand?"

"Yes. I'm sorry, Cora. I just know how precious our time is."

"Honey pie, Ben is going to be your husband. Your time with him is the most precious of all. Make him number one in your life, and he'll really mean it when he says 'till death do us part.' He loves you, Hallie. Just love him back."

"I will. I do! But if I go, you have to promise me something."

"Oh, we're negotiating now, are we?"

"Yes. You have to go up to Victoria with Christina while we're gone. Just the two of you, or maybe Barry, too. They'll make sure you're okay. I know you love it up there, and there's no reason you can't go…"

"One last time? But it might feel strange. I might not remember places I used to know."

"So? Most people never have a memory as good as yours on their best day. You might be closer to average than you usually are, that's all."

"Okay, sugar pie, you have a deal. You go on your honeymoon and, if Christina wants to go, I'll go to Victoria. And Hallie? Thanks."

"Hey, one swift kick in the rear deserves another, right? Now, I'm going to hit the shower and go accost my fiancé at his office. Will you be okay for a couple of hours?"

"Of course! Go!"

Ben sat in his office miserably trying to think of anything but Hallie. This was not the way he'd expected to be feeling a month before his wedding; the euphoria of their engagement seemed so long ago, so foreign now. Yes, he felt neglected, but even worse, he felt… unnecessary.

He glanced at the phone on his desk, willing it to ring. He wanted to rewind their lives to before Cora's diagnosis, wanted Hallie back, really back, devoted, present, deliriously in love with him.

Some movement outside his office caught his attention and he looked up to see his reflection in the glass door. In that face he saw a needy, self-absorbed, loathsome creature he barely recognized. How dare he come down so hard on Hallie, who was dealing with a painful, impossible situation? She was losing her best friend, a woman who treated her better than her own mother ever had. Did it really matter when they went on a honeymoon? Wasn't it really more important that they were getting married?

And as he berated himself, his watery image disappeared, replaced by Hallie herself, standing outside and peering in, hands cupped around her beautiful face.

In an instant he opened the door and held her close, hushing her apologies, kissing her tears. Now it was she who insisted on a honeymoon, wherever he wanted it to be.

"No, really we can wait. It was wrong of me to want to take you away from Cora right now. And trying to bully you into it the way I did... God, I'm so sorry, babe."

"No, I was wrong. You are my life, Ben, not Cora. Besides, she'll disown me if we don't go. She promised to be here when we get back. It's okay, really. And you were right— two weeks of bliss will be a nice break."

"Are you sure?"

"Absolutely. I love you, you know. More than anything. So... can you get away for a while? Go for a walk or something?"

"Actually, I shouldn't. I haven't been very productive so far today."

"Sorry."

"Don't be. I'm glad you're here."

Hallie glanced around. "Ooh, fancy office!"

"You like it?"

"Very nice. I'm glad I got to see it. But now I'll leave you alone so you can produce. See you at home!"

"I love you. Hey, next time bring Cora and I'll treat you both to that lunch I promised," Ben said.

"Deal. Love you!"

Ben smiled and waved, watching her walk toward the reception desk. At the front door, she turned around one more time and blew a kiss. When the receptionist laughed at his silly grin, he turned just slightly pink.

Sitting behind his desk again, he marveled at how completely different everything seemed now. Essence of Hallie lingered, and all was right with the world.

61

The next month seemed to disappear before their eyes, a magician's trick inspiring first dismay, and ultimately, delight. The bridesmaids' dresses required additional alterations, but were finished a few days before the wedding. The photographer Cora had recommended agreed to the date, then backed out, citing a forgotten previous commitment. But Cora had turned to Hallie and said, "Stop hyperventilating. I will take care of this." Hallie had heard her on the phone, speaking in low tones, and when she returned she only winked and said, "Problem solved."

A thousand details to oversee, a thousand things to go wrong, and yet it all came together at the last minute.

Hallie's parents arrived as scheduled, two days before the wedding. At dinner with Hallie, Ben, his parents and Cora, Hallie's mother cleared her throat and lifted her glass. "Please, everyone, I'd like to propose a toast."

"Marylou, how wonderful!" Cora said.

They raised their glasses high, waiting to hear what the mother of the bride had to say.

"To Hallie and what is hopefully her last groom."

Hallie felt her throat closing, but Ben squeezed her hand and raised his own glass even higher. "I have a toast as well. I know that marriage is hard work. Until I met Hallie, I had never experienced the kind of love and commitment that would last a lifetime. Now, I can't imagine living a lifetime, or even a moment, without her. To Hallie, my beautiful bride, my life, my love."

"To Hallie," came the chorus, and they sipped from their glasses.

A few sips later, Hallie's mother tearfully welcomed Ben to the family. When Ben's father, Alex, tried to order another bottle of champagne, Cora deftly intercepted. "We don't want to have headaches tomorrow, now do we? Especially you, sweetie," she said, patting Hallie's hand. She then took Hallie's glass and emptied its contents into her own.

"Hey! Are you cutting me off?"

"Yes, ma'am."

"But I've only had half a glass!"

"Trust me. It will interrupt your sleep and make your eyes puffy in the morning. This is not a night for drinking." She drained the glass in one gulp. "I'm only watching out for you, Hallie."

"Yeah, that's quite the sacrifice you're making for me! Thanks a lot!"

"What are friends for?" Laughter erupted almost violently between them and they held on to each other, tears streaming as they howled in fits and stops, beyond the humor of the moment, beyond reason. The others, slightly confused but amused just the same, laughed along.

Cora's family arrived the next day, driving rental cars from the airport. Hallie's jaw dropped as Kurt unpacked several cameras, still and video, a tripod, and zoom lenses of varying sizes. "What's going on?" she asked.

"Well, Christina had asked Cora what we could get you as a wedding gift. Cora said she'd call back with ideas. When she did, she suggested a few things, but then she mentioned that your photographer had bailed. So I figured this was the perfect gift! Didn't she tell you?"

Hallie caught Cora's eye and smiled, shaking her head. Kurt actually believed this had been his idea. Organizing his equipment intently, he didn't see Cora's playful shrug or notice Hallie fighting laughter. "It *is* perfect!" she said, hugging his shoulders. "Thank you, Kurt."

The house was full and chaotic, buzzing with happy anticipation. Walking into the kitchen to put the kettle on for tea, Hallie caught Cora leaving through the side door. "Where are you off to?"

She looked startled, even afraid for a brief moment. "Oh! I thought I'd just go for a little walk on the beach. Clear my head a bit."

"Would you like me to come with you?" Cora had not walked alone since the stroke, but she did seem sturdy now.

"No, honey. You stay with the families. I just need some quiet time alone."

Hallie hesitated, but couldn't really come up with a good reason not to let her go. She was fine, at least for now. "Okay. I'll have some tea ready for you when you get back."

"Thank you, sugar pie. I'll just be a few minutes."

But minutes upon minutes came and went. When an hour had gone by, Hallie went outside and looked down the beach, expecting to see Cora approaching. She was nowhere in sight.

Hallie darted back into the house and through the living room where everyone had gathered. Christina and Ben both looked up as she ran through and opened the front door.

Where? Where to look, where to begin, where could she be? Hallie thought wildly. Something was wrong, there was no doubt. She walked, looking into the windows of the neighbors' homes. She could check with George, and then just go door to door. What if she had gotten hurt somehow? *How could I have let her go by herself?*

Hallie looked up; there on the next block was Cora, walking with someone Hallie didn't recognize. Cora's head was down, and the woman with her had her arm around Cora's shoulders.

Hallie ran to them. "Cora! What happened? Are you all right?"

Now Hallie could hear her; Cora was sobbing, shaking with sorrow and grief.

"Oh, Hallie, I'm so sorry. Please forgive a foolish old woman. You're about to get married, and here you are worried about me."

Covering her face with her hands, Cora almost fell over. Her companion helped her to a bench a few feet away, and there she sat, lost in despair.

The stranger turned to face Hallie and smiled gently. "She came to my door. I live right up there. I've met Cora a few times, walking on the beach, so I recognized her right away. She said she'd been walking in a place that was as familiar as her own face, and suddenly she had no idea where she was, or where she lived. She panicked and ran off the beach to the first house she found. She had pointed out her house to me once, so I was just bringing her home. Are you her granddaughter?"

"No, I'm…"

"Funny, she said her granddaughter was getting married, and that she had to find her way back to the wedding. She was frantic, poor thing."

Now it was Hallie who thought she might topple over. A boulder suddenly seemed to be pressing on her chest.

She swallowed hard and whispered, "Thank you for taking care of her. We'll be all right now."

Hallie put her arm around Cora's shoulders. "It's okay," she whispered. "Everything is all right now."

Cora sniffed. "I know you're not really my granddaughter. I know that."

Back at the house, Christina had teased Ben when Hallie ran out the door without a word. "Guess the bride has cold feet!" But she had stood up and watched Hallie through the window, seen the look of worried panic on her face. "Excuse me a moment," she'd said, and went to the kitchen. A teapot sat on the counter, but no one was there. She ran down the hall to her mother's room. It was empty. A small sound escaped from her throat and she turned again, ran back down the hallway, through the living room and out the front door.

Now Ben was right behind her, followed by the rest of Christina's family. A block away, Hallie and Cora were walking toward them, clinging to each other for dear life.

It was just stress, they all agreed. Too much excitement, too many responsibilities. Cora was back to her old self quickly, sipping tea and joking about her little adventure.

But Hallie had seen the fear and confusion in her eyes. Cora had walked that beach tens of thousands of times, and that day she had decided to return a different way, through the neighborhood. She'd completely lost her bearings, and confusion had crept in further, deeper.

This episode was a glimpse into Cora's future, Hallie knew, the future Cora now had in store. Remembering the terror, the hopelessness, the anguish in Cora's eyes broke Hallie's heart, even as everyone continued to smile and celebrate.

Cora floated in and out of Hallie's dreams that night, bestowing rare and wondrous treasures at her feet, kissing her forehead, gently stroking her hair, drifting inevitably away; but there was no sadness in her eyes. This was a joyful farewell, for both of them.

When Hallie opened her eyes at last, there was a click as the door closed. She saw her wedding gown hanging from the bed's canopy. Her shoes were lined up on the floor. On the table by the window sat a tray with orange juice, strawberries, a croissant, a pot of tea and a cup and saucer. Inside the cup was a note: *Thought you might like a little time to yourself this morning! Love, Cora.*

Hallie sat, opened the teapot and smelled. Peppermint. She smiled. Cora would say it was to settle a nervous stomach. Was she nervous? A little, she had to admit. She wondered how Ben was feeling.

They had agreed to sleep in separate rooms the night before the wedding, and now Ben was not allowed to see her until she made her Grand Entrance. Funny, how some superstitions just wouldn't die.

She felt a pang of loneliness, of missing Ben, but as she sipped her tea and gradually tuned into the buzz of activity outside her room, she decided to savor this moment of relative quiet.

The moment was brief. Someone knocked, then opened the door without waiting for an invitation. Lonnie pushed the door closed behind her. "Good, you're up! Okay, the Matron of Honor is here, reporting for duty! How are you? Are you falling apart or anything? Wracked with doubt? Icy feet?"

"No, of course not. My feet and I are fine! Look, Cora laid out everything and brought breakfast up to me. It was all here when I woke up, so clearly I was sleeping soundly. But isn't she sweet?"

"She's a peach. But honestly, Hallie, how are you? Nervous?"

"A little. Mostly I'm excited. I'm going to marry Ben today, surrounded by all my favorite people, and tomorrow we're flying off to Hawaii. I'm so happy."

"Really? No pre-wedding emergencies that only I can fix?"

"Don't look so disappointed. Just help me carry this stuff down to the kitchen so we can get to the salon on time."

Cora heard Hallie's door open again and called out, "Bride on the staircase! Get the groom out of here!"

"Is it safe?" Hallie called down.

"Just a minute! Okay, come on down!"

In the kitchen, Hallie put the tray in the sink, then hugged Cora. "I thought it was just the gown he couldn't see."

"Oh, let's just play it safe, shall we? You look happy."

"I am! I'm..."

"Just a tad behind schedule. I checked on you a while ago and I couldn't bring myself to wake you, but I should have. So, you run upstairs, get showered and dressed and go meet everyone at the beauty salon."

"I still wish you were coming with us."

"Darling, I am your wedding coordinator. I have much too much to do here. But I promise I will look pretty when the time comes."

"You'll outshine the bride."

The doorbell rang and Cora ran to answer it, calling behind her, "Get going! You have to be there in just over an hour!"

"All right! I'm going!"

Lonnie sat at the kitchen table. "I'll be here, arranging flowers, hanging streamers and being otherwise useful until you're ready."

"I'll be down soon."

Lonnie had insisted on driving Hallie to and from the salon where they were meeting Rachel, Natalie, Ben's mother Stevie and Kim.

The appointment had included Hallie's mother, but she had declined. "Salons charge outrageous amounts for things women used to do for themselves. No thank you. I'll stay here and help Cora."

Kim had been enthusiastic in her role as bridesmaid, but the air between her and Hallie had felt heavy until Hallie finally said, "You're seeing Joe again, aren't you? It's okay if you want to bring him to the wedding."

"Really? Oh, Hallie, thank you. Yeah, he called after you and I talked about it and I decided to give him another shot. But you'd really be all right with him being at the wedding?"

"It might be a little weird, but nothing's going to bother me on the happiest day of my life. Plus, I've started trying to think of Joe as this whole new person who just happens to be dating one of my best friends. Yeah, I think I'll be fine with it."

"I'll talk to him. He'd pretty much assumed he wouldn't be welcome. I've been meaning to ask you, but I never quite found the right moment."

"That would be a difficult moment to find. But it's okay, really."

However, Joe had graciously declined, sending a note instead: *Hallie, thank you for your kind invitation. I am going to surprise you by doing the right thing and not being part of the festivities. Please accept my best wishes for a perfect wedding and happiness always. Ben is a lucky man.*

Another loose end, tied into a lovely bow.

At the salon, the women had their hair styled, enjoyed pedicures, manicures, and gathered around to watch as Hallie had her make-up applied and veil fastened in place.

"Hallie, you're gorgeous! Look at you! I mean really, look!" Lonnie said.

Looking in the mirror, Hallie tried to see herself as the others did. Her silky hair was swept back from her face except for the tendrils hanging in a perfect frame. On her head, a crystal band fit snugly among the dark curls, its veil rising upward slightly, then falling over her head and halfway down her back. Earthy tones enhanced her rosy cheeks, her sculpted lips. Her eyes, wide and dark, a freeze frame somewhere between brown and green, moistened now. She was truly beautiful.

"Don't cry; she'll have to do your make-up all over again!" Lonnie said, nearly crying herself.

"Thanks," Hallie whispered to the make-up artist. "This is just how I wanted to look."

"We'd better get moving. The rest of us have make-up to put on, too," Kim said.

"And lots of it!" Rachel said, laughing. "Hallie, this was so much fun. We'll see you at the wedding!"

Cora had planned for every contingency, including the weather. Under perfect conditions, warm, light wind, no rain in sight, the ceremony would take place outside. Anything less than perfection would call for Plan B: the bridesmaids and Hallie would walk down the curved staircase to the formal living room area, large enough to house the group comfortably.

In either case, the reception would take place throughout the main floor, the food on display in the kitchen, chairs placed in groups for chatting in every room. After the ceremony, the living room would be cleared out, if necessary, and a DJ and equipment brought in.

Heading back from the salon, Hallie eyed the clouds rolling in. "The forecast said a chance of showers. Only a chance!"

"Looks like a pretty good chance. I guess it's Wedding Plan B for us. Damn! I really didn't want to walk down those stairs!" Lonnie said.

"You did fine during the rehearsal."

"I wasn't wearing the shoes!"

"I suppose we could just come down the hallway."

"No, we're not going to change the plan. I'll be fine. If I trip and roll down the stairs it will just provide some comic relief, right?"

"Absolutely. We'll even say you did it on purpose."

"Right. All part of the plan. Good thing I'm wearing pretty underwear."

Back at the house, Hallie and Lonnie walked into chaos, clamor, and utter beauty. Flowers and ribbons in lavender, deep purple and butter yellow lined the polished wood banisters flanking the staircase. Huge flower arrangements stood in the four corners of the living room. Chairs were arranged in two sections, divided by an aisle of white fabric that curved and extended to the bottom of the stairs. Plan B was well in hand.

"Hallie's back! Don't let Ben come in here!" Cora yelled behind her as she hustled into the room.

"Cora, it's beautiful!"

"You're not too disappointed about the weather, are you?"

"No! Look at this place!"

"It's coming along nicely, but there's still a lot to do. But look at you! Oh, your mother needs to see this."

Cora turned to call Hallie's mother, and they saw that she had already appeared. "My goodness, Hallie. You are lovely. I don't think I've ever seen you looking quite so beautiful."

"I know I haven't." It was Hallie's father, standing under the archway into the kitchen. "You're breathtaking, honey. You look so happy. Are you?"

"Yes, Dad. I've never been happier."

"I'm so glad." He walked to her, kissed her lightly on the forehead. "I want to ask you something. You haven't asked, and it's okay if you have something else in mind. I know I haven't been the greatest father in the world, but I'd like to change that, starting today. I'd like to walk you down that aisle. I bought myself a tuxedo, just for the occasion. What do you say?"

The truth was, Hallie hadn't been sure how either of them would feel about following this particular convention. When Hallie married Joe, standing before a judge at the courthouse, there had been no tuxedos, no guests, no aisle, so no need for someone to give the bride away. At the time, Hallie had been relieved; her father had always been so distant, so disapproving. So this time, she wasn't sure how to ask him to give her away to a second groom. Now, here was her father impersonating a '50's TV patriarch: softhearted and loving, wise and even slightly vulnerable.

Hallie was suddenly ashamed. "Oh, Dad! I'm so sorry I didn't ask, I just... I guess I didn't find the right time. I would love for you to give me away!" She hugged him tight, smelled his aftershave: Old Spice, still. Closing her eyes, she was a little girl again, in a rare moment alone with her father: standing on Daddy's feet, grinning up into his face and holding his hands as he danced her around and around. "I love you, Daddy," she whispered, and kissed his cheek.

"Smile everyone!" Hallie opened her eyes just in time to see Kurt's camera aimed her way. It flashed, and bright dots floated like runaway balloons.

"Okay, that's it! No more kissing until after the 'I dos!'" Lonnie said. "It's time to get you dressed! Get up those stairs!"

"Call me when you're ready, Hallie, and I'll take a few shots before the ceremony!" Kurt said.

Christina had appeared, too, and stood with an arm around Cora's shoulders. "You should get ready, too, Mom. I'm done; I'll stay and supervise out here."

"All right, it's a deal. I'm going to go get dressed. I'll come up for a peek before the ceremony begins, sugar pie. Have fun up there!"

"Mind if I tag along?" Hallie's mother asked, almost shyly.

Stunned, Hallie realized there was no edge in her voice at all. She looked at her mother then, really looked at her, and tried to remember the last time she'd seen her wearing make-up. Not since she was a little girl, when her mother was not much older than she was now. "Of course not, Mom. You have to be there! I'll see you soon, Dad!"

Lonnie fastened Hallie's strapless bra and took the stockings out of their package, oh so carefully, one at a time. "You look like you're trying to diffuse a bomb," Hallie laughed.

"Hey, you want me to poke a hole in one of these things? Here."

Hallie slid them on and fastened them to the clips hanging from her garter belt. "Ooh la la, *mademoiselle!* You know Ben's going to want you to wear this for every anniversary, don't you?"

Hallie looked quickly to her mother, who had seemingly turned into a complete stranger, giggling and blushing. Laughing herself now, Hallie said, "I guess that wouldn't be such a bad thing."

Kim burst into the room. "Am I too late? Oh, good, you haven't put on the dress yet. I wanted to be here for that."

"I'm glad you're here. You're just in time."

Lonnie carried the dress over and took it off the hanger. She lowered it, and Hallie stepped inside, sliding her arms under the straps. Her mother, standing behind her, pulled up the zipper and fastened the hook at the top. Over the zipper, tiny round faux buttons slipped into place. Hallie walked to the mirror and made a few adjustments. "Well?"

"It's perfect!" called Cora from the door. She rushed in, closing the door behind her.

"How are we for time?" Hallie asked.

"T minus twenty minutes and counting," Lonnie told her. "Let me look at your face. Gorgeous! Just a little refresher on the lipstick and I think you'll be ready. Here," Lonnie gave her the tube. "Okay, now I need to throw a little more paint on myself. Bathroom across the hall okay?"

"Yes, I think that one is free right now," Cora said.

"I'll be back in ten," Lonnie said, heading for the door.

"Honey, should I go get Kurt?"

Hallie pressed her lips together and peered into the mirror to check her lipstick. "Sure, Mom. I just have to put my shoes on, oh, and I need someone to get our bouquets and someone to help me with my jewelry."

"Kim, why don't you get the flowers? I'll help with the jewelry, and by the time your mom gets back with Kurt we'll be all set," Cora said.

Hallie's mother left with Kim, headed for their assigned duties, and Hallie took a long look at Cora. Her makeup was perfect, subtly yet skillfully applied; she hadn't forgotten her lip liner today. Her hair was tied into a French twist and held in place with an abalone clip.

"Cora, you look so pretty. Lavender is really one of your greatest colors," Hallie said. Cora's dress was identical in color to Kim's, but Kim's was a smooth slip dress, while Cora's had long, sheer sleeves and a lace-edged skirt. Lonnie's dress was a deep purple, empire-waisted and sleeveless. Each dress reflected its wearer's personal style; all three women had expressed their gratitude for the lack of taffeta adorning the wedding party.

"Thank you, sweetie. You are absolutely stunning, just as I knew you would be. Now, we don't have much time and I have some things to say. First, I know you bought yourself some jewelry, but I'm hoping you might change your mind and wear this." From the pocket of her skirt, she brought out a delicate gold chain. Hanging from the chain was a single pearl. "This belonged to my mother. It was a wedding gift to her. She wore it at her wedding, I wore it at mine and Christina wore it at hers. I'd be honored if you wore it today. I think it qualifies as something old. "

"Cora!"

"You like it?"

Hallie nodded. "It's perfect with the earrings I'm borrowing from Lonnie, too! Thank you so much."

"Here, I'll fasten it for you. Need help with the earrings?"

"Yes, thanks."

"Borrowed earrings, and you've got the blue garter?"

"Yes. Lonnie's going to put it on for me when Kurt comes up."

"So all that's missing is something new?"

"Well, my dress, shoes and underwear are all new."

"I think there's something else, too."

"What?"

"You have something else that's brand spanking new. I'm fairly sure of it."

"What do you mean, Cora?"

But a crowd came tumbling through the door before Cora could answer. Kim distributed the flowers: bouquets of yellow and white roses for Cora, Kim and Lonnie, and Hallie's lavender roses were bound by yellow and white ribbons. Kim pinned on Hallie's mother's corsage of one yellow rose. "I gave Ben's mom hers downstairs," she said.

Kurt clicked away as the women exchanged hugs and compliments; then Lonnie solemnly slid the blue garter over Hallie's foot and up her leg, stopping just above her knee. Gripping Lonnie's shoulder, Hallie stepped into her shoes and let her skirt fall into place. "Is it time yet?"

Lonnie glanced at her watch, then took it off and tossed it on the table. "Yep. Want me to get your dad?"

"I'm going downstairs anyway. I'll tell him to come up," Marylou said. "Well, I love you, sweetheart. I wish you all the happiness in the world. I'm," and she hesitated, just slightly, "very proud of you, Hallie."

"Thanks, Mom. See you downstairs!" Hallie turned back to Cora. "What was it you wanted to tell me?"

"It can wait, sweetheart."

Hallie's father appeared, slightly out of breath after bounding up the stairs. "Oh, Hallie. You're so beautiful. Are you ready?"

"Yes, I think I am."

Lonnie opened the door, rushed to the landing and gave the gathering below the thumbs up signal. Back in the doorway, she grinned at Hallie. "Here we go!"

Faintly, they heard the harpist begin The Wedding March. Cora gave Lonnie her bouquet. Kim stood ready just inside the door, then Cora, and finally Lonnie, third in line. As Hallie and her father moved into place behind Lonnie Cora whispered, "Thank you for insisting I do this, Hallie," she whispered. "It's been ages since I was a bridesmaid!"

"You had to stand up for me, Cora. I wouldn't have had it any other way."

"Okay! I'm going! I love you, Hal!" Kim said, and she began her walk to the landing, and slowly down the stairs.

Cora followed close behind, grinning at Ben, who met her eyes briefly and looked back up to see Lonnie walking gracefully down the stairs and up the makeshift aisle to her place beside the other women.

Looking up again, he saw his bride holding her father's arm and arriving at the landing where she paused in the curve of the staircase. She was so beautiful; more than that, she was simply glowing, and Ben knew he would remember every detail of this moment for the rest of his life.

He watched her walk down the stairs and toward him, saw her father kiss her cheek and sit down. When Hallie joined Ben, held his hands and smiled, he thought that, as eagerly as he looked forward to the rest of their lives together, he couldn't imagine being happier than he was right now.

The minister directed them to speak their magical words and slide on each other's rings, transforming them into husband and wife. A kiss sealed their promises, making them sacred, and the guests burst into applause.

Then, the reception: Cora, ever the perfect hostess, kept the champagne and conversations flowing. She flitted from group to group, alighting briefly wherever she sensed she was needed. When it was time for toasts, she herded the crowd into the living room. "All right, everyone! Ben's best man, his brother-in-law, Sam, will now offer a toast to the happy couple."

Sam's toast was succinct. He shrugged and said simply, "Ben, I love you, and I'm so happy that you found Hallie. She's a gem. To Ben and Hallie!"

"Ben and Hallie," the rest murmured, and sipped.

"My turn!" called Lonnie, and everyone turned toward her. "Mine isn't going to be so short. Sorry. Hallie, you've come a long way in a short time. A little over a year ago, I was beginning to think you were going to end up as one of those weird old cat ladies. You know, one of those women who live alone except for about twenty cats of every size and color climbing on all the furniture and kitchen counters. You'd be a nice cat lady, of course, smiling at the children in the neighborhood, and they would all wonder what had happened to you. The answer would have been nothing. Nothing ever happened to you because you wouldn't *let* anything happen to you!

"Then one night you invited me to a karaoke bar. I could tell something was up. You were acting all antsy and strange. Before I knew it, there you were, up on stage belting out a song.

"People, I was her best friend and I had no idea she could sing! That's how private she was! But here she was, singing like a pro, and the audience got all quiet and just sat there watching this gorgeous girl singing like an angel. She came back to the table looking like a whole new person, and I knew something about her had changed. Really, deep down changed.

"I'd like to say that Ben was the reason for the change, but it didn't quite happen that way. It was Cora. Hallie met Cora and suddenly started opening herself up to the world. So Ben wasn't the reason for the change in Hallie; the change in Hallie was the reason she found Ben. What I'm saying is that none of us would be here today if it hadn't been for Cora. Everyone: please raise your glass to Cora."

" To Cora!" echoed the crowd.

"There's more!" Lonnie said. "Part B of my toast is this: Ben, I think you're a wonderful guy. And only a wonderful guy would deserve Hallie. So I'd like to propose a toast to Hallie and Ben. May you continue to make each other happy and live a long, healthy and prosperous life together."

"Hallie and Ben!"

"Thank you, Sam and Lonnie. Now I have a request," Cora said. "As Lonnie mentioned, and some of you may not have known, Hallie is a gifted singer. The DJ is setting up in the other room and we'll all be dancing soon, but before he's ready, I'd be thrilled if Hallie would play us a song. Hallie? Please?"

"Actually, I was planning on playing a song today. I have one prepared. So follow me into the piano room, everyone!"

Everyone gathered around the piano as best they could, but Hallie motioned for Cora to sit beside her on the bench. "I wrote this song," she said. "It's actually a toast, too, very similar to Lonnie's. It's called 'Toasting Cora.'"

She swallowed, hard. *You will get through this,* she told herself. "This is my gift to you, Cora," she said softly, and she began:

"What magic brought her to me that day?
A new chapter opened; I was suddenly saved.
Who else on earth could have taught me so much?
Whose hands but Cora's have so loving a touch?

To Cora, all my treasures I owe,
To Cora, for loving me so,
To Cora, a friend for all time—
I'll be toasting Cora the rest of my life.

How can I thank her for all that she's done?
For my revival, for the triumphs I've won,
For the love that has found me, the life that I live,
My debt is to Cora; it was all hers to give.

To Cora, all my treasures I owe,
To Cora, for loving me so,
To Cora, a friend for all time—
I'll be toasting Cora the rest of my life."

Hallie saw the tears in her friend's eyes and blinked back those in her own. The women continued to hug until the applause began to fade at last. "I love you, Cora," she whispered.

"I love you too, sugar pie. So very much. Thank you for my song." She kissed Hallie's forehead and stood up. "I wondered why you were playing that piano so late at night."

"I had to sneak in there when you weren't around! It wasn't easy! But I've had this melody in my head for a while, and one day I just knew it was your song."

"It's a beautiful song, honey." It was Hallie's mother. She cleared her throat. "You have talent. Much more than I ever had."

Hallie tried not to let her astonishment show. She knew how much that compliment had cost her mother. "Thank you, Mom." Hallie pulled her close, briefly, and as always felt her pull away first. "But you're just being modest. How about you and I sing a song together?"

Their voices joined tentatively at first, gradually gaining strength. On the last chorus they harmonized perfectly and Hallie's mother threw her arms triumphantly into the air.

To Kurt's particular delight, the sun made a brief appearance before it set, so the wedding party was hustled outside to the covered porch. With a backdrop of Cora's flowers, the Olympic Mountains and Puget Sound, Kurt took beautiful pictures; the best he'd ever seen, he insisted, as he previewed them on his digital camera.

The evening passed quickly. Ben and Hallie danced, first with each other and then with family and friends. They shared stories of their courtship, nibbled on hors d'oeuvres, cut the cake. They sipped champagne— although Hallie seemed to lose track of her glass every time she turned around— and kissed on command. Kurt was everywhere, his cameras clicking and whirring. And then, suddenly, it was time to get ready to leave.

Upstairs, Hallie changed into her favorite yellow dress and finished packing for the trip. They had booked a room in a hotel in downtown Seattle for the night. In the morning, they would be off to the airport for an early flight to Maui.

Hallie's clothes had already been stuffed into a suitcase. Now, just a few toiletries needed to be added to her carry-on: hairspray, lotion, perfume. Vitamins? She probably wouldn't remember to take them. Was there anything else?

Her birth control pills! She'd nearly forgotten. On her doctor's advice, she'd been taking the pill since her surgery, in the hope that her endometriosis wouldn't recur. Then when her pain had returned in recent months she'd taken the pill every day, nonstop for a while. She'd begun to feel heavy and slightly nauseous, so she'd decided to take monthly breaks again, to try having periods again. But now...when was the last time she'd taken one? She couldn't remember. She opened the case; the last pill had been taken on a Thursday. Today was Saturday. Had she taken a pill two days ago? *No. It's been longer. How much longer?*

She couldn't remember. Had it been nine days? Sixteen? When had this particular habit fallen off the radar screen?

Sitting at the table, Hallie tried to think back, to put the lapsed time into some kind of context. When was her last period?

She caught her breath. She'd missed a period, she was certain of it. The receipt! She kept all the receipts from her prescriptions in the drawer of the vanity. There it was: she'd bought the last packet of pills in July! She'd taken them Sunday to Thursday, then stopped, right about the time she and Cora had started the wedding frenzy in earnest.

Taking the pill hadn't seemed like an urgent daily requirement because they weren't really for birth control. Birth control wasn't supposed to be an issue.

Six weeks. It had been six weeks since her last period. *It's probably just messed up because of all the stress I've been under lately, that's all.* Closing her eyes, she breathed deeply and tried to tune into any signals her body might be sending out. Her breasts were a little tender; she'd noticed that when she was changing her clothes. That usually meant that her period was about to begin. But yesterday morning she'd felt a little nauseous and dizzy when she got out of bed. *Nervousness! I was about to get married. But what if...?*

Stop it! 'Your chances of conceiving are very slim,'
remember? It's just nerves.

"Hallie? You ready?"

It was Ben, already changed, suitcase in hand.

"Almost."

"Everything okay?"

"Yeah. Everything's great. My suitcase is in the corner.
I'll be right down."

"I'll take the bags downstairs and be right back."

Hallie tucked her purse inside the overnight case and
zipped it up, then climbed up onto the bed and sat, waiting.
Ben had left the door slightly open, and now Cleo appeared,
leaping onto the bed beside her. "Hey! Haven't seen you all
day. Have you been hiding?"

Cleo purred loudly, rubbing her head against Hallie's
leg. "She's going to miss you," Cora said from the doorway.
"So will I. But I'll be imagining the two of you walking on
warm sand, snorkeling with all those lovely tropical fish,
watching the sun change from yellow to orange and drop into
the ocean... You're going to love Maui."

"You've been there? You never told me that."

"It's been a while, but yes, I went there with my
husband. It was my anniversary gift to him— fifteenth, I
believe. I wanted him to take some time off and relax a bit.
Taking him on a trip was the only way I could get him to do
that. We took the kids. It was a lot of fun. Be sure to explore
the whole island, don't just stay in Lahaina."

"We will. This is my first trip to Hawaii, so I want to
see as much as I can."

"Good girl."

"You must be exhausted, Cora. Are you all right?"

"I am dragging a bit." She hesitated, and then both
women spoke at once:

"But I wanted to tell you..."

"Cora, there's something I..."

Each one's words were lost in the other's, and ultimately interrupted again when Ben reappeared at the door, quickly followed by Lonnie, Steve, Kim and both sets of parents.

"We wanted to say good-bye..."

"Good luck!"

"We love you!"

And then they were leading the newlyweds out the door and toward the stairs in a blur of good wishes and confetti. At the landing, Hallie stopped and instructed the single women to get into position. With her back to the audience, Hallie tossed her bouquet over her shoulder, then looked down to see Kim holding it high over her head and yelling, "I got it! I got it!"

Natalie, standing beside her, shrugged. "Oh, well, maybe next time, Nat," Rachel called out.

At the door, Hallie turned around, waving at her friends and family. Searching the crowd, she looked up at last to see Cora now on the landing, holding Cleo. "Cora!" she called, and the crowd hushed. But there could be no intimate words between them now. "Thank you for our perfect wedding! I love you!"

"I love you too! Have a wonderful time!"

"Thank you for coming, everyone! See you soon!"

Cora had arranged for a limousine to take them to the hotel; as Hallie and Ben walked to the car, the crowd followed them outside. Behind them, they heard someone ask: "Hey, Cora, shouldn't you have been down here trying to catch that bouquet?"

"Honey, I caught my bouquet ages ago. It was a good one, though."

The driver closed the door of the limo and Hallie looked through the window as the wedding guests watched and waved. She scanned the group until she spotted Cora, holding Cleo with one arm, blowing them a kiss with the other.

62

After checking into the hotel, Hallie shrieked as Ben swept her up and carried her into their room. The bellman brought in their luggage, showed them around the suite, received his tip and left.

Ben moved toward Hallie to hold her close, but she mumbled something about a forgotten item. "There's a drugstore in the lobby. I'll be right back."

When she returned, Hallie tried to sneak the paper bag into the bathroom, but Ben stopped her. "What's this?"

"Uh…"

"Hallie, what's going on? Are you all right?"

"Yeah, it's just, uh…"

"You're not keeping secrets from your husband already are you?"

She sighed. "It's just that I want to know for sure before I get your hopes up or upset you or however you might react."

"Hallie, what is it?" He reached for the bag; she hesitated, then gave it to him and watched as he looked inside. "A pregnancy test?"

"Yes. I just realized today that I forgot to take some pills. I forgot a lot, actually."

"How many did you forget?"

"I kind of stopped taking them six weeks ago. I know, I can't believe it either."

"Well, you've had a lot on your mind."

"Right! And I thought pregnancy wasn't even a possibility anyway. The pill was just for the endometriosis."

"I understand. But now you think you might be…"

"I missed a period. And I really just realized all this today."

"You missed a period. I thought it had been a long time, but I wondered if you'd started taking them every day again. I just kept forgetting to ask."

"It's probably just stress."

"Right. I've heard that can make you late."

"Yes! And I'm sure that's all it is."

"Okay. So take the test!"

"Now? It says morning is best."

"There are two tests in the kit. Take one now and one in the morning. Hallie! We might be pregnant!"

She looked at his face then, felt his excitement. What if she really was pregnant? What if she and Ben had made a baby? There was no doubt now how either of them would feel about it.

"Okay! I'll be right back!" She grabbed the kit back from him and hurried into the bathroom.

Pacing from the living room area of their suite into the bedroom and back, Ben glanced out the window at Lake Union. *I'm a living, breathing cliché,* he thought. *The nervous expectant father. Oh, please, Hallie, say it's positive.* It unnerved him a bit, wanting it so badly. *It might not happen,* he reminded himself. *Maybe ever.*

When the bathroom door opened, he vaulted for it, stumbling as he landed. Hallie's poker face revealed nothing. Then, from behind her back came the plastic stick. Inside the window on one end, a plus sign nearly glowed.

"We're pregnant," she whispered.

He let the words settle on them for a moment like sweet, silent snowflakes. Dropping to his knees, Ben wrapped his arms around his wife's legs and kissed her belly. And then Hallie joined him on the floor, where they rolled around, kissing, touching, laughing and weeping. Their words mingled: phrases of love and joy and hope.

Later, they sat on the bed eating from room service trays, giddy with exhaustion and their happy secret.

"Any ideas for names?" Ben asked.

"I haven't even thought about it yet. Why?"

"I've always thought about naming my kids after my parents. It's not absolutely necessary, but I'd like to consider it if that's okay."

"I don't know. I have fairly strong feelings about not naming babies after anyone. If you name them after relatives, someone will always get hurt— you know, that person is more important to you because you used her name. That sort of thing. But I'll consider it I suppose. Is Stevie short for Stephanie?"

"No. Actually, Mom's name is Mary."

"What?"

"Her maiden name was Stevens, and my dad starting calling her Stevie when they were dating. It just stuck."

"That's cute. And my mom's name is Marylou, so Mary would please both sides. And I really like your dad's name, Alexander. Not crazy about Burt, though, poor Dad. I don't know, I guess naming the baby after someone isn't out of the question. But I really don't want to think about names yet. I'm not very far along. Maybe we should try not to count on this too much yet."

"The hardest part was supposed to be conceiving, right? Now we just have to take really good care of you. Of both of you. It's going to be okay. I have a really good feeling about this."

"So do I, but I don't want to take any chances. I've already lost a baby once. I want to postpone our trip until I can see Dr. Shaw."

"That's reasonable. But let's not go home. I don't want to interrupt our honeymoon. Let's just stay here longer, and if Dr. Shaw gives us the green light, we'll just take off a day or so later. What do you say?"

"Sounds perfect. I'll call first thing Monday morning and try to get in right away."

Sunday morning, Hallie took the second test as soon as she woke up: another positive result. Glowing, they spent the day strolling around the Seattle waterfront, going through the Aquarium, watching the ferries leaving and approaching the docks. At lunch, when the waiter offered a glass of wine or a cocktail, Hallie grinned and said, "Just ice water, please."

A vague, half-thought rose in the back of her mind, a reminder of something she couldn't quite place. But Ben reached for her hand across the table and it vanished before it had fully formed.

Monday afternoon they sat in Sarah Shaw's office, holding hands and nervously watching the clock on the wall. When the nurse called Hallie's name, Ben asked if he could go with her.

Now they sat again, waiting in the exam room, Hallie on the table, Ben in a chair. Dr. Shaw knocked and walked in. "I understand congratulations are in order?"

"What? Oh! Yeah, we got married on Saturday."

"That's wonderful. So what's going on?"

Hallie inhaled sharply. "I took two pregnancy tests and they were both positive. I took one Saturday night and one Sunday morning. They were both positive." She shook her head. "I'm sorry. I'm a little nervous."

"That's okay, it's understandable. Well, I'd like to examine you and see if I can confirm the results. Ben? Would you mind waiting outside? There's a chair right outside the door. Hallie, you change into this," she said, handing her a paper gown. "I'll be right back."

Hallie removed, folded and put her clothes on the chair where Ben had been sitting. The paper gown itched a bit as she sat back up on the table. Her heart was pounding almost audibly. She took a deep breath, let it out slowly. *Maybe the pregnancy tests were defective. Maybe I read the results wrong. Maybe this is just one of those hysterical pregnancies I heard about somewhere.* She shook her head. *Please. Let it be real.*

And then Dr. Shaw was back, speaking in her soothing tone, asking the questions Hallie had anticipated.

"How long since your last period?"

"Six weeks."

"Any birth control since then?"

"No. I forgot to take it."

"Any breast tenderness?"

"Yes! And they're huge!"

Dr. Shaw smiled. "Okay. Scoot down and put your feet in the stirrups."

When the exam was over, Dr. Shaw took her gloves off and threw them away. "Well, Hallie, I love it when my patients prove me wrong like this. You're pregnant. I'd say roughly five weeks. That would mean you're due, oh, early to mid-May. Let's get Ben back in here. Do you want to get dressed first?"

"No!"

She opened the door. "Ben, would you step back in here?"

Hallie sat on the edge of the exam table, legs dangling high above the ground. In her pale blue paper gown, grinning wide, Ben thought she had never looked so beautiful. "It's good news then?"

"I'm due in May!"

"Any questions?" Dr. Shaw asked.

"Yes! With all my issues, is this a high-risk pregnancy?"

"There's probably a slightly higher risk for miscarriage than usual, especially early on. Once you're past the first trimester I'll be less concerned."

"We were supposed to leave for Maui yesterday. Should we postpone the trip for two months?"

"Normally I tell women that flying really doesn't increase the usual risks of pregnancy. It's probably true for you, too."

"What would you do if you were me, under the same circumstances?"

"I wouldn't go. Not yet, anyway. You have miscarried before. I would be extra cautious. Now, on the positive side, pregnancy is quite often an excellent treatment for endometriosis. You have nine months without periods, and sometimes the lesions just disappear altogether.

"Now. Get yourself some pre-natal vitamins. You don't smoke, that's good. Don't hang around people who do smoke. Eat a healthy, balanced diet. Exercise, within reason. Walking is good. Avoid stress as much as possible. No alcohol, of course."

"Is sex okay?"

Ben looked up, relieved that Hallie had asked.

"Yes. It's fine until the very last stages. And make an appointment for a month from now. I want to keep close tabs on you. Hallie, don't worry. I honestly didn't think you had much hope of conceiving. You've done that. I have every reason to think you'll have a normal pregnancy. I just recommend that you be a little more careful than the average mom. Okay?"

"Okay. Thank you, Dr. Shaw."

"You're welcome. I'll see you soon." And she was out the door in a white flash.

"Hallie? Are you okay?" Suddenly Hallie's happy grin had disappeared. Ben put his arm around her and saw the tears filling her eyes. "Oh, no, don't cry. It's going to be okay."

"I'm sorry about our honeymoon."

"Don't even think about it. We'll get there."

"Our baby's in danger."

"No. We're going to take special care to make sure our baby is fine."

"But what if...?"

"Babe, listen to me. I love you so much, and I believe we're going to have a beautiful, healthy baby. If it doesn't happen that way, we'll still have each other. We'll get through it together. I promise you that. For now, we have to stay positive and take this one day at a time. Okay?"

He gave Hallie a tissue from the box on the counter, then picked up her clothes and helped her into them. "Let's go back to the hotel tonight, order room service again and hide away until tomorrow. Does that sound all right?"

She nodded, leaning against him. She missed Cora, and it would have been nice to hear a few words of comfort from her, but right now a hotel room alone with Ben sounded close to perfect. "I'm not ready to face the world yet."

He turned her around to face him. "It's going to be okay. Please believe that."

"I want to. I just wanted nothing but good news today."

"We got some incredible news and a little advice to be careful. That's all."

"I know. I'm sorry. I'm just so afraid. Maybe it's hormones kicking in. I'll be fine."

They spent the evening curled around each other, talking, watching movies, eating. "Should we call Cora and Christina, tell them we didn't go to Maui and that we're coming home tomorrow?" Hallie asked.

"No, let's just tell them in person. Hey, aren't they going to Victoria?"

"That's right, I forgot. I think they're leaving tomorrow. They might not even be there when we get home. Remind me to tell George he doesn't have to look after Cleo after all."

"Will do."

In the weeks to come, Hallie would remember that utterly unnecessary request, running it through the filter of amazement and disbelief that comes in the aftermath of tragedy.

63

The sun had risen, but stayed hidden behind a wall of gray. Hallie woke in the dim hotel room, feeling vaguely uncomfortable. She lifted up onto her elbows and looked around. What was wrong? Her stomach felt a little queasy; suddenly she was wide-awake. *I'm pregnant! It wasn't a dream!* But the thrill turned to dread as she realized without any doubt that she was about to vomit.

Jumping out of bed, she ran for the toilet. "Hallie, are you okay?" Ben asked just as she began retching.

Feeling his presence behind her she asked, "You don't really want to watch, do you?" before she threw up yet again.

Ben smiled, knelt on the tile floor and pulled her hair away from her face. He kissed the back of her head and rubbed her back. "You don't have to go through any of this alone."

Finally, she spat into the bowl and flushed. "I think it's over."

"Here." Ben helped her up. "You brush your teeth, and I'll get some breakfast up here. Rachel told me that eating crackers before you get out of bed really helps."

"Lonnie said that, too. She said crackers were a pregnant woman's best friend."

"We'll have to stock up. What sounds good right now?"

"Pancakes. And strawberries."

"You got it."

Squeezing toothpaste onto her brush, Hallie heard Ben on the phone: "And could we get a few packets of saltines? Crackers, that's right. My wife is pregnant. Thank you."

She smiled. *My wife is pregnant.* He'd probably been hoping for a reason to say that. Hallie looked at her reflection in the mirror. She looked pale. Sick. "I look terrible! When do I start glowing?"

"You look beautiful!"

"Liar," she called, laughing.

In the back of the taxi, they held hands all the way home. When they exited the freeway and stopped at a red light, Ben leaned over and kissed Hallie softly. "I love you, Hallie Lawson."

She squeezed his hand. "I'm so happy! I've never imagined I could be this happy! I hope we don't miss Cora. I'm dying to tell her." The cab driver smiled in the rearview mirror.

The neighborhood was quiet; it was a weekday morning, after all. But when they turned the corner and saw the ambulance in front of the house, the quiet seemed unnatural, surreal. They looked at each other and back at the house. Hallie thought they would never arrive, that the air had become too thick for the car to penetrate. Like in a nightmare, running as hard as you can from an unseen evil, you don't seem to move at all.

But the taxi did move, of course, pulling up behind the ambulance just as the paramedics were bringing Cora out on a gurney. Christina ran along beside them, calling her mother. "Mom! You're going to be fine! I'll be right there!"

One of the paramedics touched her arm, said something, and jumped in behind Cora.

Hallie and Ben ran to Christina, saw the doors close on the ambulance, heard its siren turn on as it raced away. Christina screamed and would have fallen if Ben hadn't caught her. She saw them then, looking from one face to another as if she didn't quite believe her eyes. "What are you doing here? How did you know?"

"We didn't. Something came up, so we didn't go to Hawaii. Christina, what's going on?"

"I don't know. I couldn't wake her up this morning. They don't know what's wrong. They said she's alive, though. But this is serious. I have to get to the hospital. Will you come with me?"

"Of course. Ben, will you drive?" Hallie asked.

The taxi driver, realizing he'd brought this happy couple home to a crisis, carried their luggage to the front door. "Can I bring it inside for you?"

"That's okay," Ben said. He paid the driver, thanked him and carried the suitcases into the house. Hallie followed numbly.

Ben dropped the luggage just inside the front door. Cleo sat on the bottom stair, meowing a greeting. Hallie reached down and rubbed Cleo's neck lightly, picturing her perched on Cora's shoulder as she'd waved good-bye just a few days ago. "See you later," Hallie told the little cat. "Be good."

"Do you need anything before we go?" Ben asked Hallie.

"Just a warmer jacket. It's chilly all of a sudden."

"I'll go get one."

"Thanks," Hallie said. She looked outside. Christina was already waiting in the car. Impulsively, Hallie walked down the hall to Cora's room and stood in the doorway. She saw Cora's unmade bed, the book on the nightstand. Another chill slipped down her spine. Hearing Ben on the staircase, she closed Cora's bedroom door and joined him.

On the way to the hospital, Christina talked non-stop, trying to make sense of the morning. "She seemed fine last night, a little tired maybe, but fine. You know, I haven't even really seen signs of the Alzheimer's, except for that one incident. I mean, I notice she forgets names more than she used to. Once she seemed a little confused when she didn't remember a friend I mentioned in casual conversation. But with the wedding plans she was so careful to write everything down. She had different notebooks for different categories. I was amazed at how organized she was. I suppose she knew that she might mess things up if she wasn't careful. I helped a little once I got up here, but she really had everything under control. It seemed perfectly natural that she might be a little tired. She went to bed early last night so that she'd be rested up for our trip. I was so thrilled that she decided she wanted to go to Victoria! I listed all her favorite places so we wouldn't forget anything. It was going to be so much fun. I was glad the rest of the family went back home so I'd have her all to myself. Is that selfish?"

"No, of course not. It's probably been a long time since you've been able to spend that much time alone with her," Hallie said.

Nodding, Christina went on. "I set my alarm early enough so that we'd have time for breakfast before leaving for the boat. We were going on the Victoria Clipper this time, did she tell you that?"

"No, she didn't. That sounds like fun."

"She's always wanted to do that. So the alarm went off, I went down to the kitchen and put on the kettle for tea. I poured the water into the teapot and went to get Mom. I knocked, I called her, and heard nothing. I expected to hear her say, 'I'll be right there, Chrissy!' But there was nothing, no noise at all. I knocked again and opened the door. She looked peaceful, sound asleep. I thought that maybe she'd been up late reading, or maybe she'd had a hard time getting to sleep. I felt bad about waking her up, but I called her again, louder, and she still didn't stir. I walked over and nudged her and there was no reaction, Hallie. Nothing. I yelled, really screamed in her face and she just lay there motionless. So I picked up the phone beside her bed and called 9-1-1. The ambulance arrived, they examined her, they found a faint pulse. They said she needed to be at the hospital where tests could be run. They didn't know what was wrong, but it was serious. They kept using that word. Serious. What could it be? What could have happened?"

"It could be a lot of things, Christina. It could be almost anything," Ben said, but when Hallie saw his eyes in the rearview mirror she knew how worried he really was.

"It could be anything," Christina repeated, nodding. Hallie looked out the window.

At the hospital, they were directed to a waiting area. The doctor on call would come in soon to give them an update, they were assured. They sat, but Christina stood back up immediately. "I have to walk around. I can't…" Ben and Hallie nodded, and watched Christina walk away, disappearing down the shiny corridor.

"Do you want something to drink?" Ben asked.

Hallie's mouth suddenly felt so dry she wasn't sure she could speak. "Water?"

"I'll be right back. Hallie? Are you okay?"

"I don't know."

"We have no way of knowing what happened. Try to stay calm, all right? For the baby's sake."

She nodded. "I'll try."

Ben disappeared around the corner, heading to the gift shop. Christina appeared, smiling bravely, and left again, unable to sit longer than a few minutes. Ben returned, and Hallie gulped some water. They held hands, waiting and watching Christina walk into and out of view. Nearly an hour had passed when Christina finally returned in the company of a doctor. Hallie sat up straighter, trying to read her face, to make out what they were saying. They approached; Hallie rose to her feet. Christina turned toward her— and Hallie knew.

Cora was gone.

Christina reached for her and they embraced, rocking slowly as Christina wept with a child's abandon.

Hallie became vaguely aware that the doctor had begun speaking. "...still waiting for some test results. There will be an autopsy. I'll call you when we have the results. She seems to have passed away very peacefully; that's something to be grateful for. I'm very sorry for your loss."

"I want to see her. Can I do that? Hallie, do you want to see her?" Christina asked, wiping her eyes, but still clinging to Hallie with one arm. Hallie nodded at her. "Yes. I'd like to see her, too."

"He said she died just a few minutes ago, Hallie," said Christina, starting to cry again. "I should have ridden in the ambulance with her. I should have been there. I just didn't want to get in the way, but I..."

"Christina." Hallie's voice broke slightly, but she continued. "If she was aware of anything, she would have heard your voice before they put her in the ambulance. She knew you were coming to her. She knew how much you loved her. Don't ever doubt that."

"Thank you, Hallie. So you'll come with me to see her?"

"Of course."

"Mind if I come too?" Ben asked.

Christina simply reached out and took his hand. The doctor led them down first one corridor, then another. They saw patients being wheeled on gurneys and in wheelchairs, some urgently, some more leisurely. Family members followed or waved good-bye, their faces lined in worry, in panic, in disbelief.

Christina, Ben and Hallie gripped each other and followed Dr. Singer to a small room. He walked to a gurney and pulled the sheet down, uncovering Cora's face. "I'll give you some time alone," he said, and left, closing the door behind him.

The three of them, still holding hands, stepped closer to the gurney. Hallie's mind danced wildly around, and she thought of a scene in a favorite old movie: companions in need, once terrified and alone, together finding courage and wisdom and strength. Crazily, Hallie thought *We're off to see the wizard....*

But as they drew closer, Hallie's mind calmed. Cora looked... happy. Her eyes were closed, and the corners of her mouth were turned ever so slightly upward.

"Look!" Christina whispered loudly. "She's smiling!"

"She looks like she's dreaming about something wonderful," Hallie said.

"Or slightly wicked," said Ben.

"Good champagne," Christina suggested. "Or chocolate soufflé."

"Sunset over the Olympic Mountains. Listening to a naughty joke," Hallie offered.

"Maybe she was seeing your father, Christina," Ben offered.

She nodded, fresh tears flooding her eyes. "They're together again. I'm sure of it." She pulled the sheet further down and held her mother's hand. "Mom, if you can hear me, I miss you already. But I'm so glad it happened this way. You deserved to die this way. I hope you're flying over the Sound with Daddy right now. Tell him hi from me, okay? And if you can, come visit us once in a while, would you please? I love you, Mama."

She stepped back, and Hallie understood; it was her turn now. Taking Cora's hand, she swallowed painfully. "Oh, Cora. I had such a wonderful surprise for you today. I can't believe I'm not going to be able to share this with you. You're my best friend, Cora, the best friend I've ever had. What am I going to do without you?"

And a memory came to Hallie, a memory of Cora's voice, a promise she'd once made: "I'll be watching with a big smile on my face."

Nodding, Hallie whispered, "Keep watching, Cora. Watch over all of us, okay?"

Hallie lowered Cora's hand, patting it one last time. Turning around, she saw Ben's face, wet with tears of his own; he reached for her, pulling her close him with one arm.

Christina opened the door at last and they shuffled out. "I guess I have some phone calls to make."

"Can I help?" Hallie asked.

"I'm going to call Barry, Kurt and the kids first. Mom made all of her own arrangements and gave Barry and me the information when he was in town for your wedding. She didn't want a funeral. She wanted to be cremated; she said she agreed with Marion about the waste of using valuable land for cemeteries. She wanted her ashes to be scattered somewhere appropriate, she said. Our choice: she just didn't want them on a mantel. Too depressing. She said she wanted a party, too. A celebration of her life. You can help with all that. But first I need to call the funeral home and make… arrangements."

"I'll do that. Memory Lane?"

"Yeah. I hate that name. Are you sure you don't mind? Thanks."

The two women sat across from each other with their cell phones. Hallie called directory assistance for the phone number, but before she dialed the funeral home Ben touched her hand. "Hey. Are you all right? Physically? Do you feel okay?"

"I'm fine. I'm absolutely exhausted, though. Could it really be just 10:30?"

"I know. It's been less than two hours since we left the house. Seems impossible, doesn't it? Hallie, I know this is going to be hard, but remember that I'm here for you."

"I know. And I keep thinking about Cora, what she'd want. She actually told me I would be allowed to cry when she died, but only a little. I can't promise I won't cry a lot, but we have so much to be grateful for. I know that. Cora wouldn't want me to be sad for her. I'm just sad for myself, for everyone who knew her." She looked at Christina, who was crying and breaking the news to her family. Christina stood and walked around the corner with her phone, once again too restless to sit.

"She didn't suffer, though, like the doctor said. And she didn't have to go through the later stages of Alzheimer's. We should be grateful for all that," Ben said.

"I am grateful she didn't suffer, I really am. But why did it have to happen so soon? I wasn't ready!"

"Were you ever going to be ready? I think the important thing is that maybe she was."

"I suppose."

Digging his own cell phone out of his pocket, Ben said, "Here. Give me the number. I'll make the call."

That night the three of them sat in the kitchen eating sandwiches. They'd been discussing arrangements haltingly, and now Christina said, "Barry is the executor of her will, but there have been no changes since you two moved in with her." She sighed. "We'll have to go through her room, I suppose. Decide what to do with her clothes."

They all nodded and fell silent, chewing their food without tasting it, running private movie memories of Cora through their minds.

Finally, Christina put her half-eaten sandwich back on her plate, wiped her hands with her napkin and said, "Hey, I just remembered. You said something came up that kept you from going to Hawaii. What was it?"

Hallie looked at Ben. He reached over and touched her hand, nodding.

"Uh…" she began, and tears appeared again, unstoppable this time, streaming down her cheeks. "I'm sorry, this is so hard. I'm pregnant, Christina. I found out the night of the wedding. I spoke to my doctor. Sarah Shaw, you know her. One of your mom's flock. She said I probably shouldn't fly yet because my pregnancy may be at a higher risk than average."

"Because of your endometriosis?"

Hallie nodded. "And I've already miscarried once."

"Oh, honey, I'm so sorry. I didn't know that. But listen! This is a reason to be happy! I'm sure your baby is going to be just fine. I know it's hard not having Mom here right now. My God! You went from euphoria to devastation in a matter of minutes this morning. You poor thing. Come here." Christina drew Hallie into her arms. "I want you to remember something. Mom would not approve of all this blubbering, you know that. She would want you to concentrate on growing that little baby."

And then Christina's expression changed; her eyes grew wide, her mouth flew open. "Oh! Oh my God!"

"What?"

"Hallie, Mom knew you were pregnant! She did! She told me the day of your wedding. We were putting up decorations or something, and suddenly, casually really, she said, 'I think Hallie's going to have a baby. She doesn't know yet, but I have a strong feeling. And I think it's a girl.' She said that was why she took your champagne away at dinner the night before. Oh, and I saw her stealing your champagne all day at the reception."

Hallie gasped. "I wondered why I couldn't keep track of my glass! She knew?"

And Hallie remembered. Cora had been trying to tell her: something new, she'd said. Brand spanking new. "How could she know?"

"She knew before I did both times I was pregnant. She just had a sixth sense about it. Anyway, when she told me, I meant to ask you about it, but there was no time."

"She tried to tell me and we kept getting interrupted. It all makes sense now. Oh, I'm so glad she knew!" Hallie said, crying again.

"Hallie listen. As far as I'm concerned, you and I are sisters, and that means your baby is going to have one doting Auntie Christina. Won't that be fun? Listen: I know we're all going to miss Mom for the rest of our lives. But this news softens the blow a bit. A brand new person is joining our family and we'll all be able to share Mom's wisdom, her fearlessness, her kindness. How better to honor her life than by passing on her gifts? What a lucky baby!"

Still holding on to Christina, Hallie nodded. "You're right! Cora will be part of my baby's life, we'll all make sure of that."

A box of tissues sat on the table, a sad centerpiece, but now they laughed a little, as they all reached for it at once.

Climbing the stairs after dinner seemed nearly impossible to Hallie and Ben. "I don't think I've ever been this tired," Hallie said.

"Be sure to sleep in tomorrow; you need to get a lot of rest," Ben told her. He pulled her close and she leaned against him, around the corner and up the final flight.

In the bathroom, Hallie brushed her teeth. She was rinsing her toothbrush when she glanced in the mirror. *Why?* she asked her reflection once again. *Why now? Why couldn't she make it long enough to see my baby?* Tears streamed down Hallie's face yet again.

She tried to be quiet, but a sob escaped at last, and Ben appeared at the door. "What is it?"

"Everything feels so unfinished. We didn't get to have that conversation about the baby. We didn't get to say good-bye, and yet there was something so final about that day, didn't you feel it? She was so intuitive, Ben. What if she knew she was going to die?"

And then it hit her: Cora's sudden calm the day of the diagnosis. The strange trip to the doctor's office to get sleeping pills, which she'd never mentioned before or since.

Cora knew she was going to die. Of course she did. She killed herself! Hallie was suddenly certain of it.

"What is it?" Ben asked.

"Hold on." Hallie put her toothbrush back in its holder and ran down the stairs, with Ben following close behind.

She opened Cora's bedroom door and flipped on the light. There was Cora's purse, on the dresser. She had put the pills in her purse, Hallie remembered. Frantically, she emptied the purse onto Cora's bed, but of course the pills were gone, bottle and all.

Where could they be?

The trashcan was completely empty.

A glass of water, half-full an optimist would say, stood on the nightstand beside Cora's latest reading choice. And next to the water glass was a lovely handkerchief, one of Cora's mother's, Hallie knew; the edges were laced, ivory with age, and in one corner someone had long ago embroidered the letter *D* in bright red.

Hallie could not feel her legs; she nearly collapsed, but Ben helped her down onto the bed. "What's going on?"

"I think Cora did this, Ben. I think she took all of her sleeping pills." She had mentioned the prescription to Ben, but somehow she just hadn't remembered to tell Christina. "I knew something was wrong with all that, I knew it. Why didn't I do something?"

"Ssh. It wasn't your fault. Even if you're right, it wasn't your fault. This was Cora's decision. Listen. We can't know for sure right now. Let's go to bed and try to get some sleep.

Whatever happens, we know that Cora died peacefully, the way she deserved to. You have to hold on to that."

She nodded, and once again Ben and Hallie held each other as they climbed the long staircase to their room. But Hallie lay in the dark a long time before sleep finally caught up to her.

When her breathing at last slowed into a calm rhythm, Ben smiled gently, relieved that she was peaceful at last. He missed Cora, had come to think of her as a kind of adopted grandmother, but now he had to focus on taking care of Hallie. That's what Cora would have wanted, too.

He counted Hallie's breaths for a while, visualizing the two hearts beating inside her. *My family,* he thought. Just on the edge of sleep, an image filled his mind: a far away day, a gathering of precious people. He and Hallie, gray-haired and creased, their child, a daughter, all grown up. First steps and words, homework, proms, a wedding, all memories now, and with her a husband, devoted and kind, smiling gently at the children playing together nearby.

Family, Ben thought once more as he drifted deeper into his dreams.

As the next few days passed, time was marked by activities completed and those still left to do. The missing pills troubled Hallie, but she tried to distract herself with details.

She was reminded of Marion's death; Cora had needed her then, needed help wading through the excruciating details and decisions we all must face at the time we are least able to function. Cora had gone to great lengths to ease the process, but she could not box up her clothes or throw away her makeup. Someone else had to retrieve the urn that held her ashes, and decide when and precisely where to scatter them.

Ben returned to work; he and Hallie agreed he should save some of his vacation days for the time when they actually could take their honeymoon. He asked that some of his time off be considered bereavement leave, but his request was denied on a technicality: Cora did not fit the company's definition of family.

Word of Cora's death spread quickly, and soon the phone and doorbell rang almost non-stop. Flowers arrived in a steady stream. Hallie was amazed by some of the names on the accompanying cards: local politicians including senators, the governor, prominent business people, and even a former First Lady! And when Camilla Bryan, screen queen of the sixties, sent three-dozen roses and a note— *I was deeply saddened by the news of Cora's death. Her contributions to the field of psychiatry and to the lives of all who knew her will not be forgotten*— Hallie thought she might faint. Why had Cora chosen not to share stories of her more dramatic encounters? Had she been embarrassed by her fame? Or, was she simply protecting her clients' privacy? That seemed far more likely.

"Did you ever meet any of these people?" Hallie asked Christina.

"No. I'm sure some of them were patients. But I knew that Mom was quite a celebrity for a while. She wrote articles for medical journals, usually involving the influence of existentialism— philosophers like Kierkegaard, Heidegger, Nietsche, Sartre, Hegel— on psychotherapy. I know, it's all a little beyond me, too. They have different approaches to the same concepts: Kierkegaard was a devout Christian and spoke of the necessity to take a leap of faith in making personal decisions, while Nietzsche was decidedly *not* Christian. Heidegger believed we all must confront the meaning of our own existence. Mom's therapeutic style was to incorporate a lot of the ideas they had in common. Basically, she let her patients lead, following them on their own journeys of discovery. She never assumed she understood what anyone else was thinking, she asked for clarification. She was motivated by her curiosity about other people; she wanted to learn how her patients defined themselves and their experiences in the world. By encouraging them to vocalize those things, she allowed them to see their lives from a new perspective, and create a healthier definition of themselves, if you will.

"But she was very forward in her thinking and a woman, at that, so in the fifties and sixties she was quite a phenomenon. She was on national TV several times. I remember lying on the floor in front of the TV watching her on *The Jack Paar Show*. She was so beautiful, and of course so personable. She made psychiatry accessible, understandable. She worked hard to try to demystify mental illness. She never named them, but she told me that famous people began to seek her out for treatment.

"When she retired from her practice, she traveled around the country for a couple of years, lecturing, appearing as a keynote speaker at gatherings in the psychiatric community. But she decided she didn't want to be in the public eye anymore, so she just stopped accepting invitations. Eventually, the invitations didn't come in so often anymore, and finally they were pretty rare. People stopped recognizing her on the street. I was with her the last time someone asked for her autograph. She was very gracious, of course. It was a woman, probably about sixty, and she thanked Mom for paving the way for women in psychiatry. Mom said, 'Well, I don't know about that, but I did try to steer us away from all that dreadful penis envy silliness.' When the woman had gone on her way Mom said, 'I'd hoped all that nonsense was over. I'm no one's heroine.' I said, 'Yes you are, you're mine.' She said she didn't mind that so much."

Hallie shook her head. "She was always so interested in my life, my thoughts, my little problems. She acted as if I was the most fascinating person in the world, and all that time she was holding back so much about herself."

"But Hallie, that was the point. She really was fascinated by you, and by every other human being on the planet. That's what made her such a great psychiatrist, and such a wonderful, charismatic woman. It wasn't her in her nature to brag or recount her adventures, except when she felt her stories would instruct or serve some purpose. She would teach, suggest and occasionally offer advice, but she would never boast or name-drop. It's not that she was holding back from you, it's that she didn't want to miss any opportunity to learn more about you, or to help you in some way."

"You're right. I just wish I'd asked more questions."

"I understand. Believe me, I'm feeling a fair amount of guilt myself. Leaning on her was easy. I did it my whole life, and when I thought I wouldn't be able to any more, I sulked like a child."

"No, Christina, you were there every time she needed you. You were her rock."

"Oh, I may have hid it pretty well, but inside? Trust me, I was a petulant brat. When she was in the nursing home after the stroke, and we'd broken the news about Tom? I caught her crying. She'd actually held herself together until she was alone, but I waltzed back in and caught her in the act of being human. I comforted her as best I could; but when I left, around the corner from her room I nearly had a panic attack. And why? Because I felt I'd lost something. Like she'd changed, so I'd have to change. She was no longer *my* rock, you see? This larger than life woman had broken down, and I was now responsible for her in some way. And all I could do was feel sorry for myself."

Silently, Hallie nodded. *Guilt. How about feeling responsible for her death? How'd that be for a pile of guilt?* She shook her head. She knew she really wasn't responsible, and she knew she really knew nothing for certain, but... but there were questions, nagging, persistent questions whose voices rose and fell in Hallie's mind. Should she have told someone about Cora's pills? Should she have made sure that her doctor knew that Cora had Alzheimer's? What if she had, and Cora's death had been prevented? If Cora had made up her mind that this was her best choice, would she have ever forgiven Hallie for interfering? And now, how would Christina react if Cora's death *was* caused by a sleeping pill overdose?

Would Christina hate Hallie forever for not telling her about those pills?

Suddenly it seemed an act of cowardice to keep her suspicions from Christina. Clearing her breath, Hallie resolved to tell her, right now. She opened her mouth to speak, but Christina spoke first.

"I'm so ashamed I had those thoughts. But later I came to realize that this is what happens. This is life. Parents nurture and care for children, and when they grow old they sometimes need care and help from their children. I was incredibly lucky that my mother was kind and loving; taking care of her would have been a privilege. Think of all those abused and neglected children out there. How do they feel when they have to be responsible for their elderly parents?"

"I know, that would be awful, but…"

"But my mother died before she needed a lot of help. I couldn't imagine her in the later stages of Alzheimer's, you know. I tried sometimes, tried to prepare myself for the time when she'd be helpless and confused, when she might not even recognize any of us. But I just couldn't conjure it up in my mind. I don't think she was meant for that kind of demise. My mother was blessed, even in death. I'm so grateful that she died this way." She met Hallie's eyes at last and saw something there, some kind of conflict, some dissonance. "Aren't you?"

"Yes, Christina, I am grateful for that."

"I'm not saying I'm grateful she's gone, you know that don't you?"

"Of course. It's just…"

"You miss her, I know. She's irreplaceable. But I know in my heart that this is what she would have wanted. Do you feel that too?"

"Yes."

"In fact, I wouldn't be at all surprised if she brought this on herself."

"What?"

"The human mind is a powerful thing, Hallie, and Mom's was especially sharp. We'd just had the wedding, and she and I had a fabulous weekend together. I can see her thinking that she was finished here. I think she willed herself to die somehow. She hugged me especially hard when we said goodnight that night, and she was really vague about our trip to Victoria. The more I think about it, the more sure I feel; I think she knew she was going to die that night."

"Christina, I..."

"You think I'm crazy, don't you? I know, it probably sounds strange, maybe even morbid. But if it's true, if Mom knew she was leaving us, then we have to be happy for her because I've never seen her more content than she was that night. Honestly, she was so at peace. And there was no suffering in her death, she just slipped away. I think she had a hand in it, Hallie, I really do. And, however it happened, I'm glad for her. She died on her own terms. It's quite comforting, actually. You should be comforted, too."

"Should I?" Hallie closed her eyes, suddenly weary to her core. "Oh, Christina, I think there's more to the story. And you have the right to know the rest of it." She moved closer and held Christina's hand while she described Cora's request for the doctor's appointment and the prescription.

"Did she ever tell you she took sleeping pills?" Hallie asked.

"No. Never. And I would have been shocked if she did. It would seem so out of character."

"That's exactly how it struck me! But you know how persuasive she could be, so I told myself to let it go. I had intended on mentioning the pills to you, but, well, we were so busy with the wedding it just slipped my mind."

"You think she killed herself, don't you?" Christina said.

"Yes. I can't find the pills anywhere. And I...I just have a really strong feeling."

Sitting up straighter, Christina removed her hand from Hallie's grasp. "Well, I guess we just need to wait and see, don't we? I wish you'd told me about the pills, Hallie."

"So do I. I'm so sorry, Christina."

The call came that day; Hallie answered, and the doctor identified himself and asked for Christina. Silently, Hallie took the cordless phone to Christina in the piano room, and sat down beside her.

"This is Christina. Hello. No, she didn't seem depressed at all. She was very happy. Yes, apparently she'd been having trouble sleeping once in a while. Yes, she was diagnosed last spring. What?" There was a long pause, and Christina covered her eyes with her free hand. "All right. Thank you, doctor."

Christina clicked off the phone and tossed it away. "You were right, Hallie. Mom overdosed on flurazepam. Is that the prescription she had filled that day?"

"Yes."

"So she planned this. She chose this."

"Have the doctors ruled it a suicide?"

"No. The one who called said that because she had Alzheimer's she had probably become more forgetful than we realized, and simply took too many pills by accident, not remembering she'd already taken them. They're calling it an accidental death." She turned to Hallie. "You could have prevented this. You were supposed to be taking care of her!"

"I'm so sorry, Christina! Please forgive me."

"I can't talk to you right now. I need some time alone." And Christina was gone; Hallie listened to her footsteps down the hall, heard her close her mother's bedroom door.

Hallie was inconsolable when Ben arrived home that night. He tucked her into bed, served her dinner on a tray and coaxed her to eat a few bites. "For the baby," he said.

They spent most of the evening there, on the bed, until Hallie's tears were spent and she was too groggy to speak.

"You did nothing wrong, Hallie. Christina will come around, I promise you," he murmured.

And when she fell asleep at last, Ben went downstairs to make sure he kept his promise.

Christina had emerged from Cora's room at last, and Ben found her at the kitchen table, staring into a cup of tea. He intended on speaking gently, reasonably, but reason had suddenly left him far behind.

"How dare you! Hallie has been agonizing over this whole thing. This was your mother's choice. Don't you think she had the right to die on her own terms? Wouldn't you want that right?"

"Yes, at least I've always thought I would. I've always believed in that right, you know. The right to 'die with dignity,' as they say? But until now it's only been an abstract idea. It's a lot tougher to apply it to real life than I thought it would be."

Softening, Ben said, "Yeah, it's hard, and it hurts to lose someone like Cora. But that's what defines us as human beings, Christina. That we stand up for what we believe in when it's hard. It doesn't count as much when it's easy. I know, I sound like a saying on some stupid inspirational poster or something, but I really feel strongly about this. Cora was all about being true to herself and her beliefs, and I know you are too."

"I don't know. Maybe it's when something happens in your own life that you really see the whole picture for the first time. Maybe that's the time to clarify your beliefs. And I'm not sure I can justify what Mom did. She made this decision alone. She assumed she knew all the facts; she assumed she'd be a burden. How could she ever be a burden? After everything she did for me, all the care and support she gave me my whole life, how could she think I wouldn't be able to cope with her illness?"

"I think you're on the wrong track, Christina. Cora knew you'd be able to take care of her, and she knew you'd want to. She *chose* not to put you or anyone else in that position. She didn't want you to see her that way, to lose her that way. She wanted to spare you that pain."

"So instead she dumped this kind of pain on me? I don't know how to deal with this, Ben. Knowing that she could have lived much longer, and been healthy for quite a while, and that she chose not to. I don't understand how none of us saw that coming, especially Hallie. She was here! She drove Mom to the doctor for the damn prescription!"

"Listen, Christina. That beautiful, loving woman sleeping upstairs is pregnant with a child she wants more than anything in this world; she's terrified she might lose that baby. And you yelled at her today for telling you the truth when it would have been so much easer not to. She had no way of knowing that Cora had decided to do this. She's spent hours today crying, second-guessing and berating herself. So, you want to be mad at someone, be mad at your mother, but not Hallie. Hallie doesn't deserve it."

"I *am* mad at my mother! I'm furious! I miss her so much, and I'm going to have to live the rest of my life knowing I might have been able to prevent this."

Ben took a deep breath and pulled out a chair; he sat heavily. "Hallie said you seemed to be at peace about her death, even though you felt sure Cora had caused it in some way. Why do you feel so differently now? What difference does it make that she took a handful of pills instead of simply willing her heart to stop? Look, your mom thought dying this way was the lesser evil. Honestly, I think she might have been right. And if you really let yourself think about it objectively, you'll think so too. But Hallie is not to blame for any of this. You knew your mom better than anyone. Do you really think you could have kept her from doing what she really felt was the right thing to do?"

"No. No one could," Christina whispered. "I shouldn't have yelled at Hallie. I was just blindsided, Ben. I still think someone should have told me about those pills. But I understand how persuasive my mother was. And I understand it, the reason she chose to kill herself. I even respect it, in a way. But what she didn't understand is that her life would have been precious to me no matter how much she would have changed, how drastically she would have been diminished. I told Hallie it would have been a privilege to care for her, and I meant it. I've always admired her independence, her self-sufficiency, and I understand how abhorrent the prospect of helplessness was to her. But I lost her before I had to, Ben. It was just too soon."

"It would have been too soon no matter when it happened. You know that, too."

Christina's voice broke. "But she was my mama, and now she's gone."

Reaching across the table, Ben squeezed Christina's hand. "I'm sorry," he said simply.

She nodded, managed a smile, and reached for a tissue. "One thing, though. Please don't tell Barry. He would never understand."

"I won't say anything, I promise."

In the morning, Hallie was gone when Ben woke up and he threw on his bathrobe to look for her. The bathroom across the hall was empty, and he raced down the stairs calling her name.

"In here!" she called from the kitchen, and he found her there, enfolded in Christina's arms, gently swaying; tears had moistened their faces, but both women were smiling now.

With Ben's first glance, he caught his breath. For the briefest moment, he could have sworn it was Cora holding Hallie, keeping her safe.

The particulars of Cora's party were included in the obituary that Hallie and Christina had written together. As expected, a huge crowd appeared at the appointed time. Many more bouquets arrived throughout the day as well, from those admirers unable to attend.

George, Cora's neighbor, was devastated. "I'm ten years older! Ten years! Why couldn't it have been me?"

There were people Hallie knew, all the local vendors and artists Cora had introduced her to, Sarah Shaw, Maureen from Bridal Beauty and long time friends Cora had occasionally met for lunch. But there were many unfamiliar faces, too. People Cora had touched along the way.

There were stories of her wit, her loyalty, her intrinsic, indestructible optimism. Her goodness. There were tears, yes, but laughter rang through the house that day, too, just as Cora would have wished.

Sarah Shaw spoke slowly and softly, describing a chance encounter in a crowded coffee shop. She had run out of money, was close to dropping out of medical school when Cora asked to share her table— and proceeded to change her life. "Before I knew it, I was sobbing to this stranger, telling her all my troubles. She befriended me, took me under her wing, and gave me what she called the 'Cora Rouget scholarship for struggling female medical students who enjoy good coffee.'" Sarah paused, smiling as a few people laughed. "The truth is I never would have made it without her help."

Lonnie was relating the events leading to Lily's birth when Hallie heard a knock on the door. Another bouquet, another note of regret. "Have a nice day," the deliveryman said.

When Hallie looked up to thank him, she knew she'd seen him before. Glancing at the embroidered name on his jacket, she smiled. Here was Stan, delivering flowers to her again. Last time, they were *from* Cora, part of a birthday gift to a stranger; today, they honored Cora's memory. "Thank you, Stan," Hallie said, and she had a wild impulse to ask him to stay, to join the party. He seemed connected to Cora somehow. But Stan the Deliveryman simply gave her a generic smile and headed back to his van.

Hallie closed the door, put the flower arrangement down on a nearby table, and pulled the accompanying envelope from its perch on a plastic stake. Who would this one be from? Paul Newman? Oprah? The Dalai Lama?

The note read: *Dear Hallie, Christina, and family: I just heard the news. You have no reason to accept my apology, but I'm asking just the same. Cora was the genuine article: a good person. I'm sorry for hurting her, sorrier than you'll ever know. When she came to see me in jail, she changed my life. It's that simple. I regret a lot in my life, but I am grateful for having known Cora.* It was signed simply, *Tom Hosking.*

Hallie smiled. A note of regret, indeed. *One more story to tell.* Squaring her shoulders, she returned to her guests.

When the party was over at last, the family gathered in the kitchen to look through Ben and Hallie's wedding pictures. Kurt had placed them into two albums; he also brought the film he'd shot of the ceremony, captured on a DVD. No one felt up to watching the movie yet, but they huddled around the table to look at the still pictures.

They were beautiful, sweet and sometimes funny. There were many shots of Cora in her glory; Robin and Laurel asked for copies of their favorites. Barry especially loved one of Cora walking down the staircase holding her bouquet. "Look at that smile! Mom was so happy that day. Would you send me a copy of this one, Kurt?"

"Of course."

"Thank you so much for the pictures, Kurt. This is a wonderful gift," Hallie said as she turned another page. She gasped.

"Yeah, I thought you'd like that one so I just enlarged it right away," Kurt said.

It was Hallie, ready for the ceremony, laughing with Cora. They were looking at each other, hands clasped. Behind them was the huge window in Hallie's bedroom, beyond that Puget Sound. The sun, peeking through the thick clouds, was sending beams down in spotlights on the water. "It's so beautiful. Thank you."

In the morning, the whole group went for one final walk on beach with Cora. At the water's edge they huddled together, the urn tucked under Christina's arm. "Does anyone want to say something?" she asked.

"I do," Robin said. "Good-bye, Grandma. I love you. I'll always remember making cookies with you and going shopping and eating lunch in fancy restaurants when I was so little I had to use a booster seat. I'll miss our phone conversations. You were so smart, so full of love. Thank you for everything."

Laurel shook her head, crying too hard to speak.

Barry cleared his throat. "Bye, Mom. I wish I'd spent more time with you these past few years. But you insisted I follow my dream. You were so gracious about that. I think I've never become a parent because I knew I couldn't possibly be as good at it as you. We were so lucky to have you in our lives. I know I'll hear your voice whenever I'm about to do something stupid. You're my voice of reason and wisdom. That will never change."

Kurt was next: "I hit the mother-in-law jackpot, no doubt about that. You were always so kind, so open to me, even in the very beginning. You knew I loved your daughter, and that was all you required of me. Thank you for living with such integrity and compassion. Most of all, thank you for producing your beautiful, loving daughter. We'll miss you, Mom."

Ben said, "Cora, your generosity was astounding. You barely knew me when you offered your home to Hallie and me. I know I will be kinder, treat the world a little more gently, because you were part of my life. Thank you."

"Hallie?" Christina asked.

She shook her head. "I've already said good-bye."

Christina smiled gently at Hallie, then looked around at the rest of the group. "Shall we?" she asked.

It was only a few blocks to the ferry dock; they walked towards it in silence. Passengers lined up on foot and in cars to board the Kingston-bound ferry.

Barry got in line to buy their tickets, and Hallie kissed Ben good-bye. "Sure you won't come along?"

He shook his head. "I think this is a trip for Cora's kids. I'll hang here with Kurt and the girls."

Barry and Christina had asked Hallie to join them on their journey. The thought of a rocking boat made her slightly queasy, but she felt so honored by the request that she'd agreed to go anyway. Now, she waved at the group on shore once more, then followed Christina and Barry onto the ferry.

It was a warm fall day, the water calm and clear, and Hallie was grateful for the smooth ride. The ferry pushed on toward Kingston, taking them closer and closer to the Olympic Mountains Cora had so loved.

"Cora told me I should take this trip," Hallie said. "She said I should explore the peninsula, go see Hurricane Ridge. I can't believe it took this to get me on the ferry."

Halfway between the two shores, Christina nodded at her co-conspirators and stood up. Barry and Hallie followed her out of the cabin, outside and down the steps to the lowest level of the ferry, where cars were parked in long lines. They walked to what was, for this trip, the back of the ferry and stood next to the railing, watching the water churn beneath them.

"Ready?" Christina asked. "Okay. Here we go." She twisted off the lid of the urn and gave it to Barry. Holding the urn out over the water, she tipped it upside down and released Cora to the wind and the water. "Good-bye, Mama!" she shouted over the noise of the engine, and the three of them stood, arms linked, watching until all traces were gone.

Back in Edmonds, as Ben stood with Kurt, Robin and Laurel watching the ferry leave, something a few yards offshore caught his eye. Raising his arm, he shielded his eyes from the sun for a better look.

It was Cora's friend, the lone seal, his head above the surface of the water. He watched them intently, then dove— *his good-bye dive,* Ben remembered. They saw him rolling playfully, just once, before he disappeared.

Ben nodded, blinking back tears; one more admirer had come along to bid Cora farewell.

Barry was taking a redeye back to New York that night; he was packing in the guest room he always occupied when he heard Hallie in the hallway. "Hallie?" he called.

She'd been on her way to her own room to get a sweater, but now she went to Barry's room without stopping. "Hi," she said. "Need some help?"

"No, no, I'm almost done. I just wanted to share something with you. I saw the death certificate. I know you've been trying to hide it from me, but I spotted it and took a good look when no one was around. I know that Mom didn't die from a stroke. The official ruling was 'accidental overdose of a prescription medication,' but you know that, right?"

"Barry, I…"

"Yeah. Accidental my foot. Listen, I just want you to know that I don't blame you for anything. And I understand why you don't want Christina to know. She's so emotional. And I completely understand why Mom did what she did. Did you know?"

"Not before it happened."

"Sneaky old woman. Smart, though. She wasn't about to take any chances that someone might try to stop her. That's why she was so calm about the Alzheimer's. She never had any intention of letting it run its course, did she?"

"I don't know. I don't think so."

"That's so like her. Classy dame. I would have done the same thing."

"Really?"

He nodded. "I don't believe in holding on to life for the sake of just being alive. Sometimes your body holds up when your mind breaks down, and sometimes it's the opposite. But for me it's all about quality, not quantity. Not being able to recognize your family, take care of yourself, even remember your own life— I just don't think that would be a life worth living. That's the way *I* feel. How about you?"

"I don't know, Barry. I don't know whether it was courageous or an act of supreme cowardice. I don't know if I admire or resent her for doing it. No, I do know, actually, I'm angry! There are hundreds of people who would have lined up to help take care of her, but she didn't give us that option. Yes, she may have ended up regressing to childhood, to babyhood even, but I think Cora still would have been in there somewhere. There may have been moments of clarity, glimmers of her now and then, and she robbed us all of that, without even considering how we'd feel about it. And, I'm not Catholic or very religious at all, but maybe suicide is a sin, you know? Maybe we are supposed to trust that our lives will end as they are meant to.

"But then, in my head, I do get it— why she did it, I mean— and I suppose I respect that she died on her own terms. And I'm glad she didn't suffer, I am. It's just hard to sort all of this out. And it's hard to be without her."

"It's hard for all of us, kiddo."

"I know. But I wonder, could I have said something to convince her not to do this? Were there magic words that would have gotten the point across that she never would have been a burden, no matter what? And would that have been enough for her to hang on?"

"Hey. Hallie," Barry reached for Hallie's hand. "Don't beat yourself up about this, okay? She did what she felt she had to do. She knew exactly how we all felt about her. She just probably thought this was best for everyone."

"She was wrong."

"Maybe. Sometimes our heroes make mistakes, Hallie. Sometimes they have to be human after all. You know this wasn't your fault, don't you?"

Hallie shrugged. "It's hard not to think I had a part in it."

"Mom would have found a way. You know how stubborn she was, once she'd made up her mind to do something. And it would tick her off no end if you blamed yourself for her decision. Right?"

"I suppose you're right."

"Of course I am. But she'd also say that you have to feel what you feel before you can get over it. So be angry, with her, with yourself— just not for very long, okay? She wouldn't want that. Are you going to be all right?

"Yes. I'll be fine eventually."

"Good. Oh— one thing? Please, don't ever tell Christina, okay? She'd never understand."

Hallie bit her lip. "She might surprise you."

He shrugged. "Maybe you're right, I don't know. But she won't hear it from me.

"Hey. Thanks for everything. It's nice having a little sister, you know?" For the first time, Barry hugged Hallie close.

"You have to come visit. This will always be your home too."

"I'll be around, I promise."

As the family gathered around Barry's rented car to say good-bye, Christina was surprised by the ferocity of his hug. "I love you, Sis. Talk to you soon. Good-bye, everyone," he said with a wave.

Driving away, he took a good long look at the house of his childhood, the house that would, in his mind, always be his mother's, as it slowly shrank in the rearview mirror.

64

Since she was a child, music was an almost tangible, constant companion of Hallie's. Each morning, she woke with a song playing in her mind, one that seemed to reflect the tone of her life at the time. The melodies had changed over the years, but since Cora's death, for the first time it was a song of Hallie's own creation that seemed to be running on continuous play. It was "Toasting Cora" that formed the soundtrack of Hallie's life now.

Christina had begged Hallie to play it at Cora's memorial, but she'd refused. It had been too soon; she would have choked on the words. Now the song haunted her and she knew it was time to sit at the piano and play it, start to finish.

So, the morning before Christina and her family went home, Hallie asked them to join her in the piano room. They listened intently, and as Hallie began singing the chorus the last time, they all joined in.

Throwing her arms around Hallie, Christina said, "Thank you, thank you, thank you. Thank you for everything, Hallie, for your special gifts, for loving Mom, for being part of our family. I'm so happy she found you."

For the first time, Robin and Laurel each hugged Hallie, too. Robin squeezed her tight and asked, "Could I call you Aunt Hallie? I mean, we've never had an aunt before. Would that be okay?"

"I'd love that, Robin. You too, Laurel, if you'd like."

She nodded. "So that means your baby will be our cousin?"

"Absolutely. That's a nice thought."

"Maybe we can come up this summer," Robin said.

"Well, I'll be coming up when the baby is born," Christina said. "A brand new baby is a lot of work. You'll need some help. I'll stay for a little while, until you get settled. If that's okay?"

"I'd love that. Thank you. I'm sure I'm going to need all the help I can get."

"Okay, so I'll invade, be your nanny for a little while and then the girls and I will come back in the summer to fuss over your baby a little more." Hallie nodded, silent. Christina hugged her again. "It's going to be okay. You are going to have that baby, and you're going to be a great mother. Don't doubt that, not even for a second. Okay?"

"Oh, Christina. You have her big heart, you know that?"

"So do you. She made us all better. She always will."

Ben and Hallie had planned on going to Hawaii as soon as Hallie entered her second trimester, but Hallie found herself not wanting to leave. She wanted to work on the nursery, to shop for baby furniture and toys. Ben's disappointment fizzled quickly; he took great pleasure in watching Hallie busily nesting.

Anticipation buzzed, dim but constant, as they settled into life without Cora. Difficult moments fell on Hallie without warning, when grief covered her like a chilly blanket, and she missed Cora's voice, her face, her soft hands, so badly she ached. But she would feel the baby flutter, read a chapter in one of her many baby care books or take inventory of infant supplies, and she'd find herself smiling again.

Her parents had been in closer contact since the wedding, and especially since Cora's death. But Hallie had not yet found the right moment to share the news of her pregnancy. Now she wondered why.

Was it her fear of the inevitable warnings, the unbidden advice? Was it the ever-present doom and gloom in her mother's voice?

Yes. It was all that. Hallie dreaded her mother's tone of quiet despair disguised as support and caring, her underlying assumption of looming disaster. Hallie was grateful she had never shared the news of her miscarriage. That would surely have been a reason for her parents to assume the worst.

Marylou had been trying, had actually been fairly pleasant since Cora had worked her magic, and her father had spoken to Hallie regularly since the wedding as well. Hallie's mother was always at her best during a crisis, so Cora's death was an opportunity to present her most loving, maternal self.

But now, to open a new chapter and expect her parents to remain these new improved versions of themselves— it seemed too precarious to Hallie, too much to hope for. Cora couldn't wave her wand anymore; in Cora's absence, Hallie feared her parents' transformations might fade away. Perhaps the magic was only temporary after all and they'd return to their former selves: distant, cold and utterly, chronically disappointed in Hallie.

Telling them about the baby without Cora in the room was a frightening prospect, but it was time. *If they say something negative, I'll tell them how far along I am, how healthy I am, all the precautions I'm taking. I'll tell them I'm doing everything right.*

"You're what?"

"Pregnant! Isn't that great? You're going to be a grandma!"

"But Hallie,"— *oh God, here it comes,* Hallie thought, preparing her comeback— "you've just gotten your show business career off the ground. If you put it on hold too long you may never get it back."

"What?" This was not the objection Hallie had anticipated; she had no response for this.

"You have choices that I didn't, Hallie. You could put your career first."

"What are you saying, Mom?"

"I'm just saying that you don't have to have a baby now. You can wait. You can become a famous singer. A movie star, maybe. Your career is taking off, Hallie. Don't waste this time."

Choices. You have choices that I didn't, Hallie.

Hallie exhaled, aware suddenly that she had been holding her breath, waiting. Waiting for her mother's words to be decoded, for their meaning to be revealed, because surely she didn't mean what she seemed to be saying. Surely Hallie had misunderstood.

But now Hallie was sure she did understand; something wholly unfamiliar rose from her depths, something she had never before experienced in connection with her mother. All her anger was gone, and in its place Hallie felt only pity. How sad to live so immersed in regret, to swim in lost dreams.

"Mom, I'm sorry you couldn't make the choices that were right for you. I wish you could have had a different life. But you have a daughter who's thrilled to be alive. You can count that among your accomplishments. And now you're going to have a grandchild. That's good news. Listen to me, Mom. You're absolutely right— I do have more choices. And I am choosing this life. I want this baby more than anything I've ever wanted. Show business isn't my ultimate goal. It's fine on a small scale, as long as it fits around the important things in my life: Ben and our baby. Do you understand? Can't you tell how happy I am about this?"

"Squandered talent is a terrible thing, Hallie. You don't appreciate that yet, but just wait a few years. Wait until the wrinkles come and the men stop looking. Pretty soon no one will want to hear you sing, no matter how good you are."

"If I never sing again I'll be okay. If I never hold my baby— that would devastate me. Mom, you are still a beautiful, talented woman. Why don't you audition for a community theatre group, or a choir or something? I'll even do some research for you on the Internet. Please, will you think about it?"

"You can get information about things like in my area?"

"Yes! I'll gather it up and send it to you. All right?"

"No harm in looking, I guess."

"Exactly! Oh, Mom? One more thing. I'm due at the beginning of May."

"You're five months along? I guess you have made your choice, haven't you?"

"Be happy for me, Mom. Please."

"I will be, honey. Just give me a little time."

"That I can do."

65

Hallie continued to work a few days a week into her eighth month of pregnancy; as her belly grew, there were fewer offers for acting work, but Jim always had a jingle or voiceover for her.

As she opened the door to leave the studio one day, someone behind her called her name. Turning around, her ankle twisted, throwing her off balance, and she fell.

"Hallie! Are you all right?" The voice was closer now. There was something familiar about it, but she couldn't quite place it. She sat, rubbing her ankle and taking inventory of her aching body parts: her back hurt a bit, but that was nothing unusual these days, her ankle was a little sore, but she knew it wasn't badly injured.

"I think I'm okay. Could you help me up?" She looked up at the concerned face, and still couldn't pinpoint where she'd met this man before.

"Here," he said, holding out an arm. She clutched it and allowed him to pull her up. "Are you sure you're not hurt? I'm so sorry, I didn't mean to startle you."

"It's okay. I'm not exactly my most graceful these days. Luckily I landed on my derriere." She looked at him now, studied his face.

"You don't remember me, do you?"

"I'm sorry. I know we've met, I just…" And then it hit her. He looked amazingly different in jeans and a leather jacket, but this was Karaoke Kyle in the flesh. "Kyle? Is that you?"

He laughed. "I actually stow that name away in my closet along with the green suit. My real name is Daniel. Daniel O'Brien."

"Nice to meet you, Daniel. Karaoke Kyle is pretty catchy, though."

"That was the whole idea, I guess. I've missed you. I wondered why you hadn't been in. But I see you've been busy."

"Yeah. Life has been kind of crazy for a while. I'm really glad I ran into you, though. I understand I have you to thank for this job. Jim said you asked him to come listen to me. If you hadn't connected us, this never would have happened. I'd still be crunching numbers in a stale little office."

"So now you're singing about dishwasher detergent in a stale little studio."

"Uh-huh. Leaps and bounds beyond where I was. No, really. I can make my own hours. I've appeared in a couple of commercials, too."

"I know, I've spotted you. You're good!"

"Thanks. That's on hold for a while, but I've taken some acting classes and I'd like to pursue it a little further. I'm really enjoying my life right now, and you had a hand in it. So thank you. I kept meaning to come see you on karaoke night, but, well, things came up."

"You're welcome, Hallie. I'm glad I could help. It's nice to see talented people find a little success. It's such a hard business to break into. But you're special. You could go as far as you want."

"You know what? I think this is as far as I want to go. Maybe a few more commercials, but basically I'm right where I want to be."

"I'm glad things are working out for you. Congratulations on everything, job, baby, the whole works. Do you know if it's a boy or a girl?"

Hallie nodded. The ultrasound late in her fifth month had confirmed her suspicions. "It's a girl. I decided I wanted to know. I really didn't have a preference, but I had a feeling it was a girl. I'm due next month."

"I'm sure she's going to be just as beautiful as her mom. Have you picked out her name?"

"We're still debating."

"Tough decision, choosing a name for another person. I'm sure you'll do fine, though. Let me walk you to your car so I can make sure you're okay."

Before she closed her car door, Daniel said, "Hey! When you're ready to leave the little one with a sitter, come sing with me one night. It hasn't been the same without you. People have been asking me why you're not there."

"Really?"

"Yeah. I think you have a little fan club down there. But the public is fickle. They'll forget you eventually. Ten, fifteen years from now they'll give up and start looking for someone else to worship."

"Thanks, Daniel. I'm glad I met you out of character."

"Keep singing, Hallie. Good luck with everything."

Hallie's daughter was born the morning of May Day, three days after her daddy's birthday. Ben and Hallie spent that afternoon staring at each other and their baby as if they were the first people ever to have performed such a miracle.

Twenty-four hours later, Christina arrived; backing into the room, she turned slowly around to reveal bouquets of pink balloons and flowers. "I stopped at three stores and bought all the pink tulips I could find!"

"I'm so glad you're here!"

"I just couldn't wait to see my little niece! And just look at her! She's perfect! May I hold her?"

Ben had been holding the sleeping baby and now he stood, handing her to Christina. "She's beautiful. Just beautiful," Christina murmured, pivoting gently to and fro. "Hello, little girl. I'm your Aunt Chrissy." She looked up at Hallie, still rocking. "How are you, sweetie?"

"I'm fine. A little tired, though. I thought she might never be born."

Ben nodded. "Hallie was so brave. Fourteen hours of labor. She was exhausted near the end, but she held it together."

"I knew you'd handle it like a champ, sugar pie."

Sugar pie. Cora's voice whispered through the room. "I wish she could see the baby," Hallie said.

"Hey. I'm sure she can. She's probably been right behind you this whole time, smiling over your shoulder."

Hallie smiled. More familiar words.

Christina peered back down, just as the baby opened her eyes. "Hello, sweet girl. I'm so happy to meet you. Oh! Have you decided on a name?"

Hallie and Ben glanced at each other, and Ben nodded. "I think we have," he said.

"Well? What is it?"

Hallie smiled. "I hope you approve. We want to name her Cora. Cora Mary Lawson. What do you think?"

"I think it's absolutely perfect. Mom would be so proud. How wonderful to have a brand new Cora in the family!"

"We're going to call her Cori," Ben said.

"Perfect! She looks just like a Cori."

Christina stayed for several days, taking on the role of housekeeper and part-time nanny when Hallie came home with the baby. With Christina taking care of all the laundry, shopping and cooking, Hallie was able to concentrate on herself and Cori.

Before she left, Christina arranged for a diaper delivery and pick-up service. Hallie objected, but Christina insisted. "Trust me. You need to make this as easy as possible, because so much of it is really hard. This is my baby gift. You're paid up for six months, and then we'll see how things are going. And remember, I'm still coming up this summer with the girls. Kurt is whining about wanting to see the baby, too, so maybe we'll all come up. Unless you think you'll be overwhelmed with all of us underfoot."

"Not at all. You're all welcome here, anytime."

"We won't stay longer than you can stand us, I promise. I'll call soon." She tucked a finger into Cori's tiny hand, felt her grab on. "Good-bye, little Cori. I love you, sweet pea."

When Cori was two weeks old, Lonnie brought Lily over. "She's gorgeous!" Lonnie said. "Lily, be careful honey."

"Would you like to see the baby, Lily?" Hallie sat, with Cori in her arms, and Lily, now thirteen months old and walking, held onto the side of the couch and reached a dimpled hand toward the baby. "Lonnie, look at them! I think they're going to be great friends."

"Constant companions, no doubt about it. Isn't this just the ultimate?"

"What?" Hallie asked.

"You and me, moms together. This is my wish come true."

"Mine too. I really wanted our babies to grow up together. And I thought it wasn't going to be possible. I think there really is magic in the world."

When Cori fell asleep, Hallie tucked her in her bassinet and carried it toward the kitchen, motioning for Lonnie and Lily to follow. She put the bassinet down beside the table. "Want some tea?"

"Sure, thanks." Lily sat on Lonnie's lap, giggling as Lonnie bounced her.

As Hallie filled the kettle, she began humming absently. "That's what I've been missing!" Lonnie said. "I haven't heard you sing for a long time."

"I've been singing a lot lately, to Cori. It seems to calm her down. I think she likes her song the best."

"Her song?"

"Well, Cora's song. Now it belongs to my little Cora, too." And Hallie began singing: "To Cora, all my treasures I owe/ To Cora, for loving me so/ To Cora, a friend for all time/ I'll be toasting Cora the rest of my life."

Lily watched Hallie, her eyes wide. She wiggled a little, opened her mouth in a wide O, and began singing loud vowel sounds along with Hallie's song.

Lonnie laughed when they finished. "She does this all the time. I put on a CD and she dances and sings."

"I think I have my first student. Maybe that's why I haven't pursued teaching yet. I've been waiting for Lily."

Cleo came strolling into the kitchen then, tail high in the air, watching Hallie.

"Come on, Cleo, it's okay," Hallie called. The little cat trotted over and leaped onto Hallie's lap.

"Is she jealous of the baby?" Lonnie asked.

"Pea green. She's starved for attention, poor thing. But she seems to be warming up to Cori." Hallie smiled as Cleo leaned against her, purring loudly.

Lonnie cleared her throat. "Hallie, I have to tell you something. I feel so bad that I had Cora's help when I was in labor and she wasn't there for your baby's birth. She was so comforting, so kind. She really helped."

"Don't feel bad, Lonnie. I'm glad she was there for you. And when I was in labor, I thought about everything she said to help you through it. I could almost hear her voice. I still do, every day. I honestly feel her here with us."

"Still working her magic?" Lonnie asked.

"Always."

A year would pass before Hallie found the notes.

Ben had taken Cori that morning for a Daddy Day, something that had become a monthly tradition: a day for the two of them to share adventures, and of course to give Hallie a break. This day, she'd decided, would be devoted to spring-cleaning.

So out came the buckets, mops, sponges and rags, and Hallie cleaned the house, top to bottom. And in one of the spare bedrooms, tucked away in the corner of a bookshelf, were three little envelopes, each with a name scrawled across the front: Barry, on the green envelope, Christina on the yellow, and of course on the lavender, Hallie. All in Cora's writing.

Hallie dropped her duster and sat on the floor, staring at her name a moment before tearing the envelope open. Something jingled in the bottom, but the note was all Hallie could focus on.

Dear Hallie,

By the time you find this, I'm sure whatever shock and pain I've caused you has subsided. By now I hope you understand why I did what I did.

I wanted some time to pass before you found my little note. Hopefully, that is what has transpired. I did not want this to be mistaken for a suicide note. Mine was not an act of desperation or depression. It was simply a detour, to correct a mistake. My life was so blessed, Hallie, I can't fault Mother Nature for goofing a little at the end, especially since she still left me the final word.

Knowing doctors as I do, I'm sure my death was labeled an accidental overdose. But you know better, don't you? You're a smart girl, and I'm sure you've figured it all out, you, Christina and Barry. Perhaps you've all compared notes and discovered that I'd never taken sleeping pills before, and I'm sure you've considered certain things I did or said in an entirely new light.

So, you know I lied to you. I am sorry about that, sugar pie, truly. It was difficult for me. But, it was necessary. I couldn't very well tell you what I was up to, now could I? You would have tried to talk me out of it. You might even have tried to steal my little stash. And if I'd told you and still managed to proceed with my plan, you would have felt responsible somehow. I couldn't allow that. So, I had to be convincing in my little deception. For that I do apologize. But not for choosing the time of my own death. That was my choice to make, no one else's.

I had intended to wait much longer before leaving you all, but that little incident on my solo walk the day before your wedding seemed to me to be a sign. I knew it would never get easier, and I would never be more lucid than I am right now, as I write this. In the long run it won't matter whether I waited six more months, and if this horrible disease decided to pick up its pace, I might not have been able to make this decision much further down the line. Please trust that I'm making this choice after much thought, and I have absolutely no regrets or hesitation.

Many people, much braver than I, would have made a different choice; they would have squeezed every last minute out of their lives. But I feel greedy enough, with this life so full of love, wonderful adventures and prosperity. It's been more than full. It's been magical.

There is something else I'm sorry about, though. I regret that we didn't get to finish our conversation the day of your wedding. But by now I'll bet you know what I was trying to tell you. Was I right? Oh, I hope so. If so, you may now have a beautiful child (a girl—was I right about that too?), living there in my house with you. I wonder how old she'll be as you read this. I wonder what she'll be doing. I wish I could stick around and know your daughter, Hallie, but alas that is not in the cards.

Instead, I will watch over all of you: Ben, your little one, and you, my dearest Hallie, from wherever I am. My influence may be limited, but I will do whatever I can for you and your family. I promise you that.

I've enclosed the little pearl necklace you wore at your wedding. I am not giving it to you, but entrusting you with a sacred duty. I would like to continue the tradition of having it worn at family weddings. So, keep it close and safe, and put it on the next bride—Robin, Laurel, and then perhaps your own little girl someday. Take steps to ensure that it stays in the family (you and yours are of course included) and that the tradition is carried on.

I wish we'd had more time together, but think about this: we knew we were friends the moment we met, and that is a rare gift.

I love you, sweetheart, always and forever.

Cora

P.S. I know you'll choose a good time to give Christina and Barry their notes. Give them a big hug for me, too.

Hallie sat for a long time, reading and re-reading, breathing in the scent of the envelope, grateful that a trace of Cora's perfume lingered still. Finally, Hallie turned the envelope upside down and watched the pearl necklace fall on the floor, then picked it up and held it tight in her fist. She cried a little, but laughed too. Cora had found a way to say good-bye after all.

That night, Hallie dreamed again of a misty beach. She stumbled on the sand, frantic, looking for someone. "Where are you? Please come back!" she screamed. Through the fog, a figure grew closer. "Is that you? I'm here! I'm right here!" She ran to her beloved daughter and held her close. Her little girl was no longer lost to her. As the fog lifted, Hallie saw a dark figure moving in the water. She pointed. "Look, Cori!"

And the seal, smiling at them, blinked once. Its eyes, wide and round, were pale blue.

The young woman sat on a folding patio chair she had carried to the beach. On her lap lay a sketchbook; charcoal blackened her fingers as she outlined the Olympic Mountains in quick, sure strokes. Occasionally, furtively, she glanced up from her work. She would allow no spectators; strangers, among them possibly artists and vaguely defined experts, would surely see her efforts as average and hollow. Such exposure was simply too risky, too... final.

Hunkered over, she concentrated on the lines and shapes of the mountains, the trees, the waves.

"How beautiful!" The voice was directly behind her right shoulder. Damn! How could she have been so careless? Who was this rude person, invading her space uninvited?

"I'm sorry, how rude I must seem." The intruder was in front of her now, reaching for her hand. "I should introduce myself. I'm Hallie. Hallie Lawson."

Hallie Lawson. Where had she heard that name? "I'm Leah. I'm, uh..."

"You're busy, I know, and I'm interrupting. I do apologize. I just had to tell you— I've seen you down here before, and I've been dying to see your drawings. Now that I've snuck a little peek, I can see how talented you are."

Leah looked up, really looked at this stranger's face. Hallie Lawson was old, at least sixty, but lovely still. Leah wanted to dislike her, to dismiss her, and yet... there was something in her eyes. Some gentleness that Leah longed for. Gentleness had made only rare appearances in Leah's twenty-two years.

"You've seen me here before?"

"Many times. I live just up the beach. I've been here for, oh, thirty-two years now, and I try to walk the beach every day. Usually my husband walks with me, but he's playing golf today. Sometimes my daughter and grandchildren come along, but they're busy today too. You look a little like my daughter Cori, although she's a bit older of course."

"You've lived here for thirty–two years?"

"Uh huh, since I was twenty-nine. There are a few more houses now, more people on the beach, but it's still beautiful, isn't it?"

And without knowing quite how it happened, Leah found herself walking up the beach to Hallie's beautiful old house. Looking at pictures of Hallie's family and friends. And, strangest of all, over tea, showing Hallie all of the drawings in her sketchbook.

"I love that you use paper and charcoal. Most people use those new electronic sketchbooks now, the ones that practically draw for you."

Leah nodded. "I don't like those. I'd rather feel the charcoal, or pencil or whatever in my hand. I guess I'd rather do all the work myself."

Hallie smiled. "Gadgets have gotten fancier, but things don't really change all that much. True talent comes from within, not from a computer program. Take a look at that," and she pointed at a framed drawing on the wall behind Leah.

"I noticed that when we came in. It's beautiful. Who's the artist?"

"It was a woman who once lived here, one of the kindest people imaginable. She mentioned once that she drew occasionally, but I never saw her sketches until after she died. They were all stashed away in one of her desk drawers, can you believe it? I fell in love with that one, so I had it framed."

Leah turned to look at the drawing again. It was a simple sketch in colored pencil: a four-paned window with drawn curtains. Through the window, a view of Puget Sound and the Olympic Mountains, with the double-peaked Mt. Constance front and center. On a ledge at the base of the window, looking out at the view, sat a small black cat, its tail hanging down in a straight line.

"That was my cat, Cleo, so I'm sure Cora drew the picture after we moved in with her." She gazed at the picture, a faint smile on her face, and lowered her voice to almost a whisper. "Ironic that she would hide such a wonderful talent. I suppose she considered it inconsequential. People can always surprise you, Leah. There are secrets, thoughts they choose not to share even with their closest friends. Choices they must make alone. There truly are many paths to the top of that proverbial mountain, you know. Occasionally," Hallie nodded toward the drawing again, "there's even more than one peak."

Puzzled, Leah almost asked what Hallie meant. Instead, she crept back toward the more familiar. "You have a lot of interesting art," she said, looking at the framed photograph hanging above the arch leading into the living room. It was a close-up of a little girl blowing a puffy white dandelion gone to seed. "I love that one. It's so…calming, I guess."

Hallie nodded. "Yes. Calming and a little whimsical. I chose it to honor the artist I just mentioned. My dear friend Cora." She paused, and in response to Leah's questioning look, she added, "It's a long story."

Leah heard many stories that day, stories of people in Hallie's life, past and present. Hallie spoke of many friends, but some stood out: Lonnie, a great beauty and fitness expert, whose eldest daughter— and Hallie's goddaughter— was none other than Lily Wakefield, singer/songwriter and renowned pop icon! Hallie had been her first singing instructor, and had even written a couple of her hit songs.

That's when Leah remembered where she'd heard Hallie's name. It was on TV: a local magazine show. Hallie had been featured as one of half a dozen or so 'Local Celebrities You May Not Have Heard Of.' She had been a singer, Leah recalled, had sung famous national commercial jingles. She'd done some live theatre, a few bit parts on local TV shows. They'd even shown an old interview with her; she'd said that she wasn't at all ambitious, that she would always put her family before her career. She had turned down many offers: recording contracts and leading movie roles. They had ended the segment by revealing her connection with the great Lily Wakefield.

Leah tried not to it show on her face, but she was shocked. To be that beautiful, that talented, and choose not to become rich and famous? Well, Hallie didn't seem to be exactly poor, but she had still sacrificed what could have been an amazing career. The funny thing was, Hallie didn't seem to consider it a sacrifice at all.

Hallie also didn't seem to notice any change in Leah's demeanor; she just continued with the stories about her favorite people.

There was Kim, who had once dated Lonnie's brother, nearly married Hallie's first husband, but finally eloped suddenly with a singer named Daniel. Kim had died of breast cancer just two years later.

And George, a next-door neighbor who had lived long enough to see Hallie's daughter's first birthday.

Hallie went on, speaking of Marion, Cora's housekeeper and friend who never knew how beautiful she was; and Tom, who had once worked for— and stolen from— Cora. Hallie had helped to send him to jail, but somehow she had forgiven him and eventually grown fond of him. He was nearly ninety now, but still came to Christmas dinner at the Lawsons' home each year.

Hallie described her husband's family— his sisters and their children— in glowing superlatives and his parents, both gone now, as kind people and devoted grandparents.

"Well, that's the cast of characters," Hallie said. "I'm afraid I've talked your ear nearly off."

"No, those are great stories," Leah said, and she meant it. "What about your parents?"

Hallie smiled. "My parents were also quite inspiring. They grew tremendously over the years, really faced up to mistakes they had made and they simply decided to become better human beings. I was quite close to them in their later years. And they absolutely adored Cori."

Leah took a deep breath. "Wow. I didn't think people ever really changed."

"Oh, it happens. I've seen it enough to believe it. I hope you come to believe it, too, Leah," Hallie said, and she touched Leah's hand.

Conversation seemed to flow effortlessly that day. They spoke of many people, many of Hallie's travels and adventures. But throughout the afternoon it was Cora that Hallie mentioned most often, Cora whose story seemed intertwined with all the others. "Cora was my fairy godmother, and now she's either my guardian angel or she's off somewhere preparing to be my mother in my next life. She made me that promise once."

And when, inevitably, Hallie asked questions about Leah's life, her education, her family, Leah simply answered them without thinking. She spoke frankly and without hesitation, completely comfortable in this strange situation.

Following Hallie on a tour through the house, Leah tried not to look as impressed as she was. Hallie described the remodeling she and her husband had done over the years, but Leah only heard snippets as she took it all in: the huge bedrooms, the office, the exercise room, the library, and Leah's favorite, the little round room at the top of the house. "I sang Cori to sleep up here when she was little," Hallie said. "Now I bring my grandkids up here. And Zoë, too, of course," she added, as she leaned down and scooped up a large calico cat that had been trotting along beside them.

Leah looked out the row of windows, and felt she could see forever: a hundred shades of green stood below the dark purple and white Olympics, the matching, mirrored blues of the sky and Puget Sound. "It's amazing," she whispered.

"I believe that it's good for the soul to appreciate the beauty in the world. It's important to be in awe of it all, don't you think so?"

Leah thought of her sketches, her sacred drawings that no one else had seen until today. "Yes, I believe that, too, Hallie."

When they said good-bye, Hallie insisted that Leah come to lunch the following Sunday. "Cori will be here with her little ones. You'll get to meet them, and my husband Ben, too. Please say you'll come."

Leah opened her mouth, intending to decline, but instead asked, "What time?"

Gathering her belongings, Leah said good-bye to Hallie, thanking her for the tea and snacks. "You're very welcome, sweetie. Come by anytime. If I don't see you before then, I'll look forward to Sunday."

Walking home to her tiny apartment, Leah sighed, taking in the events of the day. Hallie Lawson was an impressive woman, kind, gentle, serene. A devoted friend, wife and mother.

In passing, Hallie had mentioned that she'd hoped for more children, but she wasn't able to have them. So Cori, her only child, was the lucky recipient of all that devotion. To love your family, your *daughter*, that much… the envy and longing physically hurt Leah.

But something about Hallie Lawson had made Leah feel so… at home. In Hallie's presence, Leah believed she really was a talented artist, a precious, lovable person. With absolute certainty, Leah knew she would be knocking on the Lawsons' door next Sunday.

I have a friend, she thought. *Someone I didn't even know this morning.* She shook her head, wondering at the strange and unpredictable nature of life. And, turning to look down the hill at the blue waters of Puget Sound, she smiled.

About the Author

Cassandra Miller, like Cora, lives in Edmonds, Washington with her husband and their family, which includes two cats. *Toasting Cora* is her first novel.

If *Toasting Cora* is your book club selection, please feel free to contact the author with questions or comments at toastingcora@verizon.net.